NEVER ENOUGH

DISCOVER OTHER TITLES BY KELLY ELLIOTT

** Title or series available on audiobook*

Cowboys and Angels Series

Lost Love

Love Profound

Tempting Love

Love Again

Blind Love

This Love

Reckless Love

Wanted Series

*Wanted**

*Saved**

*Faithful**

Believe

*Cherished**

*A Forever Love**

The Wanted Short Stories

All They Wanted

Love Wanted in Texas Series*

(Spin-off of the Wanted series)

Without You

Saving You

Holding You

Finding You

Chasing You

Loving You

(Please note: Loving You combines the last books of both the Broken and Love Wanted in Texas series.)

Broken Series

*Broken**

*Broken Dreams**

*Broken Promises**

Broken Love

The Journey of Love Series*

Unconditional Love

Undeniable Love

Unforgettable Love

With Me Series*

Stay with Me

Only with Me

Speed Series

Ignite

Adrenaline

Boston Love Series*

Searching for Harmony

Fighting for Love

Austin Singles Series*

Seduce Me

Entice Me

Adore Me

Southern Bride Series

Love at First Sight (available August 2019)

Delicate Promises (available October 2019)

Divided Interests (available early 2020)

YA Novels Written as Ella Bordeaux

Beautiful

Forever Beautiful

Stand-Alone Novels

The Journey Home

*Who We Were**

*The Playbook**

*Made for You**

Cowritten with Kristin Mayer

Predestined Hearts

*Play Me**

Dangerous Temptations (available September 2019)

Until There Was You (available Spring 2020)

NEVER ENOUGH

KELLY
ELLIOTT

This is a work of fiction. Names, characters, organizations, places, events, and incidents are either products of the author's imagination or are used fictitiously.

Published by Montlake, Seattle
www.apub.com

ISBN-13: 9781542018791
ISBN-10: 154201879X

Cover design by Hang Le

Cover photography by Regina Wamba of MaeIDesign.com

Printed in the United States of America

NEVER ENOUGH

Chapter One

Brock

"Daddy, when will you be home?"

My eyes closed, and I pulled in a slow, deep breath. I was positive the cracking sound coming from the vicinity of my chest was my heart breaking in two. Yet again. I hated that I was on the road and away from my son as much as I was, but I was trying to build our future. I only needed to bull ride, and win, for another year or two. I had plenty of money saved up, but if I could get at least one more championship under my belt, I would be guaranteed endorsements, and my son would always be taken care of.

Just a few more years of this, and then I can stop.

"I'll be home Monday, buddy. I know I've been gone a couple of weeks. I had some things I had to do for work."

"That swucks."

"Blayze Brock Shaw!" I heard my mother shout.

I forced myself not to laugh and could only imagine the look on my mother's face as my five-year-old son cursed. The result of being around my older brother, Ty, most likely.

"Blayze, you know better than to say a bad word," I scolded. "That's no way for a gentleman to talk."

"But Uncle Ty and Uncle Tanner say that word all the time, Daddy. Why can't I say it? You said so yerself: I'm a big boy."

Sighing, I raked my fingers through my damp hair. "You *are* a big boy; you're right. But you're still not allowed to say bad words. Now, you apologize to Grams before she washes your mouth out with soap."

"Again? I'm outa here, Daddy!" my son exclaimed.

I heard the phone drop and the sounds of his retreating cowboy boots taking him far away from my mother. I couldn't help the smile on my face as I heard Mom pick up the phone and call after Blayze in his mad dash to get away.

"Brock, that boy of yours is going to drive me to drinking."

"What did he mean *again*, Mama?"

"He got himself a mouthful of Ivory soap last night when he told Rose Monroe to go suck it after the PTA meeting. Of course, he throws a *w* in the word *suck* and has to make it sound all cute."

This time, I did laugh.

"Brock Shaw, it is *not* funny."

"I'm sorry. I really am, Mama. You have to admit, though, it's pretty funny, and I'm sure he's heard you say it about Rose a time or two."

When she replied, I heard the smile in her voice, and I ached to be home. Stella Shaw was the type of woman who would do anything for anyone, but piss her off, and my mama could be a bear.

"Well, I've never said it to her face. And, yes, it was a bit funny. Especially when that uptight woman tried calling me out in front of the entire PTA last night about you not being around to raise your own child."

Ouch. That hurts.

"You still feuding with her?" I asked.

"No. Yes. Maybe. Hell, I don't know. The woman talked bad about my son. That type of thing doesn't go unpunished, friend or no friend. She crossed a line when she insulted you."

"Mama, she's been insulting me since Blayze was born. You about done punishing her and ready to move on?"

"Ha! Hardly."

Rolling my eyes, I cleared my throat. "Well, I guess I'd better get me some sleep. I never seem to have a good draw in Tacoma."

"Brock?"

My breath stalled in my throat. I hated this part of our daily conversation. It was when I heard the fear in my mother's voice, even though she tried desperately not to show it. The uncertainty that me following my dreams as a professional bull rider might not be the wisest thing anymore. Especially because I was the only parent my son had. It was something I fought internally every single day.

"I know, Mama."

"I know you know, but I'm gonna say it anyway. Be careful and do your thing, but remember who's really in charge."

I nodded, even though I knew she couldn't see me, and replied, "Yes, ma'am. May I say good night to Blayze?"

My mother called out my son's name. "Blayze, Daddy wants to say goodbye! No, I'm not gonna wash your mouth out. Not this time anyway!"

I chuckled and again felt the deep ache of missing home. It didn't take long for Blayze to get back on the line.

"Daddy, I'm gonna rope me a calf tomorrow!"

The drop in my stomach nearly made me sick. "Blayze, I was gonna show you that when I came home on Monday."

"Yeah, I know, but Uncle Ty said that he could show me, 'cause you're busy."

My hand balled into a fist, and I counted to ten. I was going to kick my brother's ass. Just because he couldn't be on the circuit with me, he had to make sure I was as miserable as him. The only problem was, he was using my son to do it.

"I'm not too busy to show you how to rope, buddy. I'll teach you when I get home. I promise."

"Okay, Daddy, I'll wait for you! I wove you, and kick that bull's a-s-s tomorrow!"

Grinning, I answered, "I will, buddy. I love you too. Now, don't give Grams a hard time, you hear me?"

"Yes, sir. I pwomise to be good."

"That's my big boy."

"Bye, Daddy!"

"See ya later, buddy."

The line went dead, and I stood there in the middle of my hotel room, staring down at my phone. The emptiness in my heart was hard to ignore. Glancing down to my watch, I counted down the hours until I was going to be able to climb onto the back of a bull and feel something again. It seemed to be the only time I was able to forget.

Chapter Two

Lincoln

"I still can't believe you're leaving me for freaking Montana!"

I stepped out of the car, lifted my arms, and stretched. We were only an hour or so away from Hamilton, Montana. I smiled when I looked all around us. Emerald-green pastures were home to cattle roaming freely as they grazed. Pine trees covered the foothills, which gave way to snowcapped mountains where white, puffy clouds danced along the top. My heart felt full for the first time in years.

Any lingering doubt over making this move was completely washed away when my eyes went to the river. I nearly lost my breath. The mountain range was mirrored against the crystal-clear water. Surely something this beautiful couldn't be real. It looked like a picture. One deep breath and I could smell crisp, clean air.

This was home. A fresh start to a new life. It felt like a beautiful dream finally coming true.

"Kaylee, how can you look around and not see how beautiful it is here?"

She huffed. "Yeah, it's beautiful. Mountains, rivers, blah, blah, blah. I don't see why you need to *move* here. There are plenty of jobs in Georgia. Lots of old mansions you can design up. You made your mama cry, Lincoln. Cry! A well-raised southern woman does not make her mama cry."

I rolled my eyes. "You know the reasons why I left Atlanta. It's not about the money. It's about doing this on my own. Building a life for me on my own terms."

"Aw yes, *those* reasons. Leaving the big city for something simple? Leave the disgusting heat of Atlanta for fresh, crisp mountain air? Get out from under the control of Daddy? Start fresh? That crap?"

"Yes, those reasons."

"I know why you're really here. You want you some northern country dick."

It took everything I had not to laugh. "Northern country dick?"

She nodded.

My best friend leaned against my Land Rover Discovery, giving me a matter-of-fact look. We stared each other down, neither willing to budge.

Kaylee sighed. "It's not fair. I'm going to miss you."

"Move here! You're a book editor! You can work from anywhere you want, Kaylee. Think of how much fun it would be."

Chewing on her lip, she looked to be giving it some serious thought. I knew it would be good for her. A chance for Kaylee to get her own fresh start. Lord knows, with everything she had been through over the last few years, she deserved happiness.

The moment I'd told her I was moving, I'd seen her eyes light up at the possibility of starting over somewhere herself.

"I don't think I could leave Georgia. It's all I've ever known. I'm a southern kind of girl. I've got the twang finally down. I just don't think I could make it up here."

I raised a brow. "Did you see the hot guys in those jeans and cowboy hats at the last gas stop?"

A full smile broke out over her face. Her blue eyes lit up, and she nodded. "Heck yes, I saw them. Did you see the one wink at me? Lawrd Almighty, I thought I was gonna pass out!"

Laughing, I shook my head and did a few jumping jacks while Kaylee stretched and moaned about how tight her muscles were.

"Whose idea was it to drive to Montana?" she asked, slipping back into the passenger seat.

"I believe it was yours. 'It'll be an adventure,' you said. 'The scenery will be amazing,' you said."

She rolled her eyes as her seat belt clicked. "Well, scenery is overrated. How many more miles until we get to this little town? And is it safe? I mean, you bought this house because the guy had too many bad memories there. What happened? Was someone murdered in it?"

I paused for a moment, letting her words sink in. Slight panic raced through my veins. I hadn't asked any real questions about the house. I simply saw pictures of the old place, and the only thing that went through my mind was how I could make this my home.

Holy crap . . . what if someone *had* been murdered in the house?

Shaking my head, I pushed away my moment of freak-out. I knew what it felt like to want to get away from something, or someone, controlling you.

"Yes, it's safe, and I don't really know the full reason. All I know is, the Shaw family owns a ton of land. They have a cattle ranch and raise horses as well. Their son lived in this house and doesn't want it anymore. All his brother Ty told me was that there were memories the owner wanted to leave behind. So they broke the house and a small parcel of land around it off from their main ranch, and they're selling it for him. He didn't even want to be involved in the process."

Kaylee's arms folded over her chest. "When was this house built?"

I gave her a wide smile. "That's the best part. It was built in 1887."

"Oh Lord. Your kryptonite."

"Kaylee, the fireplace alone in the house was the selling point for me."

"The fireplace?" she asked, a look of disbelief on her face.

"Yes!" I replied with a chuckle. "It's begging to be brought back to its original state. I can picture it now: sitting in front of a roaring fire, a book in one hand and a cup of tea in the other. The kitchen is pretty big for the age of the house. And don't even get me started on the wood trim throughout the place. Or the floors."

"I'm gonna have to stay just to help you fix the place up," she stated, staring out the window.

That was my best friend's way of saying she *wanted* to stay but needed an excuse. Even though she knew I would be fine doing it all on my own, and she barely knew the difference between a hammer and a screwdriver.

"You know, I'm being serious about you moving here, Kaylee. It might be the perfect place for you to start over as well. A fresh start in a new city. New state."

She nodded. "Yeah. Maybe."

My chest squeezed as I reached over and took her hand in mine.

Two years ago, Kaylee's fiancé had killed himself. The hardest part for her was that he'd only left a note that said he was sorry. That was it. She fell into a pit of depression and refused to leave her apartment for months. The thought of seeing someplace John had loved to go caused her to nearly hyperventilate.

She had come such a long way, with help from her grief counselor. She'd finally started talking about the idea of dating again about six months ago.

"Look!" I cried out when I saw the sign that said **HAMILTON: 30 MILES**.

"Great, but your GPS says we're still sixty miles from the house."

We both laughed as I pushed a little harder on the gas pedal. Kaylee wasn't the only one ready to get out of the car.

As we pulled down the dirt driveway, I saw the little white two-story house come into view. I gasped and felt my stomach flip. The front porch caught my attention first. Immediately my mind went to adding soft blue shutters to the windows, a swing on the left side of the porch, and wicker furniture with a pop of color on the right. Plants could line the wide steps on both sides and fill the air with the aroma of lavender and roses.

I lifted my eyes and took in the second story of the house. Two high windows looked out over the front yard. Even from here, I could tell it was the original glass from the ripples reflecting the sunlight. The house had been well maintained. Right down to the new silver metal roof.

I wanted to let out a girlish scream, I was so excited.

"Oh my gosh, is that it?" Kaylee exclaimed.

My heart thundered in my chest at the sight of the house. "Yes! Isn't it precious?"

Bouncing in her seat like she was about to get a buttload of candy, Kaylee clapped her hands. "Lincoln, it's perfect! It looks like they kept it up real nice too."

I nodded. "Yep! I cannot wait to get inside."

As my car got closer, Kaylee and I both leaned forward a little to look at the guy leaning against a post on the porch.

"Who is that?" Kaylee asked.

Shrugging, I replied, "I guess that's Ty Shaw."

Her head snapped over to look at me. "Ty? The son who owns it?"

"No, his name is Brock. Ty is the brother who's been pretty much the go-between with Brock and the title company."

She motioned with her hand to stop talking. "Shut up! Do you not see how hot that guy is? Like, look at him. His chest is huge!"

I giggled. This was the first guy since John who'd had Kaylee excited. The first guy she'd really looked twice at and the first guy who was apparently making her drool. When I saw her wipe her mouth, I couldn't help but laugh.

"Horny much, Kaylee?"

"My goodness. Save a horse and ride a Montana cowboy."

I pulled up and parked to get a better look at Kaylee's cowboy. Yep, he wore the part very well.

Cowboy boots? Check.

Black cowboy hat? Check.

Tight jeans that made his ass look like you could probably bounce a quarter off it? Check.

And he was currently making his way over to my car.

"Dibs," Kaylee said, looking back at me.

"What? Did you really just call dibs on this guy?" I asked as I turned off the car.

"Yes, I really did."

Before I'd had a chance to even open my door, Kaylee had jumped out of the car. I followed her lead, and Ty stopped in front of us while we both greeted him with a smile. Kaylee's a little wide and a bit eager looking.

Ty grinned at us both before he focused on me. "Lincoln?"

I nodded. "That would be me."

He reached for my hand. "It's great to finally meet you."

"It's a pleasure."

Turning to Kaylee, his smiled widened, and he didn't hide the fact that his eyes swept over her. "You must be Kaylee."

She turned back and looked at me. Her mouth dropped open. She mouthed *I think I'm in love* before placing her hand in his. "I am. Kaylee Holden. Pleasure meeting you."

He tipped his hat. "Ty Shaw Junior."

It wasn't lost on me how Ty and Kaylee were staring at each other. It was like they were both trying to figure out what in the hell was going on. I hadn't seen Kaylee look at another man like this in . . . well, I'd *never* seen her look at a guy like this. Not even John.

I quirked a brow and studied them for a moment. I finally had to clear my throat to get them to break the intense eye contact they had going on.

"Ty?" I asked, attempting to get him refocused.

He finally looked my way, and when his eyes met mine, my breath might have caught in my throat.

Okay, I totally got why Kaylee had been lost in this man's eyes. They were bluer than the sky.

Wow.

"Like I said, it's a pleasure finally getting to meet you, ma'am."

"Ma'am?" I asked, my nose scrunching up. "Call me Lincoln, please. And you've met my best friend, Kaylee."

He tipped his cowboy hat and smiled. "Will do, ma'am—I mean, Lincoln. Yes, we've met."

The hungry look he threw Kaylee's way made her turn pink in the cheeks.

I glanced back to the house. "Wow, it's more beautiful in person."

"I'm glad you like it. My mama's great-granddaddy built this house."

"The clapboard siding is just . . . beautiful," Kaylee stated. "It's been so well maintained."

"Well, would you like to see the inside of your new place?" Ty asked, glancing between me and Kaylee.

"Very much so!" I stated.

Ty focused on Kaylee. "Are you, um, moving here from Georgia as well?"

Kaylee froze before looking my way. I arched a brow and waited for her answer.

"Well, no. I mean, I'm not really sure what my future plans are. Maybe."

The hope in Ty's eyes wasn't hard to miss. It was fast, though. If I hadn't been watching him, I'd have missed it.

Interesting.

He turned and started for the house—with a slight limp in his gait—as we followed.

"So, did you remodel this house?" Kaylee asked, practically skipping behind him.

He let out a hearty laugh. "Hell no. I'm a rancher, not a builder."

"You don't like working with your hands?" Kaylee asked.

I turned to look at Kaylee. *What in the hell kind of question was that?*

Ty shot a sexy grin over his shoulder as he replied, "I like working with my hands just fine. Do it every day on the ranch . . . and in other cases that warrant something needing a soft but firm touch. I'm pretty damn good at that, if I say so myself."

Okay, that was a serious flirt directed toward her. Kaylee's cheeks heated again, and she looked away.

Leaning closer to her, I said, "You asked for that one."

She pushed me and shrugged. "I didn't mean it that way!" she hissed.

Ty unlocked the door and then handed me the set of keys. "It's all yours now, Lincoln. Mama wanted to know if you needed anything while you were getting settled in. If you need to be shown around town or anything like that."

My goodness, are all Montana cowboys this sweet? With a polite smile, I replied, "No, thank you. I appreciate it, though."

He nodded. Then he tipped his black cowboy hat again and grinned once more.

Is that a dimple?

Yep, that's a dimple.

That was all Kaylee needed to see.

I stepped inside, followed by Kaylee. Ty walked around us once we were all inside the house.

"Back to your other question, Kaylee, I didn't remodel the house, but my brother Brock did when he married Kaci. My parents gave them this house as a wedding gift."

He smiled again, and this time his dimples were on full display. Kaylee moaned slightly from next to me, and I had to jab her in the side.

"Oh, that's so sweet . . . but why don't they live in the house anymore?"

Ty looked uncomfortable.

Lifting my hand to wave off my last question, I said, "Never mind. That's none of my business, and I'm sorry I asked."

A rush of embarrassment swept over my body. I of all people should have known better than to ask such personal questions. Here I was, attempting to start my own life over in a new town, and the first person I met, I asked a question that was truly not my business.

Ty let it go. "It's been empty for a few years now. I think you'll enjoy fixing the house up even more, with your career and all. My mother said you're an interior designer."

I nodded. "Yes, I am. I owned a pretty big design firm in Atlanta and needed a change. I sold it and decided it was time to explore something new. I'm hoping to find a simpler, less complicated life here in Hamilton."

Ty's eyes widened. "You're not from a small town, are you, Lincoln?"

"No, born and raised in Atlanta."

Glancing to Kaylee, Ty asked, "And you?"

"I was born in Georgia too."

He nodded. "Your southern accent is heavier."

Kaylee beamed with pride. "Well, I'm from a smaller town in Georgia originally, but I've been working on my southern twang for years. I think it's finally set in."

The poor man looked perplexed by my best friend. "Well, I'll let you ladies go so you can explore the rest of the house. Do you need help with your luggage?"

"Yes!" Kaylee said at the same time I said, "No."

Ty laughed. "If you pop the trunk, I'll grab your stuff."

I pulled out my keys and did just that. Kaylee and I stood there and watched as Ty stepped out of the screen door and walked down the gravel path.

"Is it just me, or does that man have an ass to die for?" she whispered.

I turned to look at her. It wasn't like I wasn't happy to see her showing interest in someone; I truly was. I believed it was time for her to jump back into the dating world. She needed to move on past the hurt. Back in Georgia, she'd never so much as looked twice at a guy, no matter how good looking he was. I wasn't about to hold her back. "No, it's not just you. He has a nice ass."

"If that's how they make the men up here in Montana, I just might be sticking around for a longer visit."

Lacing my arm through hers, I grinned. "If there are more cowboys who look like that, you might never want to leave."

"Right?" she said with a giggle.

Deep down in my heart, I prayed she would seriously think about staying. I wasn't being selfish in my reasons why I wanted her here. Of course I wanted my best friend with me. I would miss her terribly when she went back to Georgia. But I honestly felt like a new start was exactly what Kaylee needed. A place that didn't have a memory around nearly every corner she turned. A place where she could let go of the hurt and allow herself to move on. Somewhere to start over where no one told her what to do. A place to forget the past and look forward to a future.

I paused for a moment in my thoughts. Was that what I wanted for Kaylee . . . or for me?

I wanted that for both of us.

"How many brothers do you think he has? More than the one?" she asked as we watched Ty take our suitcases out like they weighed nothing.

Watching the muscles flex in Ty Shaw's arms almost felt sinful. It had been a long time since I'd even allowed myself to look at a man like this. The last time I'd given my heart to someone, I'd ended up regretting it.

With a slight chuckle, I shook my head. Maybe it wasn't time for only Kaylee to start dating but me as well. *A nice Montana cowboy is exactly what I need.* It had been over a year since I'd had a man's hands on my body. I was beginning to remember what that pleasure felt like.

I took a deep breath and slowly let it out before I said, "One can only hope."

Chapter Three

Brock

I checked my rigging bag once more before I got ready to head on out and catch an Uber to the arena with Dirk. I heard the knock on my hotel door and made my way over and answered it.

Dirk Littlewood, my best friend since first grade, stood in front of me, a wide smile on his face.

"I thought we were meeting in the lobby?" I said.

"We were. Guess what I found?"

"What did you find?"

"Kara Lane."

"Okay, I'll bite, who's Kara Lane?" I asked, motioning for Dirk to come into my room.

"She is, according to her, your number one fan. She wants to meet you."

With a sigh, I shook my head. I didn't hook up with a lot of women when I was out on tour. I did occasionally, though, when I needed the release. Dirk, on the other hand, wasn't as picky when it came to the buckle bunnies.

"Let me guess: you want something out of this."

Dirk smirked before dropping his bag and then himself into a seat.

"Normally I would say yes, but this lady has a kid with her. Cute little boy with Down syndrome. He wants to be a bull rider. She recognized me down in the lobby and asked if I could let you know how much it would mean to her and her son to meet you."

"This isn't a trick to get a hookup later, is it?"

Dirk looked slightly hurt. "You honestly think I'd make up that kind of story just to get laid?"

Rubbing the back of my neck, I sighed. "No, dude, sorry."

He nodded as I grabbed my boots and started to put them on. "You talk to Blayze?"

"Yeah. Ty was going to show him how to rope a calf before I got home."

I could hear Dirk mutter something under his breath, and I couldn't help but smile. "Dick move, right?" I asked.

"Why is he so bitter? I mean, does he not get how much it tears you up being out on the road without Blayze?"

Shrugging, I answered, "I don't think he means to do it on purpose. He's been through a lot himself."

Dirk agreed with a nod. "Still, he shouldn't be using your kid."

I stood. "I agree, a hundred percent. You got any T-shirts or anything for this?"

"Lloyd has some merchandise."

Lloyd Webster was our Wrangler sponsor and could always be found carrying a bag of Wrangler merchandise.

As we headed to the elevator, two women made their way toward us. I cringed inwardly while Dirk let a smile grow across his face.

"Morning, ladies," he purred with an accent that screamed he was country more than the boots and cowboy hat he wore.

The blonde waved her fingers at both of us and winked. "Enjoy your day, gentlemen."

When they walked by, Dirk let his gaze follow them.

He smiled wider, and I shook my head as we walked into the elevator. "I may get lucky tonight after all. You sure you don't want to go out later?"

"I'm positive. I'm sure I'll be exhausted after today and ready to hit the sack when the day is over."

"What if you ride good?"

I shrugged. "If I qualify, then I'll need to ride tomorrow, and I sure as shit don't want to have a hangover."

He laughed. "When in the hell was the last time you had a hangover, Brock?"

The elevator doors opened to the main lobby, and Dirk and I headed over to Lloyd. I saw a woman standing there with a boy who looked to be about ten. The moment he saw me, his eyes lit up. His mother followed his gaze and wore a similar look on her face. Moments like these never got old, especially when they involved little kids.

"I promised you I would find and deliver him," Dirk said as he reached the woman first. "Kara, I'd like for you to meet the current number one bull rider as of today."

Shooting Dirk a smirk, I turned to the woman and shook her hand. "It's a pleasure meeting you, ma'am."

She blushed, then looked down to her son. "Billy, this here is the bull rider you're always cheering on."

The young boy looked up at me and gave me a full-on smile. Bending down, I got eye level with him as Lloyd handed me a baseball cap and a T-shirt. I signed them both as I spoke to Billy.

"You want to be a bull rider someday, Billy?"

"Yes, sir. I'll be as good as you!"

"I bet you will be. Have you ever been on a bull?" I asked, handing him the baseball cap and laughing when he quickly put it on.

"Yes, sir. I have."

"I tell you what, Billy; I'm going to make sure you and your mom have VIP passes today. You come on back and wish me luck, okay?"

His eyes lit up like Christmas morning, and before I knew it, his arms were wrapped around my neck. "Thank you! Thank you!"

Glancing up, I smiled at Kara. She mouthed the words *Thank you.* After Billy let me go, I handed him the shirt and stood back up. I signed another hat for Kara and gave it to her.

"You don't know how much this means to me. Billy's father passed away to cancer a few months back, and this is the first time I've seen him smile. He always watched you when you rode. You were his favorite, hence the reason you're Billy's favorite."

"I'm so sorry for your loss," I said.

Dirk was now talking to the little boy and signing the back of his shirt.

"Thank you. And thank you for coming down to meet us—I know you're on your way to the arena for today's event. You'll never know how much it means to both of us."

Smiling, I reached for her hand and shook it again. "You and Billy enjoy today. Lloyd here will get you taken care of."

With a slap on my back, Lloyd moved in and began making plans with Kara. I leaned down and shook Billy's hand.

"I'll see you later, buddy."

"Bye, Brock!" he shouted, then took off running toward an older woman. I was guessing she was his grandmother. Dirk nudged me with his arm, and we headed toward the exit of the hotel to make our way to the arena. It was bull-riding time.

"Hornet's Nest. Just my luck," I grumbled as I stared at the bull.

I'd drawn the number two bull. He'd been ridden only once in twenty outs, and that was by Cord Hansen. The bastard hadn't stopped talking about it for weeks after he'd gotten the eight seconds required to get a score.

"You've got this, Brock," Dirk said from next to me.

Turning his way, I smiled. Dirk was more than just my best friend; he was like a brother to me. The fact that we got to be on tour together, both doing something we loved, had probably saved my sanity. There were plenty of moments I wanted to give in to the guilt that felt like it ate away at me every second of every day. Dirk knew; he saw it every single time he looked into my eyes or hauled my ass back to our hotel when I'd been drunk out of my mind.

Would things have been different if Kaci had chosen Dirk and not me? I had no damn idea. All I knew was, Dirk had kept me going when all I'd wanted to do was give up and walk away. He pushed me because he knew I needed it. I had never told him before, and probably never would, but he saved my life five years ago when I'd started drinking too much.

"Shaw, heard you got your old buddy."

I grunted as Cord walked up to me. I wanted to knock the smirk right off his face. The last time I'd been on Hornet's Nest, he had thrown me after two seconds, and I'd seen Cord laughing his ass off as I got up. Asshole. He was a bitter jerk and pissed because I was currently in the number one spot, and he was trailing further behind in the number two.

"Hey, Cord. How's it going?" I asked, not about to engage in his little game.

He frowned, disappointment laced on his face. Cord was like a female. Constantly trying to drum up some sort of drama.

"Good luck today, buddy," Dirk said as he slapped the shit out of Cord's back before we walked away. "Douche," Dirk whispered, glancing back to Cord.

Even after giving Dirk every reason to hate me so many years ago, he still had my back, and I knew he always would.

Growing up, Kaci had been the one girl every guy in town wanted. But Dirk and I'd had her. Not in a sexual way. She was our best friend.

The girl who went fishing with us. Hunting in the early hours of the morning. She even helped my granddaddy build the barn on my parents' ranch for the goats she'd talked Daddy into getting.

Kaci was different from any other girl I'd ever known. She wasn't afraid of anything. Gutting a deer was second nature to her. She could knock back Jack Daniel's with me and Dirk like nobody's business. She was also happy; sometimes it seemed like a forced happy, but she had a smile on her face most of the time.

Kaci could also make Dirk and me fight over the littlest things.

Everything had changed the day I asked Kaci to prom. Dirk had been pissed at me for going against our self-imposed rule. Kaci was off limits. I ignored the rule, and it had opened up a rift between me and my best friend. Neither of us knew how to deal with it besides going after each other constantly.

When it finally came to blows between me and Dirk, fighting over her, we'd told her she needed to make a choice. She knew she had to pick one of us. She picked me.

I had won and had taken Kaci from my best friend, even though I knew he loved her more than I ever could. But I was a selfish bastard and couldn't walk away from her. I was happy she'd picked me over Dirk and didn't regret for one minute marrying her. Even though everyone told us we were too young to get married.

It wasn't like I didn't love Kaci. I did. And I knew she loved me; why else would she have picked me? But I also knew how much Dirk loved her. He had a terrible way of showing her, though, and in the end, it cost him. I knew how to be romantic, while Dirk fumbled with his words. At least he had back then. Kaci only saw that side of me. The side that fantasized right along with her about the life we would have.

Something had always been missing between me and Kaci, though. It didn't take us long after we got married to realize it. An emptiness hung between us, and neither of us could figure out what was causing it. We'd thought we could make it better by having a baby. It hadn't helped that I ignored one of the main reasons we were having troubles. Bull riding. It wasn't something I was willing to give up for her. At the time, I hadn't realized how selfish that made me. Bull riding was my life, and in my mind, Kaci had known it was my life when we got married.

But Dirk was ready to give up professional bull riding for her, and I knew now he probably would have made her happier than I ever could.

A part of me would always regret that I didn't love her enough to put her first, like Dirk would have. The guilt of that ate at me constantly. Dirk never showed any bitterness toward me or Kaci, and I knew it was because he'd respected her decision. He was the true meaning of loyalty and friendship.

I glanced over to him. He seemed lost in thought, just like I was. I'd bet a million dollars he was thinking about her too.

I'd hurt Dirk not only once, but twice. Our friendship had been tested by one simple decision I'd made five years ago. A decision that had been haunting my dreams nightly since. Had our small town whispering behind my back, even to this day.

"You boys ready to kick some ass tonight?" Lloyd Webster asked, stopping directly in front of us.

I forced a smile for one of my biggest sponsors. If I rode well tonight, I'd make him one very happy man. It would show up in my wallet as well. An endorsement with Wrangler was nothing to take lightly. As long as I stayed number one on the tour, I was golden.

"Yes, sir," I answered, pushing my hand out to shake his.

"That's what I want to hear. Let's keep that number one ranking, son."

Lloyd focused on Dirk. "I have a feeling your run of bad luck ends tonight in Tacoma, Dirk."

"Let's hope so."

"You drew a good one," Lloyd added, giving Dirk a wink.

A smile grew over Dirk's face. He'd drawn Lucky Charm. He hadn't been ridden in his last ten outs.

My phone buzzed in my pocket. I reached in and answered without even looking. "Hello?"

"So, you never did tell me who day two's draw was."

Ty. I should have known.

My brother used to go on tour with me a few years back until an accident landed him in the hospital for an extended amount of time. When they told him he'd never be able to ride a bull again, you might as well have told him he'd died that day. His entire world came to an abrupt stop.

The doctors at first hadn't thought Ty would even *walk* again. He proved them wrong. He walked after just one month in physical therapy. That one victory came at a cost, though. Ty hit the bottle for months and then suffered with an addiction to pain pills that few knew about.

It gutted me when I'd realized I hadn't seen the signs. That none of us had seen the signs. When our parents found out, they got him the help he needed, but it was a long road for all of us. After a tenuous few months, Ty had cleaned up, and he worked the family cattle ranch now. I was so damn proud of my brother. I knew it had to be hard for him to fight that addiction, and I also knew it was always something he would struggle with in the back of his mind. No matter what, I'd be there for him.

"Well?"

Ty pulled me back to the present.

"I got Hornet's Nest."

The bastard laughed. "Oh, hell. Don't let him throw you after the first two seconds."

I ignored his jab at me, since I was already frustrated with him for telling Blayze he'd teach him to rope. "That's the plan," I said. "You tell Blayze you'd teach him to rope?" I knew he could hear the frustration in my voice.

"I might have mentioned it."

"Why would you do that, Ty? I'm going to teach him when I come home."

"Well, he wanted to learn, so I offered. Besides, you've been gone for a few weeks."

Anger raced through my veins at the thought of Ty showing Blayze to do something he damn well knew I'd wanted to do. The fact that he was throwing my career in my face added to how pissed off I was. "I don't see where that's any of your damn business, Ty."

"Not my business? The hell it isn't. Mom and Dad are raising your son half the damn time. Hell, *I'm* raising your son right along with them. I'm the one taking him to Little League on the weekends. Picking him up for Mama when she's got something she needs to take care of. And what are you doing? Riding a bull week after week. You seem to be more in love with the next eight seconds than you are with the next eight years of your son's life."

A flash of heat hit me hard. It was both anger and guilt mixing together to cause a rage inside of me. A rage I had worked hard at keeping buried deep within. Did he honestly think I didn't want to be home with my son? That I didn't lie in bed every night and wish it was me tucking him into his bed? That it was me coaching his Little League team?

"Seems to me that was your life a few years ago, and you had no problem with it then."

"I didn't have a kid, Brock," he bit back.

I pushed my fingers through my brown hair, knowing he was right—and hating it as well.

"Listen, I get that you got married young. You guys had Blayze in some attempt to make your marriage work. Why you thought a kid would do it, I have no clue."

"You don't know what you're talking about, Ty."

He laughed. "Yeah, whatever. I get it, Brock. You're twenty-seven. You're having a good time. I'm sure you're sleeping with a different bunny each night."

"I'm not," I stated.

Silence filled the line. Then, "Fine. Every other night. But you have a kid back home who needs his father."

I swallowed hard. "Then I'll hire a nanny and bring him with me."

"Oh, for fuck's sake. You really want him on the road with you?"

"What else do you want me to do, Ty? I fly home almost every week when I can. So I've been gone an extra week here and there. That is my *job.* You know that. Stop making me feel guilty for doing something you once loved to do as well. I can't help the way things turned out."

"Screw you, Brock."

The line went silent again.

"I'm sorry," I finally said.

Ty sighed. "Dude, I'm sorry too. You're doing a good job with Blayze, and I . . . hell, I don't know."

It was time for a subject change before we ended the call.

"So, tell me what's new back at home."

"Damn, dude. That interior designer who bought your place finally showed up, and she was *not* what I had been expecting."

My interest was piqued. "Really? What's she like?"

"Hot as hell. A body to die for. Curves like no one's business. Her friend Kaylee is even hotter. I nearly fell over when the two of them got out of the car. You said it was some interior designer from Atlanta. You didn't say she was a twenty-seven-year-old knockout who would make the cock of any guy within fifty yards stand at attention. I mean, the couple of times I talked to her on the phone, she sounded young, but I wasn't expecting someone so pretty."

I laughed. "I didn't know anything other than she was an interior designer and would be working for Karen Johnson. I didn't *want* to know. What does she look like?"

"Oh hell, dude, she's just your type. Brown hair, sort of light in color, or she puts that crap in it that makes it look streaked with lighter-colored hair."

"Highlights?" I asked.

"I'm not even going to comment or ask how in the hell you know that's what it's called. Anyway, brown hair and green eyes that I swear look like the grass on a spring morning. Her friend Kaylee is blonde, with blue eyes that I'm pretty sure were screaming *Take me to bed, Ty.*"

I laughed. My brother would never change.

"Neither of them is too skinny. You know, like half the women in town who eat nothing but carrots and celery, so they're sticks. Let's just say I'd be able to grab a nice handful of ass while either one rode me."

I rolled my eyes. "Nice, Ty. Mama would slap the shit out of you if she heard you talking about a woman that way."

"Yeah, just like she'd slap the shit out of *you* if she knew you were shoving your dick down the throat of some girl you didn't bother asking what her name was."

Sex was just a tool I used to let off steam, and not even something I did often. Finding someone to settle down with was not on my radar. I didn't deserve to find happiness, not after what I did to Kaci. I didn't want to fall in love. The fear of hurting someone again sat in the back of my head and was a constant reminder that I would probably do it again unknowingly.

"Listen, I've got to go. Have fun with the new chick in town."

He laughed. "I think I'm more interested in the friend. Besides, she's not staying, so it would be perfect. I could screw her and never see her again, except for the occasional time she came to visit Lincoln. Then we could have no-strings-attached sex. Yeah, I'm liking this little plan of mine."

What in the hell was wrong with us? It wasn't just me who was a mess; it was all three of us brothers. Not one of us could commit to a woman . . . all for different reasons.

"Yeah, well, good luck with that."

"No, seriously, though. Lincoln is a nice person, and so is her friend Kaylee. I think you'll like them both."

I *was* curious about the woman who had bought my house. "Hey, speaking of Lincoln, what did she say about the house?"

I hadn't stepped foot in that house in four years and had no desire to ever again. When I'd told my folks I was selling it, I'd thought for sure they'd want it back. They hadn't, though. They'd told me it was a wedding gift and to do what I wanted with it, so selling it seemed like the best thing.

"She loved it. I'm pretty sure she's going to change some things, though. With her being into decorating and all."

I frowned. "Kaci decorated it."

There was silence for a few moments before Ty cleared his throat. "Well, to be fair, she doesn't know the backstory, and you can't honestly expect her to never change anything."

"Yeah, I guess."

"You don't regret selling it, do you?"

"Nah, I was never going to live there again. Listen, I've got to run. Tell Mama and Dad I said hey and kiss Blayze for me. TV on so he can watch me ride?"

"Yeah, you know it's on. Will do, baby brother. Stay safe."

After we said our goodbyes, I hit end and stared at my phone. That familiar ache was starting to take hold of my chest. Only this time, I didn't know where that ache stemmed from . . . Ty riding my ass about Blayze, or from the memories assaulting me over the sale of my and Kaci's home. Either way, I didn't like it one bit.

Chapter Four

Brock

"You've got this," Dirk said, pulling on the bull rope while trying to push Hornet's Nest to move.

"Yeah," I said, getting my hand secure in the rope.

Hornet's Nest bucked in the chute, and Rob's hand, extended in front of me, kept me from hitting the rail while Dirk had ahold of my vest. Rob worked for the stock contractor who owned Hornet's Nest.

Once the bastard calmed down, I got myself adjusted, took a quick breath, said my normal prayer, and nodded.

The gateman pulled the gate open, and Hornet's Nest took off like a damn rocket. I had expected him to go left, like he always did. I guess today he felt like changing shit up.

He went right.

Then, he changed direction. For a moment, I thought I was heading down the well, which was not something I wanted to do. That meant my ass would be on the ground, and this two-thousand-pound beast would surely stomp the shit out of me. Not to mention, I wouldn't be getting paid.

I dug my spurs in to get a better grip.

"Holy shit," I grumbled as Hornet's Nest turned back.

He was all over the place—and I loved it. The feeling of this massive bull under me, fighting just as hard as I was . . . it was the reason I rode. He gave me one hell of a fight, and that had my heart racing with excitement. It never got old, this feeling of adrenaline flowing through my body when I was riding. And nothing compared to it. Nothing was able to make me completely get lost and forget everything. The moment that chute opened and it was just me and the bull, everyone and everything else disappeared. It was a fight to see who could outwit the other, and my goal was to come out on top. Every. Single. Time.

"That's it! Give it to me!" I shouted as I finally heard the eight-second buzzer.

I reached down and pulled my hand free. For good measure, the bull bucked once more as hard as he could, and I went flying. Luck was on my side, though, and I landed damn near on my feet after flipping in the air.

I pulled off my helmet and threw it as I yelled out in pure excitement.

Hank, one of the bullfighters, came up and slapped me on the back. "Best ride I've seen from you in a long time, dude!"

Smiling, I nodded and replied, "Thanks, man."

When I glanced up and saw my score, I let out a loud-as-hell "Yee-haw!"

Ninety.

Making my way through the gate, I got the usual pats on the back, the handshakes, and the "You kicked ass" comments from the other riders.

Dirk stood there, a huge smile on his face. "Looks like you showed him."

I winked. "Now it's your turn, dickhead."

"We're going to celebrate tonight."

I nodded, seeing the sports reporter and camera crew headed my way. "Later," I said as Dirk looked and laughed while he slapped my back.

After a quick interview, I made my way to the lockers to call Blayze. I didn't normally do that, but I had the urge to talk to him after my conversation with Ty.

"Daddy! You won! You won!"

Laughing, I replied, "I just got the eight seconds, buddy. I haven't won yet."

"But you will," he declared.

I loved how he thought I could do anything. In his eyes, I could never fail.

I hated that, someday, he'd learn the truth about what I had done to his mother. He'd never forgive me then, never think of me as the superhero who always saved the day.

"From your lips, buddy."

"Uncle Ty said you got lucky."

I rolled my eyes. "You tell Uncle Ty to go eat some soap because he tells lies."

Blayze laughed. "Daddy! I met a pwetty lady!"

My stomach dropped. Since when had my son started noticing women as pretty? He was *five.* They should still be gross, shouldn't they? "You met a *what?*"

"Grams says she's our new neighbor. She's pwetty!"

"Blayze, darlin', let me talk to your daddy now."

"But, Grams, Daddy called to talk to me."

My heart started to beat a little faster. *He's growing up quicker than I realized.*

"Buddy, let me talk to Grams real quick, and then we'll finish talking." I started pacing. I knew I needed to be back at the chutes to help Dirk.

"Hey, honey. Good ride."

"Mama, since when does he notice girls are pretty? I didn't think that shit happened for another few years."

She chuckled. "Calm down, Brock. He's a little boy, and he's bound to notice a pretty girl."

I sighed and ran my fingers through my hair. "Yeah. It just feels like he's growing up so fast."

"He is."

There was no doubt I could hear the sadness in her voice. It mirrored the sadness I felt in the middle of my chest. *I don't know what in the hell I'm doing anymore.*

Mom went on talking. "Lincoln stopped by to drop something off that she'd found in one of the closets. She said it was in a hidden compartment that she'd stumbled on. It's a box, and I think it belonged to Kaci."

My breath caught in my throat. "What?"

"Lincoln said it was in the largest bedroom. I guess she's making it into a master and taking the wall out to expand it for a bathroom."

Irrational anger ripped through me. "She's knocking down walls? What in the hell?"

"Brock, you sold the house. You didn't want it . . . remember?"

I sighed.

"Anyway, Blayze was out playing in the tree when I ran into the house to move the laundry, and he got excited when he saw her. He fell from the tree, but he's okay. We thought maybe he sprained his wrist, but the doctor said he's fine. Nothing a bit of ice and rest won't fix."

"What was she doing talking to a kid all alone, anyway?"

"Brock Shaw, you do not talk like that. You don't even know this woman. Don't be so mean."

Glancing at the clock, I said, "Let me talk to Blayze. I've got to get going."

Without another word, she put my son back on the line.

"Daddy! I took a picture with the pwetty new neighbor. I'll send it to you!"

I smiled. Good Lord, he had Shaw blood running through him, that was for sure. "Now, don't be going and falling in love, buddy. You've got to keep your options open for kindergarten."

"Gwoss!" Blayze shouted.

A little sense of relief washed over me that he still thought girls were gross. "Listen, I've got to go help Uncle Dirk get ready to ride. I love you, buddy. I'll see you soon, okay?"

"Okay, Daddy! I wove you too!"

I hit end and made my way out of the lockers and back to the chutes. A few people stopped me along the way to congratulate me on the ride; then my phone buzzed in my pocket.

Shit. I'd forgotten to leave it in my locker. I pulled it out, came to a stop, and stared down at the picture I knew for a fact my boy *hadn't* sent. If he had learned how to send pictures in a text message, I was in trouble.

No, this was the work of my mother.

I stared at the image of the brown-haired beauty who was bent down and nearly eye level with Blayze. His cowboy hat damn near covered his face, and Lincoln smiled from ear to ear.

Shit, her eyes.

Even if Ty hadn't told me, I could tell just from this picture that they were green. A green I'd never seen before. My gaze dropped to that pretty little pink mouth. Then my chest did some weird-ass flutter as my eyes moved up and locked on hers. There was something in those eyes, something that called to me in a way I'd never experienced before.

I was drawn to this woman—and that both scared me and annoyed the hell out of me. More so the latter.

She was beautiful, there was no doubt about it. No wonder my kid had wanted a picture with her.

The idea that my brother Ty might hook up with Lincoln bothered me. More than it should have. Why all of a sudden am I jealous of my brother being near a woman I had never even met?

"Brock! You'd better get your ass moving before Dirk climbs into that chute and on that bull."

Pulling my eyes away from the screen, I pushed the phone back into my pocket and quickly jogged back to the chutes.

The damn TV camera was in my way as I pulled on Dirk's bull rope. "Remember, you've got a left-hand delivery. He's gonna wanna turn away from you. Be ready," I said.

Dirk hit his hand to get it tight in the rope. "Got it."

"Be ready for him to change directions. He's known to fade."

"Got it," Dirk replied again.

I knew he was moments from the nod, so I didn't say another word. I let Dirk get into his head.

He gave the nod, and the gateman pulled on the nylon rope, letting the beast free from the cage.

"Get it!" I shouted as I watched Dirk get bounced around. "That's it!" I cried out. "You've got it!"

The bull swung to the left, catching Dirk off-balance, causing him to go down the well. My heart stalled, and I knew I was holding my breath. He got hung, and I watched as the bullfighters attempted to get his hand out of the bull rope.

"Get him out," I whispered, even though I wanted to shout it.

The bull swung around, and Dirk's body swung with it. He looked like a rag doll being tossed about. I flinched when I saw the bull come down on him. I closed my eyes and sent up a quick prayer.

After I opened my eyes, my prayer was answered.

His hand finally got free.

"Fucking finally!" I shouted and jumped down, making my way around to the gate where they would bring Dirk through. My heart raced in my chest. I saw him walking, so that was a good sign.

As he walked toward me, he stumbled.

"Shit!" I cried out, making my way to Dirk.

One of the members of the medical team grabbed him. "You okay, Dirk?" he asked.

Dirk's eyes met mine, and he smiled slightly. "Perfectly fine. Just another day on the job."

I knew he was lying. He wasn't fine, but like all of us, he had his poker face firmly in place.

He walked past me and winked. "Find me a blonde. I'm going to need a distraction from the shooting pain going up my side."

Shaking my head, I said, "Sex is what you're thinking about right now? How about the fact that you just missed the eight seconds?"

He groaned and then said, "When *don't* I think about sex, Brock?"

"I'll have Cord pick out a girl and send her your way!" I called out.

Lifting his hand, Dirk gave me the finger.

I smiled as I shook my head. He was going to be just fine.

Chapter Five

Lincoln

The knock on the window startled me, and I bent down and saw Ty and Blayze. I hopped off the stool and called out for Kaylee.

"Kaylee, Ty and Blayze are here."

She didn't answer, which meant she had her headphones on and was working.

"Come on in, y'all."

The screen door opened, and they walked in.

"What are ya doing, Miss Lincoln?" Blayze asked, his big blue eyes gazing up at me. I smiled and dropped down to be at his eye level. I'd met Blayze the other day when I had stopped by the Shaws' house to give them something I had found in a closet. Blayze had been a little charmer, even after falling out of the tree, and he'd put on a brave face when we all knew he was hurting.

The next day, when he and Stella stopped by to officially welcome me as a neighbor, and Blayze asked for a picture with me, my heart melted. Of course, it helped that he told me I was the prettiest girl he'd ever seen. My new little neighbor was charming his way right into my heart.

"I was attempting to hang a curtain rod."

Ty took a step forward. "How are you doing getting settled in?"

With a grin, I glanced around the house as I stood back up. We'd been in Hamilton a week, and I was already in love with it. "Slowly getting there. I've been able to get a lot done in the short amount of time I've been here."

He nodded. "Why don't you let me do that for you?"

I held up my handy-dandy electric drill. Ever since I could remember, my father had made it seem like I wasn't capable of handling simple tasks like hanging up a curtain rod. That wasn't the case anymore. "Nope, I've gone my whole life having someone try to help me with one thing or another. This house is different. Everything in this house will be because I did it."

He frowned. "You won't be admitting defeat if you let me hang a curtain rod, you know."

I grinned. "I appreciate it, but I've got this." Glancing between the older Shaw and the younger, I asked, "What brings you two here?"

Blayze proudly held up and displayed a pie. Of course I had noticed it the moment he'd walked in. "Grams said we needed to bring this to you. She sent my daddy a picture of you 'cause she said you were *real* pwetty and that he'd probably like to see a pwetty girl. He won on his bull the whole weekend. He's number one!"

I looked back at Ty, confused.

"Brock is a professional bull rider. He was in Tacoma this past weekend. Blayze said he wanted to send him the picture you'd taken with him, so my mother texted it to him."

My cheeks heated, and I hoped Ty wouldn't notice. "Oh, I see. Your mother didn't mention where Blayze's father was. I just assumed he lived here."

Ty's brows pulled in tight, and something resembling anger moved over his face. It was so quick, I almost didn't catch it.

"Yeah, well, that's not the case."

Okay then. I for sure detected a bit of anger there.

"You're not happy with what he does for a living?" I asked.

"Uncle Ty used to bull ride before he got hurt," Blayze interjected.

My eyes went from Blayze to Ty.

"Anyway, my mother wanted you to have this as a way of saying, 'Welcome to your new home.'"

And that was a serious change of subject, I mused. Did Ty simply not like talking about his brother? Or maybe it was the injury Blayze had mentioned. My curiosity had certainly been piqued.

Right then, Kaylee came walking into the living room, her headphones still on, as evidenced by her shouting, "Where's the ice cream?"

Ty's face lit up, and so did Blayze's. I had to chuckle at the way they both seemed to gleam at Kaylee. Of course, my best friend was a knockout and currently holding a hammer while asking for ice cream. Who wouldn't think that was sexy?

Kaylee pulled her headphones off her ears. "Ty! Hi. Oh, wow, that rhymed. Not that I'd tried to make it rhyme or anything. It was just a simple hello that ended up being a hi and Ty. So, yeah, not really trying to be creative with my words."

Ty laughed while I tilted my head at the woman standing before me. Cheeks red. Lust filling those blue eyes of hers. And she was babbling.

So. Very. Interesting.

"You often eat ice cream with a hammer?" Ty asked while Blayze cracked up laughing like that was the funniest thing he'd ever heard.

Kaylee held up the hammer. "What? Oh, no. I was going to try to hang up these blinds in the guest bedroom, but I sort of made a boo-boo."

I turned to face her. "I thought you were working."

"I was. Then, I got bored and decided to help you hang up the blinds, and I accidentally missed and hit the wall with the hammer."

I looked down at the drill in my hand and held it up. "*This* is what I'm using to hang up the blinds and curtains. Not a hammer!"

Kaylee's face turned red as she held up the screw. "Ohh . . . okay. I thought that little thing didn't look like a nail."

My eyes rolled as Ty attempted not to lose it, laughing. Kaylee had been raised in a very well-to-do family. Manual labor was still something new to her. She could help me move furniture around like no one's business. Loved to help me shop for decorations, but when it came time for the nitty-gritty stuff, Kaylee always disappeared.

Except for now. She truly wanted to help me with this little house. I had a feeling it was growing on her like it had on me the moment I saw it for sale online.

"It's called a screw, Kaylee."

"Even I know what a screw is, Miss Kaylee."

Moving her gaze from me down to Blayze, Kaylee smiled. "My goodness! Who is this handsome cowboy?"

She made her way over to Blayze, who stuck his chest out just a little bit more. I covered my mouth and chuckled.

"My name is Blayze Brock Shaw, but you can call me Blayze. All my friends do."

Kaylee lifted a brow and looked at Ty. "Yours?" she asked.

"What? No! *Heck no.* My younger brother's kid."

Kaylee looked down at Blayze and winked. "Bummer, I really like kids."

"He's with me nearly all the time, since Brock is traveling so much," Ty stated quickly.

I bit the inside of my cheek to keep from laughing. It was cute how Ty seemed to have a little crush on Kaylee.

Blayze turned to me. "Miss Lincoln, my papa said you bought a horse from him the other day."

"Yep, your papa is right. Would you like to see him? I could use a break."

Blayze attempted to stay calm, but his five-year-old self did a few little jumps. "Yes! Uncle Ty, can I go see Miss Lincoln's horse?"

Ty's eyes met mine. "We don't want to interrupt you from working. I know you're trying to get settled in."

"Nonsense. Besides, I think Kaylee could use some help with that . . . hammer."

When Kaylee's eyes snapped over to me with nothing but a death stare, I simply smiled.

"Come on, Blayze. Let's go see that horse."

"What? Now? You're leaving us alone?" Kaylee cried after us.

Tossing a look over my shoulder, I called back, "I'm pretty sure Ty doesn't bite—at least not hard, anyway."

Ty rumbled out a hearty laugh as my best friend's mouth dropped in shock. The girl was all talk, apparently.

Blayze reached up and took my hand as I walked him down to the barn.

"This barn used to be my daddy's."

"Really?" I asked, looking at the barn in front of us. "Did you come here a lot with your daddy?"

He shook his head. "We moved out when I was really little."

I nodded. I had to admit I was curious about this mysterious Brock Shaw. *What would make a man do such a dangerous thing for a living?*

I also had no idea where Blayze's mother was, or even if she was still in the picture.

"Do you like it here?" he asked.

"Yes, very much."

"Do you like riding horses?"

"I do, very much so."

"Me too! My daddy taught me. He also taught me how to fish, and I's can shoot a gun."

Gasping, I asked, "A gun? Aren't you a little young to shoot a gun, Blayze?"

"No, ma'am," he said, crawling up the hay bale that was sitting outside the stall. He smiled the moment he saw Thunder. "He sure is a pwetty horse, Miss Lincoln. Why's he in the barn and not in the pasture?"

"I'll turn him out here in a bit."

"Daddy says I's born to be on a horse. He's gonna teach me how to rope when he comes back home."

I grinned as I ran my hand down Thunder's neck before giving him a good pat. Blayze mimicked my action and told Thunder what a good boy he was. I couldn't help but smile as I watched him interact with the animal. It was clear he loved horses. And I loved having that in common with my new little neighbor.

Then, out of the blue, he brought up his mother. "I didn't know my mommy. Do you know your mommy?"

My heart broke for the little guy.

I nodded. "Yes. My mommy was the one who taught me how to ride a horse."

Blayze smiled. I couldn't help but wonder how old he'd been when she'd . . . left. "I bet you miss your mommy," I said, trying to picture what my life would have been like without my mother. I couldn't even imagine.

"Blayze!"

I let out a scream that spooked Thunder, making him jerk back. Blayze didn't seem fazed at all by Thunder reacting to my scream. I, on the other hand, jumped and tripped over God knows what. I landed right on my ass.

Before I could even comprehend what had happened, a hand reached down for me to take.

"My goodness, you scared me," I said as the hand pulled me up like I weighed no more than a feather.

I stumbled, and he righted me. The moment I looked up into his sky-blue eyes, my stomach tumbled.

Then, my heart seized in my chest when I focused on the rest of the man.

He was tall, but not too tall. I was five three, so he had to be five ten, maybe? Built, but not so much that you imagined he lived in a gym half his life. Oh no . . . those muscles were earned with hard manual labor that he most likely did growing up on this ranch. His brown hair gave off that sexy look of a man who likes to run his hands through it.

But his eyes. I was drawn back up to them. They looked . . . confused, maybe even a little bit sad. The way he stared at me made me take a step back. Not because I was afraid of him; it was the intensity of his gaze that threw me off.

That, and he had to be one of the most handsome men I'd ever laid eyes on. The resemblance to Blayze was uncanny.

This had to be the mysterious Brock Shaw.

Brock stared at me for another few moments, then frowned. His eyes no longer looked confused. The look was replaced with one that made me feel like I had just been sent to the principal's office.

"Daddy!"

Finally, at the sound of his son's voice, he broke the stare and turned to Blayze. He pulled him into his arms and smiled the most breathtaking smile I'd ever seen. Like his brother Ty, Brock had dimples, but his were deeper, and I'd bet they only showed up when he smiled at his son.

I thought back to a moment ago, when he had given me an icy stare, and I had no idea why he would have looked at me so coldly.

"What are you doing here?" Brock asked Blayze.

"Grams made a pie for Miss Lincoln here. She asked me if I wanted to see her horse."

Brock grinned wide, but when he turned to me, his smile dropped. I had plastered on my own smile, but when the icy stare came back, it faltered.

"What are you doing out here in the barn with my son?"

Taking a step away from him, I was stunned by the tone of his voice. I was positive the look on my face was utter shock. "Um, well, your brother is up at the house, helping Kaylee hang some blinds. I offered to bring Blayze down here to show him Thunder."

Forcing a small smile, I waited for him to crack and give me something. Surely he couldn't keep that scowl on his face indefinitely.

"So, you thought you'd quiz my son on his mother?"

My eyes widened. "What?" I gasped.

How dare this guy accuse me of that.

Wait. That's what I had wanted to do . . . wasn't it?

By my own admission, I'd wanted to know more about both Brock *and* about Blayze's mother. But it was Blayze who had mentioned not knowing her.

Placing my hands on my hips, I lifted my chin. There was no way I was going to let this guy talk down to me.

"I wasn't quizzing him. We were talking, and he was telling me all the things you'd shown him. I'm not privy to any information on his mother, so I wasn't aware that this was a subject to avoid."

Brock's eyes twitched, and he set Blayze down. "Run on over to my truck, buddy. I've got a surprise for you."

Blayze lit up like the Fourth of July.

"Bye, Miss Lincoln!" he called out.

I lifted my hand and shouted, "Bye, Blayze! Thanks for the pie!"

Once his son was around the corner, Brock turned back to me. He took three long strides and then was right up in my face. I could feel the warmth of his breath on my body, but I refused to move. The man might be good looking, but he was acting like a first-rate asshole. He leaned in closer to me, and I sucked in a breath, hoping he didn't notice.

"Don't ever ask my son about his mother again. Do you hear me?"

My eyes widened yet again, and I could feel my body trembling with anger. How dare this man come walking into my barn and throw out accusations? I may think he's hot as hell, but a rude attitude quickly makes the good looks vanish.

Taking in a deep breath, I stated, "I didn't invite Ty to come over and bring your son. They stopped by of their own free will. I wasn't fishin' for information on your wife; that is something I would never do. But let me just say, with you not wanting to be a part of the sale, you've already made this whole transaction a bit . . . weird."

The corner of his mouth twitched. "Weird? How?"

I swallowed hard and then shrugged. "I don't know. You never even exchanged an email with me. It's been your brother Ty or one of your parents handling everything. I don't know why you sold the house, and I don't care, Mr. Shaw. I just want to be a good neighbor, and since I live so close to your family, I was trying to be friendly. That's all."

Brock suddenly dropped his gaze to my mouth. I had to fight the urge to lick my now-dry-as-the-Sahara-Desert lips. When he licked his own, I swear I felt the ground shake.

One minute he looked at me like I was a bug to step on; the next he looked like he wanted to kiss me! The man made my head spin, and I'd only known him for less than five minutes.

"You want to be a good neighbor?" he asked in a low, sexy voice that almost had me wishing he *would* kiss me. Okay, maybe he wasn't such an ass.

Wait. What in the hell am I saying?

"Yes," I stated.

"Then stay out of my business and away from my son."

And it appeared the jerk was back. "I beg your pardon?"

"Did I stutter . . . *Miss Pratt?*"

There was no way I was going to let him think he could intimidate me. I folded my arms and let myself give him a good once-over.

This time, I got an even better look than a few moments ago.

Oh yes, he was built indeed. Bigger than what I'd thought he would be for a bull rider. He had a broad chest and well-defined arms, and by the way his legs fit into those jeans, I would say the rest of his body was in top form as well.

Still, good looks aside, this man would not be allowed to speak to me like this on my own property.

"Listen here, *Mister Shaw*," I retorted with my own sassy attitude, "I don't know what crawled up that ass of yours and died, but I do not appreciate being spoken to that way. This is *my* property now, and you, sir, are not welcome on it if you're going to be a cocksucker."

His brow lifted, and I swore I saw the corners of his mouth rise slightly. "A cocksucker?" he repeated.

"Yes! A dirty, rotten *asshole* of a cocksucker. Oh! And let's add *rude* in there while we're at it."

"Me, rude? You just uttered a laundry list of bad names to call me."

I scoffed. "Oh, please. I'm positive I'm not the first person to call you an asshole."

Then he looked like he wanted to kiss me again, with the way he was staring at my mouth—and, I hated to admit, I *wanted* him to.

How messed up am I that I actually want this man to kiss me?

Brock took a few steps back. It was as if he was finally noticing the heat our bodies had been creating by standing so close together.

"Does your mama know you've got a dirty mouth on you?"

Narrowing my eyes, I leaned forward some. "Does *your* mama know how you treat women?"

He flinched and took another step back.

Ha! That did it.

A guy didn't have to be raised in the South to know that if his mama found out he was being a dick to a woman, she'd be pretty pissed about it.

"Well, looks like you met my brother Brock," Ty said from the entry of the barn. "And, by the look on your face and the way you're standing, he didn't make a very good first impression."

I lifted my chin higher. "No, he didn't. Now, if you'll excuse me, gentlemen"—I glared at Brock—"and I use that word loosely for one of you, I've got work to do."

I walked past Brock but came to an abrupt halt when he reached for my arm and stopped me, whispering under his breath as I stared up at him with as much contempt as I could muster.

"I didn't mean to be so . . . rude. It's just . . . this place holds memories I'd like to forget, and I don't want my son . . . well, anyway, I'm sorry."

My eyes looked down to where his hand was holding my arm. He instantly dropped it and ran it through his hair.

"You know the way off of *my* property. Don't let the barn door hit your ass on the way out."

The good-looking jerk actually had the nerve to give me a crooked, sexy-as-sin grin. When I turned to leave, I could feel his eyes on me.

I didn't want to do it, but I glanced over my shoulder, and he was watching me walk away. With that damn smirk still plastered across his face.

Ugh! Men!

Chapter Six

Brock

Turning on the heel of my cowboy boot, I watched that gorgeous firecracker—otherwise known as Lincoln Pratt—storm out of the barn. The barn that had once belonged to me.

My eyes drifted down to the perfect ass in a pair of tight jeans. She glanced back and caught me staring.

Ty followed her out, issuing apologies on my behalf for whatever it was I had said to make her so angry. I smiled bigger when she lifted her hand to shut my brother up as she stomped off to the house.

I stopped next to Ty, and we both watched.

"What in the hell did you do to piss her off like that?"

Right before Lincoln walked into her house, she cast a glance over her shoulder once more. The look she gave me clearly said *fuck off*.

"She's a tad bit on the emotional side, is what I'm guessing," I said, knowing damn well I had been a complete jerk but unwilling to admit that to Ty. One reason was, I felt embarrassed by my reaction moments ago. Two, he would for sure tell our mother. I shuddered at that thought. I faced my brother. "What in the hell were you thinking, bringing Blayze here?"

Ty looked at me like I had lost my mind. "Why *can't* I bring Blayze here? Mama had a pie to give to the girls, and he wanted to help deliver it. Hell, Brock, he doesn't remember anything about this place."

I pointed to the house. "She was talking to him about Kaci. She ain't none of her damn business."

Ty looked down and shook his head, his hand coming up to rub the back of his neck. "Brock, at some point, you're gonna have to start talking to him about his mama. He's getting curious about her."

My shoulder hit his as I pushed past him.

"He has a right to know about his mother!"

"Fuck you, Ty."

"Yeah, fuck you, too, Brock. You're so damn scared to talk about her. It was an accident. Stop acting like it's all your fault."

I stopped, then turned and rushed him. I grabbed on to his shirt and shook him. I couldn't control the rage that was quickly building up inside of me. "Shut up! Don't talk about it. Don't you fucking talk about it! And stay away from me while I'm here."

Ty pushed me away from him. "You need help, brother. You're carrying some pent-up guilt, and if you don't get it out soon, you're going to be asking for trouble. You think riding a bull and the occasional one-night stand is going to keep it at bay? You're wrong. You've got to talk to someone about it."

"I'm fine!" I shouted, balling my fists. I'd never wanted to hit my brother like I did right then.

He shrugged. "If you say so."

I watched as he turned back to the house.

"Where are you going?" I asked.

Without looking back at me, he said, "I'm about to ask a beautiful woman out for a dinner date. Some of us still know how to treat a lady."

It felt like someone had punched me in the chest. Knowing Ty was going to take Lincoln out made me green with jealousy. Then the idea that I was *jealous* annoyed me. Yes, Lincoln was attractive. Hell, she was beautiful, and I'd be lying if I said I hadn't had a rush of confusing emotions when she first looked into my eyes. But jealous?

What in the hell was wrong with me?

"Daddy, why are you and Uncle Ty fighting?"

Somehow, I felt her watching me, so I turned to look at the house. Lincoln was standing at the window, observing the entire scene. I frowned, knowing that her first impression of me was that I was a complete dick. When she took a step away from the window, I looked down to Blayze. "It's okay, buddy. Brothers sometimes fight."

He nodded and took my hand as we walked over to my truck. "Miss Lincoln is real pwetty, ain't she, Daddy?"

Glancing back over my shoulder, I watched as Lincoln motioned for my brother to come into what had once been my house. "Yeah, she's pretty."

"You got a cwush on her, like me?"

Looking down at him, I laughed. "You've got a crush on Lincoln, huh?"

He nodded.

"Well, I don't really know her, and from what I can tell, she's stubborn as hell and probably a pain in the ass."

"Grams is gonna wash your mouth out with Ivory, Daddy."

I kissed my son on the forehead as I buckled him up in his booster seat. "Come on. I believe I promised you a roping lesson."

His eyes lit up, and I couldn't deny that the warmth in my chest made me forget almost everything. No matter what everyone thought of me, I hated being away from my son. Every time I had to pack up and leave, I felt a piece of me being left behind with him.

I shut the door and rounded my truck, and, being a glutton for punishment, I looked back at the white house.

The one thing I couldn't forget were those deep-green eyes. I'd never in my life seen anyone with eyes that color. The way they'd sparkled and seemed to catch the light sneaking into the barn . . . I'd literally had to catch my breath when Lincoln's eyes met mine.

Once I was in the truck, I shook the image away and smiled back at Blayze. "Let's go ropin'."

"Yes!" Blayze called out.

The conversation at the dinner table went in one ear and out the other. It was good to be home, but my mind was spinning, and it seemed to keep landing back on one thing.

Lincoln Pratt.

"So, Brock, Ty told me you made an impression on Lincoln today."

My head snapped up, and I looked at my brother and then back over to my mother. "Um, yeah. I headed over there after you told me where Ty and Blayze went."

Smiling, my mother said, "She's a nice girl, isn't she?"

Ty chuckled. "He wouldn't know. The last words she told him were to not let the barn door hit him on the ass when he was leaving."

I glared at my brother. The heat from my mother's stare hit me almost instantly.

"What did you say to her, Brock Shaw?" my mother insisted.

"It doesn't matter. It's over and done with. I apologized, and she chose not to accept it."

Ty laughed.

"Brock, I raised you better than that. Now, if you were upset that Blayze was over there, there's no need."

"Let's just drop it, Mama, okay?" I asked, glancing over to Blayze.

She looked at my son and then back to me, her anger evident on her face.

"I walked in on a conversation, and I might have overreacted a bit."

My mother rolled her eyes while my father sighed. Dad wasn't much of one to give his opinion on too many things. He tended to let our mother handle things like her grown sons acting like bastards.

Blayze decided it was his turn to speak up. "I like Miss Lincoln. She showed me her horse. I'd like to visit her again. She's real pwetty, and she has a nice smile."

"Well, we know the boy has good taste," Ty said as my folks laughed, and I forced a smile.

After dinner, I helped Mama clean up the dishes while my father took Blayze with him to check on the horses that were getting ready to foal.

It didn't take long before my mother could no longer handle the silence.

"Lincoln is a sweet girl, and she can't help what she walked in on. She doesn't know about the . . . issues you have with that old house. The memories that surface for you."

I swallowed hard. "It was just weird, seeing another woman there, in the barn, knowing she was changing the house and all. I let my emotions get to me."

She glanced up at me, then back to the dish she was washing. "Maybe she'll be able to exorcise some of those ghosts you think are still there."

I picked up a plate and dried it. How could I make my family understand how hard it was for me to go back to that house? How the memory of me failing at my marriage because I was a selfish bastard hit me like a punch to the gut every time I went near the place? "Out of sight" is supposed to be out of mind.

"You regretting selling the house?"

"No," I said, not even needing to think about it. "I have a house." Dragging in a deep breath, I said, "Maybe I should bring Blayze out with me for a few weeks. It would be nice to be around him."

My mother nearly dropped the bowl she was washing. "What? Take him out on the road with you? Brock, that's no life for a five-year-old boy. What in the world are you thinking?"

"I'm thinking I miss my son. I'm thinking that you, Dad, and Ty are the ones raising him. It should be me." That familiar ache of guilt coursed through me. I wanted to be with Blayze; I *needed* to be with him.

One more championship. Just give me one more.

She turned to face me, her wet-gloved hand resting on her hip. "Where is this coming from?"

I shrugged. The last thing I wanted to do was mention the fight with Ty from earlier. I hadn't even been home for an hour, and the two of us were going at it.

"Maybe you need a break. You've been doing this since you were seventeen. Maybe it's time to stop. Blayze needs you, Brock."

I looked into her eyes. I knew I was being selfish. Old mistakes were hard to break, after all. "I love bull riding, Mama. I'm number one in the world right now. I'm making good money and building a secure future for me and Blayze. I just need a couple more years."

Shaking her head, she faced the sink again and grabbed the bowl she'd let drop back into the water. "I'd think you would have learned your lesson by now."

My eyes widened in shock. She'd voiced exactly what I had been thinking. "What does that mean?"

She cleaned the bowl like she was trying to rub the finish completely off. "What does that mean? What does that mean?" she yelled as she dropped the bowl again and faced me. "It means, you have a son, Brock. A young man who needs his father, and all you can think about is how you're number one right now. Or how the next bull you draw is going to be the one you get that perfect score on. How good you feel with the adrenaline rush you get. You've always put those damn bulls first in everything, while your father and I are doing our best to help raise your son."

I felt my face drain of color as I stared at my mother. I chose to ignore the reference to me putting bull riding before *Kaci.* "Why haven't you ever told me before that you don't want to help with Blayze?"

She closed her eyes and took in a deep breath. "Oh Lord, it's not that, Brock! I love that boy like there's no tomorrow, but he needs *you.* He already doesn't have a mama."

"And I'm guessing you think that's my fault."

Her mouth fell open. "I never said that, Brock Shaw. That's something you've put on your own shoulders, and you've decided to carry that burden with you. It *wasn't* your fault."

I scoffed. Her words spoken only moments ago felt like they had burned a hole in the middle of my chest. "Like you just said, Mama, I always put the bulls first, and that's what I did that night. I put a ride first, and look what it cost me. Look what it cost Blayze."

Her hand came up and touched the side of my face. "Brock, the end result would have been the same regardless. You wouldn't have been able to change the outcome."

"It was the stress of her handling everything alone. I caused it because I was never there for her. Dirk told me not to ride; he was furious with me for climbing onto that bull."

"We both know Dirk loved Kaci and was angry at the time, but he's never blamed you." Another long breath was pulled into my mother's lungs before she let it out. "Your father and I were going to wait to talk to you about this . . . but we both agree you have to decide what your future is going to be, son. Blayze needs you, and you need to make a decision."

My heart seized in my chest. "Are you asking me to give up bull riding?"

"You have a five-year-old boy who misses you when you're gone. I know you try to fly home during the week when you can, but you're sometimes gone for a few weeks at a time. You're missing his games, and your daddy and I are getting older. We'd like to travel and see the world. I've raised my boys, Brock. Now it's time for you to raise yours."

I threw the dishcloth onto the counter. "So this is why Ty jumped all over me. You all decided to get together and have . . . what? A family talk about how shitty a father I am?"

She frowned.

"Did the three of you decide this was the right time, right in the middle of the season, to lay this shit on me? Is Ty still bitter 'cause he can't climb up onto a bull anymore, so he wants to make sure I don't either?"

"What? No! This has nothing to do with your brother, and everything to do with you being a father and your son needing you."

Her words were hitting so hard it felt like someone was jabbing me with a knife. I knew it was true. Every single word. True. "Fine. I'll hire someone to travel with me, so Blayze can come on the road with me, and we'll just stay gone. Give all of you the space to do what you want, whenever you want."

A look of horror swept over her face. "He's about to start kindergarten, Brock. You can't rip him away from everything he knows!"

"I'm his dad, remember?"

I turned away from my mother and started out of the kitchen. I needed to get the hell out of there before I said something I was going to regret.

Her words only brought to light what I worked so hard to try and keep buried. I was running. From my past. From the guilt that crept into my dreams every night. Hell, I was running from my own family. Every single time I looked Ty in the eyes, I questioned why it wasn't me who had gotten hurt. Why him and not me. I had deserved it, not my brother.

Hitting Ty on the shoulder with my own, I walked by him and out the front door, and he called out, "Who are you pissed at now?"

"Me," I whispered, low enough so no one would be able to hear.

Three hours later, I tipped the bottle back and finished off my beer. I'd lost track of how much I'd drunk since I'd walked into the Blue Moose.

"You've got Mom pretty worried."

I looked at Ty and scoffed. "Yeah, well, I'm a big boy. I can take care of myself."

A voice from my other side said, "You're drunk, is what you are."

When I turned, the entire room felt like it was spinning. My eyes landed on Tanner, our younger brother.

Tanner was on the rodeo circuit. He was part of a roping team. He was the header, and his best friend from high school, Chance, was the heeler. They were ranked number three in the world, and I was proud of them both. Mama was just glad Tanner hadn't fallen in love with being on top of a bull. He'd tried it once and had gotten thrown and stepped on. That was enough for him. His only true love was being on top of a horse . . . and a woman.

With my travel schedule and Tanner's, we didn't see each other much. I knew my folks hated that we were both gone so much. If they had their way, all four of us would be safely at home.

Four of us.

I glanced at my two brothers, and a feeling of sadness swept over me. We were missing Beck.

He'd joined the marines right out of high school. He was determined to serve his country, and my parents were damn proud of him. Hell, we were all proud of him. He'd graduated top of his high school class, and he could have gone to college anywhere but chose the military.

He was an adrenaline junkie. Loved bull riding but didn't want to make a living out of it. It was purely for fun. So, when he'd joined the military and took on some special force ops shit, we weren't surprised. He was only a few months away from getting out, told us he'd had his fun and was ready to come back home and work the family ranch.

Then, on his last mission, something went horribly wrong. We never did get the full story, but he had been shot and killed. His fellow marines had carried his body back to the pickup point, and my mama was able to bury her son and say goodbye. From that day on, she never talked about Beck. To anyone.

"Holy shit. Tanner fucking Shaw. You've got to be kidding me."

A wide smile grew over my brother's face. "You look like shit, Brock. When was the last time you got laid?"

I laughed and wrapped my hand around his neck, pulling him in for a hug. "It's good to see you, little brother," I said as Tanner slapped my back. I hadn't seen him in almost three months.

"Good to see you too. We were close by, so I thought I'd stop in for a few nights. Chance sprained his wrist and needed a few days to recover, so . . . here I am."

I smiled as I gave him a once-over. He was a male version of our mother. Dark-brown hair, hazel eyes, and a square jaw that said he was determined as hell to make his way in this world. Kid was good looking as well, or so I'd heard from the ladies. I was relieved to see no broken bones this time. "Damn, you look good."

He gave me the same once-over. "You too. Nothing broken?"

I shook my head and grinned. "Nah. Last thing I broke was my collarbone."

"I guess that's good. Means you're staying on. I try to keep up with you and all."

With a nod, I motioned for another beer.

"Where did you find this little bastard?" I asked, pointing to Tanner with my beer but looking at Ty.

"He showed up when I was leaving to come find you. Decided we would both come down to make sure your drunk ass didn't get into any fights."

They both laughed, and I rolled my eyes. "I'm not that drunk."

It was a lie. I was pretty toasted but still in control, which was why I also ordered a water with my beer.

"Holy hell. Who are those two pretty little things?"

Lifting my gaze to follow Tanner's, I felt myself sit up a little bit more when I saw Lincoln and who I was guessing was her friend. Kaylee, I thought her name was. Then I smiled. For some ungodly reason, I was happy seeing Lincoln here. What was it about that woman? She was getting under my skin already, and that hadn't happened in a long time. A very long time.

"It's the beer," I mumbled to myself. "Has to be."

Ty set his beer down and looked at Tanner, seemingly not hearing me. "That, my little brother, is Lincoln Pratt, the one with the brown hair, and the blonde is her best friend, Kaylee, whom I've called dibs on."

I pulled my brows up and turned to Ty. "You're going after Kaylee?" I asked.

"Yeah. I already told you, I like her better."

Relief washed over my body, but it was soon pushed away when Tanner stood.

"Then I think I'll go ask Lincoln to dance."

I wanted to pull his ass back down into the chair and call my own damn dibs. But I didn't. I didn't move at all as I watched him make his way over to both women. Tanner was a charmer. He had a way with women. Just a smile from him and they were putty in his hands.

The idea that he could charm Lincoln had me feeling slightly panicked. And pissed off. I couldn't pull my eyes off her. It wasn't like it was the first time I was noticing how beautiful she was either. That wavy brown hair, those green eyes. A body any man would want to curl up with at night and wake up to in the morning.

I shook my head, clearing my wandering thoughts.

"You're not interested in her at all?" I heard Ty ask from my left. "You're just going to sit there and let Tanner go after her?"

Shrugging, I stated, "What do I care? I'm not interested in getting involved with *anyone.*"

Ty stood and placed his hand on my shoulder. "It's a shame you've put yourself into this endless-punishment thing you've got going on. It's not like you have to marry her, but you could at least have some fun while you're in town. I see the way you look at her, Brock. And I ain't ever seen you look at a woman like that before—not even Kaci."

I flinched at the mention of her name. I reached for the beer and took a long gulp.

"Fine, sit here and wallow in your guilt. Looks like Tanner charmed his way in."

Scanning the bar, I saw my brother holding Lincoln in his arms as they two-stepped across the wooden dance floor.

"Doesn't matter," I mumbled. "She hates me anyway."

Ty laughed. "Whatever, dude. You enjoy your solitary night while your two brothers get lucky."

I huffed as Ty slapped my back and made his way toward Kaylee. He soon had her in his arms and was spinning her around the floor too.

After letting me sit at the bar for another thirty minutes, Tanner finally came over and dragged me to the table where everyone was sitting. As we walked up, Dirk approached the table. He gave me a knowing look when our gazes met. He nodded, and I nodded back.

"You aren't answering your phone," he said.

"I left it in my truck."

His gaze met mine again. "You're drunk, dude."

With a half shrug, I sat down, followed by Dirk. Dirk knew I only got wasted when I was pissed or trying to numb myself from feeling anything. He'd seen it enough times.

"How about some introductions," Ty said. "Kaylee, Lincoln, this is Brock Shaw. Lincoln, you had the honor of meeting him earlier today."

Lincoln looked at me and forced herself to smile. I returned it, then looked to Kaylee. "Pleasure meeting you, ma'am."

"Ma'am?" Kaylee said, jerking her head back in surprise. "My grandmother is called *ma'am*. Please call me Kaylee."

I raised my beer at her.

"Kaylee, Lincoln, this is Dirk Littlewood. Brock's best friend and fellow bull rider."

Dirk tipped his cowboy hat at them both. "Pleasure, ladies."

They both gave him a polite grin.

It didn't take long for Dirk and Lincoln to fall into a conversation. The more he talked to her, the more jealous I got, and *that* pissed me off even more. Why was I feeling so territorial over her?

It was right about then that Lincoln's gaze lifted to me, and she frowned before looking away. She shook her head and politely smiled at Dirk.

When Dirk looked my way, he lifted a brow. "Dude, is everything okay?"

I nodded. I was positive Dirk saw it on my face. Hell, even *I* kept catching myself staring at Lincoln, and I was two sheets to the wind.

"You want to talk about anything?" he asked.

Pressing my beer to my lips, I took a long pull and looked away. There wasn't anything to talk about. I was confused because of the alcohol, and Lincoln was a beautiful woman. That was all.

Dirk could read me, drunk or not. I wasn't in the mood to chit-chat. "Well, ladies, it was a pleasure meeting you both." He stood and grinned, looking between Kaylee and Lincoln. "A word of advice: stay away from the Shaw boys. They'll love ya and then leave ya."

"Fuck off, Dirk!" Tanner shouted.

Loraine Wilson was currently sitting on my little brother's lap, which meant he had given up on the idea of Lincoln or Kaylee. I was sure he had seen the way Ty was sticking by Kaylee, and I was *pretty* sure Lincoln had turned down his invitation to head out to his truck "to get to know each other better."

After finishing off my beer, I ordered another one.

"Did you drive here?"

Her sweet, velvety voice made me look across the table at her. Those green eyes were filled with concern.

Damn. She is so beautiful.

"I did. Why? You need a ride home?"

Shit. Am I slurring?

"No, but if you keep tossing them back like that, you're going to need an ambulance out of here."

I laughed. "Don't you worry your pretty little head about me, darlin'. I can take care of myself."

Lincoln rolled her eyes and folded her arms across her chest. When the waitress returned and went to put my beer down, Lincoln reached across the table and took it. "I think he's had enough, don't you?"

When Betty Jane and I stared at Lincoln, she looked like she was about to hand me back my beer, but then she pulled it to her chest.

Betty Jane let out a sigh before she spoke to Lincoln. "Honey, listen, I know you're new in town, and you city folk do things differently. But here, we take care of each other, and if Brock wants to drink himself under the table, he can. We'll make sure he gets a ride home."

Lincoln chewed on her lip, her eyes darting everywhere, as if waiting for someone to jump in and agree with her.

"Give me back my damn beer. I'm not looking for a babysitter."

"Fine," she said as she put the beer down hard in front of me. Betty Jane smiled and walked off as Lincoln went on. "Drink your stupid beer and get drunk out of your mind. It's none of my business, right?"

I saw red. Who in the hell did this woman think she was? "You're right, it's not any of your bus . . . ness. Biznestle. *Fuck.* Business."

Christ Almighty. I was drunk.

Her brow lifted. "Do you always drink like this?" Then Lincoln covered her mouth with her hand and closed her eyes before she dropped the hand and said, "I'm so sorry. I shouldn't have asked that. That's none of my business either. I got angry because all you've been doing is giving me dirty looks all night."

"No, I haven't," I slurred.

"Ha!" she said. "Listen, I don't give a rat's ass if you like me or not, but your folks are my neighbors, and they're good people. And Ty's nice, too, along with your brother Tanner. I'm positive we're going to be seeing each other around. If you don't like me, fine, but can you lay off acting like a complete dick whenever I'm in the vicinity?"

I absolutely hated that she thought I didn't like her. It was the opposite. I didn't understand why I was so attracted to her.

I looked around the bar for Ty and Kaylee. They were nowhere to be found.

"You're not worried about your girlfriend?" I asked, deciding I was too wasted to try to have that conversation with her. Hell, even I couldn't figure out how I felt about Lincoln.

She shrugged. "She's been through a lot the last few years, and if she wants to hook up with someone, that's her business. Much to your surprise, I actually am *not* a nosy person."

Ouch. That hurt.

Lifting my beer, I winked at her. She rolled her eyes again and moved so that she was facing the dance floor. I couldn't help but laugh.

Feisty. I wondered what she was like in bed.

My beer brain was in full effect right now, and a part of me wanted to know the answer to that question more than I wanted to admit.

Chapter Seven

Lincoln

I could feel Brock's eyes on me the rest of the night. Ty and Kaylee hadn't been gone long, which led me to believe nothing had happened between them.

Kaylee sat down in the chair and gave me a look I couldn't read.

"Are you okay?" I asked.

She nodded. "Yep, I'm fine."

"Are you sure?" Leaning in closer to her ear, I asked, "Did he do something?"

"No, the opposite. I wanted him to do something, and all he did was kiss me. Then he sort of freaked out on me and asked me to dance."

"Really?"

Kaylee nodded. "Yep. Guess maybe I'm a bad kisser or something."

I chuckled. "No, I sort of think these brothers have . . . issues."

My eyes glanced over to a very drunk Brock. Some little bleached blonde was sitting next to him, clearly trying to take advantage of the fact that he was wasted.

"Want to come back to my place, Brock?" she asked in a sultry-sounding voice.

I wanted to gag.

"Not tonight, Lee."

"Oh, come on! I promise to take good care of you."

"Kaylee, would you mind if I drove you home tonight?" Ty asked, causing both of us to swing our attention to Ty instead of Brock.

This was an interesting turn of events.

"You want to drive me home?" Kaylee asked, confused. "Why?"

Ty's cheeks turned a slight shade of pink, and I hit Kaylee on the leg.

"I mean, sure. Lincoln, are you going to be okay getting home alone?"

With a wide grin, I nodded. "Of course I am. This isn't Atlanta, after all. I've had only one beer, and that was a few hours ago. Um, Ty, what about your brother?" I asked, pointing to Brock.

Giving him a hard look and then frowning, Ty replied, "Betty Jane already took his keys. She'll make sure he gets to his truck and sleeps it off."

My mouth gaped open. Holy crap. Was that normal in a small town? Just put your drunk kin in their truck, and they'll sleep it off? That would be a good way to get yourself hurt back in Atlanta. "You're just gonna leave your brother here to sleep in his truck?"

With a half shrug, Ty answered, "Yep." He held out his hand and asked, "Kaylee, you ready?"

It was a little after midnight, and I was also ready to leave. I didn't want to follow Kaylee and Ty out the door, though, especially if they wanted some privacy to talk or whatnot.

Sitting back in my chair, I crossed my arms and watched the scene playing out in front of me. Lee was now rubbing her hands all over Brock's chest, his arms, even running her fingers through his thick brown hair.

It was sickening to watch. Especially since Brock seemed to be completely ignoring her.

"Come on, Brock. Let's get out of here."

Betty Jane walked up and caught me shooting death rays at Lee.

"Lee!" Betty Jane called out, making the blonde jump. "Your husband called. Said he's on his way home from his fishing trip and been trying to call your phone."

Lee jumped up. "Howie's on his way home? Shit!"

She turned and hightailed it out of the bar so fast she left a smoke trail behind her.

Then, Betty Jane handed me a set of keys. "Here, these are his. Make sure he gets out of here and safely home."

My hand instinctively took the keys, and I sat there for a few moments, stunned. When I finally realized Betty Jane was putting me in charge of getting Brock home, I jumped up and followed her over to the bar.

"Wait! Ty said you would make sure Brock got to his truck and slept it off. He didn't say anything about making sure he got home."

Betty Jane loaded up empty beer bottles onto her tray. It was then I looked around the bar and noticed it was almost empty.

"What time is it?" I asked, reaching for my phone. "It's almost one!"

She laughed. "Yep, it's been real fun watching you give dirty looks to Lee for the last hour. I figured I'd help a girl out and get rid of her for you."

When I looked back at the table, Brock had his head on it.

Good grief. Is he sleeping?

"What do you mean, get rid of her?" I asked, still trailing behind the waitress, who honestly looked to be just a few years older than me.

She stopped and faced me. "I've been doing this job since I was eighteen. It doesn't take a rocket scientist to tell that you've got a thing for our Brock. I can't blame ya, really. He's a looker. Those blue eyes and dimples. Not to mention the way the man can fill out a pair of Wranglers. Throw in he's a professional bull rider and worth some money, and you've got yourself one sought-after cowboy. He doesn't normally come in here and get drunk like this, so I'm going to guess he's had a bad day and he's trying to drink away his problems.

"Now, the way I see it is, he seems to be smitten with you, and you're smitten with him. So, it only makes sense that *you* get him home safely. What happens after that is your business, but just know that the rest of the town will most likely find out within seventy-two hours—unless you're discreet about it."

I stood frozen in place. *What in the world is this lady talking about?*

"Okay, I didn't really understand half of that, but you're very wrong on one thing. Brock Shaw is not . . . smitten . . . with me. It's really the opposite. I don't think he can stand me."

Betty Jane winked. "Ralph will help you get him out to his truck."

"But . . . I . . . my . . . I'm not . . . wait!"

Placing her hand on her hip, she rolled her eyes. "Listen, I've got to finish cleaning up and then kick everyone out of here. Just spit it out, would ya?"

"My car! I have my car here. I can't leave it."

"Oh, you don't have to worry about it being left here. It's perfectly fine."

She turned and walked away. When I called out for her again, she ignored me.

I turned around and walked back over to the table to find a sleeping Brock. Burying my face in my hands, I mumbled, "Oh my God! Why me?" Poking his shoulder, I said, "Brock! Brock, wake up!"

His head popped up, and I let out a little yelp.

He turned to look at me, and instead of frowning, he smiled for once. "Hey, pretty little thing."

He's so drunk he doesn't even know who I am.

"Um, hey. Listen, I need to get you home, so could you maybe stand and walk out to your truck?"

Brock smiled bigger, and his dimples seemed to scream out at me.

Oh. Holy. Hell.

This guy was beyond good looking. I mean, I didn't think I'd ever seen a guy smile and look so damn sexy, despite his highly intoxicated state. Even with his cowboy hat all crooked, he looked handsome as hell.

"I can stand," he grumbled out as he slowly stood.

I slipped my arm around his waist. After doing a quick scan of the table, I reached behind me and felt for my phone. I had my license and credit card tucked into my phone case, and I had my keys in my pocket.

"Okay, let's get you to your truck."

His head dropped forward, and I was pretty sure he was falling back asleep.

"Brock!" I shouted, making his head jerk up. "Walk to the door."

"What do you adore?" he asked, taking a few stumbling steps next to me as I guided him.

I chuckled. "No, I said, walk to the door!"

"I *am* walking to the door, woman!"

With a roll of my eyes, I focused on keeping this man upright. It wasn't an easy task. His stocky frame was heavy. With the way my arm was around him, I couldn't help but notice his muscles flexing as we walked . . . no, *stumbled* along. I let my silly mind wander to what he would look like without a shirt on.

Stop it right now, Lincoln Pratt!

Betty Jane opened the door for us and winked at me yet again as I walked by. "Have a good night, and don't worry about your car!"

I mumbled under my breath about being set up and then stepped out into the cool night. A shiver ran up my spine as I searched the parking lot. I'd only seen Brock's truck once, and the only thing I remembered was that it was silver.

"Where's your truck?" I asked, glancing at three trucks still parked in the lot.

Shit on a stick, does everyone here drive trucks?

Brock lifted his head and looked around. "My truck is the best damn truck in the parking lot."

"That doesn't help, Shaw. What's your license plate number?"

Brock turned, his big, drunk blue eyes gazing down at me. "You want my number, Lincoln? I thought you didn't like me."

My mouth dropped open. "Um, excuse me, but you're the one who's been shooting daggers at me all night long. Not to mention how rude you were to me earlier today."

"You didn't catch me at my best, sweetheart."

My stomach dipped at the endearment. No one had ever called me anything like that. Not baby, babe, sweetie, or sweetheart. I was always just Lincoln. Every guy I'd ever dated called me by my first name. Even in bed, I was always Lincoln.

It pissed me off how much I liked hearing that come from Brock's mouth. I liked it a lot . . . more than a lot.

Damn it. What is it about this guy?

"I didn't ask you for your phone number, you drunk fool. Your license plate number on your truck."

He frowned. "I don't know."

"You don't know the license plate on your own truck?"

"Nope!" he said, popping the *p* in the most adorable way.

I found myself smiling up at him.

"It's the silver one on the far right!" Betty Jane called out.

I looked behind me, almost losing my grip on Brock. "And I don't suppose you'd help me get him there . . . or Ralph, maybe?"

She laughed. She actually *laughed* before turning and walking back into the bar.

"Thanks for nothing," I grumbled as I guided Brock over to the truck.

I hit the button to unlock the doors, and all the lights came on. I scolded myself for not thinking of doing that sooner. When I got to the passenger side, I not-so-gently pushed him against the back door and tried to open the front.

"Damn, woman. I didn't peg you as a rough-sex kinda gal."

"If you think we're having sex right now, you're drunker than I thought."

Brock laughed, and it was magical. No, seriously, it was the most amazing sound I'd ever heard. And it went right to the area between my legs that was now pulsing after one laugh from a man I really didn't want to like but was finding myself liking anyway.

"I'ms not that dunk."

Wrinkling my nose, I said, "Huh?"

"I'ms not that dunk."

"Do you mean to say you're not that *drunk?*"

He attempted to snap his fingers and pointed one at me as he said, "Yep." And he popped the damn *p* again.

I giggled. "You are a very cute drunk."

He smiled. "I knew you liked me."

"Don't get cocky, Brock. I'm warming up to *drunk* you. Sober you is an entirely different beast."

He licked his lips and pulled me against his body. "I bet I can find a better way to warm you up."

Oh. My.

My body stilled, and I wanted to ask him what he had in mind.

I'd always heard the silly rumor that guys couldn't get hard-ons when they were so drunk. I didn't have much experience with drunk guys and sex, but what I *did* know was Brock Shaw was for sure hard. Very hard. And, from what I could tell through his jeans . . . very big.

I placed my hand on his chest and couldn't ignore the instant zap of energy that raced from his body into mine. He must have felt it, too, because he inhaled sharply. A small thrill raced up my spine at the thought of Brock reacting to my touch.

"Let's get you home, Brock."

He leaned down to kiss me, but I pulled back. There was no way I was going to kiss this man when he was drunk. No. If he truly wanted to kiss me, he'd do it sober, when he wasn't acting like a complete jerk.

The look of disappointment quickly morphed on his face, and he nodded, pushing his fingers through his hair. He turned his body and climbed into the passenger side of the truck without a word.

I shut the door and dragged in a deep breath while I walked around the truck. It was only then that it dawned on me: I could have just put him in my car. Clearly my mind was boggled around this guy. I groaned and shook my head as I climbed up into the cab.

"Tell me you've driven a truck before, princess."

Jerking my head to look at him, I asked, "Princess?"

He shrugged. "You don't like the name *princess*?"

I stared at him, not knowing what to say. I loved hearing him call me that, but it confused me more than anything. Drunk Brock was indeed throwing me for a loop. He finally looked away and sighed.

"Don't worry, I won't ever call you that again."

"No, I mean, I . . ." The words seemed to fade away in the back of my throat before I could get them out.

Dropping his head on the back of the seat, he said, "Don't wreck my truck, Lincoln."

His words were harsh, not like a moment ago, when he'd called me princess. "I'm not going to wreck your precious *truck*."

"Damn right you better not."

I sighed as I started the truck. "Just . . . pass out or something so you don't make me nervous driving."

"Fine."

Yep, we were back to the asshole. Maybe he was sobering up.

After pulling up to the Shaws' driveway, I looked around the truck's interior and saw a gate opener clipped to the sun visor. When I hit it, the giant iron gate swung open.

"Brock, are you staying with your parents?"

He snored.

Ugh.

When I hit him on the thigh, he jumped. "What? I'm up!"

I tried not to laugh. "Main house?"

The way he looked at me with a confused expression was cute. "Huh?"

"Are you staying at the main house? Tanner mentioned something about Blayze being at the main house with your folks."

He shook his head. "No, I don't stay with my folks."

My heart dropped. *Well, shit. Is he at a hotel or something?*

"Okay, well, where should I drop off your drunk ass?"

"Um . . . I live in the old foreman's cabin."

I waited for him to tell me where that was.

"Okay, Brock, I'm going to need directions there."

"The road forks up here. Go left and follow it until you see a cabin."

I remembered the last time I had been here, the road went off in two directions, and I'd had to turn to the right to get to the main house. There was a sign that marked the right turn. I hadn't noticed any other signs. When I got to the fork in the road, I turned left and followed it another mile or so.

"Jesus, how big is this ranch?"

Brock laughed. "It's big."

When I drove farther and saw a large one-story ranch-style house, I put on the brakes.

"Damn it. I must have missed it."

Brock lifted his head and looked. "Nope. That's my house."

Glancing between him and the house, I pointed to it. "That's your house, Brock? That is not a cabin! That is a house. A *big* house."

"Yeah, well, when I moved in, I wanted more room. So, I added on to it." His words were slow and drawn out, like he was trying really hard to talk normal.

After putting the truck in park and turning it off, I grabbed the keys and ran over to the passenger side.

Brock nearly fell as he got out of the truck, and then again when we climbed the porch steps. I was silently thanking God that this was a one-story and I didn't have to help him up any stairs. Brock was stumbling all over the damn place.

"My gosh, how much did you have to drink?"

He chuckled. "A whole bunches."

When we walked into the house, we stepped into a large living room. To the left was an open kitchen that made my mouth water at the amenities and high-end details. To the right was a large dining room. There were two halls that jutted from the living room.

Pressing my lips together, I kept from laughing. "Bedroom?"

"Well okay, then. Finally we're getting somewhere."

I smacked him on the chest. *My God, the man is solid.*

"You wish. Now, tell me where your room is, Brock. I'm exhausted, and trying to hold you up is testing how strong I really am."

"Um . . . let's see. Down the hall."

"Which hall?" I asked.

He pointed right. "That would be the master bedroom hall. Or, as I like to call it, the place where I'll make you call out my name when I make you come . . . at least three times."

I stilled.

What in the hell? Does he even realize what he just said?

"Do you think you can manage to get there yourself?" I asked, my heart nearly beating right out of my chest.

"Sure, I can get there."

The moment I let him go, he nearly fell over the love seat.

Grabbing his shirt, I pulled him back before he tumbled right over. "Crap! Brock, you are drunker than all get-out."

Wrapping my arm around him again, I carefully and slowly guided him down the hall. There were two doors. One on the left and one on the right. The first one on the left was an office. The last door on the right was the master bedroom.

Finally.

I kicked the door open all the way with my foot, guided Brock in, and gasped at the sight before me. "This room! It's beautiful."

Brock mumbled something about a magazine and then leaned more on me.

"Oh, wait—Brock, I can't hold you up like that!"

Spinning, I came face to face with him just as he lost the only bit of balance he had left, and we both started to stumble. I was going backward and couldn't get ahold of anything to stop.

When I felt the end of the bed hit the backs of my knees, I cried out, "Oh shit!"

I fell onto the bed—and Brock fell right on top of me.

"Brock," I gasped out. "Can't. Breathe."

He rolled off me, pulling me with him. Now, I was on top of *him*. I tried to get up and ended up straddling him.

His hands grabbed my waist and pinned me still.

Okay, this was somewhat better. I mean, at least I wasn't suffocating now, but my girlie parts were pressed against his manly parts, and . . . holy hell, it felt good. The urge to rotate my hips was powerful, but I somehow managed to get off him . . . that is, before I got *off* on him.

I tried pulling him farther up.

"Brock, scoot up more! You're hanging halfway off the bed."

He turned his head and looked at me. "Were you just on top of me?"

"No," I lied.

"Really? 'Cause I swear you were just straddling me."

"Nope." I even popped the *p*, giving him a bit of his own sass.

He pushed himself up the bed and draped his arm over his eyes. I quickly got his boots off. I contemplated attempting to remove his pants but thought better of that. Although a peek at his package might be sort of fun. He'd never remember a damn thing about tonight—thankfully.

With shaking hands, I reached for his belt buckle. It was one of those that cowboys won in rodeos and all. I leaned in closer to read it.

PBR World Champion.

My teeth sank into my lip. *Okay, why is that title such a turn-on?*

I went to work getting his belt off and then unbuttoned his pants. When I started to unzip his jeans, I froze.

"Holy hell, he's not wearing any underwear!" I whispered in shock.

Jumping back, I stopped myself.

Would I want him to undress me if I were passed out?

No! I most definitely would not.

Stop this right now, Lincoln Pratt.

I quickly looked around for a blanket. Finding one in the closet, I covered Brock, but before I could step away, he sat up and wrapped his arms around my waist, pulling me back onto the bed.

"What in the hell?" I cried as Brock quickly moved back and pulled me flush against his body. He draped his big arm over me and buried his face in my hair.

"Don't leave me alone, Lincoln. Please?"

I froze instantly. Not even breathing until I absolutely had to. I was lying in bed with Brock Shaw. The guy I was internally debating on whether I liked him or didn't like him.

No. I definitely liked him. Or maybe I liked the feeling of being in a man's arms. It had been an awfully long time since I'd had any physical interaction with a man. Over a year. And the way he asked me not to leave him . . . Why did that cause my stomach to flip?

Ugh! This was not good! Not good at all. I needed to get out of Brock's bed.

It didn't take Brock long to fall back asleep. When I tried to move, he drew me closer to him in a death grip, like he knew I was trying to escape.

Fiddlesticks. What am I going to do now?

I was stuck. Brock had pulled me into a spoon position, and not only had he thrown his arm around me, but he'd put his leg on me as well. I wouldn't have pegged Brock Shaw as a spooner, but boy howdy, he had me tied up in his body like I imagined a cowboy would tie up a calf. I was trapped—no chance of escaping from the grip he had on me.

Images of Brock tying me up went through my mind. His rough hands exploring my body while he covered me in soft kisses. I groaned and squeezed my eyes shut.

"Stop it! Stop it! Stop it!" I chastised myself, forcing the dirty thoughts out of my head. This wasn't like me at all.

"Lincoln."

I froze again. "Yes?" I whispered.

I turned my head some, only to find Brock sound asleep and saying my name while wearing the cutest grin . . . and those damn dimples were right at eye level.

My heart dropped in my chest.

This cannot be good.

Chapter Eight

Brock

I didn't want to wake up. My head was killing me, but I felt strangely at peace.

Then, I realized I had my arm around someone.

Shit.

If I'd hooked up with someone last night, I was going to kill my brothers.

I took in a deep breath and smelled something amazing. *Coconut?* No. It was better than coconut.

When my eyes opened, I saw her.

What in the actual fuck?

Lincoln Pratt was pulled up against my body. Both of us were fully clothed, but it was difficult not to notice my hard cock pressing against my jeans.

I gently lifted my arm and carefully rolled over. Staring up at the ceiling, I silently cursed myself. *What in the hell is she doing in my bed?*

When I didn't move, Lincoln did. I decided to play like I was asleep, even breathing a bit heavier.

She carefully slipped out of the bed and quietly went to the bathroom, where I immediately heard her talking on the phone. I slipped out of bed and tiptoed to the door.

"I'm sorry I didn't call! My phone was in my back pocket, and something really weird happened."

I frowned.

"Okay, let's see, after I got him in bed, I started to walk away, and he grabbed me, pulled me onto the bed, and then asked me to stay with him."

My head jerked back in shock.

"Well, of course I was fully clothed! My gosh, Kaylee!" Lincoln hissed. "I *did* try leaving, but he just held me tighter. No, I didn't sneak any peeks, but I thought about it; I won't lie. I started to take his jeans off and had to stop when I realized he was going commando."

Glancing down, I saw my belt was undone and my pants were unbuttoned. I couldn't help but smile. I bet that was a shock for Miss Goody Two-Shoes.

"I've got to get out of here before he wakes up. The guy hates me, and if he sees me in his house, he'll think I tried to seduce him or something. That's the last thing I want him to think."

Aw hell. I didn't want Lincoln thinking I hated her.

"I have to pee, then I'll try to sneak out of here. I'll be home soon."

I quickly ran back to the bed, attempting to lie exactly like I had been. The door to the bathroom slowly creaked open, and I could hear Lincoln making her way out of the room.

When the bedroom door clicked shut, I sat up in bed and scrubbed my hands down my face.

Why in the hell would I have asked her to stay with me last night?

I wasn't going to deny being attracted to her. Who wouldn't be? But asking her to stay? I must have been *really* drunk.

I crawled out of bed and had started for the bathroom when the bedroom door opened again.

I stopped instantly and turned. My breath caught in my throat when I looked at Lincoln standing there. Her cheeks were red, and she was chewing nervously on her bottom lip. I had to fight the urge to walk over to her and pull that lip out from her teeth.

"Um . . . so . . . I don't know how much you remember about last night, but I was pretty much forced to bring you home, and I left my car at the bar. I . . . I don't . . . I don't have a way to get to my car."

Bits and pieces of last night came to my mind but not a whole lot. "What do you mean, you were forced to bring me home?"

She shrugged. "Your brothers left. Ty said you could sleep in your truck, but Betty Jane said I had to drive you home, and she made me help you to your truck. And let me tell you, it was hard, 'cause you were drunk out of your mind."

She smiled, but when I didn't return it, the smile faded and she looked away.

"Why were you in my bed?"

The question was out of my mouth before I could stop it. I knew why she'd been in bed with me; I'd heard her telling Kaylee. But for some crazy reason, I wanted to hear her tell *me* why. A small part of me wanted her to tell me she'd wanted to be there. She'd wanted to stay with me after I had asked her to, as fucked up as that made me sound.

Her throat bobbed as she looked at the bed and then back to me. "It's a little hard to explain."

My brow quirked. "How about you explain it to me while I drive you back to your car."

"O-okay."

Shit. I hated how her voice sounded shaky. *Why do I always talk down to her? And why is she letting me get away with it this morning?*

That fiery personality from yesterday was gone. The woman standing before me seemed . . . defeated.

"I just need to hit the bathroom, grab some Tylenol, and then change."

She nodded. “I’ll wait on your front porch.”

I wanted to tell her that she didn’t have to wait outside, that she could make some coffee if she wanted to, but I didn’t. I simply nodded and headed into the bathroom. Lincoln didn’t need to get comfortable in my house. Bad enough I wasn’t going to get that image of her in my arms out of my head anytime soon.

After quickly brushing my teeth and washing my face, I changed and slipped a baseball cap on my head, since my damn cowboy hat wasn’t anywhere in sight.

When I stepped out into the living room, I saw Lincoln sitting on the porch swing. Her eyes were closed, and she looked like she was lost to the morning. The peaceful look on her face made me envious. I longed for that sort of peace.

“What are you thinking?” I asked, making her jump.

“Crap! You scared me. I was enjoying the sounds of the morning.”

I folded my arms over my chest. The way her eyes dragged over my body said she was thinking less-than-pure thoughts, but she looked away.

Lincoln cleared her throat and started talking. “About last night . . . nothing happened. I went to leave, but you pulled me onto the bed and asked me to stay. I was going to wait until you fell asleep and then sneak out and just walk back to my house.”

“Walk? In the middle of the night? Lincoln, do you know how far of a walk that is?”

She shrugged. “I tried to stay awake, but I guess I fell asleep. I’m sorry. I meant to be gone by the time you woke up. I don’t make a habit of sleeping in strange men’s beds.”

“So, I’m a stranger?” I asked, a slight smirk on my face.

“You might as well be,” she replied.

Okay, that was deserved, but that hurts a bit.

“Are you ready to go get your car?”

She politely smiled. "If that's okay. I'm sure you have things to do, so I was trying to think of anyone else I could call to take me. Kaylee obviously doesn't have her car here, so I can't call her."

"It's fine, and it won't take long."

With a nod, she stood. "I feel bad, pulling you away from Blayze, especially if you had plans with him today. Dirk said you'd be leaving for Billings in a few days."

I balled my fists in reaction to the instant jealousy. "Dirk?" I asked, frowning. "You talked to Dirk?"

"Um, yeah. Last night at the bar. He was sitting at the table with all of us."

Small bits and pieces of last night flashed through my memory. One of them was Dirk sitting next to Lincoln, deep in conversation with her.

"I'm not leaving for Billings until Friday. I don't know when Dirk is leaving."

Lincoln nodded. "Oh. Well, I hope you enjoy your time at home, then."

She quickly turned and headed down the porch steps toward my truck. I'd seen the keys on the inside table, so I walked in and grabbed them.

I slipped into my truck and started it, and we headed down the dirt road. We sat in silence until I pulled into the parking lot of the Blue Moose. It was one of three bars in town, and the one where most of the locals went.

Lincoln opened the passenger door and glanced over to me. "Thank you for the ride."

Before she could get out of the truck, I reached for her arm, stopping her. "Thank you for getting me home last night. I appreciate it. I don't . . . I don't normally drink like that. It was just a . . . bad day."

Her smile seemed to make the inside of the truck brighter. "No worries. I'm just glad a deer didn't run out in front of me last night on the way to your house. I'd have hated to wreck your truck, giving you *another* reason not to like me." Her hand lifted, and she said "Bye, Brock" before I could even process what she'd just said.

The door shut, and I sat there for a few seconds before I got out of the truck. "I don't hate you, Lincoln."

Her keys were in her hand, and the sound of her car beeping and unlocking felt like her way of saying she didn't want to talk to me. "It's okay. I'm sorry I said that. I have a bad habit of not thinking before I talk."

Her hand went to the handle, and she opened the door.

I pushed it shut.

When she glared up at me, I saw that feisty woman from yesterday appear.

"Excuse me, but you sure like to manhandle me, don't you? I'm not one of the bulls you ride, Brock Shaw."

I stepped closer, my heart hammering in my chest. "What did you and Dirk talk about last night?"

Her face constricted with a confused look. "What?"

"Did you dance with him?"

"N-no. He never even asked me to dance."

That brought a smile to my face. It was already getting harder to ignore how much I was attracted to Lincoln, and knowing Dirk wasn't gave me an odd sense of peace. Placing both of my hands on her car, I caged her against it. I swore her chest rose and fell at the same rate my heart was pounding.

"I'm sorry I acted like I did yesterday. It was hard, being back at my old place and knowing the changes you were making to it, and I took it out on you. But I truly *am* sorry I acted like a dick."

Lincoln swallowed. "It's okay."

"Please stop saying I don't like you, Lincoln. That's the furthest thing from the truth."

Her eyes darted up to meet mine, and when her pretty little tongue swept over those pink lips, I had to hold back a moan. "Stop *treating* me like you don't like me, then."

The corners of my mouth rose, and my gaze landed on that mouth I so desperately wanted to kiss. "I can do more than that."

Getting lost in those emerald eyes, I couldn't stop myself.

Leaning down, I softly brushed my lips over hers. She sucked in a breath—and I lost it. Pressing my lips harder to hers, I pulled her body against mine and ran my tongue over her bottom lip, asking for permission to taste more of her.

She pulled back.

"Brock . . . I . . . I haven't brushed my teeth this morning."

Laughing, I put my hand behind her neck and brought her mouth back to mine, taking it fully this time. Lincoln lifted onto her toes and wrapped her arms around my neck. My other hand went to her lower back, pulling her as tight as I could against my body, while the one on her neck pushed into her hair, giving it a tug.

Lincoln practically melted into me, like she'd been banking on this kiss as much as I had. I hadn't wanted to admit it to myself, but since the moment she'd looked up at me after falling yesterday in the barn, I'd been wanting to kiss her. *Needing* to kiss her. Afraid as hell to kiss her, and for good reason. The feel of her soft body against mine was already addicting. She gave me a warmth I hadn't experienced in a very long time. A feeling of desire that I don't think I'd *ever* really experienced before.

Lincoln's kiss felt like it was waking up a part of me I had given up on.

A throat cleared from behind us, and Lincoln promptly pulled away.

"I see you got him home safely last night," Betty Jane said, a shit-eating grin on her face.

The shade of red that covered Lincoln's cheeks was adorable. "Um . . . yes."

Turning, Lincoln slipped into her car and started it. I took a few steps back as she rolled her window down. She dug her teeth into her kiss-swollen lip before speaking.

"Bye, Brock."

My hand lifted. "See ya around, Lincoln."

I watched as she pulled out of the parking spot and made her way onto Main Street.

Betty Jane walked up next to me and bumped my arm. "You'd better not hurt her, Brock. I like her. She's got something that says she's a good soul."

When Lincoln's car turned the corner, I faced Betty Jane. "You played a little game last night, didn't you, Betty Jane?"

She acted innocent. "Why, I don't know what you mean."

"I've gotten drunk here plenty of times, and you have Ralph bring me to my truck and I sleep it off, but last night, you had that poor girl haul my ass home. Why?"

With a wink, she said, "Because I saw the way you were looking at her, and I saw the way she was looking at you. It's time you stopped punishing yourself for something you had no control over, and if that young lady can help you do that, then so be it."

Groaning, I scrubbed my hands over my unshaven face. "Ah, hell, Betty Jane. Don't be going and trying to fix me up with her. You know I'm not interested in dating. I've got Blayze, and he keeps me plenty busy when I come into town."

She huffed. "Right. You just keep lying to yourself, Shaw. I've got to go inventory the booze in that joint," Betty Jane said as she hooked her thumb over her shoulder. "Have a good one."

"You too."

As I made my way over to my truck, I couldn't ignore the way my lips still felt from that kiss. Or how my body had come to life when Lincoln wrapped her arms around me. Or how good it'd felt with her next to me when I woke up this morning.

Pushing it all aside, I decided I *needed* to ignore it. I didn't deserve a woman like Lincoln Pratt.

Not one single part of me did . . . not one bit.

Chapter Nine

Lincoln

The entire drive back to my house, I couldn't ignore how my body felt.

Because Brock Shaw had kissed me. Really kissed me.

My lips still tingled from his kiss. I'd never before experienced the feeling I got when he put his hands on me . . . *intentionally* put his hands on me, that is. I wasn't counting last night's liquid-courage word vomit he'd spewed or the way he'd touched me when he wouldn't remember one moment of it.

Holy shit. He kissed me.

By the time I'd pulled in and parked in my little driveway, I was positive the smile on my face couldn't possibly be wiped away.

Kaylee stepped out onto the porch of the house and watched me get out of my car. A wide grin grew on her face when she saw me. "Tell me you had cowboy sex or reverse-cowgirl sex—hell, any kind of sex—and that's why you have a smile on your face!"

I laughed as I made my way up the steps. "No, I didn't have sex. But I think it's safe to say that Brock Shaw doesn't hate me."

Her brows rose in question. "Do tell."

"I need coffee, and then I'll spill everything."

By the time I was finished telling her everything that had happened, Kaylee was staring at me with a shocked expression. She'd been oddly quiet as I told her everything that had happened after she'd left the bar, until Betty Jane had caught Brock and me kissing. A raised eyebrow here and there was all I had gotten from her.

"So, let me get this right. He kissed you in the middle of the parking lot of the bar."

Nodding, I replied, "Yep."

"For everyone to see?"

Taking a sip of my coffee, I replied, "Well, I think it was only Betty Jane."

"Hence what I meant by everyone. That little kiss is going to be spread through town like wildfire. You have no idea how small towns are, and you even said she'd made that comment last night about people finding out."

I brushed her off with a wave of my hand. "Nah, I don't think so. She seems cool."

Kaylee grinned wide. "If you say so. But this is huge, Lincoln."

Frowning, I asked, "Why is this huge?"

"Okay, so last night at the bar, when I went into the bathroom, I got some scoop on the mysterious Brock Shaw."

I laughed. "He's not mysterious."

"He is. Anywho, out of the two women I was talking to, I couldn't get all the details of what happened to his wife, but it was something tragic; I got that much. And Brock blames himself for it. They said he hasn't dated anyone or shown interest in anyone in a long time. I guess he's been bull riding since he was, like, ten or something crazy, started professionally at seventeen, and that he lives, eats, and breathes the crazy shit. He didn't come home a lot during his marriage, and I think that caused problems between him and his wife. Now, he tries to be home each week when he can, but he's usually gone every weekend, bull riding."

My eyes widened. "You got all that in the bathroom of the bar last night?"

She nodded. "I'm telling you. Small-town folk like to fill in the new people. I couldn't say anything to you last night, with the subject matter sitting right there."

"You said something tragic happened?" I asked, totally sucked into Kaylee's God-given talent for telling a story—and praying she wasn't about to tell me what I thought she was.

"I think she died."

I covered my mouth with my hand. "Oh no."

"Listen, I'm not really sure, but the way they kept saying how sad it all was, I sort of put two and two together. They said Brock was bound to not like you, since you bought the house that he and his wife had lived in."

Sitting back in my chair, I nodded. "Brock told me himself the house brings back bad memories when he apologized to me, so that part I believe is true."

Kaylee made a face like she agreed while nodding her head. "So, something tragic happened to the wife, and that's why he sold this house."

"I don't think it's just that. I think he loves what he does. And I can understand selling the house."

She nodded like she completely got it. "Yeah. I can understand that too."

I stood. "Well, I'm going to shower and figure out what project I'm working on today."

"When do you officially start your new job?" Kaylee asked, opening her laptop.

"Two weeks, and I'm a working girl again." Even I could hear the excitement in my voice.

Kaylee's face lit up with delight for me. She knew how much I was looking forward to this fresh start. "I'm seriously thinking of heading back to Atlanta, packing up my stuff, and moving here."

I screamed and grabbed her arm, pulling her into a hug. "Oh, Kaylee, that would be so amazing! Stay here with me!"

Laughing, she hugged me back. "Well, if you're crazy enough to move halfway across the country to start a new life, I guess I can too."

I knew part of the reason she was entertaining the idea of moving was to run away from her own ghosts. She probably understood Brock a hell of a lot better than I ever would.

"You've just made me so happy!"

She lifted a brow. "So happy you'll make me those brownies I love so much?"

"Yes! I'll even make you oatmeal chocolate chip cookies!"

The next day, when Kaylee and I made a trip into town, it was hard not to notice how everyone was looking at me.

Some even whispered, "That's her" when I walked by them.

I smiled politely, but I refused to admit to myself Kaylee had been right about the gossiping.

Kaylee was thumping a cantaloupe when I walked up to her and bumped her arm. "Is it just me, or are people staring at me and whispering?"

Kaylee looked up from the melon and took a glance around. "It's not you; they are."

She put the melon down and picked up another one like it was no big deal that two strange women our age were currently shooting daggers my way.

"Okay, what's up with the women over there, glaring at me?"

Again, Kaylee glanced up to the women and then back to me. "One word. No, wait . . . two words. No, four."

I waited for her to tell me. Arching one brow, I said, "And those four words would be?"

She smirked. "The kiss. Small town."

"The kiss?" I retorted with a laugh that screamed I knew she was right but was refusing to admit it. "Oh, please!"

"I told you that kiss was going to take off on the rumor mill. It's gotten a good twenty-four-hour run."

When I peeked back at the two women, they were walking away, but one glanced back to give me a dirty look.

"So, do you think people think I'm a slut now?" I asked in a hushed voice.

Kaylee laughed. "No, honey, they think you've snagged the golden boy, who, apparently, every single woman—hell, probably even some of the married ones—in this small town wants."

Tilting my head, I narrowed my eyes at her. "How exactly do you know all this information? We haven't been in this town that long!"

She shrugged. "I can't help it if I know how to get information."

"Miss Lincoln! Miss Kaylee!"

The sound of Blayze's voice made us both turn. The boy was coming in fast and hot, so I leaned down and instinctively held open my arms, only for him to run into them for a quick hug.

"Guess where we're going?" Blayze asked.

Grinning at his excitement, I asked, "Where?"

"The county fair! It's here all week! Daddy is gonna win me some pwizes. You want to come with us? You, too, Miss Kaylee!"

Kaylee ruffled Blayze's light-brown hair. "I wish I could, buddy, but I've got work I need to do, so I can't take any time off to play."

His lower lip jutted out, and it was the cutest thing ever.

The air around me charged, and I felt my lips tingling again, almost as if they were just as excited as I was that Brock was standing within a foot of us. And hoping for another kiss.

"Hey," he said in a deep, sexy voice that had my insides doing all sorts of jumping.

The feel of his lips on mine resurfaced in my memory, and I felt my cheeks heat.

Glancing up, I smiled. "Hey back at ya. How are you?"

The left side of his mouth rose slightly, and Lord, if it wasn't sexy as hell. "I'm good."

I nodded. "I heard y'all are going to a county fair. Sounds like fun."

Blayze spun around and grabbed on to Brock's shirt. "Daddy, can Miss Lincoln come with us? Pwease!"

For a moment it looked like Brock was going to say no, so I beat him to the punch.

"I'm sure your dad wants it to be a guys' day," I quickly said, standing and giving Brock a knowing smile. Glancing down to Blayze, I felt my chest tighten with a desire to spend the day with both father and son. That was not going to happen. But those big blue eyes staring up at me nearly broke my heart. "It'll be fun!"

"Aw, shucks. I was hoping to show you how well I could shoot the ducks!"

Laughing, I winked at him. "I'm sure you're a great shot."

I *wasn't* sure where to look. My eyes bounced from son to father. Brock just stood there, and that stone-cold face he'd worn the first time I'd met him was back. Maybe the kiss had been a fluke. A knee-jerk reaction he'd had in the heat of the moment. He probably kissed women all the time when he was traveling from town to town. Hell, I was sure he did more than that.

The thought of Brock sleeping around with strange women made my chest ache, which, in some way, surprised me. I'd known the man only two days, and I was already jealous of women he might or might not have slept with.

Good grief. Get a grip, Lincoln.

Brock cleared his throat, as if he was somehow pulling himself from a dark place. A smile grew over his face before he finally spoke. "Nah, it would be, um . . . fun to have you join us."

I could feel Kaylee's eyes boring into me. One quick peek her way confirmed she was giving me that look that said if I didn't go, I was an idiot.

Focusing back on Brock, I nibbled on the corner of my lip before asking, "Are you sure? I don't want to intrude on your time with your son."

Something in his gaze shifted when he made eye contact with me. His whole body relaxed, and his dimples popped out. "I'd love for you to spend the day with us, Lincoln."

"Then I guess it's settled," Kaylee nearly shouted, causing me to jump. "She'll go! Now, maybe I can actually get some work done without any interruptions."

Blayze jumped all around like he'd just been told it was Christmas morning as Brock and I continued to stare at each other.

Finally, he broke the moment and said, "We just need to grab some drinks for the cooler and some sunscreen. Can you join us now, or should we come pick you up at your place?"

The pained expression on his face when he mentioned picking me up wasn't hard to miss. There really *were* painful memories at that house for Brock. I wondered if the rumor about his wife was true. I tried to push away the instant sadness I felt.

"I'm fine if y'all want to grab your stuff and head over there. I'm dressed okay?"

Brock glanced down my body . . . slowly. The light-fabric dress was finished off with my favorite cowboy boots.

"You look beautiful—I mean, you're dressed perfectly. Do you have a sweater? It could turn cold."

I felt my cheeks heat.

Kaylee gave me a push, and I stumbled forward. "Yes, she has one in the car. I'll run and get it for her." She held out her hand. "Keys, please."

Before I knew what was happening, my best friend was racing out of the grocery store, telling the clerk she'd be right back to check out.

"Miss Lincoln, we're going to have fun today!"

I smiled at Blayze, and before I could say anything, Kaylee was there, panting like she'd just run a marathon. She shoved my sweater at me.

"Okay, well, have fun, y'all!" she crooned as she wiggled her fingers at us.

Brock placed his hand on my lower back, and I nearly tripped from the contact. Swallowing hard, I let him guide me around the store. It was then I noticed that nearly *everyone* was staring at us now. I wanted to tell myself it was because Blayze was jabbering on and on about how he was going to show me everything and that I had to ride every single ride with him. But I knew I was kidding myself. It was those four words.

The kiss. Small town.

Brock wore a relaxed smile, but something around his eyes said he was feeling uncomfortable as well. I wasn't sure what was making him feel that way, but I had every idea it was because of the unwanted attention he was getting from the locals who were openly gawking at us.

After getting drinks and sunscreen, we stood in line. One of the women from earlier walked up to Brock and plastered on a huge smile while pushing her chest out just a little too much.

"Hi, Brock. You gonna be at the dance tonight?" she asked, not once looking in my direction.

Turning, I focused on the cashier, willing her to hurry. Unfortunately, she was trying to listen to the conversation Brock and the woman were having, so she was moving at a snail's pace, ringing up the items.

"Hi, Lucy Mae." Taking out his wallet, Brock pulled out a twenty and handed it to the cashier while I placed the waters and Gatorades into a plastic bag. Lord knows, the cashier wasn't going to miss anything by doing her job.

"So? The dance? Maybe you can save me a spot on your dance card."

I tried not to look at Brock, but I could feel his eyes on me, so I glanced up. He smiled, and my heart skipped a beat.

Why does he have such an effect on me?

My insides felt warm, and my lower stomach pulsed with a need I hadn't felt in over a year. Heck, if I was being honest, I'm not sure I'd *ever* had a man make me feel this type of desire.

"I have a feeling my dance card will be full tonight. I'll see ya around."

And with that, he grabbed the bags from me and placed his hand on my lower back again. This time, he rubbed his thumb back and forth over the light fabric, and my insides nearly melted on the spot.

Breathe, Lincoln. Breathe.

It was refreshing to have someone care enough to take the time to guide me. Even if it was out of a grocery store with all the locals focused on us. Maybe Brock *didn't* care about the unwanted attention. Maybe this connection we felt was new to him, as well. I dug my teeth into my bottom lip, trying to hide the smile that wanted to come out at that little thought.

A small part of me wanted to look back and stick my tongue out at Lucy Mae.

What in the world is going on with me? That was not like me at all. First, I was a grown woman, for crying out loud. And second, I wasn't the jealous type, never had been.

Brock stopped walking momentarily, and I paused to see what the holdup was.

"By the way, there's a dance tonight after the fair. I hope you can go with . . . us." He'd hesitated, not wanting to make it seem like a date, and I was okay with that. There was no denying the attraction between us, but leaping right into dating, especially after our rocky start, was probably not a good idea. Or at least I told myself that.

I'd just met Brock, and I knew in a few days, he would be gone again. Besides, I wasn't sure if I was ready to open my heart up like that.

In my last relationship, I'd been betrayed. I'd sworn I would be careful next time, and something about Brock Shaw screamed the opposite of careful. His dangerous job. His past—which was clearly something he was still dealing with—and the fact that he had a son.

But when he touched me or smiled at me, my heart told me it wanted to open up and let this man in. It wanted to take the leap.

"I'd love to go to the dance with y'all."

We continued walking toward his truck as Blayze pulled on Brock's hand to hurry up.

"First thing we have to do is go to the ducks," Blayze declared.

Brock and I both chuckled as we all climbed into the truck. "Then what?" I asked.

"Then the rides! Do you like carnival rides, Miss Lincoln?"

Turning around and facing him, I smiled. "I do! I love them."

His blue eyes lit up, and I could see his father in him.

I couldn't help but wonder what Blayze's mother had looked like. *Did he get his eyes from his father? Or did Brock's wife have blue eyes as well?*

"I'm so glad you came with us! Daddy doesn't like all the rides."

My eyes went to Brock, who was now driving. "How could you not like the rides?"

He shrugged. "Never been a fan of them."

"But you ride bulls for a living. I would think you would like the rush of the rides."

He brought the truck to a stop and looked directly at me. "There are only two things I love to ride that I get a thrill out of . . . and one of those two things, the rush is shared with someone else, and it has nothing to do with bulls."

I looked away, feeling my face heat. Because I was pretty damn sure that the "someone else" comment was meant for me. Maybe I was still wound up over thoughts of that kiss. *Crap.*

"What's your favorite ride, Miss Lincoln?" Blayze asked, causing me to pull my mind away from the image of Brock and sex.

"Um . . . I'm not sure I have a favorite." *Why did my voice sound all shaky?*

When I peeked over at Brock, he was smiling like he knew exactly where my mind had just gone. Those dimples were going to be the death of me.

"Well, I don't have a favorite either! So, that means we can ride them all!"

Chapter Ten

Brock

I watched as Blayze and Lincoln rode on the Flying Dinos. My dick strained against my jeans as Lincoln laughed and let out a couple of small screams, purely for Blayze's entertainment.

I didn't want to admit that I loved seeing her with him, or how much he was enjoying it.

I'd never once brought a woman around my son. Never intended to, but after that kiss, Lincoln Pratt was the only thing I could think about. The hell with what my head was telling me to do. I wanted to be around her, and I knew she wouldn't do anything to hurt Blayze. It was pretty damn clear she was having just as much fun as he was.

"So, do you think letting a strange woman you hardly know be so close to your son is a good idea?"

I wanted to groan when I heard Lucy Mae next to me. I had dated her for a bit in high school, and in her weird, crazy world, she'd always thought we would end up together. She had hated Kaci and had gone out of her way to make her life difficult.

"I think it's none of your damn business, Lucy Mae."

She turned to look at me. "A little birdie told me she stayed at your house the other night, and you were seen kissing her in the parking lot of the Blue Moose."

My head fell back, and I laughed. "Wow, news travels fast in this town."

"So, you don't deny it?"

"Listen, Lucy Mae, what I do—and who I do—don't concern you. Lincoln is a friend of mine and a friend of my family. If I find out that you've started giving her hell, you'll regret it. Do we understand each other?"

Her hands went to her hips. "She's a city girl from Atlanta, for Pete's sake, Brock! You can't possibly be serious. All these years you push everyone away, and *this* is who you open up to?"

"Daddy! Look at me! No hands!"

I turned away from Lucy Mae and looked at Blayze and Lincoln, both holding their hands up. I gave him a thumbs-up.

"I heard that she comes from a lot of money. Rumor is, she started an interior design company there in Atlanta, and she couldn't make it work. Poor thing. Must have been so embarrassing to have to tuck tail and leave town. And that friend of hers, something creepy is going on with *her.* I'm wondering if they're . . . together . . . if you know what I mean."

"Well, considering Kaylee and my brother Ty were getting it on in his truck the other night, I'm going to say you're wrong."

The moment it came out of my mouth, I knew I had messed up. Lucy Mae would spread that bit of gossip all over town, and Kaylee would be slapped with a slut label. It wasn't even true, so why I'd said it, I had no idea.

Fuck.

"What?" Lucy Mae gasped.

Turning to her, I smirked. "Just kiddin', Lucy Mae. Wanted to see how you'd react. You still got a crush on my brother too?"

Her face went white. Lucy Mae had decided to get back at me for marrying Kaci by sleeping with Ty one night when he was drunk. I hadn't cared the least bit. I had recently married Kaci, and Lucy Mae and I had been over for some time. When I found out she'd slept with Ty, *she* was disappointed to learn I didn't give two shits.

"You know we were both drunk that night, and I told you, I thought it was *you.*"

"Right, because I would really cheat on my wife."

Her eyes went to little beads. "Well, she always did believe those rumors about you whoring around on the road."

My chest felt like someone had hit me square in it. I never understood why Kaci had believed Lucy Mae's lies. A part of me thought she *wanted* to believe they were true, for whatever reason.

Leaning in closer to Lucy Mae, I said, "She only believed it because *you* fed that shit to her. I never cheated on my wife, and you damn well know it."

"Everything okay here?"

Lincoln's voice came from behind me, her hand landing gently on my arm.

I instantly relaxed.

Lucy Mae's gaze dropped to Lincoln's hand before she smirked, turned on the heel of her boot, and walked away.

"Bitch," I mumbled under my breath. Turning, I looked at Lincoln. "Where's Blayze?" I asked.

"He, um . . . he wanted to ride the ride again with his little friend."

Darting my eyes over to the ride, I saw Blayze sitting on the ride with his friend Billy.

"Are you okay?"

Lincoln's voice pulled me back from the darkness I had been slipping into. I looked at her and smiled. "Sorry. Yes, I'm fine."

She grinned. "Don't let her push your buttons. I didn't hear what y'all were saying, but she was clearly trying to rattle you."

My eyes searched this beautiful woman's face. *Where the hell were you all those years ago?*

I instantly felt guilty for thinking that thought.

"Lucy Mae has a way of trying to rattle everyone. If she tries to say anything to you about me, will you do me a favor?"

Lincoln nodded. "Of course."

"Ignore it. We dated back in high school, and she's still bitter about me breaking up with her."

When Lincoln's eyes went wide with shock, I almost laughed. "High school! She's still upset because you broke up with her in high school?"

I chuckled. "Yeah."

She rolled her eyes and let out a chuckle of her own. "Wow. That's sort of sad."

"It is."

"Dad! Let's go shoot some ducks!" Blayze yelled out as he and Billy came running up to us.

"I like the sound of that," I stated as I ruffled his hair.

I watched him and Billy turn tail and run toward the games. Once we got there, Blayze was raring to go. He shot enough ducks to get a small prize. Then it was my turn. I shot some and got him a bigger prize.

"Miss Lincoln, you gonna try?"

She grinned. "I sure am. I used to be pretty good at this."

I looked down at the boys and acted like I was rolling my eyes at Lincoln.

"Girls can't shoot!" Billy exclaimed.

Lincoln arched a brow. "Is that right?"

I paid for Lincoln's turn, and she thanked me, picked up the gun—and proceeded to shoot every single duck down.

I was pretty sure my damn mouth was on the ground.

"She did better than you, Dad!" Blayze shouted with a laugh.

With a sexier-than-sin smile on her face, Lincoln blew at the end of her fake gun and winked at me. My damn knees went weak. They *actually* went weak.

"My daddy taught me how to shoot."

That southern accent came out in full force, and in that moment, I fell a little bit more for Lincoln Pratt.

"I'd say he did," I replied with a chuckle. "I'm beginning to think you're more on the country side than a city girl."

Her face beamed. "Well, if you're asking me if I know how to ride, I most certainly do. It's been a while—a long while—but I'm positive I'm still good at it."

I swallowed hard, trying not to notice how my dick was straining against my jeans again.

"You're talking about horses, right?" I asked, my voice a tad shaky.

Her lips pursed tight, and she shrugged before turning her attention to the attendant, who was handing her a giant stuffed dog.

Laughing, I stepped closer and pressed my mouth to her ear. "You're a very naughty girl for doing that to me."

She smiled and pulled back to look into my eyes. "Payback from earlier in the truck, Mr. Shaw."

We both fell into a lust-induced trance.

"Why are you staring at each other and not talking?" Blayze asked.

Lincoln cleared her throat while she hugged the dog a little closer.

"Where to now, buddy?" I asked.

"The merry-go-round!"

As Lincoln and I walked next to each other, I couldn't shake the feeling I had in my chest. Was that excitement? Desire? Lust? All I knew was I was confused. I liked Lincoln; there was no denying it. But why did I like her? Because she was different from the other women in this town? Or was it because, the first time I'd laid eyes on her, I'd felt something zip through my body that I'd never experienced before?

At the time, it'd pissed me off that I'd had a reaction to her. The woman who'd bought the house where I was supposed to raise a family had moved in, won the hearts of my son and my family, and made me want to kiss her the moment I met her. The last thing I'd wanted was to let someone in.

"I want the elephant," Blayze declared.

I reached my hand out for Lincoln and helped her up onto the ride. "Any certain one you want?"

She gave me a sheepish grin. "The pink horse."

I laughed. "Pink horse it is."

Blayze's elephant just happened to be right in front of the two horses Lincoln and I climbed up on. As the music began and we started to go around, I couldn't help but watch her. The way she and Blayze talked back and forth with each other. The way she laughed and let herself enjoy the moment. It was refreshing.

My mind drifted back to a memory between Kaci and me.

"This is stupid, Brock."

Her words felt like a slap in the face.

"I thought you might like coming to the carnival. You used to like it."

She scoffed. "Yeah, when I was ten. I'm a grown woman now, and I have no interest in this."

"How about if I try to win you something?"

Her frown dropped slightly. When we'd been kids, Kaci always loved it when I won her the giant stuffed animals.

"I want the pink flamingo," she demanded, hands on hips and everything.

"Pink flamingo it is."

Taking her hand in mine, I guided us through the sea of people over to the ring toss.

It didn't take long before I was handing Kaci a giant pink flamingo. Her smile was the first genuine smile I'd seen in a long time. I knew the stress of me being on the road all the time was getting to her.

"Did you cheat to win that thing?"

Kaci's eyes lit up at the sound of Dirk's voice. She turned and rushed over to him. "Brock didn't say you were back in town too!"

Dirk grinned down at my wife like he was looking into the gates of heaven. I pretended it didn't bother me that he was still just as much in love with her as I was.

Frowning, I carefully watched them.

"I've missed you, ya big dork. Are you being careful?"

Dirk nodded. "Always."

It struck me then that Kaci had said the very same thing to me this morning.

Dirk looked my way. Seeing the look on my face, he took a few steps back.

It was then that Kaci faced me. She put a huge smile on her face and said, "I'm so happy to have both my guys back. It feels right."

The memory left what felt like an ache in the center of my chest. Kaci had told me that night that she wanted a baby. I thought it was too soon. Plus, I couldn't get the image out of my head of her looking at Dirk the way she had.

We were rushing with the baby; looking back, I could see that. Rushing for all the wrong reasons. I gave Kaci what she wanted because that was what I always did. Kaci had wanted me to take her to prom our senior year, so I'd taken her instead of Lucy Mae. I wasn't dating Lucy then, but we had talked about going together. Kaci had wanted me to take her to New York City to see a ballet, so I had. Kaci wanted me to tell Dirk we were dating, so I did.

There wasn't anything I wouldn't have done for her. And I'd been completely blind to how manipulative she had been. Why? Because I had been so in love with her? Or because I didn't want her to leave me for Dirk?

Jesus. Either way, I was still fucked up in the head over her.

The sound of Lincoln laughing pulled me from my thoughts. My eyes looked past her to see Dirk standing there, watching us. He raised his hand and waved. I did the same.

A feeling of sickness and déjà vu washed over me. I needed to push it aside. This wasn't Kaci; Dirk wasn't in love with Lincoln.

"Brock? Brock?"

My eyes snapped back to Lincoln. "Yeah? Sorry, I was lost in a thought."

She raised her brows. "I'd say. You looked like you were a million miles away."

"I was," I stated, looking back at Dirk, who was now talking to someone. "Listen, how about we head on out of here and go get something to eat?"

Her eyes grew big. "You mean, like real food and not something full of grease and on a stick?"

I laughed. "Yeah, real food."

The merry-go-round ride ended, and we got off. Blayze informed me he had to try one more time at shooting ducks before we could leave. As Dirk walked up to us, I asked Lincoln if she wouldn't mind taking him, since I needed to talk to Dirk.

"Sure, I don't mind at all."

When I reached into my wallet, she slapped my hand away.

"Please, you've been paying all day. I've got this."

I watched them walk away, Blayze lifting his hand and slipping it into Lincoln's. The sight made my chest squeeze with something that felt like . . . happiness. That was something I didn't feel that often anymore.

"So, rumors around town are true?"

"What do you mean?" I asked, focusing on my best friend.

"Seems like the latest rumor mill is talking about you and the new city girl dating."

I laughed. "I've only known her a few days. She's nice, and Blayze likes her."

He nodded and rubbed his chin before throwing me a wink. "Blayze likes her. Okay, let's go with that."

"I thought you were leaving to head to Billings today."

"Thought I would stick around for a bit. Dad is working on that car. It was nice, hanging in the shop with him last night, just working on that piece of shit and drinking some beer."

I smiled. "Yeah, I'm sure they're glad you're home."

He nodded.

"I need to ask you something, Dirk."

Facing me, he smiled. "How to stay on a bull for eight seconds?"

I smirked. "Hardly. This is, um . . . this is serious, though, and I really need you to tell me the truth."

His smile faded, and he looked back toward where Lincoln and Blayze were.

"Did Kaci ever tell you she wished we hadn't gotten married?"

Dirk swallowed hard before he looked down at the ground. My heart was beating a mile a minute. When he finally looked up at me, I realized I had been holding my breath.

"No, she loved you, Brock."

"But?" I added, feeling like there was one coming.

"But nothing, dude. I won't deny I tried talking her out of marrying you, and she told me once she hoped she hadn't made a mistake."

My stomach turned, and a wave of nausea hit me. I got that he had been in love with her, but he had also been my best friend. Hearing he'd tried to talk Kaci out of marrying me almost left me feeling betrayed. "A mistake?"

Dirk didn't look at me.

"Did she mean by marrying me?"

He finally met my eyes. "Nah, dude. I know she loved us both, but she loved you more."

"And you loved *her* more."

"We don't know that."

"You would have given up bull riding and stayed with her. Made the home she wanted."

He shook his head. "She wanted you more than she wanted me. At the time it was hard for me to deal with that, and I feel bad about that, dude. I honestly do."

I rubbed the back of my neck and sighed. "I knew how much you loved her, and I didn't step aside. I wanted her too, and the thought of you having her . . ."

"Brock, it's in the past. Let's just leave it there."

My chin wobbled slightly. "I loved Kaci."

"I don't doubt that. She picked you, and I tried like hell to accept it the best I could at the time."

I looked away. My gaze landed on Lincoln. "I think I loved the *idea* of me and Kaci. I don't know if it was the type of love needed to make a marriage work. I knew that, but I wanted her more than I was willing to let her go. I'm sorry I didn't step aside."

He shook his head. "*She* made the choice between us, and I know you loved her, Brock. Don't try and compare how *you* loved her with how I did. It's not going to make you feel any better."

"I tried to make her happy, Dirk. Damn, I tried so hard to make her happy, but I always fell short."

He nodded. "She knew what she was getting into when she married you. She knew how much you loved bull riding. Truth be told, I'm not so sure either one of us would have been able to keep her happy."

Dirk's words hit me so hard I took a few steps back. I hadn't ever let myself think of it that way.

"Daddy! I won! I won!"

Blayze rushed back over to me with Lincoln in tow, skidding to a stop to say hi to Dirk.

"Hey, Uncle Dirk! Look what I won!" He held up a plastic cage that contained one lizard.

"Wow, look at you, winning a lizard. That's pretty awesome, Blayze." Dirk shook his head and laughed while rustling the hair on top of my son's head. When he looked back at me, he nodded. It was his way of saying no matter what problems Kaci and I may have had, Blayze was a product of our love. There was no denying that.

"What do you think about our small town, Miss Pratt?" Dirk asked Lincoln.

She grinned. "Please call me Lincoln, and I love it! The mountains alone are enough to make a girl want to stay."

Dirk laughed and then looked at me and winked. "I'll let you guys enjoy the rest of your day. You going to the dance?"

"Yeah, we're going to get something to eat, and then we'll be heading that way," I quickly said.

Dirk faced Lincoln. "Save this cowboy a dance, will ya?"

"Um, sure," she replied, her cheeks turning a soft pink.

"See ya later, Blayze."

"Bye, Uncle Dirk!"

A few friends of Blayze's ran up to check out his new lizard. Before I knew it, plans were made to have a campout at Billy's house.

"May I go, Dad? You can pick me up early in the morning, and we can go fishin'."

With a grin, I leaned down and asked, "What about a bag with some clothes in it?"

"Hey, Brock!"

I glanced up to see Jan, Billy's mama, standing there. "Hi, Jan."

"I hear the boys are planning a camp-over."

Standing, I blew out a breath. "I guess so. You sure you're okay with it? We'll have to run back to the house and pack him a bag."

Jan waved her hand to dismiss that. "Nonsense. Blayze can just wear something of Billy's."

I smiled. "Oh, okay. Well, good. I'll be by in the morning to get him to take him fishing."

She nodded and peeked over to Lincoln.

"Oh, hell, I'm sorry. Jan, this is Lincoln Pratt. She moved here from Atlanta and is going to be working with Karen Johnson."

"So, you're the famous interior designer from the big city? Karen has been talking nonstop about you."

Lincoln's face flushed, and it was cuter than hell. She reached out and shook Jan's hand. "Well, that is very sweet of her, but I'm not famous."

"Bullhocky! I heard you designed the governor of Georgia's country house."

My head jerked to stare at Lincoln.

"Yes, that's true," Lincoln answered, her voice low.

"And Karen said you helped design the house of some famous actress . . . oh, what's her name?"

I continued to stare at Lincoln as she gave me a timid look of embarrassment.

"It starts with an *S*. Sandra Bullock! That's who it was."

"You designed Sandra Bullock's house?"

"Well, she designed *one* of them. Which one was it?" Jan asked, moving in closer to Lincoln.

"I, um . . . well, I . . . nondisclosure and all."

Jan nodded. "Oh, I understand. Those bigwigs like throwing their weight around like that. Well, all I can say is, we're lucky here in Hamilton to have you, Lincoln. Did you see what I did there? The presidents' names and all?" Jan tossed her head back and laughed like she'd just said the funniest thing ever.

Lincoln let out a nervous laugh. "I saw. That was a good one."

"We'd better get going. You guys enjoy the rest of your afternoon and evening!"

"Blayze!" I shouted before he ran off too far. "Kiss and hug?"

"Right, Dad!"

"Dad . . . did you hear him call me Dad? What happened to Daddy?" I asked Lincoln.

After a quick hug and a kiss for me, Blayze turned to Lincoln and wrapped his arms around her legs. "Bye, Miss Lincoln!"

She returned the hug. "See ya around, Blayze."

And, just like that, Lincoln Pratt and I were alone, and Lord only knew what sort of trouble that could mean.

Chapter Eleven

Lincoln

Easy conversation flowed between me and Brock as he drove us to an Italian restaurant in the middle of the small town square. It felt as if I had known him for months. He wasn't the same guy from a few days ago who had acted like a complete jerk. Although I could tell something was bothering him, especially after the conversation he'd had with his friend Dirk.

"So, what made you move to Hamilton, Montana?" Brock asked.

"Well, I was tired of Atlanta. Tired of the hot summers, tired of my parents trying to run my life for me. If it were up to them, I'd be married with two point five kids now."

Brock laughed. "They're controlling? Like how?"

I took in a deep breath and blew it out. "I wanted to be an interior designer since before I could remember. Before I even got out of college, I was hired on with one of the best design firms in Atlanta. I was stupid and naive to think I had done it on my own merit. My father had gotten me the job; I just hadn't known at the time. He owns an investment firm in Atlanta, so he knows a lot of . . . influential people."

"He has some power?"

"You could say that. After a while, he wasn't happy that his little girl was playing second fiddle in this company, so he bought a building for my twenty-fourth birthday and told me it was mine. I could start my own business. At first, I was excited and ready to take on the challenge. Unfortunately, my father wasn't as keen on me slowly growing the business, so he brought business *to* me . . . by way of bribing people to use *me* instead of anyone else in Atlanta. It took me some time to figure it out, but eventually I did. The whole governor's summerhouse and all."

Brock smiled.

"Needless to say, I was devastated, and I started to question my own talent."

"Damn, what was he thinking?"

With a half shrug, I replied, "He was doing what he's always done. In my father's eyes, I've never really been quite capable of doing things on my own. If I wanted to try and build a piece of furniture myself, he'd tell me I shouldn't. I needed someone to do it for me, and before I knew it, there was a carpenter ready to build me whatever I wanted. Stupid things like that."

I felt a sadness in my heart that I hadn't felt since I'd sold my old design firm. "Anyway, I knew that I had to make a major change. That meant leaving Atlanta and proving not only to myself but to my parents that I could do this on my own. I started putting out my résumé. I uploaded it to a website, and Karen Johnson contacted me. Told me she was from a small town in Montana and that her business was growing, especially in Billings, which was a few hours away. She needed to be able to travel and have someone here in Hamilton. At first, she didn't want to contact me because she thought I would turn her down, but the moment I read her email, I knew this was what I wanted."

Brock pulled into the parking lot and found a spot to park. "You're not sad about leaving your family behind?"

I shrugged. "I am, but this feels right. It's something different and beautiful. I can walk outside, take in a deep breath, and feel the excitement of starting over coursing through my blood. In Atlanta, I felt like I was always suffocating. Between my folks, the business, the traffic . . . I needed something new. Not to mention, I feared for my life if I was out alone at night. Here, it's just the opposite."

"You don't think you'll get tired of being out in the middle of nowhere and want to go back?"

I got the feeling that he was asking me not purely as an innocent question. There was something more to it. I wanted to ask him if the question had a deeper meaning, but I didn't. I promised him I wouldn't be nosy, and I truly didn't want to seem like I was dissecting his every word to me.

"No. This is where I want to be, where I want to raise a family someday, and I can get back into riding here. I thought it might be fun to even teach horseback riding in the future."

"Ah, hell, Lincoln, not that fancy English-riding shit."

Hitting him on the shoulder, I replied, "Western. But I can teach English if I need to."

He smiled, and my heart felt like it skipped a beat.

"Besides, I've talked Kaylee into moving here, and she's hell bent on doing so. It'll be good for her to leave behind the past that haunts her in Atlanta."

Brock got out of the truck and quickly made his way to my door. He reached his hand out for me and helped me down. I wanted to ignore the way that made my stomach feel . . . like I had a dance party going on in there. Or the way a deliciously warm feeling had settled in the middle of my chest, something I'd never experienced.

"What's her story?"

"Kaylee's?"

He nodded.

"Her fiancé died two years ago, and she sort of fell apart. It took her a while to even get back into the normal swing of things. She was pretty depressed, and it took a lot of bestie time and a good therapist to finally pull her out of it. I've noticed, here, she seems like her old self. Ready to move on and maybe even date."

Brock held the door to the restaurant open for me. "Well, I should probably go ahead and have you warn her that my brother seems to be taken with her. And, trust me when I say, he's not the relationship type."

"I don't think that would be a problem for Kaylee. She seems to want to . . . sow some wild oats, if you get my drift."

He chuckled. "Ty would be the one to help with that."

I grinned and silently prayed he hadn't noticed my entire body shudder when he placed his hand on my lower back and guided me over to the hostess.

Why do I like that so much? Has no other guy done that before?

Surely, they had; it had just never affected me like this.

"Table for two?" the young hostess asked.

"Yes, please," Brock said politely.

Glancing around the restaurant, I couldn't help but grin. It was charming: exactly the type of place I would imagine two people going on a first date. It was only when we were walking through the dining room that I noticed everyone looking at us.

"We seem to be the center of attention," I stated as we sat down.

He took a quick look around and flashed a bright smile, tipping his cowboy hat to a few people.

"Mr. Lanser, Mrs. Lanser, how y'all doing?"

"Oh, very good. How is the bull riding going, son?" Mrs. Lanser asked.

"Doing pretty good. You going to come watch me ride in Billings this weekend?"

The older woman blushed. She actually *blushed.* "No! It would be fun, but I don't think I could stand to see you get hurt."

Brock winked as he said, "There's a reason I'm number one right now."

Mr. Lanser rumbled out a deep laugh. "That's our boy. Make Hamilton proud, son."

Brock tipped his cowboy hat again and replied, "Will do."

When he looked my way, he smiled. "Sorry."

"Don't be. I think it's great that they support you."

His eyes seemed to light up. I couldn't help but wonder why my compliment seemed to make him so happy.

The waiter came over and took our drink order before offering us a few minutes to look at the menu.

"See anything you like?" Brock asked as he studied the menu.

I chewed on my lip as I let my eyes take him in. I wanted to say yes: I saw something I liked very much that had nothing to do with Italian and everything to do with a certain bull rider.

Looking down at the menu before Brock caught me ogling him, I replied, "I think the chicken fettuccine sounds good."

I could feel Brock looking at me, so I glanced up.

By the expression on his face, I wondered if I had made a bad choice. "What? Is it no good here?"

"It's just nice to see a woman order something other than a damn salad."

I giggled. "Well, I can tell you, I have a healthy appetite, hence the reason I run every day, do yoga, and try to get in some other sorts of crazy exercise to keep my body guessing."

His brow lifted. "I'm going to have to remember that."

For the love of all that was good, I had no idea why I said what I said next.

"Well, considering I haven't had sex in forever, I could probably count that as a crazy exercise if the opportunity presented itself."

I stopped talking the moment I heard the words come out of my mouth.

Brock's smile grew bigger as my cheeks burned.

"Fiddlesticks, I have no freaking idea why I said that. I'm so sorry." I let out an exasperated breath. "I didn't mean that I thought we would be having sex. Not that I wouldn't want to—no, wait. I don't know what I'm saying. Okay, I'm going to die right now of embarrassment. I guess I just said that because . . . well, I don't really have a good reason for that one."

"Lincoln," Brock said, reaching out for my hand. "Take a breath, sweetheart, and stop talking. You're digging yourself in deeper."

"Deeper?" I said, not meaning to make it sound so sexual. I rolled my eyes and then closed them. "I'm going to stop talking now."

"Probably a good idea," Brock agreed, amusement clearly laced in his voice.

"Here are your drinks," the waiter said, setting my Diet Coke in front of me.

"I'm going to need something stronger, like a Bud Light. Please."

The waiter looked between me and Brock.

"That's what you consider stronger?" Brock asked.

I nodded.

"We'll take two."

"Okay, two Bud Lights coming up."

After the waiter delivered the beers and I nearly downed mine, we ordered.

"Do you date often?" Brock asked out of the blue.

"Not really. I mean, I've had a few boyfriends but nothing really too serious. The last one was over a year ago. I went to his apartment to surprise him for his birthday and caught him in bed with another woman. So . . . surprise!"

Brock's eyes went wide.

I shrugged. "Came back from a girls' trip early for his birthday. Best decision I ever made."

"You weren't angry?"

Giving his question serious thought, I shook my head. "No. I mean, don't get me wrong; I was extremely pissed at the time. It hurt knowing he had deceived me, and I felt betrayed. But I was angrier more than I was sad. Mostly because I hadn't seen it coming. But we were never going to work. I didn't get those butterfly feelings that I heard all my friends talking about."

"Butterfly feelings?"

With a chuckle, I said, "Yeah. Like, when a guy takes your hand and holds it in the car, your stomach sort of jumps or dips, or it feels like butterflies are flying around in there."

He smiled—and lo and behold, my stomach did every single thing I had just described.

Quickly looking away, I searched for the waiter and pointed to my beer.

"You've never felt like that with any guy?"

My eyes snapped over to his, and I held my breath, wishing that the ceiling would fall in or that someone would come up and start talking to him about bull riding. How in the hell would I ever be able to tell him that yes, I had experienced it for the first time in my life with a man I hardly knew?

Him.

The sky didn't have to fall, thankfully, because our food came, and I avoided the question.

We ate in silence for the first few minutes before I gathered up the nerve to ask about Blayze's mom.

"Where is Blayze's mother?" I asked.

Brock froze, and I instantly regretted asking.

"If I'm stepping over a line, please tell me," I said.

Damn it all to hell. Why couldn't I have just left well enough alone?

"She's gone."

I nodded. "Oh." It was the only thing I could say to such a vague answer.

Gone where? Left him? Filed for divorce? Is he still married? Did she pass away, like Kaylee thought? Maybe she ran off with another man, leaving Brock and Blayze to wonder if she would ever come back. That would explain why he wasn't dating anyone.

"So, what should I expect from this dance tonight?"

Brock looked relieved that I'd changed the subject. It was obvious he was physically pained to even think about his wife. Or ex-wife or whatever she was. I was going to have to get Kaylee to find out more information. The last thing I wanted to do was be the talk of the town.

The woman who was going after the haunted local star with a little boy.

Maybe I should just go home and not go to the dance.

"Let's see. There will be a live band."

Grinning, I said, "Of course."

"Lots of older folks gathering around to shoot the shit."

I giggled.

"Of course, there will be a lot of young folks too. Any excuse to hold a girl in your arms. It's just a good ole time with friends and family. I'm glad I'm back in town for it."

He winked, and I felt my cheeks heat slightly.

"I've been to plenty of dances but never a real country dance. I've always lived in Atlanta. My mother loves the city and honestly could do without the country life. My grandparents live outside of Atlanta, though, and that's where I learned to ride and shoot. I loved it there. They had church dances all the time, but trying to get a boy to ask you to dance at church was like pulling teeth."

Brock chuckled. "Speaking of, you ready to get out of here and head on over?"

"Are you sure you don't mind me tagging along with you?" I asked, reaching for my purse to help pay for dinner.

"I don't mind at all, and I've got dinner."

"You're sure?"

"Yes, I'm sure."

Sliding out of the chair, I flashed him a wide grin. "Thank you for dinner, then. It was good."

"You're welcome."

As we went to leave, Brock reached down for my hand, causing an instant rush of electricity to race through my body. I was hoping like hell the small gasp I'd made wasn't loud enough for him to hear.

From a nearby table, six women watched us as we walked by. Brock must have realized he was holding my hand when he noticed them staring, because he dropped it and then stepped to the side for me to walk ahead of him. I didn't want to admit it hurt a little that he cared about what they thought.

One quick peek in their direction showed they were all glaring at me like I had just stolen something precious from each of them.

I had a feeling I was going to get a lot more looks like that when I walked into this dance with Brock Shaw.

This was going to be a long and interesting night.

Chapter Twelve

Lincoln

The dance was held in a giant barn that was owned by Brad and Kimberley Littlewood, Dirk's parents. From the way they both pulled Brock into a hug, it was clear he was like family to them, which made sense, since Dirk was his best friend.

"And who is this beautiful young lady?" Kimberley asked, hope filling her voice and her eyes.

"This is Lincoln Pratt. She bought the old homestead at my folks' place."

I looked at Brock, wondering why he hadn't just called it *his* old place.

"She's becoming a fast friend of Blayze's," Brock added.

My smile faltered. I had been hoping I was becoming *his* friend as well.

"Just Blayze's?" Brad asked, shaking my hand.

"Well, the whole family. She's a friend of the family."

'Cause that made it better. That kiss was seeming more and more like a fluke.

Brad frowned at Brock and then turned to me, flashing me a big old country smile as he tried to downplay the instant awkwardness that filled the air. "Lincoln, it's a pleasure meeting you. How long have you been in town?"

"Not too long—a little over a week and a half."

"Do you like Hamilton?" Kimberley asked.

"Yes, I love it," I answered honestly.

"Well, we're glad to have you here. Is Brock treating you well?" Kimberley asked, again with a little bit of hope in her eyes.

"Um, well, yes. He's been very kind to me. His whole family has."

Brock pulled a lengthy drink from his longneck beer. He looked nervous, like he suddenly didn't want to be here. If he thought he had to babysit me, he could get that out of his mind right quick.

"Would you be able to point me to the restroom?" I asked, looking at Kimberley.

"Of course! Down that path right there will lead you to the house. Just go on in, and it's the first door to your right. We have an outhouse, but we won't subject you to that."

I chuckled. "Thank you! I think baby steps for the full-on country life is the way for me to go."

Brad tossed his head back and laughed.

When I turned to leave, Brock was looking out over the dance floor. "You should find yourself a cowgirl and dance."

His head snapped to look down at me. "What?"

Motioning to the dance floor, I repeated myself. "I said, you should find someone to dance with. You look like you're ready to jump out of your skin. You don't need to babysit me. I can take care of myself."

His brows pulled in tight. "I came with you."

I plastered on a fake smile. "Well, not as a date. I mean, I'm a family friend. Right?"

Brock didn't say anything as he rubbed the back of his neck, at least having the decency to look embarrassed for his earlier conversation.

"Excuse me," I said as I turned and quickly headed toward the house.

I needed a few minutes to rein in the emotions that were running through me. This was crazy—this stupid crush I was developing on Brock. So what that he'd kissed me? It had just been in the heat of the moment; that was all.

After staring at myself in the bathroom mirror for much longer than I should have, I took in a deep breath and slowly let it out.

"Just try to have fun and stop reading into every little thing," I whispered.

I made my way back down the path, stepped into the barn, and searched for Brock. He wasn't where he'd been standing a few minutes ago. It didn't take me long to find him, though. He was dancing with a pretty young blonde. She smiled up at him, and he smiled down at her as he spun them around on the dance floor like they had danced with each other dozens of times.

My heart instantly dropped to my stomach, but I tried like hell to pretend the sight of Brock dancing with someone else didn't bother me. After all, I was the one who'd told him to go dance, hadn't I?

Another quick look around, and I found a makeshift bar.

"Excuse me. Pardon me. I'm sorry," I said as I pushed my way through the crowd.

When I finally made it to the bar, I smiled at Dirk.

"Part-timing it as a bartender?" I shouted over the live band playing on the other side of the barn.

Dirk took one look at me and smiled. "Hey, city girl! Yeah, my parents put me as the barkeep to keep me out of trouble. You enjoying yourself?"

"Just got here."

He nodded. "Well, the party did just start. What can I get you?"

"Anything that has the word *beer* in it."

He winked. "My kind of girl. You come with Brock?"

My grin faltered. "Um, yeah."

Dirk's gaze drifted past me to the dance floor. He didn't seem to react at all when he saw Brock dancing.

I forced a smile and asked, "Y'all get much downtime when you're traveling?"

Dirk turned, grabbed a Miller Lite, and set it in front of me. "Yeah, we get some downtime."

"What do you do?"

He shrugged. "A little bit of this, a little bit of that."

I laughed. "Okay, that was vague."

"Keeps the mystery alive, little lady. Want to dance?" he asked, stepping out from behind the bar.

"Who's going to tend bar in your place if you're out on the dance floor?"

"Ah, hell, anyone can help themselves. I mostly stand back there for free drinks."

Dirk took my hand and led the way—only to have Brock step in front of us before we even touched a toe to the dance floor.

"What's going on?" he asked. His eyes filled with something that resembled anger as he stared at his best friend.

"We're headed out to dance."

Brock stepped in between us. "I don't think so."

My eyes widened as I watched the two men stare at each other like they were in a pissing contest. The fact that Brock wasn't letting me dance with Dirk really made me mad.

"Um, I'm not sure who made you the boss of me, Brock, but Dirk asked me to dance, and I said yes. Besides, you were dancing."

"With my cousin."

His cousin?

My eyes darted around until I found the blonde. She was currently sucking face with some other guy while they dirty-danced on the dance floor.

Looking back at him, I said, "Well, I still don't see why I can't dance with Dirk."

Drawing his brows in tight, Brock took a step back. "You want to dance with him? Go right ahead." He turned and walked through the crowd of people and out of the barn.

"What in the hell just happened?" I asked as I watched him round the corner.

"That would be Brock, pissed off and jealous," Dirk stated with a frown. "Hadn't seen that side of him in a while."

I shook my head. "What do you mean, pissed off and jealous? Of what?"

Dirk stared at me for a brief moment and then shook his head. "It's my fault, really. I knew he was interested in you, and I probably shouldn't have asked you to dance, but it seemed harmless enough."

Now I was really confused. "But, why would you asking me to dance be a bad thing?"

Rubbing the back of his neck, Dirk shrugged. "That's just Brock. I mean, we have a complicated history between us because of . . ." His words faded off. "He knows I didn't mean anything by asking you to dance. I think he feels guilty with *himself* because he likes you."

"He likes me? As a friend, you mean?"

Dirk tossed his head back and laughed. "Darlin', if you can't see the way he looks at you, then you might need glasses. Brock is my best friend. I know him better than he knows himself. Trust me when I say, he wants to be more than friends with you."

I blew out a breath. "Should I go talk to him?"

He gave me a wink. "That is up to you."

With a smile, I said, "Sorry about the dance."

Holding up his hands, he laughed. "Plenty of other pretty little things to dance with."

I shook my head and chuckled. Then I quickly made my way out of the barn and turned in the same direction Brock had. He was sitting on the fence of a pasture about twenty feet away from the barn.

As I walked over to him, he took a drink of beer. "I'm not in the mood, so you might as well just go back in the barn."

I stopped walking. *Does he know it's me? Or does he think it's Dirk?*

"Want to tell me what that was all about?" I asked, deciding to push forward. I stopped at the corral fence and leaned against it, turning my head to look at him.

"I thought you were Dirk."

"Nope. I'm sorry if me almost dancing with him upset you, but you're really going to have to explain to me what's going on here, Brock. You've got me all kinds of confused. You kiss me one day, then spend an incredible day with me, and then treat me like a distant friend, only to dance with some girl and then get mad when *I* go to dance with someone."

"You were the one who told me to dance. So I did."

"Because you made it seem like you didn't want to be around me."

"What?" he said, clearly frustrated.

"You introduced me as a family friend."

"What did you want me to introduce you as, Lincoln?"

I went to open my mouth and snapped it shut.

What did *I want him to introduce me as?*

"Why did you get upset when Dirk asked me to dance? If we're just friends, why do you care?"

He looked away and took another drink of his beer.

I let out a soft sigh and shook my head. "Okay then. I guess we're back to the other Brock, the one who's distant and a jackass. I think I'll go back into the barn. I can call Kaylee to pick me up if you want."

When he didn't say anything, I felt tears sting the backs of my eyelids. I'd never before let a guy make me feel this way, but for some reason, Brock Shaw could bring me to my knees without uttering a single word.

Pushing off the fence, I headed back into the barn. My heart raced, and I was trying like hell to keep my face neutral. Dirk was the first person I saw. His smile faded when he saw me. Before he'd had a chance to come my way, I pushed myself into the middle of the crowd and into a back corner. I pulled out my phone and sent Kaylee a text.

Me: I don't suppose you could come pick me up? I have no clue where I am, but I can drop you my location.

It didn't take her long to text back.

Kaylee: Oh no. What did he do?

I swallowed hard as I typed back my response.

Me: Nothing. Really. He's a moody son of a bitch, and I'm not in the mood to play games. Please come pick me up.

Pulling up my map, I got my location and texted it to her.

Kaylee: Pulling on a pair of sweats now. I'll be there in a few.

Me: Thanks, Kaylee.

Kaylee: That's what best friends are for. You're just lucky I haven't gone back to Georgia yet to pack up my shit.

I smiled. I *was* lucky. Otherwise, I would have had to ask Brock to drive me home, and that would have been a long, silent drive.

Shaking my head, I tried to figure out what in the world was going on with him.

And why did he instantly turn into an asshole? Where's the sweet guy I've spent the entire day and evening with?

I spent the next few minutes in the dark corner, hiding from everyone.

I saw Brock walk back into the barn. He searched around and then walked over to Dirk. When Brock dropped his head and looked at the ground, Dirk placed his hand on his shoulder to comfort him.

Well, isn't that nice?

They'd managed to ruin *my* evening, but they'd kissed and made up. They were both jerks, and they deserved to spend the night with each other.

My phone dinged with a message from Kaylee. She was five minutes away.

Pulling up her number, I called her and started for the door, making sure I kept along the side of the barn, ducking in and out of people.

"Hey, I'm getting ready to turn down the driveway."

"I'll head down so you don't have to pull all the way in."

"Lincoln Pratt, are you sneaking away?"

Rolling my eyes, I groaned. "Something like that."

I peeked over to see Brock was busy talking to Brad and Kimberley. Dashing out the door, I hightailed it past all the parked cars and to the gravel driveway.

"Almost there. Almost. There," Kaylee said.

"Lincoln!"

The sound of Brock's voice had me picking up my pace. I could just jump into the car, have Kaylee do a three-point turn, and hustle out of here.

"Lincoln, stop! Please."

Ugh. Why does he have to sound so pleading?

I turned around and walked backward as I forced a smile. "It's okay, Brock. I'm tired, and Kaylee can give me a ride back home."

"Lincoln, for fuck's sake, just stop. You're gonna—"

I was pretty sure he was about to say I was "gonna fall" . . . just as I started to fall.

I tripped over something, and before I could stop myself, I landed right on my ass. Hard.

"Ouch!" I cried out.

Brock was there in an instant. "Are you okay?" he asked, helping me to stand.

"Yeah. Except for my pride, I'm peachy keen."

"I didn't think you were serious about leaving. Why didn't you even say goodbye?" Brock asked.

Kaylee pulled close and stopped. I was silently praying she would get out of the car and call for me. Tell me she needed to get back to editing the book she was working on.

"I, um . . . I just thought it would be best."

"Why?"

I stared at him. *Is he for real?*

He had just ignored me a few minutes ago, and now he wanted to know why I was leaving?

"Are you for real, Brock? You just acted like a dick, and you want me to just hang around and let you take me home? Listen, I'm not looking to get involved with anyone, but I'm not going to lie. I find myself really attracted to you, and I have no flipping clue how you really feel about *me*, so I think it's probably best if we just go ahead and stop this here. I mean, it might be nothing, and I was reading into you being all sweet and kind and inviting me to hang out with you and your son today. The kiss the other day was a fluke."

"It wasn't a fluke, princess. Not one thing about that kiss was a mistake," Brock said with an intensity that wasn't his typical asshole self.

"Well, whatever it was, you're clearly putting this in the friend zone . . . at least, I think you are. I'm not even sure. I'm going to head on home. Thank you for a lovely day, Brock."

Before I could turn and walk away, he took my arm and pulled me against his body.

"You're confusing the fuck out of me, Lincoln."

My eyes went wide. "Me? *I'm* confusing you? One minute you're hot, and the next you're cold. You have my head spinning, Brock!"

He leaned down, and my breath hitched.

Oh, holy hell. He is not going to kiss me again. No. Stop him right now.

But I didn't. I actually rose up some so our lips were inches apart.

Right before his lips met mine, Kaylee honked the horn, and I jumped.

Typical Kaylee, trying to be funny in her own twisted little way. It was probably her payback for me having her come out to pick me up.

Brock smiled, and as if on cue, my stomach fluttered.

"Come to Billings."

"Excuse me?" I said, not thinking I'd heard him right.

"I want you to come to Billings with me. You can drive with me. Kaylee, too, if she wants. My whole family will be there. Let me show you what I do."

My insides went all weird on me again while my head started to pound from all the whiplash this guy was causing me. "I don't know, Brock."

"Stay with me tonight."

With a shocked gasp, I went to speak, but Brock did it first.

"No, wait. I didn't mean it like that. I meant, stay here, at the dance with me, and I'll take you home. Let me at least explain why I got so upset earlier."

I looked at Kaylee, who was sitting in my car, a shit-eating grin on her face. She probably knew all along I wouldn't end up leaving with her.

"Maybe we should call it a night," I finally said.

"Lincoln, please? I'm not any good at this. Just give me two hours, and if you still want to go home, I'll take you."

"Fine," I said with a sigh. "Let me go tell Kaylee."

A huge grin appeared on Brock's face, and a part of me wanted to slap it off of him, but those damn dimples got me every time. Not to mention he was wearing a baseball cap today. Give me a guy in either a cowboy hat or a baseball cap.

Ugh.

As I made my way over to the driver's side of the car, Kaylee started to shake her head.

"What did he promise you to make you stay? Hot sex in a stall of the barn? Lord knows, your vajayjay could use some action. That'll bring new meaning to the phrase *ride a cowboy* if you *are* gonna have sex, romping around in the hay."

Smacking her hard on the arm, I said, "Shut up! He wants to talk, so I'm going to give him the benefit of the doubt—for right now."

"Uh-huh. And the fact that he almost kissed you has nothing to do with your change of heart?"

I glared at her. "No."

She laughed. "God, you're such a terrible liar. Lincoln, just admit that you like the guy."

My eyes peeked over to Brock, who was now pacing as if he was worried I'd jump in the car and take off. Or maybe he was wondering if Kaylee was trying to talk me out of staying. Either way, nervous Brock almost made me giggle.

"I already said it . . . to him."

"What?" Kaylee shouted.

I hit her again. "Be quiet! And by the way, the little honk was totally not called for."

"But it sure was fun watching you lift up on your tippy-toes, so ready to kiss him, and then bam! You jumped out of your skin!"

Rolling my eyes, I replied, "Payback is a bitch. Listen, I'll see you in a couple of hours, if you're still up."

"I took a nap an hour or so ago. My eyes needed rest. I'll be up. Don't worry."

She flashed me an evil grin that said she planned on staying up to hear all the details of today . . . and whatever was about to transpire tonight.

"Be careful driving back."

"I will. Make sure you put a saddle on that stallion before you ride it!" she called out as I walked toward Brock.

My face instantly heated. Lifting my hand, I shot her the finger, dying of embarrassment. "Okay, you have two hours," I said to him.

Brock took my hand in his. "First, I want to dance with you."

My stomach dipped at his touch and the softness in his voice.

"Okay," I replied, letting him lead me back into the barn.

The band was doing a cover of Brantley Gilbert's "Fall into Me."

Brock pulled me into his arms and against his body. His leg went between both of mine, and his hand pressed on my lower back, drawing me in closer. I had never two-stepped this close with a guy before, but with Brock, it worked. We were practically one as we slowly danced on the makeshift dance floor. I'd never had such an amazing dance partner before. It was as if we had danced together a million times.

Neither of us said a word as we danced. Brock kept his blue eyes pierced on my gaze. His face was filled with an emotion I couldn't read. A part of my mind started to drift off, and I couldn't help but wonder how many women he'd danced with like this. He certainly hadn't danced with his *cousin* like this, that was for sure.

As he expertly guided us around the floor, the song changed to a faster one.

Brock smiled. "Tell me you can swing dance, sweetheart."

Laughing, I nodded. "I can."

"Let's show these people how to do it, then."

And show them we did. Brock spun me, dipped me, and ground against me to the point that I almost felt like I might pass out from being so close to him. I hadn't even noticed the crowd of people watching as I was spun around. Finally, he nestled his knee between my legs as he dipped me again and then slowly pulled me back up.

My heart was pounding, and it wasn't from all the fast spins and dance moves. It was because Brock was looking into my eyes like he wanted me more than the air he breathed.

Then, the shouts and clapping came, and we were both pulled out of our trance.

Dirk came up and slapped Brock on the back. "Damn, son, if I didn't know any better, I'd swear you two had done that a time or two."

I pulled in a few deep breaths as I tried to focus on the pounding in my chest and not the throbbing sensation between my legs.

"I need a drink," Brock said, taking my hand and guiding me off the dance floor.

"So I have to know . . . are all the stares because you're the local famous guy?"

"It's probably because you're the first woman they've seen me with since my wife, Kaci."

"Oh." It was the only thing I could get out. That seemed to be the only word I used when he talked about his wife, because I was afraid of asking for more information on what had happened between them.

"Come on. Let's go somewhere quieter."

I nodded as I followed him out of the barn and down a path. "Where are we going?" I asked.

"Dirk and I used to hang out in the old hunter's cabin when we were in high school. If I know Dirk's mom, she still keeps it clean in there."

We walked up a rock pathway to the cabin and stepped up two steps, and Brock fished for a key under the old mat. He held it up and smiled.

My hands started shaking at the idea of being alone with Brock in a small, private space. It wasn't that I thought he would try something; it was because I desperately *wanted* him to. This feeling of wanting him shook me slightly. I hadn't known him long, and our first interaction hadn't been very pleasant. But spending today with him had made me giddy with anticipation.

I bit down on my lip to keep my threatening grin at bay.

As we stepped inside, Brock turned on the lights and illuminated the cutest little one-room cabin. There was a bed on one side, a sofa on the other, and a table and two chairs in the middle.

Doing a quick spin, I took it all in. It was small, so it didn't take long to scope it all out. "How cute is this place?" I said.

"Yeah, I can't tell you how many times we got drunk in here or fu—uh . . . or had fun in here."

I lifted a brow. "Uh-huh. I hardly think that was what you were going to say, Brock Shaw."

His face blushed, and it was sinfully sexy. "I brought you up here so we could talk, Lincoln. I want to explain a couple of things to you about why I've been acting like I have the last few days."

I sat on the sofa as Brock pulled out a chair. He spun it around and then sat, straddling it. He turned his baseball cap backward and took a long drink of his beer.

My tongue ran over my lips while I tried to remember how to swallow. There was no denying that I was sexually attracted to Brock. No denying it at all.

"I wasn't a part of selling the house you bought because, honestly, I wasn't ready to face saying goodbye to that part of my life just yet."

"Ty said you hadn't lived there in years."

He nodded. "That's true. Kaci, Blayze's mother, died, and I never went back in the house after that."

My hand came up to my mouth as I gasped. "I'm so sorry, Brock."

He didn't respond and kept staring at the ground before finally speaking. "I guess, as much as I wanted to sell the place, knowing you bought it and were already making changes to it . . . well, it pissed me off. I don't know any other way to say it but to tell you the truth. It was shitty of me to treat you the way I did that first day we met. I'm sorry."

"It's already forgotten and forgiven."

Brock smirked. I was quickly beginning to love that smirk of his. Taking off his hat, he ran his hand through his hair. Did the man have any idea how sexy he was? Every little thing he did sent my libido off the charts.

Okay, it could be the fact that not even my vibrator has seen any action lately.

"Tonight, about the whole Dirk thing . . . I was jealous."

With a scoff, I replied, "Why on earth were you jealous? Brock, he asked me to dance; that was all."

"Were you jealous when you saw me dancing with my cousin?" he asked, the left side of his mouth slightly turned up.

"No," I lied.

"Liar. Your eyes don't let you lie, Lincoln."

My gaze dropped to the floor.

"There's a history between the two of us. Dirk and I both loved Kaci. She knew it, and we told her she had to pick one of us."

Snapping my eyes back up to him, I was pretty sure my mouth also dropped open at the same time. "You made her pick between y'all?"

With a nod, he replied, "Yes. I fought hard for her because the idea of losing to Dirk . . . well, let's just say, I don't like to lose. What I probably should have done was stepped aside and let them be together. They *should* have been together. Not me and her."

"Why do you say that?"

He shrugged. "I made her miserable. I couldn't see it at the time—or hell, maybe I did see it and didn't want to admit it. But I put bull riding before her. I hadn't done it on purpose, though. I knew Dirk loved her enough to walk away from bull riding, and I couldn't. She had begged me to stop riding, and sometimes I resented her for it. We fought a lot, and then Kaci thought maybe we should try for a baby. We had hoped it would bring us closer, and a part of me thinks she thought it would pull me off the road. Hell, maybe it would have. I don't know."

"Oh, Brock."

His eyes filled with tears. "I don't think I made her happy. She believed rumors I was cheating, no matter how many times I told her they weren't true. I should have stopped riding and been with her. Showed her how much I loved her. But I didn't. I picked bull riding over her. When Kaci picked me, I could see the distance Dirk put between us. He wouldn't come around a whole lot, and when he did, it was hard for him not to look at my wife like she hung the moon."

"Is that why you were angry he asked me to dance? Because of the past the two of you share with Kaci?"

"Yes . . . no. Hell, I don't know. Maybe? You're the first woman who's made me feel anything, Lincoln. That both excites me and scares me. I'm in territory I haven't been in for a while."

I knew how he felt, because I was experiencing the same feelings.

"Seeing Dirk walking you out to the dance floor, it made me insanely jealous. It's stupid, I know."

"It's not stupid. Like you said, I got jealous seeing you with your cousin, and I *told* you to go dance."

Brock's eyes met mine as he stood. "There's more to it, Lincoln. I'm messed up. I'm carrying around a lot of guilt, and I swore to myself I would never let another woman into my heart. I don't deserve to be loved . . . not after what I did."

Now it was my turn to stand up. "What? Why would you even say that?"

He half shrugged. "I've got a dark side, Lincoln. Dirk would be the first to tell you that. I've done things I'm ashamed of, especially after . . ." His voice trailed off before he sighed and looked back into my eyes. "You're the first woman I've ever felt something for."

My brows pulled in tightly. "Besides Kaci? You said you loved her."

His hands went into his pockets, and he looked sick to his stomach. As if what he was about to say physically made him ill. "I did love her, but probably not in the way she *needed* me to love her."

The way my heart was hammering in my chest made it hard for me to even hear Brock talking. He was barely above a whisper.

"What do you feel . . . with me . . . that's different from what you felt with Kaci?"

Brock took a few steps closer.

Everything inside my head was telling me to run. That Brock Shaw was going to hurt me like I'd never been hurt before. But my heart and these crazy feelings I felt for him had me rooted in place.

"More."

"More?" I whispered.

"When I walked into that barn the other day, I didn't want to have anything to do with you. I wasn't the least bit interested and was convinced my heart would never be able to feel things for a woman again. Everything inside me was angry and ready to lash out. But when I saw you standing there, talking to Blayze, it stopped me dead in my tracks. Your smile did something to me that has *never* happened before, and it threw me for a loop.

"I vowed I wouldn't fall for another woman, but Christ Almighty, Lincoln . . . I also never believed in falling for someone the moment I laid eyes on them, and you're all I can think about. I mean, I'm not saying I'm in love with you, but I want more. I *need* more. I want to know everything about you. What makes you laugh, what movies make you cry, who your favorite actor is, what your favorite type of food is. I want to know *more.*"

I swallowed hard. My mouth opened to speak, but I had no idea what to say. Brock's confession was not what I had been expecting. His raw, honest truth moved me beyond words. Heat radiated through my chest, and I couldn't help but notice my pulse quicken.

"I know you said you weren't looking to get into a relationship with anyone, and hell, I'm always gone, and my bull riding is one of the reasons my marriage failed. I've admitted I have some issues to work out . . . but I want more with you."

"You want to date?" I asked, finally finding my voice.

He shrugged. "I don't know. All I know is, the thought of some other guy asking you out nearly drives me fucking insane with jealousy. I loved being with you today, and I loved that Blayze enjoyed it even more."

I smiled. "I enjoyed today too."

Brock kicked at nothing on the floor. "Listen, I know there were a lot of people whispering today, and Lucy Mae may or may not be a problem."

Rolling my eyes, I groaned. "Great, the crazy ex-girlfriend from high school."

When he took another step closer to me, I held my breath.

Is this something I can do? Is it something I want to do? I was new in town and hardly even settled in. Brock was leaving in a few days. *How do you start a new relationship with someone when they're always out on the road?*

His hands came up and gently cupped my cheeks. The way his baby-blue eyes searched my face had me taking hold of his arms to hold myself up.

"Yes," I softly said.

Brock drew in his brows and asked, "Yes?"

"I'll go to Billings with you."

A breathtaking smile moved over his handsome face. Two seconds later, he was kissing me.

In that moment, I knew I would give this man more.

So much more.

Chapter Thirteen

Brock

My mother stared at me from across the barn. When I glanced over to her, she smiled. So, I smiled back.

"Blayze said he really had fun at the fair the day before yesterday."

"It *was* fun."

"Linda Ryder stopped me in the store this morning to tell me she heard a rumor going around."

Leaning against the stall, I crossed my arms over my chest. "That right? People finally find out Ty can't ride a horse for shit?"

My mother chuckled and shook her head. "You'd better not let him hear you say that."

"He never could handle the truth."

"People are starting to talk about you and Lincoln."

"So?"

Her brow lifted. "Is that a 'So, I don't care' or a 'So, what should I do about it'?"

"Mama, it was a 'I don't give two shits about what people are saying.'"

The way her eyes lit up made me laugh.

"I knew it! Ty mentioned she and Kaylee were going with us to Billings. I was just hoping *you'd* be the first to tell me."

I grabbed the bag of oats sitting on the ground and headed back to the tack room. "Mama, don't make a big deal out of this. I like her, and she likes me. We're taking things slow. Just friends first."

"Friends who kiss in public? Don't you hurt that girl, Brock Shaw, or I will have to break your legs."

"Damn, you're scarier than the bull I drew for round one this weekend. And I have no intentions of hurting her."

"I'm happy you opened up to someone. I think it will be good for you."

I nodded. But a sudden squeeze of panic hit me square in the chest.

"Talk to me, Brock. I see it in your eyes."

"What if she doesn't like me being on the road all the time? At first she's fine with it, but then . . ."

"She demands for you to stop bull riding?"

With a nod, I rubbed the back of my neck. "Or meets someone else. If I'm not here, how will I keep her happy?"

"Don't compare this girl to Kaci, Brock. That isn't fair for either of you."

"I'm not."

Her brow lifted.

"She's nothing like Kaci."

Making her way over to me, my mother placed her hand on my arm and gave it a squeeze. "You're never going to be able to move on until you forgive yourself and realize you are *not* to blame."

My heart ached in my chest. "I let her down, like I had so many times before. She didn't think I was going to show up. She knew I put that bull before her that night. She died knowing I hadn't put her first, Mama. How am I ever supposed to forgive myself for that?"

"It was tragic, but you didn't cause Kaci to die."

I nodded and took a step back. "I'm going to go for a ride before it's time to leave. I told Lincoln I'd pick her and Kaylee up around ten."

"Okay," my mother replied softly.

After thirty minutes of riding, I slipped off my horse and sat on the ground against a tree. I was out in the north pasture and had a straight view of Lincoln's house. The house I had remodeled for the happy family I'd thought I would have someday.

Closing my eyes, I went back four years to that day.

My bull was fourth up. Bending down, I closed my eyes and blocked everyone out as I said a prayer.

Standing, I took a few deep breaths before heading down and putting my bull rope over Midnight Ride. This bull was a beast and hadn't been ridden in his last ten outs.

By the time he was in the chute, I was jumping out of my skin, waiting to crawl on him. They were at a commercial break, so I had a few extra minutes to get myself in the right frame of mind.

Dirk stood there, waiting for me to crawl onto the back of the bull. Right before I did, Kendall Schmidt came running up.

"Brock! Your mother called. Kaci went into labor."

I frowned, and so did Dirk.

"She's not due for another few weeks," I replied.

Kendall grinned. "Well, sometimes these things don't always go as planned. Your mom said you need to head back. There's a complication. I'm not sure what. But as of right now, both Kaci and the baby are okay. If you leave now, you could take Bob's helicopter and be there in an hour."

I looked down and thought about it. It was only eight seconds.

"I'll go after my ride."

Dirk's head snapped my way as Kendall looked horrified. "What?"

"I'm almost up. I'll go after."

"What in the hell are you talking about?" Dirk asked, pushing me on the chest as I started to climb over the rail. "Brock, your wife is in labor, and you're going to ride?"

"She said Kaci and the baby are okay. I need this ride."

"You need to be getting your ass on the helicopter!"

I ignored him as I climbed on top of the bull.

Dirk backed away, leaving Bob, the contractor and owner of Midnight Ride, to help tighten the bull strap.

When I glanced up, I saw Dirk was leaving. He stripped off his vest and started down the steps away from the chutes.

I knew he was pissed at me for not putting Kaci first, but I had to ride this bull. If I won, that would mean a lot of money for me and Kaci; we'd be sitting really nice financially. Dirk didn't see that side of things. He only saw me putting bull riding over Kaci. But I was thinking about our future.

It was only a few more minutes. What would it hurt?

After getting my hand in position and digging in, I nodded, and the gate opened. Midnight Ride was a left-hand delivery, and he turned away from my hand. He jumped up like someone had just shot him in the ass. He tried every direction, every move he had in him, but I held on for the full eight seconds. My hand was caught for a brief moment before I got it out and jumped down to the ground. The bull tried to hook me, but I scrambled out of the way. The sounds of the crowd going wild had me smiling. I took off my helmet and threw it up in the air.

"Brock Shaw, the Montana native, just rode an eighty-nine point five, folks. You have a new leader here in Billings!"

I couldn't believe it. Not only had I stayed on and had a qualifying ride, but I'd also scored decent. When I looked up into the chutes, I expected to see Dirk before remembering he had taken off.

Kaci.

Grabbing my bull rope from Sam, the bullfighter, I got my helmet and hightailed it out of the arena. I was stopped by Kim, a CBS reporter, who asked how I felt about the ride.

"I feel great. I need to go, though. My wife is in labor."

Everyone started yelling out, and I quickly located Kendall.

"Hey, I'm ready to go if Bob is still willing to let me use the helicopter."

She nodded. "Dirk wanted to use it and leave you behind, but Bob said no."

Hell, Dirk was more pissed than I'd thought. I wasn't surprised, though.

Dirk was waiting in the helicopter, a pair of headphones over his ears. When I climbed on, Kendall handed me her phone.

"Brock? Are you on your way?" my mother asked.

"Yes, how is she?"

"Pissed you rode."

My head turned to look at Dirk, who was currently texting someone on his phone.

"How did she find out?" I asked, still staring at my best friend.

"Dirk called."

"Of course he did," I grumbled. The idea that my best friend would call my wife and tell her I rode had anger boiling in my veins. He could be pissed, but it was low to do that to me.

"Now is not the time, Brock. The baby is putting a lot of strain on Kaci. She's having a very hard time pushing."

"I'll be there soon."

Bob had arranged for a driver to be there to pick us up upon landing. Dirk still hadn't uttered a single word to me. I couldn't blame him, in a way. He would have never put a bull before Kaci. Internally, I already hated myself and wished I could go back in time.

Why in the hell did I ride? What was I thinking? I could tell myself it was for our future, but was that really the reason?

As we rushed into the hospital, Dirk was on my heels the entire time.

"Kaci Shaw?" I asked, rushing up to the desk. "I'm her husband."

The nurse nodded and motioned for me to follow her.

When I opened the door, I saw the doctor holding up the baby. Kaci dropped back on the bed and turned her head to look at me. I smiled as I glanced at the baby and then back to her.

Kaci returned my smile, but I saw the disappointment in her eyes. It nearly gutted me.

She reached out for my hand and said weakly, "Brock, we have a son."

Those were her last words to me.

I looked down at the baby boy the nurse was currently handing to me. My heart was instantly filled with so much love. "Baby, you did so good. Look at how beautiful he is!"

"Kaci? Kaci? Kaci!" my mother screamed, as I turned to see my wife lying lifeless on the bed.

Everything happened so fast. The baby was taken from me and rushed out of the room while the doctor began giving CPR to Kaci and my mother cried out for someone to tell us what was happening.

An hour later, long after they had ushered us out of the room, the doctor came out and told me that Kaci had died from what was most likely a blood clot that had traveled to her heart or brain.

I stumbled back into a chair and buried my face in my hands.

My wife died, and the last thing I did was pick a bull over her and our baby.

Dirk lost it and started screaming at me, saying it was my fault that she'd died, that the stress of the labor and me not being there had caused her to die.

It wasn't true, but in that moment, I knew I would carry that sentence with me for the rest of my life. Those words would be my scarlet letter—my self-inflicted punishment for not being the husband my wife needed me to be.

That night, I'd vowed to never let another woman into my heart again. And, besides the occasional one-night stand, I had kept that vow.

That is, until I had seen Lincoln Pratt.

As I stared at the little white house, hope bloomed once again in my chest. It had been so many years since I'd felt it. Since I'd allowed myself to think I deserved love again. All because of Lincoln. Even though I was scared as hell, I dared to believe that I might be getting a second chance.

Chapter Fourteen

Brock

"You invited her to Billings?" Dirk asked, looking at me like I had grown five heads.

"Yes."

His eyes were wide. "Lincoln?"

I nodded.

He smiled slightly. "Holy shit, you like her. You *really* like this girl."

With a shrug, I threw my duffel bag and rigging bag into the bed of the truck. Blayze, Lincoln, Kaylee, and I were driving to Billings in Ty's truck. I normally flew back to wherever the tour was, but with it being so close to home, this would give me more time with Blayze. And Lincoln.

"I can't believe it. I mean, dude, this is huge. How do you feel about her?"

Stopping, I turned to face him. "I like her—a lot. That scares the shit out of me."

His eyes looked sad as he placed his hand on my shoulder and gave it a squeeze. "I can't pretend to know what all was going on with you and Kaci at the end, but I know she loved you, and you loved her."

Shaking my head, I sighed. “I should have stepped aside for you to have a chance with her.”

“If you had stepped to the side, I would have thought for the rest of my life that I’d been her second choice. That she had loved you more than me. Dude, either way, we both got hurt. It’s time to leave it in the past, Brock. For both of us.”

We looked at one another, neither of us saying a word for a few moments.

“I know I’ve told you this before, but I never meant what I said that day at the hospital. I was angry. I know you regret making that decision, and dude, it’s time to forgive yourself and let it go. Even if you hadn’t ridden, the same outcome would have happened.”

I didn’t respond to him as I looked out over the mountains. I knew he was right, about everything.

The screen door to my folks’ place slammed shut. Dirk and I both turned to see Ty walking down the steps. He looked like he hadn’t slept in days.

“You feeling okay?” I asked as he tossed his bag into the back of the truck.

“Yeah, my leg is giving me some trouble, but it’s all good.”

Dirk and I glanced at each other.

“You don’t have to go if the drive is going to bother you.”

Ty laughed. “Nah, I took something. I’m good.”

“And you’re going to drive? With my son in the car? I don’t think so.”

The look on my brother’s face spoke volumes. He wanted to bitch me out, but he kept it in. “I took Advil, you dick.”

I felt like a complete jackass for assuming he’d taken something stronger.

“Blayze, are you sure you don’t want to ride with us?” my mother called out to my son as he came barreling out of the house and straight to me.

“Hey, Uncle Dirk! You riding with us?” Blayze asked, trying to toss his bag into the back of the truck like the big boys did.

"Nah, buddy. I'm riding in with my folks."

Blayze nodded, his ten-gallon black Stetson cowboy hat falling just a bit when he did.

I adjusted it and said, "Where did you get this, buddy?"

A wide smile moved over his face. "Uncle Ty gave it to me! Said it was your first hat you ever wore when you were a little boy."

My eyes lifted to Ty.

He stood there, smirking. With a shrug, he said, "Mama had them all saved, and I came across it in the attic the other day. Your name and age were written on the hatbox. Figured you'd want the mini version of you to have it."

I stared at my brother while a tightness in my chest caused my voice to stall in my throat. I smiled and shook my head in disbelief. "Thank you, Ty," I said.

"Hell, don't get all emotional on me, Brock. It's just a hat," Ty said as he turned and climbed into the truck. "Hurry your ass up. We need to pick up the pain in the ass and her best friend, Lincoln."

"Language, Ty Shaw!" my mother shouted.

Dirk and I both laughed before he stated, "Seems to me like that pain in the ass might have caught your brother's attention."

"That would be a first," I replied as I shook Dirk's hand. "I'll see ya in Billings."

Dirk smiled and pulled me in for a quick bro hug. Then, he said in a low voice, "I love you, brother."

I slapped his back and replied, "I love you too."

He stepped away and then, out of the blue, he threw his head back and laughed before turning and heading to his truck. "Both of the Shaw boys, smitten! I can't believe it."

When I opened the back door to get Blayze in his booster seat, Ty was watching Dirk get into his truck. "What did he say about us being smitten?"

"Nothing." I winked at Blayze. "You ready to see your daddy ride on some bulls?"

A huge smile spread over my son's face. "Yes, sir, I am! Can I ride a bull too?"

I pretended to frown. "You mean to tell me you're ready to climb up on a bull?"

He chuckled. "Yep!"

"You hear that, Ty? Blayze here says he's ready to climb up on a bull."

Ty turned around and put his hand up for Blayze to slap it. "That's what I'm talking about. My nephew, the world's youngest bull-riding champion."

I grinned as I got him buckled in.

"Daddy, Grandpa said both you and Uncle Ty won something really big while bull riding. What was it?"

"Your uncle Ty won the PBR World Finals, and two years later, so did I. Then I won another one the next year."

His eyes went wide.

"And your daddy is on his way to winning his third championship, if he keeps his head on straight and doesn't get distracted by a pretty girl named Lincoln."

Blayze laughed. "Daddy! Do you like Miss Lincoln? She's really pwetty, so I don't blame you fer likin' her."

I kissed him on the forehead. "She *is* real pretty, son. Now, let's get on the road and pick her and Miss Kaylee up."

Ty groaned as Blayze let out a loud and very excited "Yes!" along with a fist pump.

When I got into the front seat, I looked at my brother, who was now pulling out of the driveway, our parents following behind us.

"Why don't you like Kaylee anymore? She seems like a nice girl, and you guys seemed to hit it off at the Blue Moose."

He rolled his eyes. "She's everywhere. *Everywhere.* I go into town to grab a cup of coffee, and she's there. Sitting in a booth with her stupid little laptop, just doing whatever it is she does everywhere she is. She's always showing up wherever I am."

"What's a laptop?" Blayze asked.

"It's a computer, buddy, like the kind you do your games on," I said, glancing over my shoulder to Blayze, who was sitting in the middle of the back seat.

Focusing again on Ty, I said, "You know she needs it for work. Lincoln said Kaylee's an editor."

"Yeah, well, every time I turn around, she's there. Yesterday, she walked out of our parents' house with Mom. I swear, she has our mother wrapped around her finger. Did you know Mom is teaching her how to knit? What the heck does a young woman need to learn how to knit for unless she's snooping around our mother, looking for information?"

I laughed. "Such as what? The size of your underwear? Your favorite food? You sound a lil' paranoid, bro."

"I don't know. She's not even supposed to be here. She's supposed to be in Atlanta, and now she's talking about moving here. She's snarky too. Every time I say something to her, she smarts off back to me."

"She smarts off to you? What happened that night you brought her home from the Blue Moose? I thought you were both getting along fine then."

His head snapped over to look at me. "Nothing happened."

By the look on my brother's face, he was lying, but I decided to let it go. It wasn't the time or place for this conversation.

"And we did get along at first. Then she got all . . . weird . . . and now, she freaks me out."

"Why does she freak you out, Uncle Ty?" Blayze asked.

Facing my son, I replied, "Because he has a crush on her, and that freaks him out. But that's a secret between just us men. Shh, don't tell Uncle Ty, because it'll freak him out even more that we know."

Ty punched me in the arm. "Shut up. I do not like her!"

Blayze covered his mouth and widened his eyes before busting out into a song. "*Uncle Ty has a crush on Miss Kaylee! Miss Kaylee! Uncle Ty as a crush on Miss Kaylee! Miss Kaylee! Uncle Ty and Miss Kaylee, sitting in a tree. K-i-s-s*—oh, shoot, I don't remember how to spell the rest."

Looking in the rearview mirror, Ty shot Blayze a warning look. "Stop singin' that, Blayze, or you're walking to Billings."

Blayze covered his mouth again and froze. Trying so desperately to hold in a giggle. I missed these moments with Blayze and my family.

It didn't take long to get to Lincoln's house. Ty and I both got out of the truck and made our way to meet both women. When Ty reached for Kaylee's small bag, I couldn't help but notice how they looked at each other.

Both of them were clearly attracted to each other. My brother was a lying bastard. Didn't like her, my ass.

"Why, thank you!" Kaylee said, giving Ty a wink and bouncing over to the truck. "I call shotgun!"

"Oh Lord," Ty grumbled as he made his way back over to the truck.

Turning to Lincoln, I smiled. "Hey," I softly said as she stepped down off the last step.

"Hey back at ya."

I quickly scanned the front porch of the house. Lincoln had four rocking chairs, two on each side of the door, and plants everywhere. Some hanging, some in planters, and some in planter boxes she had on the rails. She even had potted plants going up the steps.

"Looks cute out here."

She glanced back over her shoulder. "Thanks!" Facing me again, she added, "I love flowers, and I don't think you can ever have enough."

I took her bag and motioned for her to follow. "Blayze loves helping my mom in her garden."

"He's a sweet little boy."

"He's excited to see you again."

Lincoln gave me a soft smile and walked silently next to me as we made our way to the truck.

"Did you get your hotel room booked okay?" I asked, setting her bag in the back of the truck.

"Yep. I booked one room for both me and Kaylee. It has queen beds in there. I think we got the last room!"

I almost told her she could always stay in *my* room. I was glad I caught myself. I didn't need to scare her off before we even got out of the driveway.

I opened the passenger door and held her hand to help her get in. She paused and looked at Ty and Kaylee, who were arguing about what radio station to put on. When I glanced back down to Lincoln, she smiled, and her eyes practically lit up like Christmas morning.

"What?" I asked.

She leaned closer to me and whispered, "You look nice in a cowboy hat."

I tipped it and moved closer to her. "You've seen me in a cowboy hat before, Lincoln."

Her teeth sank into her lip, and my dick strained against my jeans at that simple gesture. I gave her a crooked smile and then winked. "I'll be sure to wear them more often."

"Daddy, what are y'all whispering about?"

Ty and Kaylee stopped talking, and both of them turned to look at us. Lincoln had her back to everyone and closed her eyes, a soft smile on her face. She opened them and pursed her lips before turning and climbing into the cab of the truck.

"Hey there, Blayze! Your grams told me you helped deliver a baby calf yesterday!"

My heart squeezed in my chest as my son looked at Lincoln with the happiest smile I'd ever seen. The way she launched so effortlessly into a conversation with him was amazing. She genuinely enjoyed talking with Blayze, and he loved the attention from her.

"Yes, ma'am!" And off he went, giving Lincoln a very long and detailed description of a baby calf being brought into the world. It wasn't lost on me that she gave him her entire focus. As if she hung on every word he said.

I shut the door and made my way around the back of the truck, trying to remember how to breathe.

Chapter Fifteen

Lincoln

We were only an hour outside of Billings when I decided I needed to learn more about what Brock did. I knew he rode bulls. I knew he must have made good money from it, by the looks of his house, and I knew he traveled a lot.

Blayze was crashed in his car seat, his headphones on and a movie on the DVD player. I figured now would be a good time to ask questions.

"So, how long have you been riding in the rodeo?"

Ty nearly choked on the water he was drinking.

Kaylee reached over and slapped his back, probably harder than she should have, a small smile tugging at her lips. "You okay there, cowboy?" she asked, the smirk clear in the profile of her face.

Ty shot her a look and nodded as Brock let out a laugh.

"Brock, you'd better set your girl straight," Ty said with a laugh.

Turning to look at Brock, I lifted a brow. He actually blushed, which made my insides go all soft and gooey, like a hot chocolate chip cookie when you broke it apart.

"Um, I don't ride in a rodeo. I'm on the PBR tour. It's a group of professional bull riders—the best of the best, if you will."

"The guys who ride in rodeos aren't professional bull riders?" I asked.

"They are. A lot are members of the PBR."

"There is a difference, though," Ty interjected.

I waited for Brock to keep talking.

"So, in the PBR, we ride bulls only. In the rodeo, they have to do other events as well, not just bull ride. The bull riders in the PBR are the highest ranked, and so are the bulls. So, it's at a different level. I ride in the Built Ford Tough Series. There are other series under that. I started out at rodeos, then worked myself up to the Velocity Tour, and then debuted on the Built Ford Tough, where I rode good enough to stay on tour. I won rookie of the year my second year on tour, and then the following year, I won my first of two PBR World Finals. Ty also won a PBR World Final."

Kaylee and I both looked at Ty.

"Did you get hurt on a bull?" Kaylee asked.

Ty looked straight ahead and simply said, "No."

That was our clue Ty wasn't ready to talk about his days of riding or how he'd gotten hurt.

"And you've won two PBR World Finals?" I already knew that part from my internet search of him after we'd first met.

Brock smiled. "Yes, ma'am."

"And this season, he's been jumping from number one to three to number two, and is now back at number one. Whoever is number one at the last event in Vegas is world champion."

My stomach jumped. *Is it the excitement, knowing how good he is, or is that pride I'm feeling?* It was an unusual emotion that I couldn't quite identify, as I'd never felt anything like it before. "Wow, so you're on your way to maybe winning another?"

Brock shrugged. "Maybe, but anything could happen. I could get hurt tomorrow and be out the rest of the tour. With bull riding, you never know. It's unpredictable, and you'd better make damn sure your head is in it, or you could get killed."

"Why do you do it if it's so dangerous?" I asked.

Ty and Brock exchanged a passing look in the rearview mirror.

"I love the feeling of crawling on the back of a bull. Knowing it's me against him, and that only one of us can come out on top. I'm addicted to the adrenaline it gives me."

"Have you been hurt a lot?" Kaylee asked.

Brock laughed. "Yes. Broke my first bone at ten, getting flung off the back of a bull."

"Ten!" Kaylee and I both said at once.

He nodded and went on. "I've had stitches, broken ribs, broken hand, a collapsed lung, pulled muscles, and a concussion, to name a few."

My mouth dropped open.

"When I nod my head to let them know to open the gate, I know what could happen. It doesn't scare me or make me nervous. It's just what I do."

I chewed on my lip. My mind raced. *Can I really get involved with a guy who does something so dangerous?*

Every time he got on a bull, I'd be a nervous wreck. I made a mental note to talk to Stella, Brock's mom, about how she handled it.

Brock looked like he wanted to say something else, but he turned his head and stared out the window.

"Does Tanner bull ride?" I asked.

Ty laughed. "No. He's tried it before, but he doesn't like it. He team ropes."

"Team ropes?" Kaylee asked.

"Yeah, he works with a partner. They let the calf out of the chute, and Tanner ropes his neck, and his partner—Chance, he's the heeler—ropes the back legs. It's timed. The faster you do it, the better you rank."

Kaylee seemed enthralled by all of this. "Are he and his partner good?"

"They're number three in the world right now," Brock said. I could hear how proud he was of his brother.

"So, they're in rodeos?" I asked sheepishly.

Brock nodded. "Yes. PRCA."

"OMG, all these acronyms!" Kaylee said with a chuckle.

"Professional Rodeo Cowboys Association," Brock clarified.

Ty added, "Like how the PBR has the world championship, the PRCA has the NFR—National Finals Rodeo."

"My head is spinning. Please tell me you're not going to quiz us on all of this," Kaylee said.

We all chuckled, and Blayze stirred just a little. Not because of us, since he had his headphones on.

Ty was soon pulling into the Ledgestone Hotel in Billings. "Okay, let's get checked in."

Ty Senior and Stella pulled in behind us as everyone climbed out of the truck. I didn't even think about it when I reached in and unbuckled Blayze. It felt so natural to get him. As I pulled him out, he woke slightly and wrapped his arms around my neck, and I held on to him. Kaylee looked at me and smiled—but it was the look Brock gave me that made me think I might have overstepped.

"I'm sorry. I wasn't even thinking when I reached over and got him out."

He stood there. Not uttering a word. I'd started to make my way to him, to hand him his son, when Stella stepped in front of me.

"He always falls asleep in the car. When he was little, Brock used to have to drive him around to get him to even go to sleep." She faced Brock. "Is he in your room or ours?"

"He mentioned wanting to stay in your room."

Stella turned back to me. "He knows he'd probably be in there anyway. The nights can get long for a five-year-old."

I nodded, still not sure what to do with the sleeping boy in my arms.

With one last look at his son, Brock turned and headed into the hotel, following Ty, Kaylee, and their father.

"Stella," I asked. "Did I do something wrong, taking him out of the truck? Brock was looking at me like I had."

Her soft smile made me relax some. "No, honey. I think it's because it's always been Brock and Blayze and, of course, us. He's never had a mama, and I can see by the way my son looks at you that he wants you in his life in a more *meaningful* way."

She winked, and I blushed.

"Well, we haven't really known each other for very long."

She waved me off and then covered Blayze's ears. "I met Ty Senior on a Wednesday at a church youth group meeting. We went on our first date the following Friday night after the football game, and by Sunday, I had given him my virginity and known he was the man I was going to marry. Some folks don't believe in love at first sight, but I do. And, like I said, my son looks at you like I've never seen him look at another woman. Not even Kaci." Her head nodded down to Blayze. "Don't think so much, Lincoln, honey. Live life and have fun."

I grinned. "Would you mind if we grabbed something to drink later? I have something I need to talk to you about."

Stella beamed with the thought that she might be able to talk girl talk with me. "Heck yes. Let's get settled into the room, and then we'll head to the bar and get us something to drink before dinner. You ask me anything you need to know about falling for a man like my Brock."

And with that, she turned and walked into the hotel.

I stood there, holding on to a sleeping five-year-old boy and wondering how in the hell his grandmother had been able to just read my mind.

Kaylee poked her head out the hotel door. "You coming in or what?"

After walking into the hotel, I realized that this little boy was heavy. I made my way over to the couch and sat down. Blayze held on to my neck tighter, and I found myself falling even more for him, just like I was falling for his daddy, who was currently checking in.

My eyes swept over his body.

I stared at the black cowboy hat. *Yummy.*

Moving my gaze down, I took in the long-sleeved blue ranch-style shirt he had on. It fit him perfectly and showed off his broad chest. I'd always thought bull riders were on the smaller side, but Brock had muscles. Not like a bodybuilder, but he was built in all the right places. *Chiseled* was how Kaylee would describe him. I'd gotten a feel of those muscles when I'd danced with him.

My eyes landed on that perfect ass nestled in those Wranglers. His jeans didn't fit him loose; they were snug on those thighs.

Is it getting hot in here?

A little farther down, and there was the cherry on the cake. The cowboy boots.

I'd always been a sucker for a cowboy, and being from Georgia, we had our fair share. But none of them were like Brock Shaw. None of them had made my insides quiver and my lower stomach pulse with desire. None of them had made me want something more, like I did with Brock.

Kaylee turned to head my way. When she stopped in front of me, I glanced up at her.

"Have you no shame, Lincoln Pratt?"

"Huh?" I asked, confused.

"You're holding the man's son and looking at him like you want to strip him right here and take him."

"He'd probably like that," Ty said, making Kaylee jump and me giggle, my cheeks heating.

"He's heavy, ain't he?" Ty asked.

"Yes, he his. But he's sleeping so soundly. I don't have the heart to wake him up."

About that time, Brock walked over with his room key in hand. He stood in front of me and grinned. I guessed the initial shock of me taking his son out of the truck had worn off.

"Let's bring him up to my room for a bit," Brock said, lightly pushing the hair back from his son's forehead. The sweet gesture touched me and made me sigh internally.

"We're in room two twenty-seven. Here's a key," Kaylee said, handing me a key card to our hotel room.

I somehow managed to slip it into the back pocket of my jeans.

"Okay, kids, we've got a room on the first floor—one nineteen," Ty Senior stated as he looked between his two sons, almost as if to reassure them that their parents wouldn't be anywhere near their rooms.

Brock was the first one to reply. "Sounds good, Dad. I'm going to take Blayze upstairs with me, and then we'll all meet for dinner."

I stood, careful not to wake up the sleeping prince.

"Lincoln, call me when you're ready for that drink."

"Yes, ma'am," I said to Stella. "I will."

Brock focused his gaze on his mother, then me, before offering to take Blayze from me. "Want me to carry him? I know your arms have to be on fire by now."

"No, he's okay. I can bring him up to your room, so he doesn't wake up."

A slow, sexy smile spread over Brock's face.

Okay, so I might have been using the excuse of not waking his son because I really wanted a few extra moments with Brock. It might have been wrong, but in that moment, I didn't want to be right. It was shameful, but I was hoping for another one of those mind-blowing kisses he'd given me.

Little did I know how much more I'd be getting.

Chapter Sixteen

Lincoln

The ride in the elevator was quiet. Kaylee and Ty stood on complete opposite sides while Brock and I stood next to one another. The heat between our bodies was hard to miss, and I knew he felt it too.

The door opened, and Brock carried his bag along with mine. Downstairs, Ty had offered to take Kaylee's, but she'd politely declined.

Kaylee stopped at the door to our room. Brock brought my suitcase inside and then stepped out into the hall again, where I was waiting for him. Before she shut the door, Kaylee gave me a look that said she knew what I was up to.

Ty's room was next. He told Brock he'd meet him down in the lobby before dinner and slipped inside.

Then, we were standing in front of room two thirty-eight. Brock's room. For a brief moment, I let myself pretend we were a little family, heading into our weekend retreat, where Blayze and I would watch his dad ride on a bull, and then we'd all head home and play house.

I snapped out of it at the sound of the door shutting.

What in the hell are you doing, Lincoln? This man has a son. He has a dangerous job, and you want to play house.

We walked into the room, and a king-size bed sat in the middle. A small kitchen area was to our left, with the bathroom to the right.

Brock pulled the covers back on the bed, and I gently placed Blayze down and covered him. He looked so precious as I slipped the headphones off and leaned down to kiss him on the forehead.

Yes, this little boy was jumping right on into my heart, and there was nothing I could do to stop it. Even if things didn't work out between me and Brock, I'd still adore Blayze.

Taking a step back, I turned and headed toward the door, Brock on my heels.

"I guess I'll see you for dinner?" I asked, turning before opening the door.

His hands came up and landed on the door, framing my body against it.

My heart raced in my chest as I looked up into his eyes.

"The more you're near me, the more my body aches for you, Lincoln."

I swallowed hard, my mouth opening to tell him that I felt the same. Brock didn't give me a chance to answer, though. He cupped my face, his mouth instantly on mine.

My knees felt weak as I reached up and placed my hands on his hips. This man could really kiss me senseless. It was the only thing he had done, and I couldn't even imagine what it would feel like to have his hands on all the other parts of me. Touching me and bringing me to utter pleasure.

Brock pulled me into the bathroom. My heart raced as I looked over his shoulder, and he shut the door.

"He's out cold. Kid can sleep through a tornado," Brock whispered.

Swallowing hard, I realized I was about to find out *exactly* how it felt to be touched by Brock.

His hands shook slightly as he lifted me and set me on the counter. They shook even more as he slipped his hand under my shirt. I gasped as his thumb rolled gently over my nipple.

My back arched, the need to feel him touching me nearly driving me mad. This wasn't my normal behavior, to make out in the bathroom of a hotel, but with Brock, I was a different person. I found myself wanting to do anything for him, and have him do anything to me. It felt naughty to mess around in the bathroom of his room.

"I need more," he panted before pressing his lips back to mine.

My breathing increased, and I felt the heat move into my cheeks.

Brock broke the kiss and placed his hand on the side of my face. "You're so beautiful when those cheeks of yours blush."

His hands moved down, and he lifted my shirt over my head.

"Brock," I gasped, my head falling back while his lips kissed a path around my neck. My head was dizzy with every emotion I could possibly have. Need. Desire. Nerves. Excitement. It was all swirling around in my head. He brought out a side of me I was beginning to like. A lot.

When his finger trailed along my bra line, I opened my eyes and looked at him.

"May I touch you, Lincoln?"

Swallowing hard, I reached behind my back and unclasped my bra. My hands were shaking as well, and I instinctively held my bra over myself.

"I don't normally do this sort of thing, Brock. And Blayze is—"

He pressed his mouth to mine again, kissing me senseless. We weren't going to have sex; I knew that. Not with his son in the next room.

Brock pulled back and brought his forehead to mine. When his hand touched the one holding my bra, I jumped.

"Do you want me to stop?" he asked in a raspy voice.

I shook my head. "No," I whispered as I let my bra fall to the floor.

The way his eyes took me in made my entire body heat up. He slowly let his tongue move over his lips before he took my breast into his hand. "Lincoln, what are you doing to me?"

My chest rose and fell faster. His eyes lifted to mine. When he pinched my nipple, I gasped.

"Do you like me touching you?"

I nodded. "Yes."

His mouth was back on my skin, kissing right above my breasts. I couldn't believe I was letting him do this to me. I grabbed on to his shoulders and choked out, "Brock, wait."

He stopped instantly.

"Blayze."

"Is asleep."

I smiled, feeling a naughtiness I had never possessed.

"One taste," he said softly as he placed his mouth over my breast and slowly teased me with his tongue. We both moaned as my hands slid down his arms. My entire body felt like it was on fire. There was no way I could come from a man simply playing with my breasts . . .

I dropped my head back and let the feel of his hands on my body relax me into a euphoria I'd never experienced before. I didn't have to orgasm; this was still one of the most erotic moments of my life.

When I felt his mouth moving back up my neck, I tried to keep my breathing even.

"You scare me, Lincoln Pratt." His words were spoken so low, I almost missed them.

Pulling my body back, I caught his gaze. "Why?"

Slowly shaking his head, he said, "Because you're the reason my heart is pounding so hard in my chest right now. I've never felt like this before. I feel lost, and that scares me. I don't know how to give someone my heart. I've kept it to myself for the last five years. I've got all these . . . demons running around in my head, telling me I don't deserve someone like you. You're beautiful, exciting, thrilling, and I'm not going to pretend I don't want you. I just don't know how to open up that part of my heart."

I went to speak, but his next words stopped me.

"Ever since I first met you, you've been a beautiful dream that plays alongside a nightmare."

My heart ached for this man. He had been hurt, and I didn't know how . . . but I knew I would never cause him more pain.

"I don't know what's going on in that head of yours. All I know is that I feel something for you, Brock. Something that I've never experienced either. I feel like I've known you forever, yet I don't know you at all. I *do* know for a fact that the last thing I would *ever* do is hurt you or Blayze. I'm not asking you for something you're not ready to give, but I think I knew from the moment we met the other day that there was something between us. I can't deny that."

Leaning his forehead against mine again, he whispered, "I'm so damn terrified that you're going to see what I do and run as fast as you can."

Placing my hands on the sides of his face, I lifted his gaze to mine. The thought of being with someone who rode bulls scared me a bit, but not enough to not see where this was going. "I'm not going to run. I promise you."

He smiled so big, it made my stomach flutter.

"You've set something inside me into motion, cowboy, and I want to see where this goes. I'm not asking for your heart right now. I'm asking for a piece of you. A chance to get to know you." I leaned forward and gently kissed him before whispering against his lips, "I sort of feel funny, sitting here half-naked on your bathroom counter."

He grinned. "We can take all your clothes off, if that would make you feel less funny. Although, if more of your clothes come off, I can guaran-damn-tee ya that you *will* be feeling something, and it sure as hell won't be the least bit funny, doll."

My face flushed even brighter at his admission. But I knew the type of man Brock was and that he'd take this as slow as I needed.

He lifted me off the counter and helped me get my bra and shirt back on. He might be a bit of a bad boy, but he was also a gentleman.

When I was fully dressed, he took in a deep breath. "I'm not going to pretend like I've been a saint since Blayze's mother. I've slept with a few women, but I'm not a man-whore. I can promise you that, if we do this, I'm one hundred percent committed to *you* only . . . and I expect the same in return."

A flurry of butterflies took flight in my stomach. "Of course," I somehow managed to get out.

I was agreeing to date a cowboy.

No. I was agreeing to date a man who had a son and clearly had relationship issues . . . and something from his past haunting him. Let's not forget that he also rode bulls for a living.

His hand slipped behind my neck, and he drew me in for another mind-blowing kiss. Every doubt about where this was going simply slipped away.

"I'd better go," I said against his lips.

"Yeah, you better."

We both smiled as Brock opened the bathroom door and I headed to the hotel room door. Brock opened it and gave me a smile that nearly had me tripping. When I took off down the hall, I glanced over my shoulder to see him watching me. I pulled the key card out of my back pocket and slipped it into the door.

The moment I set foot in the room, Kaylee was in front of my face.

"Oh. My. God. You had sex!" she hissed. "Fast sex. Was it eight-second sex?"

My eyes widened. "I did not!"

Her head tilted, and her left eye narrowed, like she was really looking me over. "Then, you had an orgasm."

"Wrong again. Do you really think we'd have sex in his hotel room with his son in there?"

Pointing to me, she replied, "Something happened. Spill the beans."

I felt my cheeks blush. "Yes, something happened."

Kaylee started dancing around the room like a child getting a new toy.

I fell onto the bed and sighed. Kaylee followed my lead.

"So? Tell me what happened."

I rolled over onto my back, stared up at the ceiling, and giggled like a schoolgirl.

"I want details. I need to live through you. Mouth? Fingers? What did he do?"

"Oh, Kaylee. He pulled me into the bathroom, and the next thing I knew, his hand was under my shirt, and then my shirt was off. Then my bra."

Her mouth fell open.

"He actually asked me if he could touch me."

She smiled. "That was sweet."

I nodded. "Then he placed his mouth over my nipple, and I thought I might actually have an orgasm. It was pure bliss."

"Well, damn. Either it's been a really long time for you, or he has a magical mouth."

I giggled. "Both."

"And? What else?"

"I could tell he was as nervous as I was."

Her brows lifted. "Bad boy mixed with a little bit of good. I like it. Keep going!"

My cheeks heated. "That was it. Then he admitted to being scared about how he felt for me. He's dealing with some inner demons, that's for sure. We both decided to just see where this goes."

"You're okay with how fast y'all are going?"

Facing her, I scrunched up my nose. "I didn't have sex with him. How many times have you let a guy feel you up on a first date?"

She shrugged. "On a first date? Maybe twenty percent of them. Depends on if I knew them before or if we had a connection."

"Well, it wasn't even a date. And we sort of went on a date the other day at the carnival and dance." I paused. "Oh my God, I'm a slut, aren't I? I let him do that to me with his son sleeping in the other room!"

"Was the bathroom door shut and locked?" she asked.

"Yes."

"Were you both quiet?"

I nodded.

"Then you're not a slut. It's sort of hot to think y'all messed around a bit in the bathroom, though."

I grinned.

"Do you want more with him?"

"Yes, I do."

She dropped back and groaned. "Girl, I would too. Have you *seen* him? I mean, holy bull-rider hotness. I'd let him tie a rope to me and hold on tight, if you catch my drift."

I laughed as I joined her again, staring at the ceiling. "Ty's handsome. He has a nice body."

"Yeah, he *is* good looking, and funny too. I get the feeling he's pretty messed up in the head, though, and I've heard he's a player."

I swallowed hard. "Yeah, I sort of get that about Ty too. Where did you hear he was a player?"

"Oh, I overheard a group of girls talking at the café the other day. Ty walked in and grabbed a breakfast taco to go. One of the girls said she got it on with him a few months back. I guess he likes to screw them and leave them."

Letting out a breath that made my lips rattle, I said, "Brock admitted he had some demons that kept telling him he didn't deserve me. I guess he feels like he can't open his heart up to anyone."

She quickly sat up. "Really? This is interesting. Did he elaborate?"

"No," I stated, sitting up and facing her. "It has something to do with his wife, though. I get the feeling he blames himself for the reason she died."

"What makes you think he blames himself?"

With a half shrug, I replied, "I don't know. It's a weird feeling I have that I can't seem to shake. I want to ask him more questions about how she died, but I don't think he's ready to answer them. I don't want to push him."

My phone rang, and I pulled it out to see Stella's name. "Oh gosh, how do I talk to her after her son just had his mouth on my boobs?"

"With a big-ass grin on your face—that's how." Kaylee laughed and reached over, swiping my phone to answer it before passing it to me.

"Um, hello? Stella? Hi!" I fumbled around with my words. I hadn't been planning on Kaylee answering the phone for me.

"Tone it down," Kaylee whispered.

"Hey, sweetheart. You ready for that drink?"

I dragged in a deep breath. "Sure. I'll be right down." I hit end and climbed off the bed. "How do I look?" I asked, running my hands over my body.

Kaylee stood and gave me a once-over. "Like you just had an incredibly hot moment with a good-looking guy in his hotel bathroom."

When she winked at me, I felt my entire face heat. Again.

"I hate you."

Chapter Seventeen

Lincoln

I saw Stella the moment I walked into the hotel bar. She had on a long-sleeved white shirt, jeans, and cowboy boots, and her hair was pulled up into a ponytail. She didn't look a day older than forty.

"Hi," I said softly, sliding onto the barstool next to hers.

I glanced around and saw a few other people in the room. A table with four guys caught my attention. They all had on cowboy hats, and on two of them, I could see their big buckles, just like the ones Brock, Dirk, and Ty wore.

"Bull riders?" I asked, motioning over to them with a jerk of my head.

Stella glanced that way. "Yes. Brazilians. They're big in this sport."

"Really?" I asked.

"Yep, who would have thought, right? Beer?" Stella asked as she pointed to her Miller Lite.

"Sure."

Lifting her beer, she motioned to me, and the bartender nodded. "So, why don't you just get to what's on your mind, sweetie?"

I dragged in a deep breath and slowly blew it out. "How do you do it? I mean, two sons who ride bulls and another who rodeos? How are your nerves not shot?"

She laughed and took a drink of her beer. The bartender set mine down in front of me, and I followed Stella's lead. Only I took a longer drink. My nerves were still on edge, and I hoped Stella couldn't tell why I was flustered.

"I wish I could tell you it's easy, loving a man who does something like bull riding for a living. Ty Senior did it when we first met. He won the state high school bull-riding championship. At first, I thought it was sort of sexy. Then I fell in love with him, and I did whatever I could to encourage him. It was something he was passionate about. Luckily for me, though, when I had Ty, something in his father switched, and he just stopped. Worked full time on my daddy's ranch, the one we live on and work now. He walked away from bull riding and never looked back."

My brows pulled in some. "Why didn't Brock do that when he got married and had Blayze?"

She hesitated before taking a deep, cleansing breath. "I can't tell you why he kept riding. Some guys just do. They get married, have kids, and keep on the tour. I can, however, speculate. Kaci and Brock were not meant to be together. At least, I think they were both just too young. They thought they knew what love was, and maybe they did."

I sucked in a breath. "You don't think they were meant to be together? Why?"

Stella faced me. "It's not my story to tell, and when Brock is ready to share it with you, he will. But he's holding on to some serious guilt about more than one thing. You're the first woman he's even looked at since he married Kaci. When she died, I think he went on a few benders and had a one-night stand or two. Probably did some things he regrets, but for the most part, he swore off ever falling for another woman."

"He's opened a little bit with me, but I don't want to push him."

Stella gave me a grin and went on. "I think Kaci figured once they got married, Brock would walk away from bull riding. Of course, that never happened. Since her death, he's been struggling, and the mistakes of his past have made him the man he is today. Brock just has to figure out who that man is, and find the right woman to share that man with."

I took a swig from my beer.

Stella took my hand in hers. "Lincoln, Brock is a wonderful son, an amazing father, and one heck of a good guy. He likes you, I see it, and I'm pretty sure you like him just as much. Just go slow, be patient with him, and let him come to you when he's ready. He'll get there, but it might take longer than eight seconds, if you know what I mean."

I wanted to ask her more, but the sound of Blayze's voice from the lobby had us both looking that way.

Stella smiled and said, "The gang is all ready for dinner. You'd better call Kaylee and tell her to get down here. Once these Shaw men get hungry, that's it."

With a chuckle, I pulled out my phone and sent Kaylee a text to come to the lobby. She texted back that she was already there, talking to Dirk.

I paid for my beer and followed Stella out into the lobby. I couldn't help but smile as I took in everyone. Brock seemed so happy to be with his family. He loved his job, but I was positive he hated that it took him away from his son.

Blayze ran up to me, grabbed my hand, and began pulling me toward the door. "Sit next to me, Miss Lincoln!"

Laughing, I asked, "Where?"

"At the restaurant, silly!"

There was a steak and seafood restaurant right across from the hotel. Ty Senior had made reservations, so when we got there, we were seated immediately.

"So, what can we expect from tomorrow?" Kaylee asked, tossing a piece of bread into her mouth.

Everyone looked at Brock.

"Well, I've got passes for everyone, and a behind-the-scenes tour set up for Lincoln and Kaylee, as well as Mom and Pop."

"Me too?" Blayze asked.

"Of course for you too." Brock ruffled his son's hair. "Then, round one starts. If I qualify, I move on to round two on Sunday. The fifteen/fifteen bucking battle is after that, and then the championship round."

"What's the fifteen/fifteen bucking battle?" I asked.

"It's the top fifteen riders in the world competing against the fifteen highest-ranked bulls at the event. Points count toward the season standings."

I nodded.

"Are you ready for Tiny Devil and Moonshine?" Ty Senior asked.

Brock nodded. "They're both good bulls. Moonshine is currently ranked third, and Tiny Devil is tenth."

Kaylee and I exchanged a look of utter confusion. She made a face, and I tried not to laugh.

"Moonshine is a left-hand delivery, so he's gonna turn away from your hand," Ty Senior added.

Brock nodded. "Doesn't bother me any. I wouldn't be surprised if he went right."

Blayze tapped my arm, causing me to glance down at him. "Daddy is takin' me to see the bulls. Will you come with us?"

I peeked over to Brock. He was still talking to his father. "I'd love to, if your daddy says it's okay."

"He will. He likes you. Just like Uncle Ty likes Miss Kaylee. Daddy said Uncle Ty has a crush on her! And I made up a song about it. Wanna hear?"

Kaylee nearly choked on the salad she'd just put into her mouth.

Stella chuckled, and all three Shaw men stared at Kaylee as she grabbed her water. None of them had heard what Blayze said.

"What's wrong?" Ty asked, clearly worried about Kaylee.

Holding up her hand, she took a drink and managed to get out, "I'm fine."

Her eyes were watering, and she shot a glance in my direction, shock on her face and in her eyes. I had to admit, I was a bit shocked as well. Ty had seemed to have pulled back on his flirting with Kaylee, and now he acted as if she annoyed him more than anything. Kaylee had told me after they'd shared a kiss at the Blue Moose, Ty had grown distant. I wanted to dig deeper into that, but I needed to focus on Brock first before I even attempted to figure out Ty Shaw.

Kaylee kept coughing, and Ty stood up. "Kaylee, are you okay?"

With her hand lifted in a thumbs-up sign, she nodded.

Ty grabbed her now-empty water and walked over to the waitress to ask her to fill it. I had to admit it was a sweet thing to do. When he came back and handed it to her, I knew Kaylee thought so as well. She seemed awestruck for a few moments as Ty sat back down.

"What in the world happened? Something go down wrong?" Ty Senior asked.

I looked at Brock and nodded down to Blayze, moved my eyes to Ty and Kaylee, and then nodded to Blayze again.

Brock frowned and mouthed, *What?*

Clearly, I needed to work on my covert skills.

I leaned around Blayze's back and whispered to Brock, "Blayze announced that his uncle Ty has a crush on Kaylee and something about a song he made up, right as she was taking a bite of salad."

Brock pulled back and stared at me, and then he looked to Kaylee and his brother.

Then, he lost it, laughing, and I couldn't help it; I followed right along.

Kaylee shot us both daggers as she quietly said, "I hate you." Then, she proceeded to kick me under the table.

"What's so funny?" Ty asked.

I wondered when Blayze would speak up, and he didn't disappoint.

"I think Miss Kaylee swallowed her salad all wrong when I told her you had a crush on her. I know you said I'd have to walk to Billings if I didn't stop singing my song, but we're here now, so I want to sing it for *her* too."

The entire table stilled—well, with the exception of Kaylee, who was groaning.

Ty stared at his nephew. "I do not have a crush on Kaylee, Blayze. We already went over this. And you'll walk back *home* if you start that song."

"What?" Kaylee asked, glaring at Ty now. "You went over this? When?"

Ty looked at her. "It was before we picked you both up. Blayze misunderstood something his daddy said. Right, Blayze?"

The little boy winked at his uncle and replied, "Right." He leaned across the table and whispered loudly, "We're tellin' a white lie, ain't that right, Uncle Ty?"

This time Ty moaned, and Kaylee tried to keep from laughing.

"Well, moving on from that conversation," Stella said with a huge smile, "girls, I'd love to get some shopping in while we're here, if you're both up for it."

"Shopping? I am always up for shopping," Kaylee stated.

Stella giggled, as did I.

The rest of dinner was spent with the men talking about ranching, bulls, horses, and what they were going to plant in the north pasture. Stella and I talked about me starting a garden, possibly offering a few riding lessons, and she even offered to board one or two of their horses in my barn for the lessons. I told her about how excited I was to start my new job. Then, I played tic-tac-toe with Blayze to keep him occupied while we waited for the check. Brock picked up the tab and told his father he could get it next time, to which his father argued back that Brock had said that *last* time he'd picked up the check.

I couldn't help but notice how Ty's mood had seemed to slip. He hardly said a word the rest of the night. After dinner, he mentioned something about heading back to the hotel and meeting up with a few friends for some drinks.

Brock invited me to go along with him and Blayze to see the bulls, and that made both me and Blayze happy campers. Stella and Kaylee excused themselves and acted like two schoolgirls as they set off for their shopping trip.

"You sure you don't want to go with Mom and Kaylee?" Brock asked as we headed toward Ty's truck. He was letting Brock use it since he would be with friends.

"I'm positive. I'd rather spend the time with you and Blayze."

The way Blayze smiled up at me made my chest squeeze tightly with adoration. This boy had a way of wrapping you around his little finger.

As we walked along and looked at the bulls, Brock gave me their stats.

Ruthless Outlaw had been ridden the full eight seconds only once in the last six outs. Brock was the one who had gone the full eight on him last. Pride bubbled up inside me.

Steel Bullet was a spitfire bull. Small, but he packed a lot of power. Brock loved riding him.

"What did it mean when your father said one of the bulls was a left-hand delivery?"

"When we get to the event center tomorrow, I'll show you. But basically, it means that the bull is left-handed, so to speak. He likes coming out of the chutes on his left side. Most bulls are left-handed. So, most of the bulls you see tomorrow will be a left-hand delivery."

I nodded. "And him turning away from your hand?"

Brock smiled. He seemed to like me asking questions.

"If I'm right-handed, I've got my hand in my bull strap like this." He motioned like his hand was slipping under a strap. "If the bull turns away from my hand, or to the left, he's turning away from me. If he turns into my hand, goes to the right, he's turning into me. Most guys like it when the bull turns toward his hand."

My brow lifted. "And you?"

He shrugged. "I don't mind either way. I just keep my chin tucked and keep my free hand in control."

I leaned against a fence, taking in the smell of the small ranch just outside the arena. "I'm not going to lie: I'm nervous about watching. I pulled up some videos on the PBR site and searched your name."

Brock's face lit up. "You researched me, did ya?"

"Did you see my daddy winning?" Blayze asked, pride filling his voice. "He's the best there ever was when it comes to riding a bull. That's what Papa says."

Brock reached down and grabbed Blayze, putting him on his shoulders. "Your granddaddy has to say that, buddy. I'm his son."

Blayze laughed like that was the funniest thing he'd ever heard. Even slapped his hand on his leg. "That's a good one, Daddy!"

Brock and I looked at each other before laughing. It was evident how much Brock loved his son, and how much Blayze loved his daddy.

"You feel like hanging out with us tonight? We're gonna watch *Finding Nemo*."

I smiled. "That's one of my favorite movies."

Blayze shouted, "It's mine too!"

I shot my gaze between both Shaw men. "I'll watch the movie with y'all on one condition."

"Anything!" Blayze offered up.

"We have to have popcorn and black licorice."

Both Brock and Blayze scrunched their noses. "Gross," they said at the same time. Except one sounded more like *gwoss.*

Like father, like son.

"Who likes black licorice?" Brock asked, a mock expression of horror on his face.

"Or popcorn?" Blayze said.

Gasping and placing my hand on my chest, I looked at Blayze. "You don't like popcorn?"

He shook his head, his sweet little blue eyes beaming down at me. "Daddy doesn't like it, so neither do I."

How adorable is that?

"Well then, what will we eat while we watch the movie?" I asked.

It took only a nanosecond for them both to respond, "Pretzels and chocolate chip cookies."

And I just fell a little bit in love with both of them.

Chapter Eighteen

Brock

Blayze was passed out, his head on my lap and his feet on Lincoln's. *Finding Nemo* had long since ended, and Lincoln and I had been sitting there, just talking. She asked me questions about bull riding. How the bulls were bred, the average bull age, if anyone rooted for the bulls. That one was my favorite.

"A lot of people root for the bulls. They keep stats on them and everything."

"What happens if you draw a bull whose riders make eight on him a lot?"

"The stock contractors will usually put him down a level. He'll go to some more inexperienced riders. That way, he can throw them and build his confidence back up."

She nodded. "Get him a little ego boost, huh?"

"Yeah, something like that," I replied with a chuckle.

Glancing down at Blayze, she asked, "Do you ever worry that you'll get hurt?"

"I'd be stupid not to. I don't so much worry as I try to focus on *not* getting hurt. I work out, do yoga, try to stay in shape. The better shape I'm in, the better I'll heal when I do get hurt."

"When, not if?"

"Yeah, baby. It's always when."

Lincoln looked to be in deep thought before she glanced back at me and smiled. "I'm excited to see you in your element tomorrow."

I lifted my brow. "Oh yeah? I'm excited to show you."

"I won't be a distraction, will I?" she asked, suddenly nervous.

"No, just don't wear any Daisy Dukes or tell me you're not wearing panties, and I'll be golden."

Her face blushed, and she looked at Blayze. "Brock Shaw!" she said, playfully hitting me on the shoulder. She then shook her head and took in a deep breath. "I'd better get back to my room. I hope Kaylee is back."

"I hope she wasn't embarrassed about the whole Ty having a crush on her. My brother is a bit awkward around women. He's never really had a girlfriend."

Her brows rose. "Really? He's so . . ."

I quirked my head. "He's so what?"

"Um, I was just going to say, he's so kind and . . . well, handsome. I find it hard to believe he's never dated."

I chuckled. "He's had his fair share of women, if you catch my drift. None that ever caught his eye. Well, until Kaylee."

"Kaylee's caught his eye?"

I nodded. "I think so. At least, he sure looks at her like he's interested, but then says he's not."

Lincoln thought on my words for a bit before she snapped out of it. Smiling, she moved Blayze's feet off her lap and slowly stood. "What time should we be ready to go?"

"Let's all meet down in the lobby for breakfast. Eight sound good?"

Her eyes lit up with what clearly was excitement. "Sounds perfect."

I moved Blayze so that I could stand and followed her to the door. Before she had a chance to open it, I placed my hand on her arm.

"Lincoln."

Her body trembled at my touch, and that did something to me right in the middle of my damn chest. Kaci had never reacted to me like Lincoln did. Her body hadn't shaken under my touch. Her cheeks hadn't flushed a beautiful pink when I touched her, and she hadn't looked at me the way Lincoln did after I kissed her. That knowledge messed with my head, but I tried to push it aside. I knew Kaci loved me, but I was beginning to wonder if our love had been enough.

She turned and leaned against the door. Her chest moved faster as her breath quickened. She was so beautiful; it was hard to breathe when I looked at her. It was hard not to get lost in those green eyes of hers. Hard to forget how soft her lips had felt against mine. Even harder to forget how beautiful she was on the inside.

Lincoln Pratt was like no other woman I had ever met before.

Leaning down, I brushed my lips across hers. She tasted like chocolate, and I moaned when my tongue slipped into her mouth.

Her arms wrapped around my neck, and I drew her body to mine, lifting her slightly off the floor when I kissed her. She wasn't very tall, maybe five three, but she fit against me like we were made for one another. I couldn't get enough of this woman, and it took everything I had not to call my mother to come get Blayze so I could explore every single inch of her.

We were lost in the kiss. Lost in each other. If it felt this amazing to kiss, what would it feel like to make love to her? I should have been scared of these feelings I was having. And I *was* scared, but there was something else there. Something so much stronger, pushing the fear back.

Our mouths finally broke apart as I set her on her feet, and our foreheads rested against one another.

"Your kisses," she breathed heavily, "they're addictive."

"I feel the same."

"Brock," she whispered, her head drawing back, her green eyes locked on my blue, "thank you for letting me spend the evening with you and Blayze."

Smiling, I leaned down and rubbed my nose to hers. "Tomorrow night, it's just you and me."

Her breath hitched, and her eyes closed for a brief moment.

I lifted my hand and pushed a strand of hair behind her ear. "We don't have to do anything you're not ready for, sweetheart."

Lincoln's eyes snapped open as her mouth parted slightly. "I've never wanted anyone like I want you."

My heart felt like it had slammed against my chest as I crushed my mouth to hers, pushing her into the door.

"Daddy? Are you and Miss Lincoln girlfriend and boyfriend?"

We both froze before I stepped away from Lincoln. Her lips pressed together as we stood there with our eyes locked.

Glancing down at my son, who was now standing next to me, I didn't even have to think twice with my answer. "Yeah, buddy, we are."

Her eyes sparkled, and a smile spread over her face before she looked down at the ground and then cleared her throat. "Night, Blayze! I'll see you in the morning."

He waved to her. "Bye, Miss Lincoln! Don't let the bedbugs bite."

Her smile faltered, and she said, "Ugh, not what you want to think about in a hotel."

I laughed and opened the door. I watched as she walked down a few doors. Blayze was standing in front of me, also watching Lincoln. He waved when she waved to him. Her eyes lifted to mine, and she dug her teeth into her bottom lip.

"Night, gentlemen."

"Night!" Blayze loudly called out before I covered his mouth and winked at her.

"Sleep good, sweetheart."

Lincoln nodded and slipped into her room. Blayze took off, running back into our room. It took me a few seconds to get my composure and join him. He was on the bed, jumping.

"Someone got his second wind."

"I like Miss Lincoln. You like her, too, huh, Daddy? You were kissing her!"

Pulling him down, I rustled his hair. "I do like her, buddy."

"Is she gonna be my new mommy?"

Everything came to a sudden stop. At least it felt that way. My heart stopped. My breathing stopped. The happy feeling I'd had vanished.

"What?" I managed to get out.

Blayze shrugged. "Dalton's dad has a girlfriend, and they're gonna get married. She's gonna be his new mommy. I never had a mommy, and I want one."

Panic started to build inside me. I liked Lincoln a lot. She was the first woman who'd made me want something more than a quick fuck in my hotel room. Dating her was a huge step for me.

The idea of marrying her . . . that freaked me out.

"Give me a second, buddy."

I turned and walked into the bathroom, shut the door, and leaned against the counter. I pulled in one deep breath after another. I wasn't ready to think so far into the future. I wasn't ready to let Lincoln into my heart like that, yet I'd let her into my life, and my son's life, so easily. Maybe too easily.

"Fuck!" I softly said as I dug my fingers into my hair. "What did you do, Brock?"

I'd brought a woman into Blayze's world all because of how my body had reacted at the first sight of her.

What if things don't work out? What if she ends up realizing this isn't the life she wants?

I had a son, and a job that was dangerous. She had moved to Montana looking for a new life.

But does she want a guy with baggage and a kid in tow?

Her own words flooded back into my head.

"I'm not asking for your heart right now. I'm asking for a piece of you. A chance to get to know you."

Opening the bathroom door, I found Blayze sitting on the bed, watching the Disney Channel.

"Hey, buddy, can I talk to you for a second?"

He looked my way and said, "Sure, Daddy."

My heart nearly exploded with love. Kaci and I might have had our share of problems, but I knew in my heart we'd loved each other. Maybe our love wasn't the type of love other married couples shared; I didn't know. All I knew was that we had made this beautiful creature in front of me. Kaci had given me something I treasured with all my heart, and I would always be grateful to her for that.

I scrubbed my hands down my face and took in a breath. I felt my son's hand on my shoulder.

"Daddy, are you worried that Miss Lincoln don't like you back? I'm pwetty sure she does if she let ya kiss her."

Grinning, I nodded. "Lincoln and I do like each other, buddy, but we're just getting to know each other. I don't want you to get your hopes up. Things might not work out, and we could just end up being friends."

Blayze looked away from me, like he was really letting my words settle in. Then, he looked me straight in the eyes. "Daddy, will you ever get married again, like Dalton's daddy?"

My heart fell. I hadn't ever allowed myself to think how it must be for Blayze to not have a mother in his life. I wanted to give him the answer he desperately needed to hear, but I could only tell him the truth. "I don't know, buddy. I honestly don't know."

He smiled, like he knew something I didn't. Then he patted my shoulder. "Don't be afraid, Daddy. Mommy wants you to be happy and for me to have a mommy here to take care of me."

My breath caught in my throat. "Mommy?"

Blayze nodded. "She visits me in my dreams, and she tolds me that. She tolds me I was supposed to tell you it was okay to wove someone. That she knows you woved her."

Pulling my son into my arms, I held him as I felt the tears fall from my eyes. "I love you, Blayze."

His little hand gently patted my back, as if he was trying to comfort me. "I wove you, too, Daddy."

I glanced to my right to see Lincoln and Kaylee standing off to the side. They were talking to Roy MacMore, one of the stock contractors. They, along with my folks and Ty, had gotten to be behind the scenes with me and Dirk today. Ty was currently helping George Ryder, another bull rider, tighten his bull rope. I knew my brother missed all of this and loved being immersed in it again. He had asked me to help him set up an agricultural-education program for raising bulls. And he wanted to teach younger kids about how the bulls used for riding are taken care of and educate them on professional bull riding, which I was all for.

Dirk walked up next to me, his vest on, his helmet in his hand.

"You ready?" I asked.

He nodded.

"You have a late night last night?"

Looking my way, he smiled. "Is that your way of asking me if I hooked up with anyone?"

I shrugged. "Just making sure you know Kaylee is off limits."

He tossed his head back and laughed. "Dude, I think Kaylee is nice and all, but I'm not the least bit interested. Besides, I was with Ty last night, and a few friends. We all got caught up in a game of Texas hold 'em, and lady luck was not on my side."

I glanced over to Ty. He was holding on to George's vest and keeping his other hand out in front of him in case the bull decided to throw George forward. The beast George was on was getting impatient.

"I know this is hard for him, being here and all."

"He's tougher than you think, Brock."

"Yeah, I know he is. I can't help but worry about him."

Dirk placed his hand on my shoulder and gave it a hard squeeze. "I think this is good for him. Shows him he can be a part of the world without climbing onto a bull. He's okay."

I nodded and gave my best friend a smile.

My eyes looked past Dirk to Lincoln. My folks were standing next to her. She turned my way and waved. I smiled and waved back to her. Blayze was already up in the stands with my cousin Kristin. I watched as my folks guided Lincoln and Kaylee to their seats. Where I had them sitting, they would be able to see everything happening at the chutes and during the bull riding.

Dirk was up first. He did his normal routine of doing a few jumps and dropping to a knee, saying a quick prayer, before he got up on the bull. Ty walked up and grabbed the bull rope. Dirk glanced at him and nodded, then ran his hand over the rosin on the rope.

After Dirk got his rope where he wanted it, Ty pulled as I held on to Dirk's vest.

"He's probably gonna go to the left. You know he likes that," I said.

Dirk positioned himself. "Ty, get him to turn," he said, wanting the bull not to look to the back of the chute.

Reaching his foot over, Ty pushed hard on the side of the bull, making him jump a little so that Dirk could get settled over the bull exactly how he wanted.

A quick nod, and he was out of the chute. Ty and I both watched as Dirk rode almost flawlessly. He kept his hand up and moved right along with the bull. That bastard bull damn near jumped straight up, almost sending Dirk flying, but he held on. He dominated the ride as the bull attempted to throw him, but Dirk wasn't having any part of it.

"Yes!" I shouted. "Do it! Do it!"

Ty yelled right along with me. "Dig in, Dirk! Hell yes!"

The buzzer went off. I watched as he got his hand free, and Striker, the bull he was on, launched him into the air. When he landed, he hit hard but got up fast and out of the bull's way.

"Hell yeah," I said, slapping Johnny G, the stock contractor for Striker.

He laughed and shook his head. "I thought for sure that bull was going to kick his ass."

The announcer came on with Dirk's score: 87.5 points.

"He rode good. Now, ride better and show them why you're number one," Ty said to me as I rolled my neck.

I glanced up into the stands and saw Lincoln.

"Get her out of your head, man. Come on. Stay focused," Ty said.

With a nod, I put my helmet on.

My father walked up next to us and slapped me on the back. "Moonshine is feisty today."

I laughed. "When ain't he?"

Cody Harris was riding, and I watched as he slid down the bull's side.

"Shit, he's going into the well," Ty said.

Cody's hand got caught on the rope. The worst thing you want to do is start sliding to the side of the bull with your hand caught.

"Shit!" Ty and I both said.

We watched as the bull jerked him around like a rag doll. Once he finally got free, the medical crew was out there, attending to him.

"Let's go," my father said to me, giving me a light pat on the back.

I dragged my gaze off Cody and climbed onto the back of Moonshine.

"He's up and walking it off," Ty informed me as he held up my rope.

Running my hand over the rope, I took a deep breath and positioned my hand. "Tighter," I said, grabbing at the rope and pulling along with my brother.

I knew the camera was there, but I stayed focused. I couldn't hear Kim, the CBS Sports reporter who was with us every weekend. I couldn't hear the crowd. The only thing I heard was the sound of the bull breathing and me breathing.

My father's voice cut in. "Chin down, arm controlled, Brock."

"Yes, sir."

Adjusting myself on the bull, I felt my heart kicking up as the sounds of everything around me flooded back in a rush.

The beginning notes of Van Halen's "Runnin' with the Devil" started. It was the intro song the PBR had used the first year I was a rookie and drew Diablo. Damn beast had bucked me my first three times on him, and I'd never gotten to eight with that bull.

I could hear the crowd going nuts when the music started. The beat echoing in my ears. I smiled as I put my mouthpiece in.

I loved this shit. Lived for it.

One more adjustment, and I was there. A prayer and then a nod, and the gate flew open. Moonshine didn't go left. He went right and spun. He bucked forward; I adjusted. He kicked and I dug my heels into him. When he changed direction, I changed with him. That bull was doing everything in his power to get me off, and there was no way I was letting him win.

I heard the buzzer and reached down to loosen the bull rope. Moonshine spun and gave one hard, pissed-off kick. He knew I'd won, and he was not happy.

Somehow, I landed on my feet, pulled my helmet off, and tossed it up into the air.

"Yes!" I shouted as the bullfighters came up to me, each one slapping me on the back and fist-bumping me.

I turned to look for Blayze. He was clapping, and I pointed to him and then pointed up. My mama had taught me to always thank God for a safe ride, and I did. When I looked back, I saw Lincoln. She was smiling and clapping.

As I started out of the arena, they announced my score.

Ninety-one.

"Fuck yes," I muttered to myself as I walked up to the CBS reporter.

After I gave a quick interview, the only thing I could think about was getting to Blayze and Lincoln.

Chapter Nineteen

Lincoln

I watched as Brock stood there, waiting to get on the bull. Ty Senior and Junior were both there.

Turning to Stella, I asked, "Does he have to have a qualified ride to stay number one?"

"Well, if he doesn't, or if he has a low score, he just opens the door for someone to move up. Like Dirk, for instance. He just rode the best I've seen him ride in weeks. He'll move up in ranking, especially if he does good in round two tomorrow."

Nodding, I took a deep breath as I observed Brock climbing onto the bull. Everyone around him was leaning in and doing something. Ty pulled on the bull rope as Brock rubbed his hand up and down it.

"Okay, the rosin is sticky and helps him hang on to the rope, right?" I asked Stella.

"Yep! You're a quick learner, Lincoln."

"I have a good teacher."

Stella grinned.

The announcer came over the loudspeakers. "All right, everyone, we've got the local kid from Hamilton, Montana—and current number one leader in the standings—up next."

A song started up, and the crowd went nuts. The beat of the song matched the pounding of my heart.

Keeping my eyes on Brock, I tuned everyone out and focused on him. He hit at his hand and adjusted himself before he gave the head nod. I held my breath as the gateman pulled the gate open, and Moonshine came barreling out. My eyes widened in shock at how athletic that giant bull was. I had watched the videos of Brock riding, but live, seeing it in person . . . *holy. Shit.*

The bull under Brock was filled with rage. Snot flew from his nose as he forcefully jumped so high into the air, I gasped and grabbed on to Stella. The moment he landed, he kicked and twisted in a frantic effort to buck Brock off.

I watched as Brock looked like he was being tossed around on top of the bull. His head whipped back, then his body jerked forward—but he stayed on, his free hand never once coming down and touching the bull.

How in the world is he staying on that thing?

Stella screamed next to me, and Blayze did as well. Kaylee grabbed my hand as we heard the buzzer go off. Brock reached down to release his hand and was launched into the air. I gasped and jumped up when he landed.

He took off his helmet and threw it in the air. It was then that he turned and pointed to Blayze.

"Go, Daddy!" Blayze yelled as Stella stood next to me, screaming out her son's name and clapping.

Then, his blue eyes found me, and he smiled. Dimples and all.

My heart melted, and I knew I had just fallen even harder for him. Not to mention it was sexy as hell watching him ride that bull.

"Is it wrong that this stuff is a huge turn-on?" Kaylee whispered into my ear, making me laugh.

Brock headed out of the arena. When they announced his score, Stella nearly knocked me over with a hug. I knew it was a good score from my earlier conversations with Brock.

Sitting back down, I searched for him. I had seen other riders come back up and hang out at the chutes. Ty was still up there, helping other riders, but Ty Senior had made his way toward where Brock was.

When round one was almost over, Stella stood. She took Blayze's hand and looked at me. "He's going to win this round. Let's head down there."

"Oh, okay," I said, quickly standing.

Kaylee stayed behind with the boys' cousin, Kristin.

As we made our way over, people reached out to shake Stella's hand and congratulate her on the fine job Brock had done. Blayze had asked me to carry him, so I was currently holding him as we made our way over to the side of the chutes. People smiled at me, but I knew they were wondering who in the world this new girl was.

Brock was being interviewed again. He laughed at something the pretty sports reporter said and shook his head. He held a buckle that was framed in a case in his hands. My eyes roamed over him. The cowboy hat, the dark-red shirt, the chaps.

Good Lord, those chaps.

I was getting more turned on by the second as my mind went to a few different naughty images of Brock in only those chaps. And how wrong was that, with me holding his son?

He turned and saw me, and a wide grin covered his face. A few guys who worked for the PBR were telling Brock to head on out to the middle of the arena, but he motioned for me. I figured he wanted to take Blayze from me to bring with him.

I was right; he reached for Blayze—but then he grabbed my neck and pulled me in for a kiss.

The fact that the CBS camera was still on him didn't seem to faze him at all.

He stepped back, winked at me, and walked out into the arena.

I stood there, stunned, watching him and trying not to look at the camera that was still pointed at *me* now. When they realized they weren't getting anything out of me, the camera crew followed Brock.

Stella walked up next to me and bumped my arm. I looked at her as she said, in a very country drawl, "I daresay, my son has made a very loud and clear statement."

The heat on my face was intense, and I immediately prepared myself for all the things Kaylee was going to say to me. She was going to have a field day with this. Swallowing hard, I replied, "Please tell me that wasn't on national TV."

Stella laughed and clapped her hands. She was enjoying this a little too much.

Dirk and Ty were both now standing next to us, grinning with pride. The way they supported each other made my heart soar.

I looked at both men. They were smiling and calling out Brock's name. I glanced back out to see Brock. He had his cowboy hat off, waving it around. Then he went into an interview with two PBR commentators. I held my breath, hoping they wouldn't mention the kiss.

They didn't, and I let out the breath I'd been holding when Brock and Blayze made their way back to us.

The celebration dinner was packed with people, including Charles—who was one of Brock's sponsors—a few bull riders and stock contractors, and family I hadn't met until tonight.

Every time Brock's leg hit mine or he brushed his arm against me, it nearly drove me insane. My body was building up sexual tension I'd never experienced before. I was the epitome of a horny woman desperately wanting sex.

When Brock laughed, my insides shook. When he leaned in to whisper something to me, the pulse between my legs grew. Hell, when Brock ate, drank, talked to Blayze . . . all of it was whipping up a frenzy inside me. I wasn't sure if it was the atmosphere, Brock winning today,

Brock looking so sexy, or just the idea that maybe he'd make me his tonight—or all of the above.

I turned to Kaylee, who was sitting next to me. "Is it just me, or is it really hot in here?"

She took a bite of her food and shook her head. "No, it's hot in here, but a different sort of hot. I'm pretty sure it's from cowboy overload. I'm ready to strip off my clothes and ask for one to take me right now."

I giggled and bumped her shoulder. "Well, anyone catch your eye?"

We kept our voices down, especially since Ty was sitting directly across from Kaylee. I couldn't help but notice every time he stole a glance or two her way.

With a half shrug, Kaylee replied, "Yeah, I don't know if I'm ready for that after all."

"All talk, no action, huh?"

She chuckled. "I guess so."

I glanced over to see Ty watching us. I looked away and focused on the handsome cowboy sitting next to me. It was then I caught a glimpse of a blonde staring at Brock. Or was she staring at me? I smiled politely, and she looked away.

I reached under the table and placed my hand on Brock's leg. I needed to touch him in some way. I was feeling a bit brave, so I moved it to the inside of his thigh. My heart sped up, and I knew if Kaylee'd had any idea of how brazen I was being, she would be proud. I couldn't help but notice that Brock seemed to tremble for a quick moment. My stomach flipped with excitement at the idea that my touch could make him react like that.

The gentleman across from me started to ask questions about what I thought of all this. It was Brock's uncle Danny. I absentmindedly rubbed the inside of Brock's thigh and didn't even realize how far up I'd moved on his leg, because I was lost in a conversation with Danny and Stella—until Brock grabbed my hand and stopped me, making me jerk with surprise.

I glanced his way with an apologetic look.

He leaned closer to me and placed his mouth against my ear, so only I would hear him. "Are you trying to get me to come in my pants? Because if you keep inching closer to my cock, I'm going to do just that."

My mouth dropped open, and I managed to whisper, "No."

"Then stop. I already want to be inside you, sweetheart. Keep this up, and I'll be doing it in the restroom of this restaurant."

I sucked in a breath of air. The idea both shocked and thrilled me. I was almost tempted to tell him to meet me in the women's bathroom.

Who is this risk-taker Brock Shaw has brought out?

He kissed my cheek and kept his hand over mine.

It was then I noticed the blonde again. This time, she was glaring at me.

Is she someone Brock slept with in the past?

I wasn't stupid, and I knew he'd most likely slept with a number of women on the tour. Even though he'd said he wasn't a man-whore, it didn't mean he hadn't slept around. If I was going to be with this man, I needed to realize I might run into women who may have shared something with Brock in the past.

I noticed Stella and Ty Senior standing.

"Are y'all leaving?" I asked.

Stella nodded. "Yes, we're going to get Blayze back to the hotel. The little guy is ready to pass out."

Peeking around Brock, I giggled. Blayze had his head in his hands, groaning about something.

Brock stood, picked up Blayze, and gave him a hug and kiss. He whispered something into his ear that made the little boy light up.

When he set him down, Blayze made his way over to me. He threw himself into my arms, and I hugged him.

"Good night, sweet boy," I said against his head, and then kissed him on the cheek.

"Night, Miss Lincoln."

He made his way around the table to the people whom he knew, which was pretty much everyone. It was almost like young Blayze Shaw was working the table, as if to say, *I'm going to be the next bull rider in this family, and you'll be able to say that you knew me when.* The thought made my stomach ache at the idea of him being hurt.

After Stella, Ty Senior, and Blayze had left, other people began to excuse themselves. Charles picked up the tab for dinner and told Brock he had done a good job before reminding him of the autograph session he had tomorrow.

I turned to ask Kaylee what her plans were, but she was lost in conversation with Dirk. It didn't appear to be a serious conversation, but she wore a slight smile.

The idea of Kaylee moving here still made me so happy. I knew if she were to stay in Atlanta, we would both feel like two lost souls. She was fitting in so well with Brock's family and friends.

Ty joined in their conversation, and I had to chuckle when I realized they were arguing about which was the best Disney movie. Only Kaylee could get two rough-and-tumble cowboys to talk about Disney movies.

Laughing, I turned my attention away from them. It was then that the blonde who had been staring at Brock stood. She approached Ty and started talking to him as Dirk also stood and announced he was turning in for the night. And Ty was quick to follow, with Kaylee doing the same. The blonde disappeared from the table, and, for some reason, I breathed a sigh of relief, and I had no idea why.

Brock stood next, but not before leaning down to say into my ear, "Let's go . . . now."

I nearly knocked my chair over from standing so quickly.

Lifting his brow, Brock smirked. "In a hurry?"

With a polite smile, I replied, "Slightly."

"Thank you, Charles, for dinner. I'll see you in the morning," Brock said with a tip of his hat to the older gentleman.

"Yes, see you then, Shaw."

Brock slipped his hand in mine and led me toward the exit. The blonde from earlier was standing outside, down a ways from us, waiting for her car to be brought up.

"Who is that?" I asked, motioning to her.

Brock looked her way and frowned slightly. "No one important."

Okay then.

"She was staring at you almost through all of dinner. Do you know her well?"

I had no clue why I couldn't let the subject go. It was clear that Brock didn't want to talk about her.

"Yes."

That piqued my interest, and I found myself needing to know if he'd had a relationship with her. But "Oh" was all I replied.

Brock turned me to face him. His hands came up and framed my face. "Not like that. She was Kaci's best friend and hooked up with Ty off and on in high school; that's all. She works for Charles now as his personal assistant."

I tried not to let the relief show on my face, but I smiled, which earned me one in return from Brock.

"Were you jealous, Miss Pratt?"

"No."

His lips brushed over mine as he whispered, "Liar."

I wanted to get lost in the kiss but remembered we were in public, and I needed to tamp down the urgency of wanting this man's hands all over me.

When I broke the connection, I took a step back and caught the dirty look being shot my way from the woman who had been Kaci's best friend. Now, I somewhat understood the evil eye she'd been sending my way. It only made me want to ask Brock more questions about Kaci, but I wasn't about to ruin the way I was feeling tonight. Or the way Brock was feeling. I needed to let it go and move past what was clearly me being insecure.

It wasn't like me to act this way. Maybe it was all the emotions I had been feeling today. Excitement, fear, happiness, desire. Lord, it was all swimming around inside me, having a party.

When the Uber pulled up, Brock nearly dragged me to the car. In the back seat, his thumb moved lazily over my hand. Each sweep sent tingles through my body that ended up settling right between my legs. Every now and then, we would exchange glances, both of us knowing how much we wanted each other.

When the driver pulled up to the hotel, Brock gently guided me out of the car, causing me to laugh. As we walked through the lobby, a few fans stopped Brock for a photo or for him to sign something. I stood patiently off to the side, a grin on my face as I watched the interactions.

My eyes drifted to the bar. Ty was sitting there with another guy on his left. A woman approached both men, said something to them, and then walked off. I figured they had excused her—until I saw Ty get up, throw money onto the bar, then turn and head in the direction the woman had gone. They met up at the elevator, and both got on.

My heart dropped some. I wasn't sure why. Maybe it was because I knew Kaylee actually liked Ty, or maybe it was because my hope that he liked *her* had just been thrown out the window.

"Ready to go?" Brock asked me, pulling me from my thoughts.

"Yes!" I said, a little too eager.

The ride up in the elevator was heated. We stood next to each other, but another couple was with us, so we had to behave. Even walking down the hall to Brock's room seemed to take forever.

The key card slid in. The door opened. We both walked in.

Then, Brock was all over me.

He pushed me against the door as his mouth came crashing down on mine. Our hands were everywhere on each other in a flurry of touches. Mine were desperately trying to untuck his shirt, unbutton it, and push it off his shoulders. His hands lifted my shirt over my head and cupped my breasts, and he moaned when my nipples poked against my bra.

Brock kicked off his boots, making me do the same. I hadn't really wanted our first time together to be rushed. But there was no denying the passion between us.

My shaking hands undid the belt buckle, and I silently wondered if I'd have the guts to push my hand into his jeans. Biting on my lip, I did just that. I found his very impressive, hard length ready for me. Wrapping my hand around it, I groaned, and he did the same. His hips involuntarily pushed into my hand.

Brock jerked my hand away from him and panted sharply. "If you keep touching me like that, I'm going to come before we even get to the good stuff."

The hammering of my heart echoed in my ears, and I watched as Brock dropped to his knees and took off my jeans and panties. His blue eyes lifted, and he smiled.

"Please tell me you're okay with me tasting you now?"

Gasping for air, I asked, "Taste me?"

Lord Almighty. I knew what he was asking, but my head couldn't wrap around the idea of *his* head being buried between my legs, doing incredible things that I knew he was capable of with that tongue of his. I wouldn't last five seconds.

Brock stood. His eyes hooded over with a lusty haze. "Has a guy ever gone down on you?"

I snapped out of my fantasy and nodded. "Yes. One guy, and he wasn't a fan, so it wasn't very often."

Brock grinned from ear to ear before scooping me up in his arms and carrying me over to the bed. He laid me on the bed and told me to crawl back. I watched as he pushed his jeans down, and then his boxer briefs. I tried to remember how to breathe as I got my first real look at him completely naked. My eyes traveled down his perfectly toned body and landed on his dick.

I am going to be so sore.

It was rude to stare, but I had to. It was big and thick. The veins seemed to pulse as he stood there. When he wrapped his hand around himself and slowly started to pump, my breathing picked up, and I felt a flood of moisture between my legs.

Brock crawled onto the bed and spread my legs wide. Any other man, and I would have been embarrassed. But this man . . . this man brought out a side of me that wanted to be a little dirty. I wanted things I never imagined I would want.

With Brock, I needed it all.

Then, he did what I'd almost been about to beg him for. He kissed me on the small bundle of nerves that pulsed with need.

"Oh God," I whimpered, the feeling of ecstasy building so fast that it left me dizzy and breathless. His mouth was on my clit, my lips, my inner thigh, then back to my clit again. When I felt him spread me apart with his fingers, I lifted my hips, silently begging for more.

"You're so fucking perfect, Lincoln."

I gasped for air as I felt his tongue move slowly over me, then flick my clit.

"Jesus!" I cried out. My hands fisted in his hair as my body took over.

When I felt his tongue moving soft over my clit, I let out a low moan. The feel of his fingers slipping in and out of me as he sucked harder on my sensitive nub had me arching my back off the bed and calling out his name.

My orgasm ripped through my body in a rush so blinding, I swore I saw the sun burst into the room. I let it consume me completely, and

I felt my body tremble even as I was coming down from my euphoria. I'd never in my life experienced such a rush of ecstasy.

And holy hell's bells. This man knew what to do with his tongue and fingers.

I could feel Brock kissing up my body. He removed my bra, and I still felt like I was half in a dream. He stopped at each nipple, sucking gently. I thought I could possibly come again just from that. Then his mouth hovered over mine.

"Can I kiss you?"

I focused on the most beautiful blue eyes ever. Everything was a fog, except for one thing.

Brock.

Everything about him was clear. My feelings for him. How much I wanted him inside me. How desperately I wanted his mouth on mine, regardless of where it had just been.

"Yes," I breathed out in a heavy voice.

He pressed his mouth to mine, prompting me to open to him. The salty taste of my own body hit my tongue, causing me to moan. Brock did as well, his fingers slipping inside me once again. He quickly found the spot that began to build my next orgasm. One press of his thumb on my clit, and another round of pleasure was gifted to me. Brock stopped kissing me as my body shook and trembled with my orgasm.

"God, I'm already addicted to watching you come," Brock whispered.

I opened my eyes and smiled.

Then, I heard foil ripping.

"I wanted to go slow our first time, baby, but I'm going to die if I don't get inside you."

I watched him roll the condom onto his length. My lower stomach ached with desire and anticipation.

Brock moved over me, resting his weight on his elbows as he held on to my head. Our eyes locked, and time stood still. It was just me and him in this moment. I pulled in a deep breath and blew it out, Brock's name flowing with it.

He closed his eyes and slowly pushed inside me.

I wrapped my legs around him, guiding him into me. I felt my body stretch to accommodate his size, and I gasped a couple of times, making him still. The immediate connection I felt sent a rush of heat through my body. This felt beyond amazing. It felt so damn good . . . better than I had ever experienced.

"More," I whispered as I nudged him with my legs. When he was completely buried inside me, he leaned his forehead against mine. I knew he felt the connection too.

"I'm so glad you moved to Montana, Lincoln. You've brought me back to life."

His words hit me so hard in the chest, I felt my emotions about to tumble out. I wanted to tell him exactly how I felt. That he was the man I hadn't even known I was waiting for. Longing for. That he would now forever hold a piece of my heart with him.

That heart quickened as I looked at him.

Brock didn't move. He simply kept himself inside me, his eyes still closed, and a million emotions crossed his face. I wanted to know what he was thinking. Feeling.

I placed my hand on his cheek and whispered, "Brock?"

When he snapped those baby blues open, our gazes locked again. He pulled out, a pained expression on his face, confusion in his eyes.

When he pushed back in, he mumbled, "I don't deserve something so beautiful as you. As this."

My fingers sliced into his hair, pulling his mouth to mine. I kissed him with everything I had. I needed him to know what he meant to me. That he *did* deserve me.

Then he moved. The rhythm was slow at first. It didn't take me long to find my own pace that matched his. I pulled him deeper into my body, and we both let out a moan of pleasure. It was beautiful. The mad dash to be together had slowed to a romantic pace that had my heart feeling like it would explode at any moment. The closeness I felt to this man was mind boggling.

Brock pressed his mouth to mine as he moved faster. His control slowly starting to slip.

When he pulled back and our eyes locked, I knew he felt what I was feeling. That this was beyond amazing.

I panted, "More."

His sky-blue eyes quickly turned to a deeper, darker shade, and the corners of his mouth rose into the sexiest grin I'd ever seen.

"I've been waiting for you to tell me that," he replied.

Lifting to his knees, he grabbed on to my hips and gave me exactly what I wanted.

Harder and faster.

Brock's name fell from my lips as he brought out another orgasm. I came so hard, I wasn't even sure what I was crying out. His name, maybe? How good it felt? God, it felt beyond good. Lord Almighty, the man could pull out the pleasure in me like he'd been doing it for years. Like he already knew how to make my body react to him in every single way.

He slowed again as he took my hands and laced our fingers together; then he pushed them over my head. The weight of his body on mine was amazing. I'd never had a man look at me with such an intensity in his eyes like Brock was. He was watching everything I did. Listening to every noise I made when he moved inside me. He was learning what pleased me.

"Brock, I'm—"

Before I could tell him I was going to come, yet again, he pressed his mouth to mine.

There was no turning back now. I had given Brock Shaw a piece of my heart that would forever remain his. It felt like this was my first time. My first love. My soul mate.

I squeezed my eyes shut, forcing my tears to stay back as we came together.

I would never forget this moment for the rest of my life, and I knew that no man would ever make me feel like this again. I knew I'd never want anyone other than Brock.

Chapter Twenty

Brock

This feeling was unlike anything I had ever experienced before in my life. I was making love to Lincoln. The walls I had so carefully built around my heart fell piece by piece as I moved inside her, slowly, memorizing every single thing she seemed to like.

I didn't make love to women. I fucked them.

This, though . . . fuck, this was so different. I never wanted this moment to end.

The movement of her hips began to match mine. The slow, steady pace of our lovemaking wasn't going to last much longer.

Then, she opened her eyes, and I saw it. At first, it scared the hell out of me.

Lincoln Pratt was giving me a piece of herself. And, being the greedy asshole I was, I was going to take it.

All of it.

"More," she begged, squeezing my hands.

"I've been waiting for you to tell me that," I said.

I gave her what she asked for.

"Yes," she whispered. "Oh, Brock, yes!"

My name on her lips nearly drove me to slow back down, but I wanted her to come again. When she did, I got lost watching her fall to pieces. It was the sexiest thing I'd ever seen. I wanted to see that look on her face every single day.

"Brock," she whispered, her fingers moving softly up my chest as our eyes met once again.

She was stunning. The most beautiful woman I had ever seen.

I laced her hands in mine and slowed things down. Our bodies moved together flawlessly. As one. My heart sped up, and I tried not to compare making love to Lincoln with making love to Kaci.

With Kaci, I had never felt this connection, this closeness. Sex was good with her, but it was more like fucking. We had fun, then it was over. She didn't look deeply into my eyes, or run her fingers gently over my skin. With Lincoln, it felt so different. Like she was a part of my very soul. I felt like I could stay inside her for the rest of my life.

Her body tightened around my cock, and I held my breath.

"Brock, I'm—"

Her words were stopped when I crushed my mouth to hers. Both of us moaned as we came at the same time. Her fingers in my hair, grabbing and pulling me closer to her.

It was the best moment of my life. A moment I never wanted to forget for as long as I lived. Being with Lincoln damn near felt like my first time again, yet so much better.

I pulled out of her slowly, instantly missing her warmth.

A beautiful pink filled her cheeks as we stared at one another.

She giggled, and I loved how it made my stomach jump and my chest squeeze. I smiled as I ran my thumb softly over her cheeks.

Lincoln rubbed her kiss-swollen lips together a few times before she spoke. "That was so amazing, Brock. I don't think I can—nor do I want to—hide how amazing that felt."

I kissed her nose. "It did feel amazing."

"I wish we could stay in this room for days, making love and learning everything about each other."

Laughing, I gently rubbed the tip of my nose down her neck, causing her to let out a contented sigh. "Me too, sweetheart. Me too. Will you take a shower with me?" I asked.

Nodding, she replied, "Yes."

When I stood, I pulled the condom off and wrapped it in a Kleenex before tossing it in the trash. I ran the water for the shower and let Lincoln get in first. It was a stand-up shower, big enough for the both of us. I was silently thanking God for that one.

I poured the body soap into my hands and started to run them over Lincoln's body. The need to be with her again was growing stronger, and I could see it in her eyes as well.

She whispered my name so softly as I washed her breasts, it nearly brought me to my knees.

I wanted to make love to her again but knew fucking her against the shower wall would make her even sorer, so I pushed the thought right out of my head.

Turning her body to face mine, I shook my head as she gazed up at me with those stunning green eyes of hers.

"Tell me what you're thinking, Brock."

I swallowed hard. "That I don't deserve you. That if you knew the truth about Kaci, you would hate me."

Tears filled her eyes and she shook her head. "I could never hate you. Ever. Whenever you're ready to tell me, I promise I won't think any less of you."

My mouth pressed to hers, and we kissed until we both needed air.

Reaching behind her, I turned off the shower and stepped out.

I wrapped a towel around my waist and then dried Lincoln. She seemed to be in heaven, and I loved that I was the one making her feel that way.

After drying myself, I picked her up and carried her to the bed. I gently laid her down, dropped the towel, and slipped under the covers with her, pulling her flush against my body.

I wasn't sure how long we lay there before she finally talked.

"Penny for your thoughts."

I closed my eyes. I'd been thinking that she was the first woman I'd held in bed since Kaci. And the guilt eating away at me was because I *loved* holding Lincoln. I loved seeing her smile. Hearing her laugh. It felt like I was betraying what I'd shared with Kaci, because this connection I felt with Lincoln was so much more intense.

I'd never once felt that way when I'd slept with another woman. But when I'd made love to Lincoln earlier, it had felt so real. So intimate. Unlike anything I had experienced before in my life, and that confused me.

Why had I not felt that with Kaci?

"That I love holding you like this."

It wasn't a lie. I had been thinking that.

She nestled into me more. "I do too."

I listened to her breathing grow steady. Then I let the reality of it all sink in.

Can I really do this? Let myself dare to dream that I can be happy with a woman like Lincoln? Even after how miserable I made Kaci? How I stole her happiness because I was a selfish bastard? Am I really going to be given a second chance?

I rolled onto my back and stared up at the ceiling.

Something had happened tonight between me and Lincoln. Hell, something had happened the first time our eyes ever met.

The question was, Could I let her in completely?

Could I let myself fall in love again?

Ty hit my back. "You here, buddy?"

I nodded as I watched Stetson James get bucked off at five seconds. He was the reigning PBR World Champion, and he'd had a string of bad luck this year. He was currently ranked tenth in the world standings.

"Ouch. Damn, that had to hurt," Dirk said from the other side of me.

Not saying a word, I tried not to think about this morning. Waking up with Lincoln's head on my chest. Rolling her over and making love to her again. I'd almost forgotten to put on a condom, but luckily, Lincoln had still had her wits about her. I'd never forgotten one before. When I was with Lincoln, though, I seemed to be lost in everything.

Ty bumped my arm. "You're a million miles away, Brock."

"I'm not. I'm trying to keep my head clear."

He looked at me, not believing a damn word I'd said. His eyes looked past the chute to where our family sat. Where Lincoln sat.

"What's going on? Did something happen between you two?"

"No. I mean, yes. We slept together last night," I quietly said.

Ty groaned. "Oh hell, Brock. Why?"

I narrowed my eyes at him.

He rolled his. "I know why, but couldn't you have waited until tonight?"

Dirk was helping Jose, one of the top Brazilian riders, with his bull rope. Dirk had already ridden and got thrown two seconds into the ride. He was pissed but refused to hide out in the locker room.

"I wanted to wait, but things got a little hot and heavy last night."

"Did you fuck her this morning?"

Turning, I grabbed on to his shirt. "Do *not* talk about her like that."

Ty held up his hands and looked around. "Jesus, dude, settle the hell down."

Quickly letting him go, I put my helmet on, glancing around to make sure there hadn't been any cameras near us to catch my little temper tantrum.

"Listen, I don't know what's going on in your head, but I have a feeling you're starting to feel guilty for being with Lincoln. Why? I have no damn clue. But believe it or not, you're allowed to find happiness with someone, Brock. What happened with Kaci sucked big-time, and you've punished yourself enough. Lincoln came into your life for a reason, so stop overthinking it."

I turned to look at my brother, my brows pulled in tight, and I was sure he could see my expression, even with my helmet on.

"Yeah, I can be deep when I need to be. Now, get your head out of your ass and think about Tiny Devil. You picked this bull. Now, you fucking ride it."

I nodded and watched as Tiny Devil came into the chute. The moment I saw him, I forgot everything else. This was my happy place. The place where nothing could bother me. The place where I had only one mission.

To win.

Once my rotation was up, I climbed onto Tiny Devil. Ty started pulling on the bull rope, and I rubbed my hand on the rosin. The intro to "Runnin' with the Devil" started as I adjusted my hand and then my position on his back.

"He's gonna roll to the left and then the right," Ty said. "Don't let him get you into the well."

Hitting my hand to make sure I had a good grip, I adjusted once more and said a prayer.

Then I heard Ty shout, "Cover this bull!" It was our way of saying beat the bull at his own game and ride him the entire eight seconds.

I gave the nod.

The gate flew open, and Tiny Devil did exactly what I'd known he would. Bucked so fucking hard I had to dig in to stay on. I adjusted to every move he threw at me. Toward the end of the ride, he spun as fast as he could. Giving a good buck to show he wanted me off his back.

The buzzer went off, and I reached down and got my hand out. When I jumped, Tiny Devil's hoof got me in the back. My breath was instantly knocked out, and I landed hard, stealing what little breath I'd had left. Never mind that the bastard had spun so fast, I was dizzy as well.

Hank, one of the bullfighters, moved over me as I got up on all fours, trying to pull in some air. The medical staff was there in an instant, and Stan, one of the doctors, was right by my side.

"Hey, talk to me, Brock." He saw me trying to catch my breath. "Wind knocked out of you?" he asked.

I somehow managed to nod. He reached up and took my helmet off. It was then I heard my score: 88.5.

My eyes looked up and went straight to where Lincoln was sitting.

She sat next to my mother, a look of concern plastered on her face, but my mother was saying something to her, making Lincoln nod with understanding. When her eyes met mine, she smiled.

She freaking *smiled.*

It felt like my lungs opened up and air flowed right on in. As if the power of her smile had affected me in a way I'd have never thought possible.

I stood, lifted my hand to the cheering crowd, and made my way out of the arena.

Kim, the CBS reporter, was right there, ready to interview me. "Brock, that was an impressive ride. Looks like Tiny Devil got one last shot in as you were getting off."

"Yeah, he knocked the wind out of me some, but I'm all right. He's a good bull. I'm happy with the ride."

"And so you should be. So, there you have it from our still top-of-the-points leader, Brock Shaw. Out to you, Bill."

The camera went off, and Kim reached for my arm. "Off the record, who's the pretty brunette you kissed?"

I grinned and said nothing, making Kim give me a look that said she was disappointed but totally got it.

When it was all said and done, I won Billings and kept my number one ranking. Dirk was in fourth and 470 points behind me.

I grabbed my rigging bag and headed out to meet up with everyone. I caught a glimpse of Dirk talking to one of the buckle bunnies. He signed something for her; then he leaned down and said something into her ear. I rolled my eyes and walked faster. I'd thought Ty was bad. Dirk made Ty look like a schoolboy.

I smiled when I saw Lincoln holding a sleeping Blayze. He'd gotten into the habit this weekend of wanting Lincoln to hold him when he was sleepy. It didn't bother me, but I had to admit, it did give me a thrill to see her holding him.

"You're going to build some serious arm muscles if this keeps up," I said, leaning down and kissing her on the cheek.

"I know!" She chuckled. "The little guy doesn't look heavy, but after a few minutes of holding him, it gets to ya."

Moving like an expert, I took Blayze out of Lincoln's arms.

"We ready to get on the road?" Ty asked as he tossed his bag into the back of his truck.

"You're heading back with us, right?" Lincoln asked.

"I am. I have to leave on Friday for Ohio."

"Ty said you had Vegas the next weekend after that?"

I nodded. "You want to come?"

Lincoln grinned. "I'll have to see how my work schedule is looking. I'm starting a bit earlier than expected. Karen asked me if I could come in tomorrow. If I can make it work, I'd love to be there."

"I need to be there early for a meet-and-greet event for Wrangler. I can fly you out that Friday night and have you home Sunday night."

She glanced down at Blayze. I was wondering if an entire weekend of us being alone was what she was thinking about. "Us, all alone." I waggled my brows, and she blushed. God, I loved how easy it was to make her do that.

"That would work."

"Then it's settled. After Vegas, I've got a couple of months off." We started toward Ty's truck.

"You're not riding in any other events?"

"I'll ride in a few on the lower level, just to keep my score up, but I'd like to give my body a break some too. I feel like I've got a good lead on the guy sitting in the number two spot. I'll have to watch and see what he does and how much he rides."

After I got Blayze in his seat, we all climbed into the truck.

It didn't take me long to pass out. I slept the entire drive back to Hamilton. When I finally woke up, it was because Ty had hit my leg.

"Hey, Sleeping Beauty, you're home."

I rubbed my eyes and saw we were parked in front of my house. Turning, I saw Blayze was out like a light still. Lincoln and Kaylee were gone.

"Where's Lincoln and Kaylee?"

Ty got out of the truck. "I dropped them off at Lincoln's place."

A part of me was disappointed that Lincoln hadn't come home with me, but I knew why. And he was currently crashed in his booster seat.

Ty grabbed Blayze's duffel as well as mine, and the rigging bag. "You did good this weekend, little brother. You're on fire. Keep it up."

"Thanks," I said, giving him a tap on the arm before getting Blayze out of his seat.

As I walked up the steps to my house, an empty feeling came over me, knowing it would be only me and Blayze tonight. I wondered if it was because I hadn't realized how lonely I'd truly been before Lincoln showed up in my life.

"Mom said if you need her to watch Blayze for any reason, just let her know."

"I will," I said, placing my son down on the sofa and covering him up. "You need to leave right away, or you want to grab a beer?"

Ty glanced at his watch. "I can knock back a beer."

After grabbing two beers out of my refrigerator, we headed to the back porch. I kept the door open so I could hear if Blayze got up.

We spent the first few minutes staring out over the mountains before Ty broke the silence. "I gotta say, you sort of shocked me with this whole Lincoln thing."

I laughed. "Yeah, I sort of shocked myself, but it's all good, man."

"You serious about her?"

"I guess as serious as you *can* be after a week, but yeah, I want to date her. Exclusively."

He nodded and took a drink. "You don't think she'll distract ya?"

"She didn't this weekend."

"What about your vow to never fall for another woman again? You ready to put all that shit behind you now?"

"I'm still struggling with a few things, but I really want to see where this goes with us. I invited her to come to Vegas and spend the weekend with me there."

Ty let out a gruff laugh. "Well, that's where she differs from Kaci. She actually supports your bull riding. At least, right now she does. We've both seen women do a one-eighty with that in this business."

I pulled in a long drink of beer and sat there for a few minutes before I responded. "I've been pretty up front with her about what I do. She's not going in with blind eyes."

Ty sighed. "Kaci didn't either."

I nodded, knowing he was right. Kaci had always supported me and Dirk and knew we both loved bull riding. When we got married, though, that all changed. *She* had changed. Hell, maybe we both had changed.

Ty's voice made me jump slightly. "I *will* tell you something about Lincoln Pratt. She's different from other women. I figured that out when I was doing the real estate deal with her. She's set in her ways. When she wants something, it appears she goes for it, and she's not afraid to take on something . . . broken."

My head snapped over to him. "You think I'm broken?"

"I think you're as fucked up as I am—different reasons, but still a little fucked up."

I sighed and raised my beer to his. "Isn't that the truth."

He grinned before taking a drink.

We sat silent again before Ty turned to me. "Do you think two guys like us are really ever going to be able to keep a woman happy?"

Shrugging, I finished off my beer and answered him honestly. "I have no damn clue, but it sure will be fun trying to."

He scoffed. "You have fun trying. There are plenty of women around, so no need to have to worry about pleasing just one."

Staring at my brother, I wanted to ask him what he was so damn afraid of, but I let it go. After all, I had my own fears that were trying to bubble up to the surface.

Chapter Twenty-One

Lincoln

Karen showed me all around the office, including where the coffee was stored and how to make the type of coffee she liked. And, if I wanted something else, I could feel free to bring in another pot.

"The most important thing I need to show you is this. Where the extra M&M'S are when the candy bowl gets too low. I have to have them to survive."

I giggled. "Got it."

Making a mental note to buy more M&M'S, I headed to my office.

I smiled gleefully at my mountain view. Karen explained she had a new client coming in who wanted to remodel her living room, kitchen, and dining area, and it would be the first client I was going to handle. Since I had owned my own business back in Atlanta, she was giving me full rein. I was over the moon.

Then she delivered even better news. "The office is closed on Fridays, and as you found out today, we come in later on Mondays."

I would be able to go to Vegas early now and spend the whole day with Brock on Friday. Maybe I would surprise him and fly in on Thursday night.

A knock at my door had me glancing up to see a young woman standing there. She was dressed entirely in blue. And when I say blue, I mean at least three different shades of blue, from her shoes straight up to the large-brim hat she wore.

"Lincoln Pratt?" she asked, stepping into the office when I motioned for her to come in.

"Yes! Julia Kent?" I asked, rounding my desk.

"That's me." Her gaze ran over me with interest as she sat in the chair in front of my desk.

As I made my way back around to my chair, I took up a notepad and pen and smiled. "Karen tells me you want to remodel your entire downstairs."

Pursing her lips, she tilted her head to examine me. "I'm sorry, but are you even old enough to know what you're doing?"

I tried not to laugh, considering this woman looked to be the same age as me. "Yes. I have a degree in interior design and owned my own company back in Atlanta for a few years before moving to Montana."

"What brought you here?"

Okay, this was going to be a personal interview, it appeared. "Well, I was looking for a change, cooler weather, distance from my parents," I added with a lighthearted laugh.

"Hmm."

That was her only reply.

Taking in a breath, I said, "Okay, well, should we talk about your redesign? Karen said you have a theme you want to go with."

"Are you dating Brock Shaw?"

I nearly choked on my own tongue. "Excuse me?"

Clearing her throat, Miss Kent repeated her question. "Are you . . . dating . . . Brock Shaw?"

I leaned back in my chair. "I'm not sure what my personal life has to do with redesigning your home, Miss Kent."

"It doesn't, Miss Pratt. It's purely a nosy-ass question on my part."

A tight smile formed on my mouth. "I see. Well, to answer your question, yes, I am."

A huge smile erupted on her face as she leaned in. "Shut! Up!"

Okay, there was her age coming out.

"Why is that so shocking?"

She waved her hand about. "Okay, where do I *even* begin? First off, his wife died, and he totally blamed himself for her death. The man has been filled with guilt ever since."

Kaylee should have sought out *this* girl for the town gossip.

"Don't even get me started on his brother Ty. He's hot, and he knows it. I'm pretty sure he's slept with most of the women in Hamilton. Word has it, though, he has someone in Billings, I think. He's cooled it down on the one-night stands the last few weeks. As a matter of fact, there have been no reports of any hookups."

"Reports?" I asked.

"Oh yeah, Ty often gives the rumor mill a run for its money."

Oh yeah, I need to hook Kaylee up with Miss Kent.

"Now, if you're interested, a few of the local single guys always go to the Blue Moose on Wednesday nights. But then, you did say you were dating Brock, so you might *not* be interested."

She winked, and I attempted to get her back on track with our conversation.

"So, your design—"

"You'll probably want to avoid Lucy Mae. She's nothing but trouble, and has a thing for Brock that she hasn't been able to let go of since he dumped her for Kaci."

My eyes widened. "Avoid her?"

I had no idea why I asked and egged her on to keep talking.

"Yes! She'll fill your head with tales of Brock and his whoring ways. That's what she did with Kaci."

Frowning, I wanted to ask why, but I was not about to start gossiping about Brock's deceased wife and his ex-girlfriend.

"So, a theme?" I asked, again trying to get the conversation back on her project.

"And whatever you do, don't eat at the Rusty Pig."

I pressed my lips together in an attempt not to giggle. This woman was hell bent on getting me caught up on all of the town's gossip.

"And why would that be?" I asked. A glutton for punishment.

Julia placed her hand over her mouth and pretended to gasp. "I hope you haven't eaten there already! He barely passes the health inspections, and I'm almost positive he uses cat for his meat."

"I'm sorry . . . what did you just say?" I asked, leaning in closer. "Did you say cat?"

She nodded. "It hasn't been confirmed yet."

Blinking a few times, I slowly shook my head and took in a deep breath. No wonder Karen had given me this client. Was this some sort of test? Handle the town gossip and you can handle anything?

"So, back to your remodel. Did you have any color scheme you wanted to keep with?"

She nodded. "Blue."

Thank the Lord, we were moving on.

"You know Dirk, Brock's best friend?"

I let out a frustrated sigh. "Yes. I know Dirk."

Leaning in closer, she gave me a saucy grin. "He's *really* good in bed—or so I've heard." She winked. "Okay, so maybe we did hook up once or twice. The man has a cock like no other."

My jaw dropped. Then my eyes went to her wedding ring, and she laughed.

"It was before I got married. Now, your best friend, is she moving here as well?"

My head was spinning. How did this woman switch topics so quickly?

"Kaylee is not a subject open for discussion."

She looked apologetic. "Lord, I'm sorry. You're new in town *and* not ready for the ins and outs of Hamilton, probably," she said with a lighthearted laugh.

I forced a smile and decided enough was enough. "My goodness, Mrs. Kent, we should really talk about your design theme."

She sat up straighter and cleared her throat. With a big toothy grin, she said, "Right. I want to go with an ocean theme. Blue everywhere and fish decorations galore!"

I almost laughed, but I realized quickly that she was serious. Especially when she pulled out the three-ring binder with pages of ideas she'd taken from Pinterest plastered inside.

I looked from the binder to Julia and back to the binder.

Oh, hell, this is not the first job I'm taking on in Hamilton . . . is it?

Walking into my barn, I took a deep breath. It was Tuesday night, and I hadn't seen Brock since Sunday. I wasn't the type of girlfriend who was clingy, and truth be told, I had needed the distance between us to wrap my head around these intense feelings I was having toward both Brock and Blayze. And I'd just gotten off the phone with Julia. I needed to get my mind out of the ocean and back to real life. I'd also learned from Karen that Julia was the town go-to person when you needed to find out anything. Of course, she'd informed me a little too late. I'd figured that out on my own.

I'd passed that information along to Kaylee. She'd rubbed her hands together, and an evil grin had spread over her face. "I think I'll go introduce myself to Mrs. Julia Kent."

"Be warned," I'd advised her last night, "she probably already knows you and Ty danced and left the bar together a couple weeks back."

Walking up to Thunder, I smiled. "Hey, handsome. How was your day?"

"Long."

I spun around at the sound of Brock's voice. My mouth instantly went dry when I saw him. Cowboy boots. Tight jeans. White T-shirt. White cowboy hat.

He looked delicious.

"Hey," I said, realizing how happy I was to see him.

"Hey back at ya."

He moved toward me in easy strides, making my insides quiver with anticipation. All thoughts of whatever else I had been thinking about vanished. The only thing I could think about was Brock kissing me. Touching me. Taking me right here, in the barn. I was turned on simply from the sight of him.

"Lincoln?" he softly whispered as he stopped in front of me. "You're looking at me like you want me."

With a barely there nod, I replied, "I do."

He pushed his fingers into my hair. "I'm sorry I didn't get to see you yesterday. It was a crazy day on the ranch. Dad takes full advantage when he's got all three of his boys home."

"It's okay. I was exhausted from work. I have a client who wants an ocean theme in her living room, dining area, and kitchen."

He grinned. "Julia Kent?"

I gasped. "How did you know?"

"She's always been obsessed with the ocean. I bet she was dressed all in blue too."

My eyes widened in shock. "Yes! I thought she had done that for inspiration!"

Brock laughed and wrapped his arm around my back, pulling me closer. "She's also a big gossip."

With a small grin, I replied, "Yes, I found that out quickly."

Then, his mouth was on mine. And I was lost. There wasn't anything I wouldn't do to have this man kiss me.

His hands moved down my sides, gripping my ass and lifting me up like it was nothing for him. My legs wrapped around him, his hard length pressing against me.

"Lincoln," he gasped when our mouths pulled apart.

He winced when I squeezed my legs, trying to feel more of him.

"Are you hurt?" I asked.

With a smile, he rubbed his nose over mine. "Cracked rib from my ride last weekend."

"What?" I nearly shouted. "Brock, put me down!"

He laughed. "Hell no. I want you."

"Then take me into the house, and we can be careful."

Something moved over his face. The idea of taking me into the house was what had caused it.

Is it because he shared that house with Kaci? I am so stupid. Of course that's what it is.

"I want you right here, in the barn."

My stomach burned with desire. "Brock." It was all I could manage to get out, and even then, it was with a heavy breath.

Before I knew what was happening, he had me back on the ground, my right boot had come off, and my pants and panties were pulled down and off that leg. He didn't even take the time to remove everything. My hands shook as I undid the button and zipper on his jeans. The sound of my heart hammering in my chest filled my ears. What in the world did this man do to me? I was willing to have sex right here in my own barn, knowing anyone could walk in at any moment. The idea of it thrilled me.

Brock pulled out his wallet and took out a condom, quickly ripping it open and slipping it on.

I wanted him. Just like this. Intense and passionate. Something I had never experienced until I'd met this man.

His fingers pushed inside me, and a deep growl came from the back of his throat. "You're so wet."

"Yes," I panted. "You make me that way, just by being near you."

His eyes filled with lust, and he picked me up again. I carefully wrapped myself around him as he lowered me onto him. He filled me so full I had to hold my breath to adjust to the size of him. Not to mention I was still a bit sore from last weekend.

"You feel like heaven."

He walked us back and pressed me against the wall. He moved slowly at first, then went faster. Harder.

I cried out, and he stilled. "Shit, are you okay?"

I nodded. "Yes. Do it again."

He smiled, and I felt my heart open up more to him.

"Tell me what you want from me, sweetheart."

Our eyes met. I knew what I wanted—but did I have the guts to tell him? "I want . . ."

He slowly pulled out, barely keeping himself inside me. When he arched a brow, I realized he wasn't going to move until I said it.

"I want you to not be gentle. I want it harder. Faster."

Those beautiful blue eyes turned dark, and he did just what I'd asked of him. It didn't take me long to come. I cried out his name, feeling him grow bigger. He buried his face in my neck, pushed in deeper, and trembled as he cried out my name.

He stayed inside me as he walked us back and kicked open the door to the tack room in the barn. A bed was in there, and up until that point, I hadn't paid much attention to it. It wasn't uncommon for small beds to be found in tack rooms of stables or up in barns. Especially for when a mare was foaling. For a moment, I was surprised he knew it was there, and then I remembered that this used to be his barn.

He laid me on the bed and then pulled the condom off. His eyes stayed glued to mine as he lay on top of me. His still-semihard dick rubbed over my sensitive bundle of nerves, and I moaned in delight.

"Oh God, Brock."

If he was able to make me come this way, I knew he would ruin me for all other men.

"I want to make love to you, but I don't have another condom."

I opened my eyes. My green staring into his blue. It felt like I'd known him forever instead of the short amount of time we had *actually* known each other.

Am I ready to open myself up completely?

I still had unanswered questions, but at the moment, I couldn't remember a single one. "I'm on the pill."

He stilled. Then, he moved farther down, the tip of his head pressing at my entrance. I lifted, silently begging him to push inside me, stunned he was hard again so soon.

"Yes," I whispered.

Then—something happened.

Brock looked around the tack room and stilled. He pulled away slightly. His brows constricted, and a look of anguish grew on his face.

"What's wrong?" I asked.

It hit me then that he hadn't been offering to have sex with no condom.

Brock quickly got off me, pulled up his jeans, and took a few steps back, still staring at me, but now with a look that said he was confused. Maybe even angry . . . but not with me, more at himself.

I was still half-dressed, and for some reason, I suddenly felt dirty. Like I had offered my body to a man who didn't want it.

"I'm sorry. I wasn't thinking and was caught up in the moment."

When I stood, I reached for him to help steady me as I got dressed, but Brock jerked away. Like my touch was something he couldn't stand the thought of.

I froze. My eyes instantly filled with tears. He'd told me Kaci had thought a baby would bring them closer. Maybe he thought that had been her way of getting him off the PBR tour.

My stomach sank as dread coursed through my veins. What if he thought I was doing the same thing?

"Brock."

I couldn't even think of any words to say. The way he was looking at me, it left me speechless.

Finally, he spoke, and the words that came out of his mouth nearly dropped me to my knees.

"I can't do this."

Turning, he pushed open the door and left.

He left me alone in the room and wondering what in the hell had happened.

Chapter Twenty-Two

Brock

Two weeks had passed since that day in the barn. I'd ridden in Ohio and placed second, and then won the Last Cowboy Standing in Vegas. Lincoln never came to Vegas. Probably because she hadn't heard from me since the day I'd walked out of the barn and left her there.

Alone.

No explanation as to why I'd freaked and left.

Hell, I hadn't even been back home. Mama was riding me hard for not seeing Blayze. Ty hadn't talked to me in three days, and I'd gotten six text messages from Kaylee, describing in detail what she was going to do to me when I got back to Hamilton. The last one might have scared me a bit.

"Hi, how's it going?"

I glanced up from my beer to see Jenny Webster standing there. She was Lloyd's daughter, and Lloyd was one of my sponsors. "Hi, Jenny."

"You look like you need a friend. Or maybe a warm body?"

I knew it had been a mistake sleeping with her a couple of years back. I'd had no idea who she was, and my first thought had been that she was just a buckle bunny. Until I fucked her and she told me her name afterward.

"I'd rather be alone."

Her hand landed on my arm. "The girlfriend didn't last long? What happened? She tell you to stop riding bulls?"

I pulled away from her and took a long drink of my beer before setting it down and turning. "Jenny, you're barking up the wrong tree. I'm not interested."

She frowned. "She doesn't have to know."

Rolling my eyes, I grabbed my wallet and pulled out a twenty. Tossing it onto the bar, I tipped my hat at her. "Have a good evening, Jenny."

Before she could say anything else, I walked out of the bar and into the casino. I had to stay an extra day in Vegas for an event Wrangler was putting on. My phone buzzed in my pocket, and I pulled it out. It was a text from Dirk.

Dirk: Where are you, Brock? I'm worried about you, dude.

Dirk had been trying to babysit me all damn weekend. I'd told him about what had happened in the barn, and how I'd freaked out and left after I'd told Lincoln I couldn't do it.

To say he was disappointed in me was an understatement. To his credit, though, he never actually said anything; he simply let me talk it out.

I typed back my reply—In the casino. I'm fine—and shoved the phone into my back pocket.

Making my way outside, I dragged in a couple of deep breaths and then reached for my phone again. I pulled up Lincoln's name and stared at it.

How in the hell can I tell her the idea of making love to her without a condom freaked me the fuck out? It had been so soon, and for her to suggest it had completely thrown me for a loop.

It was in that very room in the barn where Kaci and I had decided to try for a baby. I had made love to my wife on that very bed in an attempt to save my marriage.

When I had glanced around and realized what in the hell I was about to do, it almost felt like déjà vu. Not that Lincoln was trying to get pregnant; I knew that. In my mind, though, nothing had made sense at the time.

Making love to Lincoln without a condom would have meant things were different between us. The only woman I'd ever had sex with without a condom was Kaci. And, even then, it had been in an attempt to save our marriage.

Guilt ripped through my body. I had wanted to make love to Lincoln in that barn. In that room, without a condom. When Lincoln said she was on the pill, I realized in that very moment that I wanted her more than I had ever wanted my own wife.

I felt something so much stronger for Lincoln than I had for Kaci. But how could I make love to Lincoln in a place I'd had sex with my wife as well?

When I recognized the one emotion that had surfaced in that tack room, I panicked. I wasn't ready to let love in yet. And realizing I *wanted* to make love to Lincoln with no barrier between . . . I'd wanted to feel what she felt like more than I'd wanted my next breath.

"Kaci, I'm so sorry."

Pushing my hand through my hair, I closed my eyes and cussed. Lincoln had laid her heart out for me, and I'd destroyed it. When she'd looked at me with tears in those green eyes and said she was sorry, I'd wanted to tell her that I loved her.

When I'd realized that, I'd had to leave. Needed to get out of that room. The emotions of everything had hit me so hard all at once, I'd felt like I was drowning in them.

I'd let my guilt over falling in love with Lincoln hurt her. I'd not only let Kaci down, but now I'd let Lincoln down as well. When I'd told Lincoln I couldn't do this, I had meant I couldn't betray Kaci. But was I really betraying her by falling in love again?

"Fuck, I've messed everything up."

I owed Lincoln an explanation.

Hitting her number, I took a deep breath.

Her voice mail picked up. "Hey! This is Lincoln Pratt. Sorry I missed you. Leave your message, and I'll call ya back!"

The sound of the tone alerting me to leave a message made me jump.

"Hey. It's me, Brock. I need to talk to you. Explain why I left. I'm, um . . . I'm still in Vegas until tomorrow. Please call me back."

I hit end and then dialed my mother's number.

"Daddy!"

A warmth completely filled me to hear the sound of my son's voice.

"Hey, buddy. What are you doing? Where's Grams?"

"I just finished riding! Grams is talking to Miss Lincoln."

My heart stilled in my chest. "Lincoln is there?"

"Yep. She came by to ask if me and Uncle Ty would look after Thunder, her horse."

I swallowed hard. "Why?"

"I dunno. Something about her going back to Atlanta."

Nearly dropping the phone, I tried to keep my legs from going out from underneath me. "She's going back to Atlanta?"

"Yep. Her and Miss Kaylee."

I scrubbed my hand down my face. "Hey, can you take the phone to Grams? Fast?"

"Okay! Are you coming home tomorrow?"

"Yeah, buddy, I'll be home tomorrow."

I heard him yell out in happiness. "Grams! Grams! Daddy needs to talk to you. Fast!"

Nodding, I said, "That's it, Blayze!"

"Hello?" My mother's voice was tight and held no emotion. That was how she'd spoken to me for the last two weeks, since I'd left for Ohio.

"I need to talk to Lincoln. I tried calling her cell, but it—"

"She left already."

It felt like my heart had plummeted to the bottom of my stomach. "She left?" I repeated.

"Yes. What time does your plane get in tomorrow?"

I couldn't even think. I wanted to ask my mother a million questions. *Is Lincoln coming back? Is she just taking Kaylee back home? Is it a one-way ticket or a round trip?*

"Brock? What time do you get in? I need to let Ty know."

Rubbing the back of my neck, I said, "Ten."

"Okay then, we'll talk after you get home. You have some explaining to do. I *know* I raised better men than this. I don't think I have to tell you how upset I am with you. *Disappointed* is a better word to use."

"Yes, ma'am." It was all I could say. I knew every word she spoke was the truth. "Is Lincoln coming—"

The line went dead. She hadn't even said goodbye. Or to have a safe trip. Nothing.

I felt sick. I instantly ran to the side of the building and threw up.

The moment I stepped out of the airport, I took in lungsful of crisp mountain air. It didn't take me long to find Ty. He was leaning against his truck, a smug look on his face. As I made my way closer, he pushed off and walked over to the front and climbed into the driver's seat. I put my stuff in the back and then made my way into the passenger seat.

"Hey, bro," I said, shutting the door.

Ty looked at me and shook his head. Then he pulled out of the parking spot.

"You want to tell me why you're pissed at me?"

He laughed. "I think I'm the last person you need to worry about. Our mother is on a damn tirade and ready to blame you for the collapse of everything right now."

"Why?"

Ty glanced my way, a look of disbelief on his face. "Are you for real? You left, Brock. You only said goodbye to Blayze, and you took off for two weeks. And I don't know what you did to Lincoln, but she walked around town for a solid week in a daze.

"Kaylee was ready to rip your head off, and since you were nowhere to be found, guess who she came after? Me! That's right. She unleashed on me about how you broke her best friend's heart. How all men were dirty, rotten bastards, and how she wanted nothing to do with this town. So then I got pissed, and yelled back at her, telling her she didn't belong here and needed to take her happy little ass back to Atlanta . . . which was not the right thing to say, because that's exactly what she did." His voice went from angry to sad at the end.

"Why did you tell her to leave?" I asked.

He took off his cowboy hat and dropped it next to us. "I don't know. She made me mad. She's always making me mad, and I have no idea why."

"Maybe it's because you like her and don't want to admit it."

Ty didn't respond at first before he let out a frustrated sigh and spoke again. "Anyway, when Kaylee said she was going back to Atlanta, Lincoln wasn't far behind."

A heavy thickness grew in my chest, and a feeling of sickness hit my stomach. "For good? Is she going back to Atlanta for good?"

He shook his head. "No. Lincoln isn't. I'm not sure about Kaylee, though. Lincoln told Mom she would be back Sunday night."

I breathed out a sigh of relief. The thought of not seeing her for another four days gutted me.

"Warning, though, little brother: I don't think she'll be anxious to talk to you. Her sadness turned to anger. When Tanner took them to the airport last night, he said he asked about you, and Lincoln told him you'd made it perfectly clear you were no longer interested in her, and she informed him that she was going to move on—and had a date on Monday night."

Balling my fists, I gritted my teeth. "What? Who with?"

Ty shrugged. "I don't know, and Tanner didn't ask."

Lincoln has a date? Well, that's just great. I've messed things up more than I thought.

Chapter Twenty-Three

Lincoln

"You sure you're okay?" I asked, closely watching Kaylee as we stood near the security line at the Atlanta airport.

"Yes."

"I'm going to miss you not being in Hamilton with me."

She gave me a warm smile. "I need to get everything settled here, and I promise I'll be back. Except this time, I plan on finding my own place. It's time I started to build a new life. Maybe find someone who wants to help with that." Kaylee waved her hand around in the air and laughed. It didn't reach her eyes. I knew deep down she had been hurt when Ty told her to leave. She hadn't been acting the same since that day.

"Kaylee, he didn't mean it when he told you to go back to Atlanta."

She scoffed. "Who? Ty? Whatever. Okay, I admit I had a crush on him when we got there. He's the opposite of . . ." Her voice trailed off.

A sadness swept over her face, but I didn't get the feeling it was for John. She liked Ty more than she was letting herself believe.

"I don't think Ty Shaw is the type of guy who wants to settle down, and that's okay. I'm not looking for that."

Lifting a brow, I sighed. "You're coming, though? Promise me you're moving to Hamilton. I know you liked it there."

"I did, a lot. That's why I finally decided it was time to come back home, face reality, and handle my stuff. I'll be there soon. I promise, Lincoln. Are you going to be okay? Dirk said that they had the next few months off, and that both he and Brock were back home now."

I chewed on my lip. The idea of seeing Brock made my heart drop. I wasn't sure if that was because I *wanted* to see him or if I didn't want to *risk* seeing him. "The idea of seeing Brock is . . . well, I don't know what it is. I spooked him; I know that. But for him to just leave me like that, to say he couldn't even try . . . I don't know if I can risk falling more for him and having him make me feel like that again."

She gave me a knowing look. "You said he called."

"Yeah, I could hear the sadness in his voice." Tears threatened to spill. "I'm not sure I'm enough for him."

"What do you mean?"

I shook my head, lost in my own confused thoughts. "I don't know if Brock Shaw is willing to let me into his heart."

"He is," Kaylee said with more confidence than I could muster.

"Kaylee, all I mentioned was having sex without a condom," I whispered. "He freaked. He ran so fast from me, it made my head spin."

"As much as I love you, and I'm on your side, Lincoln, y'all hadn't been dating that long. For some guys, that's a huge step in commitment. For women too. Now add in Brock's past and imagine what was going through the guy's head. Not to mention you said he sort of seemed to realize where he was when he looked around the tack room. Maybe the idea of being in *there* was what freaked him out."

I blew out a frustrated breath. "I know; I know. I messed up and shouldn't have suggested it. Especially knowing how gun shy Brock is. At any rate, I've got a date tomorrow night with a really nice guy. I'm not really looking to start dating anyone, but I think I'll still go. Maybe that's what I need to move on."

Her head tilted as she studied me. "Even though you're head over heels for Brock? You might not want to admit it, Lincoln, but you've fallen in love with him."

When I opened my mouth to disagree, nothing came out. Instead, I said, "I'd better go get checked in. I'll see you soon?"

She nodded, pulling me in for a hug, and her voice cracked as she replied, "I'll see you soon."

When I walked out of the Hamilton airport a few hours later, I smiled at the sight before me. Tanner Shaw and Chance Miller, his team roping partner, were both there with signs that had my name scrawled across them.

I shook my head. I'd gotten to know them both pretty well the last two weeks while Brock was MIA. Chance had gotten hurt, so they had taken a few weeks off from the circuit and had been using my corral to practice in.

"How did you know when I was coming back?" I asked the younger Shaw. He looked so much like his older brothers. The only difference was, he had hazel eyes instead of the blazing blue that Ty and Brock had.

"Mom. She told us to get our lazy butts up here to pick you up. Plus, she was worried Brock might try to be here, and she wasn't sure you were ready to see him."

I swallowed hard. "Is he still in town?"

"For now," Tanner answered.

"For now?" I asked, trying not to seem like I really cared.

"He's riding in a rodeo on Friday night."

"A rodeo? Why?" I asked.

Chance laughed. "It's for a benefit. They called him and Dirk up and asked if they wouldn't mind doing it. Help raise money for a little girl in the community who has cancer. With two big names like Dirk and Brock, both in the top five of the PBR, they'll bring in a lot of money."

My chest squeezed at the thought of Dirk and Brock doing that. I knew Brock had mentioned wanting to give his body a rest, and Dirk was ready to be home for a couple of months. "How far away is it—where they're riding?"

Tanner took my small bag and put it in the back seat of his truck, next to Chance, while I slipped into the front seat.

"Ah, hell, not far from us at all, just down the road. Most of Hamilton will be there in support of the little girl," Tanner stated as he started up his truck.

"Y'all aren't riding, are you?"

Chance sighed. "I'm not, but Tanner's got him another heeler, so he'll ride."

"Not much on the line. Not doing it for money. It's mostly just to help the family out. Honestly, it's Brock and Dirk who will be bringing in the money. Mama said Brock made a donation at the bank the other day, but he told them not to say who it had come from."

My heart melted. "That was sweet of him."

"Yeah. I wasn't supposed to tell you, but if I have to watch my brother mope around another day, I might go insane. He's been home only a couple of days, but this is crazy. You guys need to make up."

Chance leaned forward between Tanner and me. "Yeah, he wasn't even this depressed when his wife died."

"Chance!" I shrieked.

"What? He wasn't! He was feeling bad; don't get me wrong. But this is a hell of a lot different. Ain't that right, Tanner?"

Tanner simply shrugged and looked at me.

I sat up straight. "Well, I still have a date tomorrow night, and I don't intend on breaking it, so I'm not at all concerned about what's going on with Brock's issues."

"With who?" Tanner and Chance both asked.

"Nathan Kesler. It's nothing serious. He asked me to dinner to get to know me, since I'm new in town and he works for the city."

Tanner pulled over to the side of the road and slammed on the brakes of his truck. "Nathan? You're going out with Nathan?" He laughed and shook his head. "No way in hell are you going out with Nathan Kesler."

Folding my arms over my chest, I arched a brow. "And why not?"

"Nathan Kesler makes Ty and Dirk look like virgins!"

I rolled my eyes. "I find that hard to believe."

"No, I'm being serious, Lincoln. Listen, I like you a lot, and you're the first girl to pull Brock out of the nightmare he was living in. I want to see you get back together; that's no secret. But I'm not warning you away from Nathan for selfish reasons. He's a douche. He's the city manager, and he's a dick. Seriously, he treats people like shit, and I can't tell you how many secretaries he's banged on his desk and then had to fire because they wanted more."

I stared at him while his words settled. I shook my head in disbelief as I replied, "The Nathan I met in my office was a gentleman who asked me to dinner to get to know me, and that was all. It's nothing serious. I'm not looking for that. It's bad enough I fell for your brother as hard as I did."

Chance laughed. "Did you hear that, Tanner?"

Tanner gave me a wide smile that showcased his dimples and made him the spitting image of his older brothers. "I heard it."

"Heard what?" I asked, glancing back at Chance, and then at Tanner.

Pulling out onto the two-lane highway, Tanner didn't say another word. Both men sat quietly in the truck cab, leaving me alone with my own thoughts and wondering what they'd meant.

The knock on my office door made me glance up. *Shit.* I'd forgotten to lock the office when I got here.

It was Friday, and normally my day off, but I'd needed something to keep my mind off knowing Brock was home. I had somehow, by some small miracle, avoided seeing him the last four days. That didn't mean he wasn't on my mind nearly every moment of the day. Work was the only way I could keep him out of my head. What better way to do that than dig myself in to Julia's underwater remodel?

I gave a polite smile when I saw who had knocked, even though I was surprised to see him.

Nathan and I had gone to dinner on Monday night as planned. He had spent most of the night comparing himself to one Brock Shaw. His house was bigger than Brock's. His bank account impressive for not being a local celebrity, like Brock. Compared his charity work to Brock's.

It felt like the entire dinner was a case he was building for me to like him better than Brock. Julia must have let him know I had been dating him. As short lived as it was.

I'd wanted to set the poor man straight that night. He'd never hold a candle to Brock. Ever.

And, on Wednesday, when he'd slid into my booth and invited himself to have lunch with me, I was pretty sure the waitress had slipped him her number.

Clearly, Nathan and I were not a match—not that I had been looking for anything other than friendship. Even if I had wanted it to be something more, it wouldn't have worked. I knew it the moment he'd picked me up for dinner, and I had wished he was Brock.

"Nathan," I said, standing and smoothing my pencil skirt as I made my way around my desk, "what brings you here?"

"Hello, Lin."

I gritted my teeth. I had corrected Nathan at least a dozen times on my name. "You refuse to call me Lincoln. Why?" The rough edge to my voice was evident. I was knee deep in whales and schools of fish for Julia's kitchen, and I wasn't in the mood for this crap.

"It's just such a boy's name."

My mouth opened slightly in surprise. "Well, I'm not even sure what to say to that, Nathan, other than I'm busy, and I can't chat right now." I spun on my black high heels and started to walk back to my desk.

Nathan reached out for my arm, turning me back to him. He stepped closer, totally invading my space. Just like he had on Monday night, when he'd dropped me off at home and walked me to my door.

Of course, had he seen Tanner, Chance, and Ty all down at my corral, I hardly think he would have moved in and tried for that kiss. I'd quickly shut him down when I raised my hand and said no. I got the feeling that Nathan didn't like being told no. Once the guy had gotten into his BMW and driven off, the group of men had laughed their asses off. "I'd have lost respect for you, Lincoln, had you let him kiss you!" Tanner had shouted.

Now, glancing down to Nathan's grip on my arm, I cleared my throat.

"I'm sorry. I didn't mean to hurt your feelings. I'm kidding. Lincoln is an adorable name."

I forced a smile. This was why I didn't date—and why I'd told Nathan, again, at lunch on Wednesday, that I didn't see this going anywhere past friendship, which I didn't.

A part of me was still hanging on to the hope that Brock would walk through my door any day now. I hadn't returned his call yet, so I guessed the ball was in my court.

"Listen, I wanted to see if you wanted to go to the rodeo with me tonight."

My head jerked back. "Huh?"

He sighed. "Go out with me tonight? Rodeo? Let me show you off on my arm."

Crossing my arms over my chest, I started to talk but noticed Nathan's eyes were on my breasts. "Excuse me—my eyes are up here. I believe I already told you: I'm not interested in dating you."

He gave me a look of pity. "Still holding out hope for that lost cause Shaw, huh?"

Dropping my arms to my sides, I balled my fists. "You don't know a damn thing about Brock. He's ten times the man you are and fifty times more of a gentleman. Now, if you'll please excuse me, *Nate*, I have work to do. I'm pretty sure that young waitress at the café will be getting off work soon, so take her."

Nathan smirked. "Okay, well, don't say I didn't give you a chance."

I rolled my eyes. I swore I had a built-in magnet that attracted douchebags. It must have been broken when Brock had walked into that barn.

When my office door shut, I let out a long groan. This was stupid. I had feelings for Brock, and I knew he had feelings for me. I was being childish by not returning his call.

I quickly walked over to my desk, pulled up his number, and hit it.

"Hello?"

My breath caught in my throat when a woman answered Brock's phone. I pulled it away from my face and looked at it. The name *Brock Shaw* was on my screen.

"I'm . . . I'm sorry. I must have dialed the wrong number."

"No! Lincoln! Wait!"

I froze. *How does she know my name?*

"How do . . . how do you know my name?"

She chuckled. "Brock has you programmed into his phone. I know he's been waiting—well, hoping—you'd call."

Who is this girl?

I couldn't speak for a moment. My thoughts were running a million different ways.

"I'm sorry, but who is this?"

The girl laughed. "I'm so sorry! You're probably freaking out about now. This is Lynn, Dirk's younger sister."

My eyes widened. "I didn't know Dirk *had* a sister."

Another laugh. "Well, I go to boarding school in Billings, and I'm home for the summer. I was helping the boys with their gear for tonight's rodeo. Brock is with one of the stock contractors and the bulls. He gave me his phone, and boy howdy, will he be glad to know you called! Are you coming to the rodeo tonight?"

I paused, letting it soak in that my first thought on who the girl on the phone was had been so wrong. "Um, yes. I plan on going."

"Oh, yay!" I could hear her clap, her voice muffled from probably tucking the phone against her chin. "I can't wait to tell him! Be sure to sit with his mama and daddy."

"Um, okay." I *had* planned on sitting with them, since they were the only people in town I really knew.

"I can't wait to meet you, Lincoln!"

A smile moved over my face. It was the first real smile I'd had in the last three weeks. "I can't wait to meet *you*, Lynn."

The phone went dead, and I sat down in my chair. I was suddenly scared to death to face Brock tonight . . . but also excited at the possibility of being near him.

Chapter Twenty-Four

Lincoln

I'd called Stella and arranged to ride to the rodeo with her and Blayze. To say he was excited to see me was an understatement. I could hear him running around the house, singing, when I was speaking to Stella on the phone. A sting of guilt ripped through me, because I'd distanced myself from Blayze and hadn't meant to. Well, I had intended to the week when Brock had come back into town, but I'd figured Blayze would be happy to see his dad after not seeing him for two weeks.

Ty Senior was with Brock, and Ty was driving with Tanner and Chance.

When we got to the rodeo, Ty took Blayze to go see all the horses and bulls and to wish Brock good luck. For a moment, I'd almost asked to go too. I enjoyed the excitement of being behind the scenes. The only difference at the rodeo was, there were no TV cameras anywhere.

When I scanned the area, I saw Lucy Mae. She was dressed in jean shorts that made her ass stick out. Even though it was the end of May, it still felt too chilly to wear shorts. My jeans and black T-shirt that read *#TeamBrockShaw* in bright pink were perfectly fine for me, thank you very much. Of course, when Stella had seen the shirt, she'd grinned. I guessed she'd forgotten she had sent it over to the house earlier this afternoon with a card that said, *Please wear this. The rest of the family will be wearing the same, and Blayze will love it.*

I should have known Stella was up to no good. Currently, I was the only person wearing the T-shirt. And said T-shirt earned me a dirty look from Lucy Mae.

Ty brought Blayze back to us as we headed to our seats. It didn't take but two minutes for Blayze to ask to leave again. "Grams, can I get a chili dog?" Blayze asked as we took our seats.

Stella sighed. "Blayze Shaw, we just sat down."

"I can get it. I don't mind," I said as I winked at Blayze. He looked so much like his father it made my chest ache.

If Brock and I had kids, what would they look like?

Stilling, I tried to figure out where in the world that thought had come from. I hadn't even talked to Brock in three weeks, and here I was having thoughts like that.

"You don't mind?" Stella asked, looking flustered as she tried to settle a very rowdy Blayze.

"Nope. Just a chili dog?" I asked the little boy.

"And some onion rings!"

I pulled in my brows. "I don't think they have those, buddy."

His shoulders dropped. "Well, dang it. I had me a hankerin' for some."

Pressing my lips tightly together, I tried not to laugh.

"Chips will be fine," he added.

Stella mumbled under her breath, "Like father, like son. Apples don't fall far from the trees in this family."

That time, I did laugh. I made my way down the stands and behind the bleachers.

I was stopped by Tanner. "Hey, I need you to follow me."

"Oh. Well, I was going to get Blayze a chili dog and chips."

"Yeah, he doesn't want any. I told him to say that. I figured you'd offer to get it. Mama doesn't like leaving her seat once she's settled."

I stared at Tanner as he pulled me along. "You used Blayze to get me down here?"

"Hell yeah. The little shit comes in handy sometimes."

"Tanner Shaw!" I gasped.

He simply laughed.

"Where are we going?"

"Brock wants to talk to you."

My heart started to beat rapidly in my chest. "Right now?"

"Yep. Said he can't ride until he talks to you."

"Now?" I asked again, feeling the nerves flutter in my stomach.

My anger over what had happened had cooled, and I was now in the lovesick stage again. I wanted to see Brock, but at the same time, I was okay with waiting. At least, I thought I was.

The moment I saw him standing there, talking to a group of older cowboys, I lost my breath. He had on jeans, blue chaps that had *Blayze* on one leg and his favorite Bible verse on the other, a dark-blue long-sleeved shirt that I knew would make his eyes stand out, and a black cowboy hat. He didn't even have to turn to look at me, and I was already captivated by him.

I pulled Tanner to a stop and whispered, "I can't do this."

He frowned. "Do you not want to try to work things out? He feels something awful about what he did, Lincoln. He misses you, and when you called him today, he thought that maybe you wanted to talk."

"I do! I *do* want to talk, but I'm feeling really emotional for some reason, and I . . . I feel sick to my stomach."

Brock turned then, and our eyes met. He smiled—and my insides melted.

Every doubt I'd had about us, about Brock's feelings toward me, vanished with that smile. I could see it in his eyes. The torture he'd put himself through. The guilt that had plagued him.

"Brock," I whispered.

"I take it you've changed your mind about seeing him?" Tanner asked with a slight chuckle.

Without saying a word, I rushed to him. He took a few long strides, and I threw myself into his arms. His mouth crashed to mine, and I didn't care who saw us or what they thought.

I loved this man, and I wasn't going to let him go. I'd made him a promise that I wouldn't run, and I wasn't going to.

We kissed until we were breathless. When our mouths parted, we both mumbled, "I'm sorry."

Laughing, we kissed again. Brock's hands went to my hair, grabbing it and pulling my forehead to his. "I'm so sorry I freaked out and left you. I didn't mean to say what I said. I didn't mean it at all. I've got so much shit going on in my head that I—"

I pressed my fingers to his lips. "Not now. It's okay. I pushed us somewhere you weren't ready to go, and I'm sorry. I've missed you so much, Brock."

He closed his eyes. My name was like a soft breath on his lips. Then, the next words out of his mouth left me stunned.

"Lincoln . . . I love you. It took me messing up things with you to realize that all of this stuff—the fame, the money, the spotlight on me every weekend—it could never be enough if you weren't there with me. You've shown me that there's another dream inside my heart that I never knew was there. I need you with me to start it."

I stared up into his blue eyes. Tears pooled, and my heart was beating hard in my chest. I didn't have to think twice. I had known the moment he walked into my barn that he was mine. He'd always be mine.

"I love you, too, Brock. And I told you, I'm not a runner."

A wide smile moved over his face. His dimples were out in full force, and I felt heat pool in my lower stomach.

"Brock! We need to get to the chutes," someone called out.

Sighing, Brock shook his head and said, "I'm sorry. I'll see you after my ride, and I'll explain why I left you like I did."

I nodded. "It's okay."

He went to leave, but I grabbed his hand and pulled him to me. Lifting up on my toes, I cupped his face with my hands and kissed him, pouring as much as I could into the kiss. "Be safe."

He winked. "Always, sweetheart."

After grabbing the chili dog and chips, I rushed back to my seat. The bull riding was about to begin, and Dirk and Brock were pretty far down on the list. They were saving the best for last.

Blayze devoured the chili dog and his chips. I couldn't help but chuckle. He had a hearty appetite, that was for sure.

"How are Brock's ribs?" I asked.

Stella was keeping stats on a clipboard and looked up at the chutes. "He says he's fine, but he also said that when he rode in the world championship with a broken hand."

I gasped. "Was it his riding hand?"

"No, but still, these cowboys ride with some serious injuries. The fact that Brock didn't take any time off after Billings worried me. Ty said he was moving around fine, but Ty Senior gave me a different report last week. Said he saw him flinch when he was picking up the hay bales."

I shook my head. My heartbeat slowly increased as each rider went. I didn't want Brock or his family to think I was going to be someone who would make him give all this up. I would love it if he didn't have such a dangerous job, but I would stand by him, 100 percent supporting him.

"Stella, Tanner said you handled all the booking and travel arrangements for both him and Brock."

She nodded, not looking up from writing down the last rider's stats. "Yes, it's a handful."

I wrung my hands in my lap, not wanting to overstep. "Well, I'm sure you love doing it, but I was going to say, I could take care of Brock's travel arrangements. I mean, if you'd be okay with that."

She stilled, and then slowly looked my way.

Oh fiddlesticks, I've overstepped.

A huge grin broke out over her face. "Okay with it? I'd be over the moon if you took that on! Are you sure? I've been doing it since day one, and to have Brock's schedule off my list would lighten my load."

I wanted to ask her why Kaci never did it, but I let it go. "Honestly, I'd love to do it. That way, if I decide to travel with him some weekends, I can easily book us together on flights."

Her eyes filled with tears, and she reached for my hand. "Thank you. Not for taking that on, but for supporting my son and being a part of something that means a lot to him. I know you talked to him before you got Blayze's food. That little boy is a terrible secret keeper and spilled the beans as soon as you left."

I chuckled, glancing over to Blayze, who was sitting on Lynn's lap. Lynn was indeed a young woman, seventeen at the most, and it was obvious she had a heart of gold. She clearly loved her family and adored Blayze. She had done nothing but shower him with attention since she saw him.

My hand covered my mouth, and I nearly started to cry. This was not like me to be so emotional. "Oh, Stella! I have to tell someone or I'm going to burst. I tried calling Kaylee to tell her the news, but she didn't answer."

"What is it, sweetheart?"

Another rider came out, and Stella held up her finger. We watched him ride the full eight. She wrote it down on the day sheet next to the rider's name.

Then she focused back on me. "Go . . . before another rider comes out!"

Chewing on my lip, I blurted out, "Brock said he loved me."

Her eyes widened, and I heard someone gasp from behind me.

Damn it. I'd said that really loud. I didn't even want to know who was sitting back there and had overheard.

"Oh. My. Stars. What did you say?"

I grinned. "That I loved him. I mean, we have to talk about everything, but I've known from the moment Brock stepped into my barn that he was going to change my entire world."

Stella wrapped her arms around me and squeezed. I did the same.

"Why you two huggin'? Can I have a hug?" Blayze asked, pushing the two of us apart.

I reached down, pulled him onto my lap, and hugged him.

"I wove you, Miss Lincoln."

And there went my heart. The last piece given to a five-year-old little boy with blue eyes like his daddy's. "Blayze, I love you too."

From the corner of my eye, I watched Stella quickly wipe away a tear. I wasn't sure if saying it to Blayze was the right thing. I didn't want to confuse him, but at the same time, I did love him. I loved him like he was my own.

"Will you do me a favor?" I asked Blayze as he settled onto my lap and stared out at the arena.

"Sure!"

"Call me Lincoln, not Miss Lincoln."

He didn't bother to look at me when he replied, "When can I call you Mommy?"

Stella and I both froze. My eyes widened, and I snapped my head over to her, my breathing suddenly increasing tenfold.

What do I say? I mouthed to her.

Doing what she did best, Stella cleared her throat and acted like Blayze's question had been the most natural thing in the world. "When your daddy and Lincoln get married, or when your daddy tells you that you can call Lincoln Mommy."

I must have opened and closed my mouth ten times.

"Catching flies with that thing?"

Hearing her voice, I turned to see Kaylee standing there.

"You weren't hard to spot with that shirt, Lincoln."

I jumped up after sliding Blayze off my lap. "What in the world? How? When? Why didn't you tell me you were coming so soon?"

Kaylee shrugged. "Turns out, I have nothing back in Atlanta at all. I put my condo on the market, fully furnished, and told my folks to trash or get rid of everything else. Packed up my car Tuesday night and drove pretty much straight here."

"Kaylee, I'm so glad you're here!" We hugged like we hadn't seen each other in months, when in reality, it had only been a few days. "You must be exhausted!"

With a half shrug, she sat down in the empty seat next to me. "I'm fine. I told Dirk I'd be here and to make sure there was an open seat next to you."

"I'm going to kill him for keeping this from me."

She giggled. "Why? It was sort of fun, pulling one over on you."

The announcer mentioned Dirk's name, and we all focused on the arena.

Blayze called out, "Get 'em, Uncle Dirk!"

Kaylee yelled out her own good-luck message, which was about the same: "Give him hell, Dirk!"

I glanced her way and laughed. Never in a million years had I thought my best friend would get into bull riding.

The chute opened, and the bull came charging out, hell bent on getting Dirk off his back. He rode him like it was nothing. Everyone jumped up and cheered. Dirk turned, looked directly up at Blayze, and pointed to him. He took off his helmet and smiled and then looked behind us to his parents.

"Ladies and gentlemen, we have the great honor of announcing our last bull rider of the evening. He's currently ranked the number one bull rider in the world and a locally grown cowboy. Give it up for Brock Shaw!"

The crowd went a bit crazy. My eyes were locked on the chute, where Brock was already on top of the bull. Ty was holding on to Brock by his vest while Tanner was pulling the bull rope tight. Ty Senior was on the other side of Tanner, telling his son something. I smiled. It was really a family affair. I snuck a peek at Stella. She was smiling, too, but I saw the same worry in her eyes that I knew had to be reflected on my own face.

Swallowing hard, I focused back on Brock. They didn't play any songs for the introduction like they did on the PBR tour. A regular rodeo was a low-key event.

He hit his glove, making sure he had a good hold. He looked up, and I knew he was praying. Adjusting himself on the bull, he nodded, and the gate shot open.

The bull's name was Sweet Cupcake, but there wasn't anything sweet about that giant beast. The snot shot from his nose, and he bucked as hard as he could. He went to the left, and then he changed it up and went right. I didn't want to take my eyes off Brock to look at the clock.

Then, the buzzer went off, and Brock reached down. The bull gave him another buck, and Brock was launched into the air. He landed and quickly got to his feet.

I jumped up and started clapping and screaming like a silly girl. Brock did what he always did: he took his helmet off, threw it up in the air, and looked up into the stands. Our eyes met, and my stomach fluttered.

From the corner of my eye, I saw a bullfighter running toward Brock.

Brock turned to see what was happening. The bull had been heading back into the pen, but then it took a sharp right and headed straight for Brock.

The bullfighter got between them, but the bull took both of them out. He tossed the bullfighter and chased Brock to the fence. Before he had a chance to jump on it and get away, the bull had lowered his head and gotten Brock in the back, hooking his horn on Brock's vest.

The last thing I remembered was Brock going up in the air—and then the bull running over him when he landed.

I heard Stella screaming from beside me, and I grabbed Blayze. He was crying and calling out for his father.

I stood there, motionless, as they finally got the bull away from Brock, and they carried him out on a stretcher. I hadn't even noticed Stella taking Blayze from my arms and leaving.

Kaylee's arm was around my waist as we walked through crowds of people.

"Ty!" she cried out when we finally got through the crowd.

"They airlifted him to Billings." His voice pulled me from my daze.

"What?" I asked, staring into Ty's eyes.

Ty looked at Kaylee and then back to me. "Mama and Dad are already headed to the hospital."

"Blayze!" I cried out.

"He's with them."

I nodded. "We . . . we need to get to Billings."

Kaylee turned and guided me as we followed Ty.

"Where are Dirk and Tanner?" I asked as I climbed into the back of Ty's truck.

"Tanner was taken to the hospital with Brock."

I gasped. "What? Why?"

"Tanner ran out there, tried to get the bull away from Brock, and got kicked. He went in the helicopter too; they think he broke his ribs, but they need to make sure there's no internal bleeding."

My hand covered my mouth. "Dirk?"

"He went in the helicopter with Brock. They weren't going to let him, but somehow, I don't know how he did it, he got on."

I nodded. "Good, good. So he's not alone."

Turning, I stared out the window as the night sky went by. All I could think about was Brock telling me he loved me. Most people would say it was way too soon to be sharing those words, but I knew in the depths of my soul that we both meant them. Then I thought about Brock telling me he'd had another dream in his heart.

What was his dream? What is our dream together?

"Can you pull over, Ty? I feel sick."

He pulled over, and I jumped out of the truck, rushing out before I vomited. My insides hurt as I threw up violently.

"Brock . . ." I cried as I stood there afterward, my entire body trembling with fear before Ty gently guided me back to his truck.

Kaylee got into the back with me, letting me bury my head in her chest and cry.

Chapter Twenty-Five

Lincoln

"Lincoln."

I stirred and opened my eyes. Kaylee was looking down at me with a soft smile.

"I thought you might want some coffee."

I stared at the cup in her hand, but just the sight of it made me feel nauseous. "No, I don't want any."

She frowned. "Then, will you at least come with me to eat?"

My eyes traveled past her to Brock. He was lying in a hospital bed, an IV dripping into one arm, a blood pressure monitor on the other. His face was bruised, and the cut above his eye showed where the doctors had stitched it shut.

I swallowed hard. He was still unconscious as he lay there, machines beeping and oxygen being pumped into his body. My chin trembled as I thought back to the doctor and his laundry list of things wrong with Brock.

A concussion. No bleeding in the brain, which was good. His major injury, besides the head, was a costochondral sprain. It was making breathing difficult for Brock, especially with him still being unconscious. He'd be out of the PBR for two months. Maybe three. Complete rest was ordered, which I was positive Stella and I would make sure happened.

Also, he had a cut on his leg from the bull stepping on it. Forty stitches required for that one. The cut above his eye had only needed fourteen. *Only.* He had a black eye, and it looked like someone had beaten the hell out of him. That was the result of the bull throwing him in the air and Brock coming down and hitting his own helmet lying on the ground.

"I'm not hungry," I finally managed to say.

"Lincoln, you have to eat to keep up your own energy. Do you want to help take care of him when he wakes up?"

Tears filled my eyes. "Yes."

"Then, let's go eat."

I nodded. "Give me a second, okay?"

Kaylee sighed and then looked at Brock as she replied, "Two minutes, and then I'm dragging you out."

As I made my way over to the side of the bed, I took in a deep breath. I reached for Brock's hand, lifted it to my lips, and kissed it.

"Hey," I whispered. "Please wake up. I *really* need you to wake up. I know the doctor said you were going to be okay, but if you could just wake up and tell me yourself, that would be great. I need to see your smile. Hear your voice. Feel you reach up and touch my cheek. Tell me you love me again, because I *really* need to tell you how much I love you, too, and know that you hear me."

My head dropped down, and I focused on not crying. I had to be strong for him, and standing here, begging him to wake up to comfort me, was not what Brock needed.

Clearing my throat, I lifted my head. "So, while you're lying here napping, I've been dealing with the drama that is Kaylee and your brother Ty. That's been interesting. I'm not sure if they like each other or hate one another." I chuckled. "It's pretty entertaining, watching the two of them, though. And Blayze has been keeping me on my toes. That boy has more energy than the Energizer Bunny."

Pulling in another deep breath, I kept my voice steady.

"Don't even get me started on Tanner. He has three broken ribs. His career as a bullfighter was stripped from him before it even started. He's a big baby too. I mean, he tries to act all cool, but when it's just me and him, he whines. It's sort of funny."

My eyes searched Brock's face for something. Anything.

I sighed and leaned over, gently kissing him on his bruised cheek. "I love you. I'm going to grab something to eat. I'll be back."

The door to the room opened, and I shot Kaylee a dirty look. "I'm coming," I said in a low, growling voice.

After grabbing hospital cafeteria food, we sat at a table. Ty, Dirk, and another cowboy friend of theirs joined us. His name was Pitt. I thought I recognized him, and it finally hit me who he was.

"You're a bullfighter, right?" I asked.

Pitt looked at me and grinned. "Yes, ma'am, I am."

"It's sweet of you to be here."

He tipped his cowboy hat at me. His honey-brown eyes had specks of gold in them that caught the light more when he smiled. "Brock's a real good friend of mine. Known him since he first came on tour with us. I came right when Dirk called me."

I smiled and noticed the wedding ring on his left hand. "Do you have any kids?"

He seemed surprised at my question and then glanced down to his ring. "Nah. We're separated. She doesn't like all the traveling and says my job is insane."

I frowned. "Did she not know what you did for a living when y'all got married?"

Pitt laughed, looked at Dirk and Ty, and nudged his thumb in my direction. "I like her. I see why Brock does too."

Kaylee sat pretty quietly next to me the entire meal. I picked at most of my food, not in the mood to eat, and when I stood, the room started to spin.

"Whoa," I said, reaching out for something to steady myself.

"Lincoln!" Kaylee yelped, grabbing on to me right as I sank to the ground.

And blackness took over completely.

My eyes flew open, and I instantly panicked. *Where am I?*

Sitting up, I glanced around to see Ty and Kaylee both in chairs, sleeping. My head was pounding, and I felt a little sick to my stomach.

"Wh-what happened?" I mumbled, touching the side of my head with my hand.

Ty and Kaylee both jumped up. They wore goofy smiles on their faces as they looked at each other and then back to me.

"I'll let the nurse know she's up," Ty said, squeezing Kaylee's hand.

Okay, am I dreaming, or did I just witness a kind gesture between the two of them? "I'm dreaming, right?"

"No. Why?"

"I swear I just saw Ty grab your hand."

Kaylee pulled the chair up next to me and sat down. "We called a truce."

"Good."

"So, I have something I need to tell you."

A feeling of dread swept over me. "Brock—"

"Is fine!" she said, cutting me off. "He's not awake yet, but he's fine."

I let out a breath of air.

"But I think you might have something to tell him that could possibly nudge him into waking up."

My brows lifted. "I do?"

Her face broke out into a wide grin. The door opened, and Ty walked back in. Kaylee looked up at him and shook her head, causing him to come around and stand next to her. The two of them still wore the goofiest of smiles.

"Have y'all been drinking?" I asked, my gaze bouncing between them.

"No!" Kaylee said. "But we wanted to be the first to tell you, because I'm pretty damn sure you're clueless!"

Drawing my brows in tight, I said, "Huh? Okay, you know what? You two have fun with that. I need to get out of here."

Ty placed his hand on my shoulder as I started to get up. "The nurse is getting the doctor. He wants to take one last look at you, and then you'll be able to go to Brock."

"They *admitted* me? For fainting?"

Kaylee nodded and said, "They had to give you an IV and such because you were dehydrated. But who cares about that, Lincoln? We've got some pretty big news, so I need you to take a deep breath, slowly let it out, and hold on to your boots."

Ty leaned down so he was at the same eye level as Kaylee.

"Holy hell, you two slept together!"

They both frowned, looked at each other, and then back to me.

"I wish," Ty said.

Kaylee slapped him on the chest. "No, that's not it. Lincoln—you're pregnant."

Ty and Kaylee both smiled. Big. So big that it was sort of creepy.

I chuckled. "What?" Her words replayed in my head, but they were so ridiculous that I had to laugh.

"You're pregnant," Ty repeated. "You've got a bun in the oven. You're knocked up. There's a bat in the cave. You're in the family way. There's a pea in the pod. You are preggo. Preggers. A baby Shaw is kicking around in there."

"Are you done?" Kaylee asked as I slowly sat straighter and stared at them. "Seriously, did you google all that in the last few hours?"

Ty smirked. "You're just jealous you couldn't come up with any of it."

"What? I'm the one who said there was a bat in the cave! You took that from me!"

Rolling his eyes, Ty said, "It's *my* nephew."

"Well, it's *my* niece."

"Not by blood."

I shook my head and buried my face in my hands. "Wait. What?" I mumbled as Ty and Kaylee went at it.

But then the realization of what they'd said sank in.

"Stop!" I nearly screamed, making them both turn my way to give me those creepy smiles again. "I can't be pregnant! I'm on the pill, and Brock wore a condom each time. So there's a mistake. We've only had sex . . . a few times!"

Kaylee pulled in a breath and blew it out before she said, "I hate to break this news flash to you, but it only takes once. You're pregnant. They drew blood, and it came back saying you were preggers. Now, I did have to lie and tell them I was your sister to get said information, but it was a lie I'm glad I told!"

Ty grinned and said, "Kaylee and I figured you're not that far along. Maybe a month, if that."

My mouth fell open as I stared at them both. Tears filled my eyes as I let their words really sink in.

"But . . . *how*? I don't understand."

Kaylee cleared her throat. "Well, the P goes into the V. Then the guy ejaculates in the woman."

"That's the best part, really," Ty added.

Kaylee nodded and then continued, "Well, as long as the woman comes before he ejaculates."

"Right. A man ain't a cowboy if he doesn't take care of his lady first," Ty stated.

"You are so adorbs. Anyway, then the little sperm make their way to the egg. They have to be strong swimmers."

"Shaw swimmers are strong. Just sayin'," Ty interjected.

"Then, one of the buggers gets in, and *bam*, a baby is on its way."

With a groan of frustration, I closed my eyes. "I know how a baby is made! How did we make a baby with two different types of birth control?"

"Okay, one part of that is easy to explain. Remember when you got sick right before we moved, and they put you on those antibiotics?"

I nodded.

"Yeah, well, some of those sort of work against the pill. I think you finished up the bottle right about when we got here. You and Brock hooked up about five days or so after your last pill, which meant your birth control pills were all jacked up."

"And if Brock used an old rubber—"

"Ew. I hate that word. Say *condom*," Kaylee said.

Ty glared at her and went on. "If Brock used an old *condom*, it could have broken."

"I would have felt it. He would have noticed!"

"Not really," Ty and Kaylee both said at once.

Taking my hand and kissing the back of it, Kaylee gushed, "Either way, kiddo, y'all are having a baby. I hope you kissed and made up."

"They did. He told her he loved her."

Kaylee gasped. "What? *What!* Why am I just now hearing this?"

The doctor walked in. I launched into the whole *How could I be pregnant? We used birth control!* questions. He repeated pretty much what Kaylee and Ty had said.

After I signed the papers to discharge me, I made my way to Brock's room. I sat in the chair next to his bed and stared at him.

I'm pregnant. What are you going to do when you find out, Brock?

He still had so many demons he needed to work through. *We* needed to work through together. My head dropped onto my hands, which were holding his. No matter what happened, I wasn't running. I'd wait for him. For as long as it took.

I pulled in a deep breath and slowly let it out. There was no denying I was scared shitless . . . for a few reasons. This pregnancy was totally unplanned. I was starting a new career and a new relationship in a new city. Brock spooked easily and was a flight risk. And Blayze . . . how would little Blayze feel about another baby to share his attention with his father?

My head swirled with all the emotions. Happiness seemed to keep coming up to the surface above all the others, though. Was it wrong for me to feel joy in my heart? I didn't think so. I'd always known I wanted to be a mom. I'd even dreamed of it with Brock and Blayze that day I stood outside his hotel room.

Slowing my breathing down, I calmly let it settle in.

I was pregnant.

I was having Brock's baby.

I was going to be a mother.

Lifting my head, I felt the tears run down my cheeks as I looked at the man I loved. How could I feel so insanely happy yet scared to death? How would Brock feel when he found out I was pregnant? Happy? Trapped? Spooked?

I closed my eyes tightly. This was going to change everything. I prayed it would change it for the better.

Chapter Twenty-Six

Brock

The light poured in as I slowly opened my eyes. My head was pounding, and my mouth felt like it had been stuffed with cotton. I attempted to move and quickly stopped when the pain in my ribs stilled me.

"Shit," I whispered.

Soft breathing made me look to my right. Smiling, I gazed down at the woman I loved.

Lincoln.

Her cheek was lying on my hand, and she looked uncomfortable. Hell, she was going to have a massive crick in her neck after sleeping like that.

I lifted my other arm, the one that had an IV attached to it, and gently brushed a piece of her light-brown hair away.

She whispered my name, and that word felt like it launched right into my body and pierced my heart.

"Lincoln."

She didn't move.

I tried to reach her cheek, but the twisting action shot pain throughout my body. So, I gently lifted my other hand, causing her head to move. She slowly sat up—and then grabbed on to the bed. Righting herself as if she was dizzy.

"Hey," I said with a smile.

Her eyes lit up with happiness . . . and relief. "Hey back at you." She shook her head, tears streaming down her face, and she stood. Her lips pressed against mine. Lincoln kissed me like it was our first kiss. When she pulled back, her eyes drifted up above my eye, and then she did a quick sweep of my face.

I remembered my face coming down on my helmet, so I was positive that I looked like shit.

"I'm not going to lie to you: I was so scared."

My chest ached. I could see it in her eyes. No woman had ever looked at me like this before. With such love mixed with worry. Not that Kaci hadn't worried about me; I think she was just used to seeing me banged up.

The way Lincoln was looking at me right now, though, I knew this thing between us was entirely unlike what Kaci and I had shared. Not to take away from my love for my first wife, but I had to admit to myself that things felt completely different with Lincoln. I wasn't going to let myself feel guilty for loving her like I did. Not anymore. Life was too short.

"I'm sorry. It was stupid of me to take my eyes off the bull. I wasn't thinking."

Her head shook. "Please tell me I wasn't a distraction, because if I was, I'll never sit in the stands again."

My brows furrowed. "What?"

"If I distracted you, and that's the reason you got hurt, I'll never forgive myself."

This woman was like no other. I fell in love with her even more in that moment.

"Lincoln, it wasn't your fault. It's my job, and it's dangerous. And honestly, I was expecting a lecture about how you couldn't love a man who rode bulls and to come find you when I was done."

She giggled and kissed me again. "I told you, I'm not a runner. I know what you do, and I know you love it." Her eyes turned serious. "Brock, I promise you right now: no matter what happens, on or off a bull, I will never ask you to give up riding."

The tightness in my chest wasn't from whatever injury I had. It was from the knowledge that Lincoln would stand by me no matter what. She knew what I did for a living, and she was willing to support me. My chin wobbled some as I tried to speak.

"I love you, Lincoln. The way I feel about you is unlike anything I've ever felt before."

It was clear in her eyes she wanted to ask about Kaci.

"I loved Kaci; I did. But with you . . . it feels like my soul has finally found what it was searching for."

More tears filled her eyes, and she leaned over to kiss me. "I love you, Brock."

It hit me then—my son.

"Blayze," I said, a worried rush to my voice.

"He's fine. He was upset for a couple of days, but your dad took him back home and will be back tomorrow."

"A couple of days? How long have I been out?"

She pulled in a breath and said, "Three days. The last eight hours or so, you've been sort of waking up off and on. Not opening your eyes, but moving a lot more. You're probably really sore."

I nodded. "So, what damage did he do?"

The door to the room opened, and the nurse came in. "You're awake, Mr. Shaw! Thank you for letting me know." She glanced at Lincoln, who was now retreating away from me.

I tried to lift my brow in question but stopped when I felt more pain. Lifting my hand, I felt the stitches.

"I pushed the call button when I kissed you," Lincoln stated.

The nurse took my vitals and asked if I wanted some water.

Lincoln jumped at the chance. "I'll go get it."

The moment she left the room, the nurse started chatting. "So, I hear from your wife that you're a bull rider."

My breath stalled. "My wife?"

She was messing around with my IV bag but stopped to look at me. "I'm so sorry. I just assumed you were married. She certainly loves you very much. Her friends nearly had to drag her out of the room each time to get her to eat. That's the only time she's left you alone."

I licked my dry lips and focused on my words. "I could see why you thought we were married. I love her too. We haven't been together very long."

Her brow rose. "Really? Well, I have a feeling the two of you are going to make . . . a beautiful future together."

She had paused, and I couldn't help but wonder why. I smiled, though, and agreed with her. "I do too. She's an amazing woman, and to be honest, I'm not sure what she sees in me."

With a chuckle, she stopped and looked down at me. "Oh, I see it, Mr. Shaw." Then she winked and headed to the door. "The doctor will be in shortly. I've let him know you're up. Let me know if you need any painkillers. You got some in the IV a couple of hours ago, but now that you're up and moving around, I can give you more."

"Thank you."

Lincoln came rushing into the room. "I've got water!" she declared.

I laughed and then promptly stopped because of the pain in my side. Hell, all over, if I was being honest.

Her hands shook as she poured it, then slipped a straw into the cup. I asked her to raise my bed some, and she did. Never once taking her eyes off my face so that she could read my reaction to moving. Little did my cowgirl know I hid pain well.

"That's good," I said when I needed the movement to stop.

Lincoln handed me the cup, and I drank.

"Not too much. You don't want to get sick. Take small sips. I stopped at the nurses' station to see if they could get you some lunch."

I stared into her hauntingly beautiful green eyes. They were the color of a meadow on the first day of summer. Damn, I could get lost in them, and had . . . more than once. "So, tell me what's wrong with me and why my side hurts like hell."

Lincoln pulled up a chair and sat down. "Well, the worst of your injuries is a costochondral sprain."

I stared at her, confused. "What in the hell is that?"

She pulled out her phone from her back pocket and grinned.

God, she's beautiful. Especially when she smiles.

"I had to look it up too. So, basically, your rib bone separated from the cartilage of your sternum."

"Ouch."

With a nod, she mumbled, "Yeah. The doctor said you need complete rest."

"For how long?" I asked, holding my breath, which made my ribs hurt.

"Two . . . maybe three months."

I closed my eyes and cursed under my breath. "Fuck."

"But, if you relax and take it easy—that means no working on the ranch—you'll heal faster. They've prescribed pain pills to help with the pain and breathing. Deep breaths will hurt."

A frustrated sigh slipped from my mouth. "What else is wrong?"

"A concussion, but there was no bleeding on the brain, which is really good. A deep cut on your leg from the bull stepping on it. You got forty stitches on that one. Then, the cut above your eye got fourteen."

"Huh. He must have gotten me good on the leg."

"They think he stepped on it and then horned you. Your face is pretty bruised, but it's already looking better after a couple of days."

"Blayze. How was he when he saw me?"

As she chewed on her lip, I could tell she was hesitant to tell me. "Well, he cried and was really scared when it happened. Then, he cried when we brought him in to see you. The first night, he slept with me over on that little sofa."

My gaze drifted across the room. "You let him stay with you?"

"Of course. You're his father, and he was worried. I *will* give you a heads-up. Your son is a major flirt, and I'm pretty sure at least three nurses here have fallen in love with him."

I laughed and then stopped again.

"I'm sorry."

"Don't be. I like hearing stories about him. I also like knowing you were both here."

Her cheeks flushed.

"Those are all my injuries?"

She nodded. "You've had a plethora of people here to see you. Pitt has been here. He's a nice guy. Going through a rough patch right now with his wife and all, but a super nice guy."

"Yeah, he's good people."

Her gaze moved down to her hands, and then back up at me. "He's sort of mad at you for getting hurt at a rodeo."

I tried not to laugh. "He'll get over it." Lifting my hand, I placed it on the side of her cheek. "How are *you*, sweetheart?"

"Um . . . I'm good. Tired. Probably need to eat some."

Right then, the door to the room opened, and the nurse from earlier walked in, carrying two trays of food. "I figured you might be hungry too. You need to eat." Her comment was directed right at Lincoln.

She simply nodded. "Yes, I'm starving."

She winked, and Lincoln smiled.

"Broth?" I asked as I opened the lid to my dish.

Lincoln opened a pack of crackers. She put one in her mouth and dipped the other, handing it to me as she said, "Think of it as pieces of steak."

I took it and put it in my mouth. "Mmm . . . yeah, that's not working."

After eating, I asked for some pain meds and quickly fell back asleep.

I stayed in the hospital another couple of days, just so they could make sure I was breathing clearly, and then I was discharged and sent home.

Lincoln had packed up some things and was staying in the guest room of my house. I loved hearing her and Blayze every morning in the kitchen. It took me a while to get around the house, but I knew the more I walked around, the better it would be for my ribs. It killed my leg, though, and Lincoln insisted I use a cane. It helped, even though I refused to admit it did.

After managing to get up and dressed on my own this morning, I called my mom; then I headed toward the sound of Lincoln's and Blayze's voices.

"What if I want it in the shape of a cow?"

I walked around the corner and saw Blayze sitting on the large island, far enough away from the stovetop where Lincoln was cooking pancakes but close enough to be involved.

"A cow? Ugh. Why couldn't you say a heart?"

Blayze snarled his lip. "Gwoss."

"Why is a heart gross?"

He shrugged. "Dunno."

"Well, I think my pancake that I made for your daddy is going to be a heart, because he owns mine."

A lump formed in my throat.

With a chuckle, Blayze asked, "How can Daddy own your heart, Lincoln?"

He hadn't called her Miss Lincoln. That was interesting.

"Well, it really just means that my heart belongs to your daddy. I love him and only him."

"You don't wove me?"

Lincoln stopped what she was doing and moved closer to Blayze. "Yes! Wrong words to use. Blayze, I love you so very much. You own a piece of my heart too."

"I do?" he asked, his voice filled with hope.

She nodded. "And I want you to know something. No matter what happens and who comes into our little world that the three of us are building right now, you will *always* have such a special place in my heart."

"Like a mommy would have for her baby boy?"

"Yes. I might not be the mommy who grew you in her tummy, Blayze." Her head shook a little as she gazed down at him with nothing but love. "But I would be so honored to get to be the mommy to help your daddy raise you into a fine young man, like he is."

My eyes filled with tears at Lincoln's answer.

He wrapped his arms around her, and they held each other for the longest time as I let go of a bit more of the guilt I had been holding on to.

Chapter Twenty-Seven

Lincoln

"Hey, good morning, you two."

I jumped at the sound of his voice. Blayze turned and smiled when he saw his father walking into the kitchen. Stella and I had both explained to him where Brock was hurt and that hugs were off limits for now. So, Blayze stuck his arms out in the air and pretended to hug him before Brock leaned down and kissed him.

"Morning, buddy. What's going on here?"

He moved over to me and turned me toward him. He placed his finger on my chin, and my whole body instantly warmed. He slowly bent and kissed me. He certainly wasn't afraid of showing his emotions for me in front of Blayze. It was Brock who had explained to him that I would be staying for a while to help him get better, but that I would be in the guest room.

"Lincoln was making pancakes for us. I asked her to make a cow, but she didn't know hows to."

Brock smiled and then peeked in to see me lifting out a heart-shaped silicone mold so I could flip the pancake. "You're cheating, using that!"

With a laugh, I replied, "Hey! I might be an interior designer, but I never claimed to be a good cook!"

"Speaking of, is Karen okay with the amount of work you've missed?"

"Yep, I took care of some work while you were in the hospital. When I couldn't sleep and my mind needed to focus on something else. Right now, I'm finishing up Julia's makeover. I swear, if I see another fish or whale or dolphin, I might get sick."

"Like you did this mornin'?" Blayze asked.

I froze.

"You were sick?" Brock asked.

I quickly took the pancake out and placed it on a plate for Blayze. "That food last night must not have agreed with me. I had a bit of an upset stomach."

Brock placed his hand over my stomach, and I stilled. Then, it hit me. My out-of-whack emotions the last few weeks . . . at least now I knew why I had been so emotional lately.

"How's it feel now?" he asked as I looked up into his eyes. When he saw the tears building, he frowned.

"It feels amazing."

He smiled. He thought I meant his touch, which . . . yes, that did feel amazing, and I instantly wanted more of it.

"I see," he purred, kissing me once more.

"Gwoss . . . all this kissin'. Can I eats my pancake in the living room?" Blayze asked.

I chuckled. "Sure, I'll bring it in there."

Blayze jumped off the island and bolted out of the kitchen. I quickly cut his pancake into sections and poured a small amount of syrup into a bowl. Blayze liked to dip his pancake into the syrup rather than have it poured over it. Brock poured more batter into the pan.

"Let me take this to him," I said, taking the plate and bowl and heading into the living room. "Here ya go, buddy. One heart-shaped pancake cut up like little pizzas for my favorite little boy!"

Blayze beamed as he looked up at me. "Thank you, Lincoln!"

I ruffled his hair as I said, "You are so welcome, buddy. Remember what we talked about: eat over your bowl so the syrup doesn't get everywhere."

He nodded and got to work eating his pancake while he watched a cartoon.

When I walked back into the kitchen, my breath caught at the sight of Brock standing over the stove. Even broken and bruised, this man was a sight to be seen. My heartbeat quickened, and I tried to swallow the lump in my throat.

"How do you feel?" I asked.

"Better. It's always good to get up and walk."

I shot him a warning look. "Take it easy."

"I will." He popped a strawberry in his mouth. "Mom's on her way over to get Blayze."

"Why?" I asked, slipping a perfect heart-shaped pancake out of the pan and onto the plate. I buttered it and poured a bit of syrup on it before following Brock to the table.

"I asked her to. I wanted to talk to you. It's time I told you everything about me and Kaci."

"Brock, what's in the past is in the past. I don't need to know."

He chuckled and then held on to his side. "If you've spent more than five minutes with Julia, I'm sure you and I need to talk. According to her, it was a heartbreaking love triangle between me, Dirk, and Kaci. In a way, I guess it was. But I need you to understand why I was distant for so many years and then attempted—but failed—to keep you away."

"We can talk, but I need you to know that I'm not pushing you into anything. I would never do that. So, no matter what happens here the next few weeks, I'm going to go at your pace, Brock. No more spooking you away." I chewed anxiously on my lip. "At least, I hope not."

"That's not going to happen. I promise you."

I gave him a forced smile. *Oh Lord. If sex with no condom spooked him, a baby is going to freak him the heck out.*

Pacing the kitchen, I wrung my hands while Brock ate. Maybe I needed to wait to tell Brock. This was moving so fast.

A baby.

We were having a baby.

My hand covered my stomach as I tried to keep the bile down.

The doorbell rang, and I let out a small scream.

"Jesus, Lincoln, what's wrong?" Brock asked. "You're pacing a hole in the floor."

"Sorry. I'll go let your mom in."

I rushed out of the kitchen and barely beat Blayze to the door.

I opened it to see Stella standing there. "Good morning! I'm here to see if a certain little boy wants to go to the park with me and Papa? Maybe fly some kites?"

Blayze's eyes lit up as he said, "Yes! I want to go!"

"How fun is that going to be!" I said with a chuckle as Blayze ran out of the room and quickly came back with his on-the-go toys that he always had at the ready.

"You excited, buddy?" I asked with a chuckle.

"Yep," he said as he flew past Stella and rushed to his grandparents' truck.

"Well, I'd say he was a bit more than excited. Bye, Blayze!" I called out.

He merely lifted his hand and climbed up into the truck. Ty Senior buckled him in.

"He just ate a pancake for breakfast."

Stella smiled. "Sounds good."

"Hi, Ty!" I called out as I waved my hand.

He replied with a smile and a good morning. Then I felt Brock next to me.

"Hi, Mama. How's it going, Dad?" he called out.

"Good. How are you feeling?" Ty Senior asked as he shut the truck door.

"Better now that I'm home."

Stella reached up and kissed her son on the cheek. Then she turned to me and did the same. She moved her mouth to my ear and whispered, "Don't be worried. He's going to be over the moon."

My eyes widened and my mouth dropped.

She knows about the baby?

"Ty can't keep a secret for his life," she whispered.

After a quick hug, she waved her fingers in the air and officially declared it grandparents' day.

I was still in shock as I watched her climb into the truck and drive away.

"You okay? What did she say to you?" Brock's voice snapped me out of my moment of daze.

"Oh, girl stuff. You know."

He rolled his eyes and took my hand. "Come on. Let's talk."

Swallowing hard, I followed him into the family room. Brock's house was decorated with a rustic design. I loved every part of the house. It screamed of Brock everywhere you looked. We sat down on the leather sofa, and he took in a slow, steady breath and then winced.

"Do you need a pain pill?"

He shook his head. "No."

I wondered if he was avoiding the pills because of Ty becoming addicted to painkillers after his accident. "Are you sure?"

He nodded. "I'll take one later this afternoon."

I turned and faced him, patiently waiting for him to tell me what weighed so heavy on his heart.

"I know I've told you a little about Kaci before, but I left one important piece out. How she died."

"Okay." My voice sounded shaky.

"Has anyone told you?"

I shook my head. "No."

He furrowed his brows and then closed his eyes only briefly before speaking. "I never really understood why I couldn't make Kaci happy. For a while, I wondered if it might be because she regretted picking me over Dirk. A part of me wishes we had never forced her hand on it. But over the years, I've looked back . . . and there had *always* been signs of how unhappy she'd been, even before we got married. I guess I just ignored them."

I reached for his hand.

"Anyway, after we got married, Kaci started to pressure me into giving up bull riding. She wanted me to go to college, get into law. She worried about me riding and said the stress was too much. We fought a lot; Dirk put a lot of pressure on me as well to try harder to make her happy. Sometimes I wonder what her life would have been like, had she loved Dirk more than me."

He shrugged and got lost in his thoughts for a moment before continuing. "I tried so hard to show her I loved her. I did love her, Lincoln."

I squeezed his hand gently. "I know you did."

He slowly let out a breath and tried to hide the pain he was in. "After a while, I started to grow resentful toward her. The constant complaining about me being gone, wanting me to give up what I loved, and she got it in her head I was cheating. I never once cheated on her. Then, one day, she said she thought a baby would bring us closer. It was in the barn, in that tack room we were in. That day you asked me to make love to you in there, that memory came rushing back to me . . . and I felt like I was betraying Kaci. It's been part of the reason I haven't allowed myself to fall in love again. The guilt that I couldn't seem to make her happy, and the fact that I was a selfish asshole for not putting her first."

"You're not betraying her by loving me."

A soft laugh slipped from his lips. "I know that . . . *now*. Being in that room and wanting to make love to you, knowing we felt such a powerful connection, made me feel guilty. I wanted to tell you, but I *couldn't* tell you I was falling in love with you . . . not in that room."

The room fell silent as Brock seemed to get his thoughts together.

"About a week before Kaci went into labor, everything in our world seemed great. She was happy; she wasn't pushing me to go to college; I thought things were going to work out. That the baby was already bringing us closer. The night before she went into labor, though, she called me. She was angry and not really acting like herself. She gave me an ultimatum."

"An ultimatum?" I asked.

"Yeah. She told me if I wanted to be a part of our child's life, I had to slow down on the tour, or she would leave me."

My hand came up to my mouth. "What?"

Brock nodded. "I was so pissed at her. I told her she knew what I did for a living when we got married, and it wasn't fair that she was asking me to walk away from it. We fought a bit more, she said something, I said something, and she hung up on me."

"Why would she suddenly demand this from you?"

He shrugged. "I don't know. I think she was in a dark place; I just didn't know it at the time. Kaci suffered from depression. I also didn't know *that* until the day of her funeral. Her mama pulled me to the side and told me. I was so angry, but Kaci had made her parents promise not to tell me. Things might have been different, had I known. Dirk didn't know either. She kept it from both of us."

A tear slipped down Brock's cheek, and I reached over and gently wiped it away.

"The day she went into labor, I wasn't that far away, at a PBR event. I was about to ride when I was told she was in labor, too early, and there was a problem." His voice shook and he closed his eyes. "The helicopter was waiting to take me to her, and I . . . I was up to ride. Dirk was yelling for me to get off the bull, but I kept telling myself it would only be one to two more minutes. I could ride and still get out of there and to Kaci."

My chest grew heavy with sadness for him. "Brock," I whispered.

"I made the eight. Then reality came crashing in on me. I was putting bull riding first over my wife, and now I was also doing it with my unborn child. I cursed myself the entire trip back home. Dirk didn't utter a word to me, and I couldn't blame him. I couldn't even believe I had done it. The guilt was ripping me in half. In my mind at the time, I had made the right decision. I needed the win for a big sum of money. I justified it because of that."

He paused again, and I dropped onto the floor in front of him. Holding on to him. I could see the emotions growing, and I knew Brock had been carrying that guilt with him for so long.

"I got there just after Blayze was born. Kaci smiled the moment I walked into the room. She knew I had ridden because Dirk had called to talk to her. He told her. It took me some time to forgive him for that, but I understood why he did it. He loved her, too, and was scared, wasn't thinking clearly himself. Anyway, she told me we had a son. Those were her last words to me."

I lost my battle to keep my tears at bay.

"The next thing I knew, my mother was screaming Kaci's name and they were pushing us out of the room. The doctor later told me she died from a blood clot that must have come loose when she was delivering Blayze. Dirk flipped out on me and said it was my fault that it happened. He didn't mean it, of course; I think he was upset with himself as well for telling her I rode."

I sat there, stunned. Every emotion I could possibly feel rushed through me. I was angry with Dirk for blaming Kaci's death on Brock, angry at Kaci for forcing Brock's hand, hurt for how Brock had carried around the guilt of her death, and helpless because he blamed himself. What a mess.

"After all that, I vowed that I was never opening my heart again. I could never let someone get that close to me. I let her down when she needed me the most, and I wouldn't do it again."

"Brock," I whispered, taking his hand and kissing the back of it.

"Then, I met you, and my entire world turned upside down. When I'm with you, Lincoln, I feel something so powerful and so real. It's beautiful, and sometimes I feel like it's beyond words."

Tears filled my eyes. "I feel the same. I need you to know something, though. *None* of what happened with Kaci was your fault."

He closed his eyes.

"It wasn't, Brock. I know if you could go back, you'd change some of it, but nothing you did led to her death. If she had a blood clot, that was not something you'd caused. And the day she went into labor, you can't know why that happened. There could have been any number of reasons why she went into labor early. This guilt you're holding on to—you need to let it go."

"I know," he whispered. "I want to, and I feel like I *have* let a lot of it go, with you being in my life." Brock's eyes met mine. "I'm so sorry about that day in the barn, Lincoln. I was confused and scared. Still holding on to a lot of guilt."

"I understand why you ran away that day. But we have to promise each other that we'll talk about everything we're feeling. We have to be honest."

He nodded. "I know."

I closed my eyes and took in a deep breath. I wanted to push off talking about our future to another day. I wanted to pretend like we didn't have this facing us head-on in a new, very fragile relationship. But we did. And I'd just preached about being honest with each other, so here went nothing . . . or everything.

I climbed back up onto the sofa and turned to face him. "Where do you see us in five years?" I asked.

This time, he slowly turned his body, and we were sitting face to face. "That's easy. Married. Maybe a baby or two. I'll be working full time on the ranch. I imagine you'll still be working if you want, but you won't have to. I've got enough money now to retire. Dad put me in touch with an investor, and I've done well with my sponsors and winnings. I thought maybe I needed another championship to really secure my future, but my eyes have been opened to more important things other than money."

"I don't care about money, Brock. I care about spending the rest of my life with you and Blayze."

"Then marry me."

My eyes nearly popped out of my head. "Wh-what?"

"Marry me. I know I love you, I know Blayze loves you, and you love us. Why not?"

"Um . . . well, people will think it's too soon . . . but then again, we sort of have a good reason."

"Hell yes, we do. We love each other, and I don't give two shits about what other people think. We can have a big wedding or a small one. Hell, we don't even have to tell anyone."

I shook my head. "No . . . if I marry you, Brock Shaw, I want to shout it from the tallest mountain."

He smiled, and his face lit up.

"But I do have something important that I need to talk to you about."

"Okay."

I wore a concerned look on my face as I said, "It's kind of . . . well, I'm not sure how you're going to react."

He tilted his head and studied me. "Okay."

"Promise me one thing. You won't freak."

"Uh . . . I'm sort of already freaking, Lincoln. Is something wrong with you? Are you all right?"

I giggled. Suddenly, the happiness of knowing I was carrying this man's baby hit me all over again. I felt like I was floating in a cloud of euphoria. I wanted this more than I could have ever imagined. Now, I just hoped he wanted it too.

"I'm more than all right. I'm amazing. I'm overjoyed. I'm shocked as hell."

He pulled his brows in with confusion. "Shocked about what?"

Blowing out a breath, I closed my eyes, counted to five, opened them again, and just said it. "I'm pregnant."

Brock sat there for a few moments in utter disbelief.

I gave him some time to let it sink in before explaining, "When you were in the hospital, I wasn't eating very well. I was also feeling sick, and I got dehydrated. I fainted."

"What?"

I held up my hand for him to let me finish. "They admitted me and did a few tests. One of the blood tests showed I was pregnant. I was stunned when Kaylee and Ty told me."

His eyes widened. "They know?"

"Yeah, the doctor told them because Kaylee said she was my sister. I asked how it'd happened, because I was on the pill and you'd worn condoms. I had been on some antibiotics that affected the pill. I had finished them up that first week we met. Then, I guess one of your condoms failed, and . . . well, we have a baby as the result."

Brock stared at me for the longest time before I saw a tear slide down his cheek.

I wrung my hands. "Please tell me what's going on in your head, Brock."

"We're having a baby?"

I nodded. "Yep. Surprise!"

His hand went behind my neck and he pulled me to him. Our mouths crashed together, and he kissed me.

This kiss felt so different from all the others. Maybe it was because we had told each other we loved one another. Or because everything between us was out in the open now. Brock wasn't holding back anything from his past. Or maybe the knowledge that we had made a child together made us feel closer. Whatever it was, I could feel his love pouring into me through that kiss, and it made every nerve ending in my body tingle. It was magical. Beautiful. Intense.

Then he stood, pulling me up with him.

"Come on. I need to make love to you."

"What? No! You can't! You're in no condition to have sex. And—wait, you haven't said anything about the baby. I mean, after that kiss, I can guess you're happy. Are you feeling anything else, though? Scared? Tell me, please."

He tossed his head back and laughed. Then he held on to his side and pierced my gaze with his. "I'm fucking over the moon, Lincoln. I'm freaked out, yes. Scared? I don't think so. I feel, happy. We're having a baby. We are having a baby!"

My own tears fell now, and he reached up with both thumbs and wiped them away.

"I love you. And, because of this bit of information, I want to marry you even more. As soon as possible."

I nodded. "O-okay. I want that too."

"Just family? Here or in Atlanta?"

There was no thinking twice about my answer. "Here."

He smiled and kissed my nose. "Now, come on. Let's get creative about this sex thing. You can be on top, but I want to be inside you right now."

Chapter Twenty-Eight

Brock

My heartbeat was racing as I guided Lincoln to my room.

We're having a baby. Holy shit. This is happening so fast—and I love it!

It was amazing how things had changed for me the last few weeks. How admitting my love for Lincoln and telling her what had happened with Kaci had set me free. A weight felt like it had been lifted from my soul.

"Brock, I'm not sure this is a good idea."

"You just told me you're having my baby. Plus, you said you would marry me. I want celebratory sex!"

She giggled as she walked up to me and pulled my shirt over my head, dropping it to the floor. Then she pulled my sweatpants down, careful to avoid my stitches. She kissed gently around the stitches, leaving me breathless and weak in the knees. I stepped out of my pants and kicked them to the side.

"Commando, huh?" she whispered.

"You should probably know that happens a lot when I'm home."

"Duly noted," she replied in a sexy voice.

Then she stood, and I was silently thanking God that she hadn't wrapped those pretty lips around me, or I would have lost it.

She quickly stripped, then took in my bandaged-up side. She looked sad, but she quickly let it slip away before looking up into my eyes. "I love you," she whispered.

Those three words, in that moment, seemed to shatter away the remaining brokenness I'd felt. My body felt light. I was happy for the first time in years. I was hopeful for my future . . . and I knew exactly what I had to do.

I walked back and carefully lay down on the bed. Lincoln followed, trying not to touch anywhere I was injured.

"Lincoln," I whispered as she moved onto the bed next to me.

Her fingers trailed lightly over my chest as I lay there, trying not to breathe too hard and forcing myself not to roll her over and bury myself inside of her.

Then she stilled, as if reading my own thoughts. "I'm so afraid I'm going to hurt you."

"Don't be. Please, I want you."

She smiled and slowly moved. Careful not to touch my chest or my stitched-up thigh. "Brock. I—"

"Please, sweetheart. *Please.*"

Her eyes filled with tears as she positioned herself over me. Her teeth dug into her lower lip, and I wanted to pinch myself to make sure I wasn't dreaming.

Her eyes burned with passion as she slowly lowered herself onto me. Our gazes were locked on each other, and I held my breath as I felt myself enter her body for the first time with nothing separating us.

"You're so beautiful, Lincoln. And you're mine."

She nodded. "Forever."

When she began, I grabbed on to the sheets, trying to slow this train down, because I needed her to come before I did, and in this position, that was proving more difficult with each of her hip rotations. I had been dreaming about making love to her again and being inside her; knowing she was pregnant with my child, knowing we had a future together, it was more than I could take.

My hand slipped between our bodies, finding her sensitive clit and rubbing it slightly. Every movement fucking killed my side, but I ignored the pain.

Lincoln dropped her head back, placed her hands on her breasts, and cried out my name as she came.

She squeezed around my cock, and I lost all control. Not even caring almost every inch of my body was in pain. All I cared about was this woman.

I placed my hands on her waist and pumped into her fast and hard. The way she reacted to our lovemaking had me falling in love with her even more, if that was at all possible.

"Brock. Brock, yes!" she cried out.

The pain in my side was almost too much to bear, but I ignored it still, along with the pain in my leg. The pure bliss of being inside her, raw and passionate, outweighed the pain. "Lincoln, I'm coming."

I orgasmed so hard, I swore I saw stars exploding in the room.

When we finally stilled, she climbed off me and made her way to the bathroom. I heard the water running, and then she reappeared. She used a warm washcloth to wipe me off. It was the sweetest thing anyone had ever done for me after making love. The way this woman cared about me blew my damn mind.

Then, she carefully inspected every inch of me. "Are you okay?" she asked.

I nodded, my eyes still closed as I reveled in the bliss of our lovemaking. "I could use a pain pill now, though."

She sighed and pulled my shirt over her head as she dashed out of the room.

As I lay there, I thought about everything that had happened this morning. The conversation I'd overheard Lincoln and Blayze having, the news that we were having a baby, and the idea that Lincoln was going to marry me.

Then I thought back to Blayze, telling me his dream about Kaci.

"Thank you for giving me Blayze," I said out loud. "I'll always love you, and I promise to make you a part of your son's life."

A feeling of warmth spread over my body, and that last little bit of guilt that I had been holding on to slowly slipped away.

"You do know if Lincoln sees you doing that, she'll kick your ass."

I glanced over my shoulder to see Ty standing there. "She won't know unless you tell her. I can't sit in the house anymore. It's been two and a half months, and this weekend, I'm riding. I've got to move around some or I'm going to suck and not make the eight."

"You've been cleared to ride?" he asked, grabbing a bale and putting it in one of the pens.

"Yep. Completely healed. Not that the doctor was happy that I would be climbing back on a bull."

He laughed. "How's the pain?"

"Pretty much gone."

"Good. You take it easy on the pills?"

I stopped and looked at him. The worry in his eyes was evident. "Yeah, I was careful."

"Put the shit you have left over up and away. Or better yet, get rid of it."

With a nod, I replied, "Okay."

He stopped and took a deep breath. "I almost took one of your pills."

Freezing, I asked, "What?"

"They were on your kitchen island, and I picked up the bottle. Went so far that I opened it."

A wave of disappointment in myself hit me like a brick wall. I'd left that temptation out for him and hadn't even realized it. "Damn it. I should have told Lincoln to keep them up. She usually kept them high up, so Blayze couldn't get to them. What stopped you from taking one?"

He scoffed. "Kaylee. She walked in, and I hadn't even seen her; I was so lost in my thoughts."

"What did she do?"

Swallowing hard, he rubbed the back of his neck. "She didn't say a word, but she took them from my hand and set the bottle down, and then . . . she kissed me."

My eyes widened in shock. "She kissed you?"

"Yeah," he said with a slight laugh. "Instantly made me forget all about the pills."

"I can imagine."

He sighed. "I've never had a woman kiss me like that before, Brock. It wasn't like she was attempting to distract me from taking the pill with a simple flirtatious kiss." He shook his head and smiled slightly at the memory. "It was more like she was letting me know *why* I shouldn't take the pill. I felt something in her kiss. Like she gave me a piece of her but wasn't expecting anything in return. I don't really understand it, so I might not be explaining myself right."

I got exactly what he was trying to say.

"Then what happened, after she kissed you?"

"She took the bottle of pills with her and walked out of the kitchen."

"Damn."

"Yeah."

"Do you think you would have taken one?"

"I don't know. I didn't want to; I know that much. I really didn't want to . . . but the urge was there. I felt it."

Swallowing hard, I asked, "You go back to counseling?"

He nodded, and I barely heard his reply. "Yes."

"Good."

"What are you doing?" Lincoln demanded.

Ty and I both turned to see my sexy-as-hell fiancée standing there, hands on her hips and a pissed-off look on her face.

"Um, just loosening my muscles."

"That's what the gym is for. This work is for Ty."

"Gee, thanks. I can't even get Tanner to help me."

Lincoln folded her arms over her chest. "Do you remember he took on a bull to save your brother and broke his ribs?"

Both Ty and I huffed as I replied, "Hell, Lincoln, he's back on the circuit, roping."

She rolled her eyes. "You're all crazy. I really came down here to tell you that my folks called, and they'll be here tomorrow morning."

A wide smile moved across my face. We were getting married in two days.

"They happy to stay at your place?"

She waved her hand. "Yes. Kaylee is over the moon to have them there. I'm glad I convinced her to just rent my place from me." Her eyes moved over to Ty. "Aren't you, Ty?"

He shrugged and tossed another bale of hay into a pen. "Makes no difference to me."

"Uh-huh," she replied, and then winked at me.

"Everything all set for the ceremony?" I asked, stopping in front of her to kiss her.

"Yep, it's all set. You nervous?"

"Hell no." I placed my hand on her stomach and asked, "You?"

She wore a breathtaking smile and replied, "Heck no. I'm ready to be Mrs. Brock Shaw."

"Damn, that has a good ring to it. Doesn't it, Ty?" I called over my shoulder.

"You both make me sick with your lovey-dovey shit."

I leaned my forehead on hers. "I'm sorry we can't take a honeymoon right away. I promise I'll make it up to you."

Her hand came up to my face. "I don't care about that. All I care about is you, Blayze, and this little baby growing in my stomach."

"You'd better be feeding my nephew. Shaw men like to eat."

Lincoln laughed and went to reply, but Kaylee did first. She must have gotten tired of waiting in the car.

"I'm sorry, Shaw. Keep dreaming. That baby is a girl. Have you seen how sick she's been?"

Ty leaned against the fence, and I couldn't help but notice how Kaylee swept her eyes over my brother. I lifted a brow in Lincoln's direction, and she smiled.

"So, the more morning sickness you have, it means it's going to be a girl?" Ty asked.

"Yep!" Kaylee proudly declared.

Ty shook his head. "There you have it, Brock. Women are a pain in the ass, even in the womb."

Kaylee's hands balled. Then she pointed to Ty. "You . . . you . . . you—"

He pointed to himself. "Me?"

She let out a scream. "Ugh! You drive me crazy, Ty Shaw! Crazy!"

Turning, she stomped away, mumbling something about how she wanted to junk punch him. Prompting Ty to cover his junk and then laugh.

Shaking my head, I focused back on Lincoln. "I'm about done, and then I'll head up."

"Okay. Take it easy. I don't want you getting hurt before the wedding *or* this weekend."

I knew deep down that she hated I was heading back on tour, but she'd never once uttered a word. She had booked flights for me, her, and Dirk. Gotten the hotel rooms and arranged a dinner with a few of my sponsors, who wanted to check to see how I was before I climbed onto a bull this weekend in Nashville.

Kissing her nose, I replied, "I promise."

"Bye, Ty!" she called out.

"See ya around, Lincoln."

When she was out of earshot, he walked up next to me. "Have you told her?"

Smiling, I answered him. "Nope."

"When are you planning on telling her?"

I faced my brother and hit him on the side of the arm. "After I win the world championship."

A wide grin spread over his face. "That's what I'm talking about."

Chapter Twenty-Nine

Lincoln

I stared at myself in the full-length mirror of my old bedroom in the little white house. I'd officially moved out of my house and in with Brock and Blayze. I still kept my stuff in the guest room, but most nights, I slept in Brock's room.

We had been careful not to let Blayze see either of us sneaking out in the mornings. We had told him last night that he was going to be a big brother, and he'd had the same reaction as his father. He'd cried tears of joy and then declared he had to call everyone to tell them. We'd let him call my folks first. He was the one to actually break the news to them—and much to my surprise, my mother had said she already knew.

I had flown to Atlanta for a weekend wedding-shopping trip. It had just been me, Kaylee, Stella, and my mother. Stella and my folks had hit it off amazingly. My mother had said she knew the moment she'd looked at me that I was carrying a baby. Plus, with the rushed wedding, my folks had put two and two together. There were no lectures, no *Are you sure you should get married?* comments. It was like they knew I was happy, and they were happy for me.

It took me selling my business and moving thousands of miles away to prove to my father that I could make it on my own and find happiness without his help.

Of course, when they'd started talking about moving to Montana, I had to admit, I wasn't thrilled with the idea. I loved my parents, but I loved them more from a distance.

My thoughts returned to the dress. It was a simple lace gown that perfectly hugged my body yet flared out at the bottom with layers of lace ruffles. I still wasn't showing, except for a small bump that was hardly noticeable. I lifted the dress to reveal the blue cowboy boots Kaylee had bought me. They were my "something blue." Well, those and the baby-blue panties I wore that read *Bride* on them. I was sans bra, since the dress was strapless, with a sweetheart neckline.

The tap on the door caused me to jump.

I covered my stomach and laughed. "Come in."

"How's it going in here?" Kaylee asked, walking up behind me and smiling. "You look stunning. Brock is going to shit his pants when he sees you."

I chewed on the corner of my lip. "Why am I so nervous all of a sudden?"

"Well, your emotions are out of whack with the baby. So, I'm sure, here in a minute, you're going to want to cry. Then you'll probably turn into bridezilla, and then be back to being nervous. It's a cycle."

Laughing, I blew out a breath. "I can't wait to see him. Have you seen him?"

She nodded. "Yes. And I know he's the father of your baby and fixin' to be your husband, but, girl, oh. My. God. He's in a tux. He didn't shave, so he has that whole five-o'clock-shadow thing going on. Christ Almighty, the man is too good looking. I mean, he even makes *my* stomach flip."

I hit her on the hand that was still resting on my shoulder. "Stop that."

"It's true! Did you know there's a website out there that's made up of nothing but women who hate you?"

I spun around and looked at her. "Me? Why?"

She rolled her eyes "Um, you took one of the sexiest eligible bachelors around off the market. Women in the PBR fan world are pissed."

"Oh, come on. You're kidding, right?"

When she tilted her head with a look that said she was dead serious, I groaned.

"Oh my gosh. They set up a *website*?"

She nodded. "Yep. Some of the comments on a photo of that famous kiss . . . Dirk, Ty, and I were cracking up at them."

My hands went to my hips. "How long have you known about the site?"

Holding up her hands in defense, she said, "Since last night. Dirk showed it to us."

I was sure my mouth was on the floor.

"Don't worry. They'll forget all about Brock, and they'll all move on to Dirk. At least, that's his hope."

We both chuckled as my mother poked her head in.

"Girls, it's time. Your father is ready to come in. All set?"

I nodded as my father walked into the room, carrying my bouquet of fresh wildflowers.

"Oh. My. Princess, you look like a . . . well, like a princess!"

I smiled and tried to hold back my tears. "Thank you, Daddy."

He placed his hand on the side of my face and slowly shook his head. "I wouldn't have agreed with this going as fast as it has, if I hadn't seen the way that boy looked at you. It's like you hung the moon."

My chin trembled. "I love him, Daddy. I would be marrying him even if I wasn't pregnant."

"You follow your heart. You've always been that way, Lincoln. You were hell bent on coming to Montana, and I truly believe this was your destiny. All those years I butted in, thinking I was helping, but all I did was push you away."

A tear slipped down my cheek. "No."

"Yes," he said, carefully wiping it away. "But it brought you to Brock. And, as much as I hate that he does what he does, if he makes you happy, then I'm happy."

"He makes me very happy."

"Then, there ya go."

I chuckled. "There ya go."

"Let's do this."

Kaylee hadn't been lying. Brock was the most handsome man I'd ever seen, and dressed in a tux, let's just say I stumbled when I saw him. Thankfully, my father was at the ready and steadied my feet. Brock smiled bigger. I didn't think it was possible, but every day, I was feeling more and more in love with him.

When my father placed my hand in Brock's, I didn't hear anything else. I was lost in his eyes. A blue sea of pure love. The way he rubbed his thumbs over my hands during the ceremony left me breathless. I barely made it through my vows and lost it when Brock cried during his.

Blayze stood behind Brock, next to Ty. Kaylee stood behind me, handing me a hanky that my mother had given to her right before she walked down the aisle.

Of course, Ty had nearly fallen over at the sight of Kaylee in her deep-red, curve-hugging, sequined bridesmaid gown, and I know I wasn't the only one in the room who saw him stealing glances her way.

The preacher finally told Brock to kiss the bride.

He cupped my face in his hands and said, "Hey, Mrs. Shaw."

Another round of tears fell as I somehow managed my reply, "Hey back at ya, Mr. Shaw."

He kissed me. Softly at first, and then he deepened it.

It was Ty who leaned in and said, "Seriously, y'all, you make me sick with this mushy crap."

We both laughed, and then the preacher introduced us as Mr. and Mrs. Brock Shaw as we walked down the aisle.

We had gotten married in Brock's favorite place on their property. It sat on top of a hill and overlooked the entire ranch. Stella had been worried about it being too windy, but it turned out to be a beautiful August day.

The reception was held in a giant tent with twinkle lights strung everywhere and decorations that made any other wedding I'd ever been to pale in comparison. It was perfection. Kaylee had ended up doing almost everything for the wedding. All the plans, the decorations, the cake, the photographer—she had taken care of all of it. She had done such an amazing job that a few people asked her if she would consider planning more events. I hoped she would give it some thought. I knew she loved editing books, but I could also see she was longing for something more. And Hamilton could use a good wedding and event planner.

Warm breath hit my neck, and I instantly melted into Brock's body. The reception had been going strong for almost two hours, and things were beginning to wind down.

"Hey," he whispered before kissing my neck. "I'd like to spend some time with you and Blayze for a bit, before exhaustion overtakes you both."

I laughed. "That sounds wonderful."

He winked. "I have an early appointment with the mayor's office before we fly out to Nashville tomorrow. But I wanted to take you somewhere first. Me, you, and Blayze. You down for a drive?"

I spun around and looked up at him. "A drive?"

He nodded.

Blayze pulled on my dress. "Please, Mommy, please!"

My heart jumped to my throat. Blayze had called me Mommy. I fought to hold back my tears as I looked up at Brock. He was doing the same.

"O-okay," my shaking voice said. "Let's go for a ride."

Brock announced we were slipping out to spend a bit of time together with Blayze. He helped me into his truck and then put Blayze in his seat. We headed down a dirt road that led to the mountains. After driving up a pretty winding and twisting road, we came to a clearing. I gasped at the view.

"Oh my goodness! This is . . . this is . . ." I faced Brock.

"It's not the tallest mountain in the world, but it's the tallest one on the ranch."

Blayze chuckled.

With a wide grin, I said, "Let me out of this truck. I have some shouting to do!"

Brock's eyes filled with happiness as he rushed to get Blayze out. We walked hand in hand with Blayze and stopped at the edge of the plateau. It overlooked the entire ranch valley.

"Why didn't we get married up here?"

"I'm pretty sure my mother would have had a fit."

"Pwus, it's super windy!" Blayze added, clearly remembering all the comments Stella had made about the wind.

"You ready?" Brock asked me.

I nodded and pulled in a deep breath. Then, I screamed as loud as I could, "I'm Mrs. Brock Shaw!"

Blayze jumped up and down, screaming out what he wanted the world to know as well. "I have a mommy, and I'm going to be a big brother!"

I dropped down, pulled him into my arms, and held him. Brock had been talking more about Kaci to Blayze lately. He had always had a picture of her at the side of his bed, but now Brock had gotten into the habit of telling Blayze stories of when Kaci was pregnant with him. It made my heart so full, and I knew Blayze loved hearing about his mother.

Then Brock shouted, "I'm the happiest man in the world and married to the love of my life! Mrs. Lincoln Shaw!"

I lifted Blayze in my arms and let Brock engulf us both in a large hug. Burying my face into his chest, I cried tears of happiness.

Nothing would ever top this moment in my life.

The next morning, Brock had stopped by the mayor's office to finalize the plans for the park that he was helping to raise money to build. It was going to be an amazing community park, named in Kaci's honor, with a playground, a skate park, and an arena for kids to show their animals as well as a large building that would house an indoor pool, a gym for older kids and adults, and classrooms for the agricultural-education students and local residents to use. There were even plans being set up to help people who suffered from depression, anxiety, and other mental health issues, which Brock was working on with Kaci's parents.

Brock didn't want anyone to know, but he had been a major financial contributor in getting the project for the community park up and going. It seemed to be therapeutic for him while he'd been recovering from his injuries.

As we walked out of the mayor's office, Brock reached for my hand. "I think she would be proud of this project."

I smiled. "I know she would be. Plus, it's a great way to honor her memory, and one that Blayze will forever cherish."

Brock simply nodded as we made our way to his truck. He stopped at the passenger door and paused.

"Is everything okay?" I asked.

Looking into my eyes, he smiled. "I have never been so happy in my life, Lincoln. Thank you."

I placed my hand on the side of his face and returned his smile. "For what?"

"For saving me from the darkness. You're the light I didn't even know I was searching for."

My chin trembled as I fought to hold back my tears. "I love you," I whispered, right before Brock's mouth pressed against mine.

◆ ◆ ◆

The next three months flew by. I was five months pregnant, and a clear belly bump was showing.

By the time he'd returned to the tour in Nashville, Brock had slipped to number two in the rankings. He hadn't seemed worried about it, so neither was I. Since then, he'd been riding amazingly and was bumping in and out of first and second place in the standings. We would be heading to Vegas tomorrow for the world finals.

Brock was currently sitting on the fence of a corral, looking out at a bull.

"Penny for your thoughts," I said, climbing up next to him.

"Don't be climbing on this, Lincoln."

I sighed. "I'm fine. Stop worrying. Now, if I were to climb down and walk over to the bull, that might be another story."

Brock chuckled. "Ah, hell, he's a pussycat. He'd let you love on him, no problem."

"I think I'll stay here."

He nodded. "Probably a good idea."

Bumping his shoulder, I repeated my earlier comment. "Penny for your thoughts."

"Just trying to get into the right frame of mind for finals."

"You'll do great."

Brock looked at me. "You have to say that; you're my wife."

"No, I'm saying it because I know how good you are and how much you want this. Don't worry about anything else. You *will* do great."

"I love your confidence in me."

I smiled, causing him to return one. "Besides, the more pregnant I get, the hornier I seem to be."

His brows rose. "Come again?"

"Yep. So, between you riding those bulls, you're gonna have to ride your wife. I hope you're ready for a busy week."

Brock stared at me for a few seconds before jumping off the fence, then getting me down. "We'd better start practicing. Now."

I giggled as he nearly pulled my arm out getting us back into the house.

Chapter Thirty

Brock

The camera was in my face as I tried to walk back to the locker room.

Kim wasn't about to let me walk away without an interview. "Brock, how does it feel to win the fourth round? You've got to be feeling good."

I smiled. "I'm feeling good, yeah. Just need to focus on the next round and keep my head in it."

"How do you feel about riding Diablo?"

I smiled. "I've been waiting to get on his back again."

She nodded. "So, you're ready for the rematch?"

"Yeah. Should be fun."

Kim faced the camera. "You heard it here. Brock Shaw is ready for the ride that could very well make him a PBR World Champion for the third time."

After the camera went off, I pulled Kim to the side and spoke into her ear. She drew back and looked at me with a stunned expression.

"Can you help me out?" I asked.

She nodded and replied, "I'll lead into it for you, no problem."

"Thanks, Kim. I appreciate it."

We parted ways, and I walked back to the locker room to change before meeting Lincoln to head back to the hotel to attend a dinner.

Once I'd returned to the hotel, Lincoln walked out of the bathroom in a dress that showed off how incredibly sexy her pregnant body was. I smiled, and she held up her hand.

"As much as I want you, we don't have time, Brock Shaw."

"Sure we do. I can be fast."

Lincoln chewed on her lip as she thought it over. She wasn't lying when she'd said the pregnancy was making her horny. She would get up in the middle of the night to use the bathroom and decide she needed to feel me inside her. I would wake to her placing soft kisses on my chest. It wouldn't take me long to wake up fully, flip her over, and make love to her.

I loved seeing the bump on her belly. Loved moving my hands over our baby, especially when I was inside her.

Finally, she shook her head. "You'll be late. And it gives you dessert to look forward to."

My dick jumped in my pants. "I do like dessert."

She chuckled as she laced her arm around mine, and we headed down to dinner.

Most of the people at this dinner were sponsors. My agent was here as well, since this was the national championship. If I won it, that would mean big money in promotional ads, and she was ready to jump on any offers.

Small conversations went on around the table, but I couldn't keep my mind from wandering. I didn't hear half of what was being said.

"Hey, what's going on in that head of yours?" Lincoln asked, lightly bumping me on the leg.

I looked around the table. "I'm ready to leave."

With a soft smile, she replied, "I can make up an excuse. Maybe I'm not feeling well?"

As tempting as Lincoln's offer was, I knew we just had to make it a little bit longer and then we could head on out. "Nah. Let's just push through it."

She squeezed my hand.

Another hour went by, and finally, we were all getting up to leave. Lincoln and I headed to our room, where I jumped into the shower once more. When I walked into the bedroom, she was sound asleep.

Damn.

She looked too peaceful to even think about waking her up. I pulled the towel off my waist and crawled in next to her. I drew her to me and wrapped my hand around her, resting it on her belly. With a smile on my face, I drifted off to sleep. I'd never felt so happy and content in my life.

I pulled Dirk's bull rope tight. He wrapped it around and tucked it into his glove.

"You get an eighty-five or above, and you're there, buddy."

"Yeah," he said simply.

"Cover this bull."

Dirk hit at his hand to tighten his hold. Titan's Boy jumped, causing Dirk to fly forward, but Ty grabbed him. He—along with Tanner, my folks, and Blayze—had gotten here earlier this morning. I glanced out to the stands to see them all sitting there. Lincoln was holding Blayze on her lap, laughing at something he was telling her.

I turned my focus back to Dirk. "He's gonna roll right, but don't be surprised if he rolls left. He's a testy little bastard."

Dirk laughed. Adjusting himself, he took in a deep breath and gave the nod.

The gate swung open, and Titan's Boy jumped straight up so damn far we all yelled out.

"Ride him, Dirk! Ride him!" I yelled out as Ty yelled next to me for Dirk to hang on.

Titan's Boy gave Dirk everything he had, but it wasn't enough. He rode the entire eight seconds. The buzzer hit, and I watched as Dirk jumped off. Pounding his fist into his chest and then sticking up his hand. The crowd went wild, and I couldn't wipe the smile from my face. Then his score of eighty-nine came in, and Ty and I both yelled out in celebration.

"You haven't told him this is it, have you?" Ty asked as we moved down to the chute I'd be at in a bit.

"Nope."

He laughed his ass off. "I'm glad you haven't told him."

Smith Morley was up next. I watched as he climbed onto his bull. If he rode his eight seconds, it was going to be neck and neck between us for number one. He'd gotten a good jump on me when I was out for those two months by riding in a few events during our off time.

The chute opened, and I watched him cover the bull. His score was eighty-six.

Taking a deep breath, I watched as they loaded Diablo. My bull rope was around him, and I swore the bastard knew that it was my rope as he looked up at me.

"Oh, hell. He's got you in his sights, bro," Ty said with a laugh.

"Yeah, I saw that."

The cameras were there, and Kim was talking in the background.

I remained silent as I climbed onto Diablo. Ty grabbed the bull rope, and I ran my hand over it. My heart was pounding, but I had never been more ready to ride a bull in my life.

I could hear Kim as she stood next to Ty. "What can Brock Shaw do on Diablo to get him to number one? We're about to find out."

Ty pulled the rope, and I adjusted it.

He grabbed my vest, and I looked up at him. I could hear the intro music playing but quickly tuned it out as I focused solely on my brother.

"Do this, Brock. Do. This. I know you can, bro. I know you can. All you need to do is stay on him."

I didn't say a word as I slipped higher up on the bull. I could feel Diablo shaking under me. He was just as ready for this rematch as I was. The last time, he'd won. This time . . . I planned on winning.

After adjusting myself once more and saying a quick prayer, I gave the nod.

The gate flew open, and Diablo jetted out like the pissed-off motherfucker he was.

I let my body relax and followed him as he tried his best to throw me. The more seconds ticked by, the more pissed off he got. He kicked hard and spun as fast as he could. I swore I felt my ribs come apart again. I gritted my teeth and matched him. He spun again and tried his best to throw me off-balance, but it wasn't working.

No way was I getting thrown from the last bull I was ever gonna ride. He was *mine*.

The buzzer went off, and I reached down and got my hand out. Diablo kicked once more, throwing me clear up, causing me to do what I was guessing was an impressive flip in the air. I landed damn near on my feet with a stumble; luckily, it hadn't been on my bad side.

The crowd went wild, and I looked to see where the bull was. He was angry and going after Pitt—until he saw *me*. He came right for me. I ran to the side and jumped up to get out of his way. When they finally got him through the gate, I launched my helmet up and had three bullfighters rushing toward me.

I turned to find Lincoln. Jumping the fence, I made my way over to her. People slapped me on the back, and I smiled as I passed them.

She stood and made her way to me. Wrapping her in my arms, I buried my face in her neck . . . and then heard my score.

"Ladies and gentlemen, Brock Shaw and Diablo have a score of ninety-three! With his combined scores and only one rider left, no one is going to be able to beat that score. That means Brock Shaw is a three-time PBR World Champion!"

"Oh my God! Brock, you did it!" Lincoln shouted.

"Holy shit!" I carefully lifted Lincoln and hugged her. Putting her down, I cupped her face and kissed her. "I love you."

She laughed as she wiped her tears away. "I love you too. So very much."

Reaching down, I kissed Blayze. "I love you, buddy." Then, I quickly went back to the arena and hustled out so the last bull rider who was left could go.

When I saw Kim and her camera, she smiled. "How do you feel?"

I shook my head. "I'm not sure. Ask me again when this is all over."

She laughed and looked into the camera to talk. I was pulled away from Kim by Ty, Dirk, and a few other bull riders as they all congratulated me.

Holy freaking shit. I just won my third PBR World Finals.

Ty smiled. "I knew you could do it. I knew it!" he shouted in my ear. "Lucky three!"

Everything was a whirlwind as they got ready to present me with the trophy. Lincoln and the rest of my family were down near the chutes. The moment I saw her, I rushed over. I was being told we needed to go out into the arena, but I didn't give two shits. I needed to hug her again. Tell her how much I loved her . . . and give her a warning.

She threw herself into my arms. Cameras were all around us as she cried into my neck.

"I love you, baby," I said as I held her tighter. Then, I moved my mouth to her ear. "That was my last ride. I'm retiring."

She pulled back, a look of confusion on her face. "What?"

"Brock, we need you out there now."

I winked at her, then followed Kim.

The camera light went on, and Kim started. "Brock Shaw, you are the PBR World Finals Champion, with this being your third time winning. How are you feeling?"

With a chuckle, I replied, "Pretty darn good. It was a rematch I'd been waiting for, and this was the best place for it to happen. I'm glad he was the bull I got to go out on."

"By 'going out on,' what do you mean, exactly?"

Looking at Kim, I smiled. "That was my last ride. I'm retiring from professional bull riding."

I could hear the gasps from the crowd. I looked past Kim to see Lincoln standing there. She and my mother both looked as white as ghosts.

"Why retire now, Brock? You're at the top of your field."

I stared at Lincoln, not taking my eyes off her. "Bull riding has always been my number one dream. Then I met someone who changed everything. I'll always love this sport, but I married the love of my life a few months ago, and I really want to be there as we grow our family."

Kim smiled. "Does that mean you'll share if it's a boy or girl?"

My head tossed back with a laugh, and I shook it. Damn if the woman didn't try. I winked at her. "That's it for now."

The rest of the evening was a blur. I did more interviews and private autograph sessions. Met with sponsors and talked to others about future opportunities. It was insanity. When we finally made it back to the hotel, Blayze was asleep, and Ty took him to his room.

As soon as the door to our hotel room shut, Lincoln gave me that look. "How long have you had this planned?"

I started to strip out of my clothes. "Winning? Hell, since the beginning of the season."

Her hands flew up to her hips, and she wrinkled her nose. It was the cutest damn thing ever. "No, Brock Shaw. Retiring. Why didn't you tell anyone?"

I sat down on the bed. "Let's see. The retiring came to me right after you told me you were pregnant. I'd missed everything with Blayze. When he said his first word. The first time he walked. He'd started kindergarten, and I hadn't been there that day. I refuse to be a missing dad anymore. I don't want to miss anything else, especially this pregnancy."

Her face softened. "This is really what *you* want? Because you know I will support you if you want to keep doing this. I would never ask you to stop riding."

I reached for her hand, pulling her to me. I placed my hand on her belly and closed my eyes. "This is what I really want, Lincoln." When I opened my eyes, our gazes locked. "Bull riding has always been a passion of mine. But I'm twenty-seven years old, almost twenty-eight, and I want to spend the rest of my life on my *other* passions. You and Blayze. And this baby we have coming. My dream has always been to help my dad run the ranch. This. Is. What. I. Want."

She pushed me back onto the bed and pulled her dress over her head. Kicking her boots off, she then shimmied out of her panties and unclasped her bra.

"I'm filthy, Lincoln."

Crawling over my body, she smiled. "My God, I hope so."

Epilogue

Brock

Four Months Later

The sound of a beeping horn drew both my and Ty's attention toward the racing ranch truck coming down the dirt road.

"Who in the hell is driving like that?" Ty asked.

"Probably Tanner. You know how much he likes driving in fresh snow."

The truck came to a halt, and Kaylee jumped out.

"Oh, hell. Her behind the wheel is an even scarier thought," Ty mumbled.

"Brock! Lincoln's water broke!"

I dropped the fence cutters. "What?"

"Her water broke! Come on!"

Ty knocked me out of the way as he ran by, causing me to slip and fall. He started toward the truck as Kaylee let out a shout.

"What in the hell, Ty?" I cried out.

He stopped and saw me on the ground. "Shit! Sorry. Come on!"

He pulled me up, and we both took off.

"Get out of the way. I'm driving!" I shouted as Kaylee damn near dived into the back seat.

"Go! Go! Go!" Ty yelled. "I still don't see why you can't tell us what you're having," he continued, his arms crossed and a pout on his face.

"Lincoln and I decided it was too much fun watching you and Kaylee argue about it."

Kaylee huffed in the back seat as Ty did the same.

"Just get to your wife, you ass," Kaylee said.

As I pulled into the front yard of my house, Tanner and Blayze were helping Lincoln into the front seat of my truck.

My mother and father were pulling up the rear. Dad was carrying Lincoln's suitcase. Ty rushed for it as I made my way to Lincoln.

"Hey," I said as I skidded to a halt.

She looked up at me and smiled the most beautiful smile I'd ever seen on her face. "Hey back at ya."

"You ready to have a baby?"

"Yep. You?"

I nodded and pulled the seat belt around her, trying to keep my hands from shaking. Tanner was getting Blayze into his seat. "Most definitely. You're going to be amazing, sweetheart," I said, leaning in and softly kissing her.

Her eyes closed, and she pulled in a deep breath as she placed her hands on her belly. I felt her stomach then and knew she was having a contraction.

When it passed, she stared into my eyes. "I'm scared, Brock."

I kissed her. "I am too. Just know that I love you."

"I love you more," she replied.

Shaking my head, I whispered, "Impossible."

I backed out of the truck and shut the door.

"She called Dr. Cannon already. Be careful driving! We'll be right behind you," Mom shouted.

Waving, I called out, "Okay! Thanks, Mama."

It didn't take long to get to the hospital, but Lincoln's contractions were beginning to come faster.

"Is it supposed to happen this quick?" she asked, breathing through another contraction as the nurse hooked her up to a bunch of machines.

"It can. Usually, first births don't progress this fast, but you could stall out, so . . . let's just get you comfy."

Lincoln nodded, then turned to me. I could see the fear creeping into her eyes.

I fought to keep my own fears at bay and kissed her hand. "It's okay, baby. It's all going to be okay."

"I know. I just can't believe the day is here. She's coming, Brock. Our little girl will be here soon."

Tears stung the backs of my eyelids. "I know. Ty is going to be so pissed."

She laughed. "Only because Kaylee was right, but he'll love her so much."

"He will."

"Where is Blayze?" Lincoln asked.

"He wanted to explore the hospital, so Tanner took him on a little adventure."

"Oh, boy."

"Yeah, I thought the same thing."

"Let's hope he doesn't run into any pretty nurses on that adventure."

The door to Lincoln's room opened, and Dr. Cannon walked in. "Well, hello there. Let's go ahead and see how you're doing." She examined Lincoln and then turned to the nurse. "She's fully dilated. Let's do this."

"What?" Lincoln and I said at the same time.

"You're ready to push, Lincoln."

"But . . . but I just got here!"

The doctor laughed. "Good thing too! It's baby time."

I smiled as I looked at Lincoln. It appeared everything in our relationship was going to move at top speed.

An hour and a half later, I walked into the waiting room to find it filled with people. My parents jumped up first. Then everyone else followed.

I smiled and looked around the room.

"Well? Are you going to just make us all suffer?" Kaylee asked.

I motioned for Blayze to come over to me. Bending down, I whispered into his ear, "You've got a baby sister."

He wrapped his arms around my neck and squeezed. "I'm so happy! I pwomise to take care of her, Daddy!"

My eyes filled with tears as I picked him up and stood. I looked at my parents and said, "Morgan Elizabeth Shaw has arrived."

The waiting room erupted.

"A girl!" was heard coming from everywhere.

I couldn't help but notice how Ty and Kaylee exchanged a hug—and then backed away when they realized what their excitement had led them to do. They quickly retreated to standard behavior.

"I told you it was a girl," Kaylee said with a smirk.

Ty simply rolled his eyes.

"Let me have Blayze meet his sister, and then everyone else can."

My mother walked up and kissed my cheek. "Well done, sweetheart."

"Thanks, Mama. But it was all Lincoln."

She winked, and I turned and brought Blayze back to Lincoln's room. When I opened the door, Lincoln was feeding Morgan.

"Blayze, meet your little sister, Morgan," Lincoln said softly.

I set him on the bed, and he got on his knees to get a better look.

"Wow! She's pwetty. Just like you, Mommy."

Lincoln smiled. "Thank you, sweet boy. I see your daddy's charming ways are rubbing off on you."

I winked, and Blayze continued to stare at his sister.

"Where's her hair?"

Lincoln rubbed the dark-colored patch of hair on our daughter's head. "That's her baby fuzz. She'll grow some soon."

Blayze nodded. "Okay. 'Cause I want to put her hair in pigtails, like Lindsey in my class wears."

Lincoln's eyes darted up to mine. "Who's Lindsey?" she asked while staring at me. A smirk on her face.

With a shrug, Blayze nonchalantly said, "My girlfriend."

I scrubbed my hands down my face and groaned while Lincoln let out a giggle.

"It's not supposed to happen this soon," I mumbled under my breath as Lincoln shook her head.

"Do you want to hold your sister?" Lincoln asked.

I thought Blayze was going to fly through the roof. "Yes! Yes! Yes!"

"Daddy will get you all fixed up over there on the couch. Go sit down. You have to be very still when you hold her. Remember what we told you?"

Blayze climbed up on the couch and sat all the way back while I put a pillow under his arm. I smiled as he said, "Yes. She's very delicate, and she doesn't know how to hold her head up. So I have to be a stwong big brother and pwotect her. I'm always going to pwotect her."

I walked over and took Morgan from Lincoln.

"I know you will. You're already such a good big brother," Lincoln said, wiping her tears away.

I sat down next to Blayze and placed Morgan in his arms. He stared at her for the longest time and then began singing one of his favorite songs, which he had been having us play every time we got in the truck for the last two months—Dan + Shay's "When I Pray for You."

My heart nearly exploded in my chest as I turned to look at Lincoln, who had her hand covering her mouth as she cried.

I wiped my own tears away and looked into my beautiful wife's eyes. "Thank you," I said softly.

She sucked in a breath and shook her head as she attempted to find her words.

I stood and walked over to her, gently kissing her on the lips.

"This is the most amazing moment of my life," she whispered against my lips.

With a smile, I said, "Oh, baby . . . this is just the beginning."

THANK YOU

To Kristin, Tanya, and Laura: For being the first eyes on *Never Enough* and telling me what you thought of the story.

To the amazing contractors who gave me a behind-the-scenes tour of the PBR event in Tacoma: Your information was so incredible and helped me out more than you know!

To Darrin and Lauren: Thanks for not complaining when I watched hours of PBR bull riding every week.

To my readers: Y'all have waited a long time for this story to come out. I hope it was worth the wait!

ABOUT THE AUTHOR

Kelly Elliott is a *New York Times* and *USA Today* bestselling contemporary romance author. Since finishing her bestselling Wanted series, Kelly has continued to spread her wings while remaining true to her roots with stories of hot men, strong women, and beautiful surroundings. Her bestselling works include *Wanted*, *Broken*, *Without You*, and *Lost Love*. Elliott has been passionate about writing since she was fifteen. After years of filling journals with stories, she finally followed her dream and published her first novel, *Wanted*, in November 2012.

Elliott lives in Central Texas with her husband, daughter, and two pups. When she's not writing, she enjoys reading and spending time with her family. She is down to earth and very in touch with her readers, both on social media and at signings. To learn more about Kelly and her books, you can find her through her website, www.kellyelliottauthor.com.